OXFORD WORLD'S CLASSICS

A SENTIMENTAL JOURNEY

AND OTHER WRITINGS

LAURENCE STERNE was born in 1713 at Clonmel in Ireland, the son of an army ensign, Roger Sterne, and his wife Agnes. In 1723 or 1724 he left Ireland for school near Halifax, proceeding in 1733 to Jesus College, Cambridge. He graduated BA in 1737 and entered the Church of England as a deacon, being appointed curate at St Ives and obtaining the living of Sutton-on-the-Forest in Yorkshire the following year. In 1741 Sterne married Elizabeth Lumley. In 1759 he published the first two volumes of *The Life and Opinions of Tristram Shandy, Gentleman* in York, and found himself immediately famous. Extravagantly praised for its humour and roundly condemned for its indecency, *Tristram Shandy* was an enormous literary success and Sterne was lionized both in London and Paris. Seven subsequent volumes of *Tristram Shandy* appeared between 1761 and 1767. In 1760 Sterne published two volumes of his sermons under the title *The Sermons of Mr Yorick*, adding two further volumes in 1766. In 1767, he met Mrs Elizabeth Draper, 22-year-old wife of an East India Company official, with whom he enjoyed a brief but intense sentimental friendship which bore literary fruit in *The Journal to Eliza*. In February 1768 he published the two volumes of *A Sentimental Journey through France and Italy*. Sterne died in London of consumption on 18 March 1768.

IAN JACK is Professor Emeritus of English at the University of Cambridge, and General Editor of the Clarendon Edition of the novels of the Brontës. Among his books are *Augustan Satire, English Literature 1815–1832*, and *Browning's Major Poetry*. He has also edited Emily Brontë's *Wuthering Heights* for Oxford World's Classics.

TIM PARNELL is lecturer in English at Goldsmiths' College, University of London. His publications include *Constructing Christopher Marlowe* (co-edited with J. A. Downie), essays on Sterne and Swift and a critical edition of *Tristram Shandy*. He is currently writing a literary life of Laurence Sterne.

OXFORD WORLD'S CLASSICS

*For over 100 years Oxford World's Classics have brought
readers close to the world's great literature. Now with over 700
titles—from the 4,000-year-old myths of Mesopotamia to the
twentieth century's greatest novels—the series makes available
lesser-known as well as celebrated writing.*

*The pocket-sized hardbacks of the early years contained
introductions by Virginia Woolf, T. S. Eliot, Graham Greene,
and other literary figures which enriched the experience of reading.
Today the series is recognized for its fine scholarship and
reliability in texts that span world literature, drama and poetry,
religion, philosophy and politics. Each edition includes perceptive
commentary and essential background information to meet the
changing needs of readers.*

OXFORD WORLD'S CLASSICS

LAURENCE STERNE

A Sentimental Journey
and Other Writings

Edited by
IAN JACK *and* TIM PARNELL

With an Introduction and Notes by
TIM PARNELL

OXFORD
UNIVERSITY PRESS

OXFORD
UNIVERSITY PRESS

Great Clarendon Street, Oxford OX2 6DP

Oxford University Press is a department of the University of Oxford.
It furthers the University's objective of excellence in research, scholarship,
and education by publishing worldwide in

Oxford New York

Auckland Bangkok Buenos Aires Cape Town Chennai
Dar es Salaam Delhi Hong Kong Istanbul Karachi Kolkata
Kuala Lumpur Madrid Melbourne Mexico City Mumbai Nairobi
São Paulo Shanghai Taipei Tokyo Toronto

Oxford is a registered trade mark of Oxford University Press
in the UK and in certain other countries

Published in the United States
by Oxford University Press Inc., New York

Editorial matter © Tim Parnell 2003

Database right Oxford University Press (maker)

First published 1968 by Oxford University Press
First issued as an Oxford World's Classics paperback 1984
New edition 2003

British Library Cataloguing in Publication Data

Data available

Library of Congress Cataloging in Publication Data

Data available

ISBN 0–19–283996–9

1 3 5 7 9 10 8 6 4 2

Typeset in Ehrhardt
by RefineCatch Limited, Bungay, Suffolk
Printed in Great Britain by
Clays Ltd, St Ives plc

CONTENTS

ACKNOWLEDGEMENTS

IN preparing this revised version of my Oxford English Novels edition, first published in 1968, I have been helped by two friends: Mr John Oates, of Cambridge University Library, and Professor Arthur H. Cash, now acknowledged as the leading authority on Sterne.

I. J.

My greatest debts are to Arthur Cash's two-volume biography of Sterne, Lewis Perry Curtis's edition of the *Letters*, Melvyn New's edition of the *Sermons*, and Gardner D. Stout's edition of *A Sentimental Journey*. Although I was unable to make use of the forthcoming Florida edition of the *Journey* and *Journal*, Mel New was typically generous in answering questions and sharing his unrivalled knowledge of Sterne.

I should also like to thank Chris Baldick for his translations of Sterne's French and Peter de Voogd for instant responses to queries about illustrations of the *Journey*, and for kindly allowing the use of an image from his own collection for the cover of this edition. Thanks, too, are due to Blake Gerard, Joanna Gibbs, Tom Keymer, Judith Luna, and Simon McVeigh.

T. P.

INTRODUCTION

IN early January 1768, Sterne travelled from York to London to see the first two volumes of *A Sentimental Journey through France and Italy* through the press. He had begun the book in earnest in June of the previous year, but bouts of serious illness and domestic distractions had hampered his progress on what had been conceived as a work in four volumes. Thus when *A Sentimental Journey* appeared on 27 February, the subscription copies included a loose-leaf 'Advertisement' assuring subscribers that 'The Work will be compleated and delivered . . . early the next Winter'. Some days later, Sterne wrote to his daughter: 'My Sentimental Journey, you say, is admired in York by every one—and 'tis not vanity in me to tell you that it is no less admired here—but what is the gratification of my feelings on this occasion?—the want of health bows me down'. At 'death's door . . . with a pleurisy',[1] Sterne was confined to bed in his Old Bond Street lodgings. A consumptive since his student days, he died on Friday 18 March, leaving *A Sentimental Journey* tantalizingly incomplete with the account of the Italian portion of Yorick's journey still unwritten.

Although he did not live long enough to see many of the earliest reviews, Sterne might have derived particular satisfaction from the response of Ralph Griffiths in the *Monthly Review*. The *Monthly* had enthusiastically greeted the first instalment of *Tristram Shandy*, but the discovery that the witty author was a divine led to increasingly censorious responses to the sprinkling of Rabelaisian bawdy in the later instalments. Delighted with Sterne's 'affecting' and 'touching' new book, Griffiths clearly felt that the *Monthly*'s criticisms of volumes III–IX of *Tristram Shandy* had been vindicated:

Now, Reader, did we not tell thee, in a former Review . . . that the highest excellence of this genuine, this legitimate son of humour, lies not in his humorous but in his pathetic vein?—If we have not already given proofs and specimens enough, in support of this opinion, from his *Shandy*, his

---

[1] *Letters of Laurence Sterne*, ed. Lewis Perry Curtis (Oxford: Clarendon Press, 1935), 417, 418.

Sermons, and these *Travels*, we could produce more from the little volume before us.[2]

Other early readers generally concurred with Griffiths' judgement that *A Sentimental Journey* was Sterne's 'best production', and it was his 'pathetic vein' as much as his humour that earned him classic status in the decades after his death. Indeed, while Sterne is now celebrated as a sophisticated and playfully sceptical innovator in the history of the novel, he was credited in the later eighteenth century as 'the founder of a school of sentimental writers' and widely regarded as the unrivalled delineator of 'the feelings of a tender heart, the sweetness of compassion, and the duties of humanity'.[3]

When death cut short Sterne's literary career, he had produced two of the most popular and influential books of the second half of the eighteenth century. Yet only eight years earlier he had travelled to London with the aim of promoting a book he had had to risk his own money to print. Having failed to persuade a London bookseller to take a chance on a quirky book by an unknown Yorkshire clergyman, in December 1759 Sterne financed the York and Dublin editions of the first instalment of *Tristram Shandy* and speculatively sent half the print run to London. When he arrived in the capital in March 1760, the copies had sold out and a contract for a second edition was swiftly signed with the leading London bookseller, James Dodsley. Within weeks, *Tristram Shandy* became a sensation and its author a celebrity courted and entertained by the luminaries of the London social scene.

Enjoying his celebrity status, Sterne publicly played the roles of both *Tristram Shandy*'s heteroclite divine, Yorick, and the book's eponymous hero. If, on one level, the roles were no more than playfully donned social masks, they also came to represent two aspects of Sterne's authorial identity that some of his first readers found hard to reconcile. On the one hand was the anarchic and notoriously naughty humorist, and on the other an idealized portrait of the artist as parson, whose credentials as a giver of both instruction and delight Sterne may have hoped to underscore in publishing his own sermons as *The Sermons of Mr. Yorick*. The distinction between Tristram and Yorick was not, however, strictly maintained and, as

---

[2] *Monthly Review* (March 1768), 174–85, in Alan B. Howes (ed.), *Laurence Sterne: The Critical Heritage* (London: Routledge, 1974), 199–200.

[3] *The Beauties of Sterne* (London, 1819), p. xi.

the attribution of serious pulpit discourses to a fictional court jester suggests, humour and more sober piety rarely remained altogether discrete. Encouraging the conflation of his own personality with that of his characters, the clergyman-author whose fiction encompassed bawdy comedy, pointed satire, and moving pathos appeared as mercurial in his person as in his writing.

Freed of qualms about the literary decorum appropriate for an Anglican minister, modern readers have been more willing to let Sterne's fiction speak in its own serio-comical integrity. Yet the contrasts within Sterne's small *œuvre* and the trajectory of his writing career—from the traditional satiric allegory of *A Political Romance*, through the Rabelaisian idioms and themes of *Tristram Shandy*, to the ambiguous 'sentimentalism' of *A Sentimental Journey* and the tearful intimacies of the *Journal to Eliza*—are such that modern commentators have sometimes figured Sterne as a flighty opportunist willing to write what the public would pay for. Deflected from his natural predilection for robust satire by the strictures of the reviewers, Sterne, the argument goes, wrote *A Sentimental Journey* with a calculating eye on the potential rewards to be had from the burgeoning market for sentimental fiction. Because it is belied by the significant continuities discernible across his canon, the image of Sterne as opportunist perhaps reveals more about modern criticism's discomfort with the 'sentimental' rhetoric and themes of eighteenth-century fiction than about the complex of factors that helped shape his writing career. No less than any professional writer, Sterne wanted to make money from his fiction, but this does not mean we should see commercial instinct as the principle informing his literary choices or too readily dismiss his own claims for the underlying morality of his art.[4]

There is no template for the career of a novelist in any period, but this is especially true in the eighteenth century when both the cultural standing and the generic conventions of the emerging novel were far from certain. As the period in which the novel emerged as a significant cultural form, the eighteenth century rivals the twentieth as a great age of experiment and innovation in prose fiction. Writing before the conventions that we associate with the nineteenth-century novel had been concretized, all the major

[4] For Sterne's defence of his motivation for writing *Tristram Shandy*, see *Letters*, 88–91.

eighteenth-century novelists can be seen as both pioneers and experimenters. Set alongside the relatively homogeneous canons of, say, a Jane Austen or a Thomas Hardy, Sterne's canon looks much odder than it does next to that of a contemporary such as Henry Fielding. Like Sterne, Fielding turned to fiction in his mid-forties and, like Sterne too, he began his career with a short satire and ended it, ten years later, with a novel whose 'sentimentalism' seems to belong to a quite different world. Because neither Fielding nor Sterne began writing fiction with grand plans or clear models of how a novelist's career should unfold, their respective paths from the boisterous satire of *Shamela* (1741) and *A Political Romance* to *Amelia* (1751) and *A Sentimental Journey* should not surprise us in any way. Moreover, our modern sense of the incompatibility of satire and sentiment creates an anachronistic dichotomy that did not obtain in mid-eighteenth-century fiction, where the happy cohabitation of irony, comedy, and pathos is commonplace.

Given Sterne's tentative entry into the book market and the essentially experimental nature of his fiction, the search for absolute consistency or unity of purpose in his canon is as potentially flawed as the discovery of spurious significance in apparent inconsistencies. Thus while *A Political Romance* stands as the catalyst for his writing career and clearly prefigures some aspects of *Tristram Shandy*, it would require some over-ingenious interpretation to discover in it meaningful connections with *A Sentimental Journey*. With the sermons Sterne published between instalments of *Tristram Shandy*, the situation is different and the five sermons included in this edition give a clear sense of the common ground that the fiction and pulpit discourses share. To read the sermons alongside *Tristram Shandy* and *A Sentimental Journey* is to be made aware, among other things, of Sterne's consistent preoccupation with the ethical dimensions of feeling and compassionate response. Indeed, the notion that Sterne reinvented himself as a sentimentalist with his last work is difficult to sustain in the light of the concerns of the sermons. Although it is quite unlike anything else Sterne wrote, *The Journal to Eliza* too gives further testimony to Sterne's considered engagement with the complex of ideas associated with the 'culture of sensibility'.[5] Written

---

[5] For an illuminating account of this culture, see G. J. Barker-Benfield, *The Culture of Sensibility: Sex and Society in Eighteenth-Century Britain* (Chicago: University of Chicago Press, 1992).

as he worked on *A Sentimental Journey*, and inhabiting a generic no-man's land somewhere between intimate correspondence and fiction designed for public consumption, the *Journal* illuminates as well as complicates our understanding of Sterne's much-debated 'sentimentalism'. Before looking more closely at these related works, however, it is fitting to begin with the work that fortuitously launched Sterne's literary career.

A Political Romance

When Sterne began to write *A Political Romance*, it is unlikely that he had ever contemplated becoming a professional writer. The satire was written partly for his own amusement, but primarily in support of the dean of York, John Fountayne, in his dispute with the York lawyer, Dr Francis Topham.[6] Although Fountayne was a college friend of Sterne's, he was also, more importantly, a potential patron for a lowly member of a profession in which patronage was a principal route to preferment. As he had done a number of times during his twenty-two years as a clergyman, Sterne put his wits and pen at the service of a superior in the hope that his talents would be rewarded. On this occasion, however, Sterne had to suffer more than the thwarting of his hopes for advancement in the church. Having contributed the only imaginatively distinguished blow in a local paper war over ecclesiastical rights and privileges, Sterne was denied a significant audience for the fruits of his creative labour by the archbishop of York's decision to end what had become too public a squabble. On the brink of its public dissemination, *A Political Romance* was withdrawn and its print run of several hundred copies consigned to the flames. Partly because the disappointment stung, the aborted publication was a crucial element in Sterne's subsequent decision to try his luck as a professional author. The archbishop's command to suppress the work seems to have underscored Sterne's sense of dependency and helped persuade him to exchange the role of hack for that of independent writer. Convinced of the pointlessness of 'employing [his] brains for other people's advantage',[7] Sterne

---

[6] For full details of the origins, writing, and printing of *A Political Romance*, see Arthur H. Cash, *Laurence Sterne: The Early and Middle Years* (London: Methuen, 1975), 262–77.

[7] *Letters*, 84.

now had a new self-confidence stemming from the discovery of hith-
erto hidden talents. As he told an acquaintance who visited him
when he was writing *Tristram Shandy* in June 1759, until 'he had
finished his [*Romance*] . . . he hardly knew that he could write at all,
much less with humour, so as to make his reader laugh'.[8]

While most of the credit for the humour of *A Political Romance*
belongs to Sterne, enough comedy inheres in his subject to more
than justify the archbishop's desire to take the dispute out of the
public domain. The satire focuses on the attempt of Dr Topham
(represented in Sterne's allegory as Trim the disreputable village
sexton and dog-whipper) to rewrite the patent for his post as church
commissary so that his son would inherit it. To add further weight to
his ridicule of Topham's design, Sterne also alludes to other petty
and undignified disputes between the lawyer and Dean Fountayne
(John the honourable parish clerk) that had been rumbling for nearly
ten years. In January 1751, an ongoing power struggle between
Fountayne and his allies and the faction comprised of Archbishop
Hutton (the late parson of the parish), Sterne's uncle, Jaques, and
Topham manifested itself in a quarrel over the appointment of substitute preachers. With Topham apparently deliberately stirring
things up, the conflict reached a head in a farcical scene in which
Fountayne's appointed preacher locked himself into the pulpit of
York Minster while the archbishop's appointee, sermon in hand,
angrily rattled the locked door. From such real-life absurdity, it is
only a short step to Sterne's satirical rendering of the quarrel over
the dean's powers as a squabble about the comparative heights of the
clerk's and parson's desks. Like the broader device of representing
the eminent clergy of the see of York as low-ranking officials in a
rural parish, Sterne's reductive allegory is as effective as it is simple.

Had the animosity between the dean and Topham remained at this
general level of factional strife, the paper war Sterne was about to
join in January 1759 would not have broken out. Topham, however,
had a personal gripe with Fountayne based on promises of preferment, which the latter allegedly made to the lawyer when he was
appointed dean of York in 1747. In particular, Topham felt he had
been cheated of the promised commissaryship of the spiritual court
of Pickering and Pocklington when Sterne was preferred to the post

[8] From an anonymous letter, dated 15 Apr. 1760, first published in the *St. James
Chronicle*, 24 Apr. 1788, in Howes (ed.), *Laurence Sterne: The Critical Heritage*, 60.

in July 1751. Sterne thus rubs salt into Topham's wounds by appearing in *A Political Romance* as '*Lorry Slim*, an unlucky Wight' with a 'light Heart' who cherishes the worn pair of plush breeches (the commissaryship) because 'he knows that *Trim* . . . still envies the *Possessor* of them,—and . . . would be very glad to wear them after *him*' (p. 161).

Disappointed and angry though he was in the summer of 1751, the lawyer's grievances were not made public until Fountayne's refusal to support his attempt to secure the patent of the Commissary of the Exchequer and Prerogative Court (allegorized as an old watch-coat) for his son led him to publish *A Letter Address'd to the Reverend the Dean of York* in December 1758. Fountayne responded swiftly with *An Answer* and Topham 'sallied forth again' (p. 163) with *A Reply* on 13 January 1759. A number of handbills, ballads, and broadsides added to the fun and Sterne prepared to join the fray by writing the first part of *A Political Romance* shortly after the publication of the dean's *Answer*. With the surprise appearance of Topham's second pamphlet, Sterne added the 'Postscript' and an expanded version of the satire was printed in York.

For all the comic brilliance of Sterne's ridicule of Topham, it would be vain to claim that *A Political Romance* completely transcends its immediate occasion and the inevitable limitations of local satire. None the less, the work is a success on its own terms and it tells us much about Sterne's literary tastes and predilections at the point when he began to work on the first instalment of *Tristram Shandy*. With the primary aim of laughing Topham's case out of court, Sterne looked to the great satirists of the early eighteenth century for his models. Thus Swift's practice in *A Tale of Tub* and *The Battle of the Books* of 1704 is the most palpable influence on the *Romance*'s central satiric strategy of reductive allegory. Similarly, the 'Key' appended to the satire proper draws on a satiric tradition developed by the writers of the Scriblerus Club—Dr Arbuthnot, the earl of Oxford, Thomas Parnell, Pope, and Swift—and exemplified in Pope's mockery of arcane readings of *The Rape of the Lock* (1714) in *A Key to the Lock* (1715). Like Pope's, Sterne's 'Key' offers a range of spurious allegorical interpretations, which for all their playfulness serve, paradoxically, to confirm that there is no doubt about the satire's real targets. The 'Key', though, adds nothing material to the satire of Topham and Sterne clearly began to enjoy himself in

creating the members of the York political club whose private
obsessions enable them to discover such 'a Variety of Personages,
Opinions, Transactions, and Truths' behind the 'dark Veil of
[the *Romance*'s] Allegory' (p. 172).

The Sermons of Mr. Yorick

Regretting his support for Fountayne and feeling his treatment of
Topham had been unjust, Sterne made no effort to publish the
Romance in the wake of *Tristram Shandy*'s triumph. Thinking more
highly of the sermons he had been writing and delivering throughout his clerical career, however, Sterne planned to publish them if his
book succeeded as he hoped. Having skilfully integrated one of his
two previously published sermons, 'The Abuses of Conscience Considered', into a scene set in Shandy Hall in *Tristram Shandy*'s second
volume, Sterne has Tristram inform the 'world': 'That in case the
character of parson *Yorick*, and this sample of his sermons is
liked,—that there are now in the possession of the *Shandy* Family, as
many as will make a handsome volume, at the world's service,—and
much good may they do it'.[9] The sample was well liked and when the
first two volumes of *The Sermons of Mr. Yorick* appeared in May
1760, they did so with an impressive list of subscribers and eventually
ran to more lifetime editions than the best-selling *Tristram Shandy*.

   In spite of their popularity in the 1760s and the decades after his
death, Sterne's forty-five sermons are now the most neglected part
of his canon. In part, the neglect can be understood in terms of the
distance between the sobriety of the sermons and the wit and
exuberance of the fiction. More importantly, the specialization of the
category of the literary that began in the nineteenth century has
tacitly informed the view that sermons and fiction belong to properly discrete realms. That Sterne's first readers happily read his
sermons alongside his fiction is, however, a useful reminder of an
eighteenth-century print culture in which no such distinction
obtained, and in which readers of imaginative literature were also
avid consumers of a variety of devotional texts as well as works of
history, philosophy, and science. Although prose fiction became

---

   [9] *The Life and Opinions of Tristram Shandy, Gentleman.* The Florida Edition of the
Works of Laurence Sterne (henceforth Florida edn.), vols. i–ii: *The Text* (henceforth
TS), ed. Melvyn New and Joan New (Gainesville, Fla.: University Presses of Florida,
1978), II. xvii. 167.

increasingly prominent in the second half of the eighteenth century, religious works continued to dominate the book market and the sermon remained, as John Brewer puts it, 'the single most important literary form'.[10] Written primarily for delivery in his Yorkshire parishes and without expectation of future publication, Sterne's sermons offer at once an illuminating context for his fiction and a broader insight into the values of a culture in which Anglicanism played a major role.

The Anglican discourse is among the most significant in the complex of discourses and ideas that informed the eighteenth-century 'cult', or culture, of sensibility.[11] Partly because the so-called 'sentimental' novel[12] develops from the 1740s onwards, this culture is generally seen as a mid-century phenomenon. However, many of the debates about human nature that are central to the culture of sensibility, and with which novels as diverse as Richardson's *Clarissa* (1747–8), Fielding's *Tom Jones* (1749), Goldsmith's *The Vicar of Wakefield* (1766), and *A Sentimental Journey* engage, have their roots in the late seventeenth century. Thus the arguments associated with Thomas Hobbes's *Leviathan* (1651, 1668) were contested by moral philosophers, political writers, novelists, and sermonists throughout the eighteenth century. Contrary to the Aristotelian view of man as a social animal, Hobbes saw human beings as essentially selfish, governed by warring appetites and held in check only by fear of private or state retribution. The perceived threat of these views to Christianity was such that the major divines of the late seventeenth century—the shapers of Anglican thought of the next century—took considerable pains to counter them. Consequently, many sermons emphasized sociality, good nature, and benevolence as primary

[10] John Brewer, *The Pleasures of the Imagination: English Culture in the Eighteenth Century* (HarperCollins: London, 1997), 172.

[11] The earliest and most influential treatment of the relationship between Anglican teachings and mid-century 'sentimentalism' is R. S. Crane's 'Suggestions towards a Genealogy of the "Man of Feeling" ', *ELH*, 1 (1934), 205–30.

[12] As John Richetti observes, 'the term "sentimental novel" is broadly uninformative', because most 'eighteenth-century fiction explores moral problems, meditating on the difficulty of regulating the passions and navigating virtuously through a vicious and unjust world' (*The English Novel in History, 1700–1780* (London: Routledge, 1999), 247). Similarly, the stock motifs, character types, and pathos associated with sentimental fiction are ubiquitous in the writing of the period. Thus, for example, the predominantly comic novels of Fielding and Smollett, which have much in common with Sterne's writing, are liberally sprinkled with tearful and pathetic episodes.

virtues. Without denying the importance of faith, Anglican *practical* divinity stressed the active, social virtues of charity and philanthropy, and its model of Christian behaviour has clear affinities with the types of the 'good-natured man' and 'man of feeling', who appear with increasing regularity in the mid-century novel.[13]

Accounts of the relationship between 'sentimental' fiction and Anglican theology sometimes suggest that novels and sermons share a naively optimistic understanding of human nature. Yet even in the sentimental text *par excellence*, Henry Mackenzie's *The Man of Feeling* (1771), anxiety about the unworldliness of the virtue the novel recommends is manifest. In Anglican sermons, the terms in which, and ends to which, ministers sought to vindicate human nature qualify the broad optimism of their teachings.

In his charity sermon, 'Vindication of Human Nature', Sterne argues against the view that man 'is a selfish animal' (p. 190), insisting instead that 'spontaneous love towards those of his kind' is 'one of the first and leading propensities' (p. 193) of human nature. Yet even where the conventions of the charity sermon require the minister to accentuate the positive,[14] Sterne's approach is pragmatic. Urging and cajoling his parishioners to cherish 'social virtue and public spirit' (p. 192), Sterne's defence of human nature is qualified in its admission that ' 'tis one step towards acting well, to think worthily of our nature'. Lest his listeners forget, Sterne reminds them that 'GOD made man in his own image', and that in spite of the fall and humankind's 'depraved appetites . . . 'tis a laudable pride and true greatness of mind to cherish a belief, that there is so much of that glorious image still left upon it, as shall restrain him from base and disgraceful actions'. While the divine residue is stressed, there is a simultaneous acceptance that human depravity often obscures it. Having depicted the ideal, Sterne devotes the rest of the sermon to largely practical arguments for disinterested sociality, based on an implicitly hard-nosed notion of 'mutual dependence' (p. 195) as a necessary societal cement.

In the different context of the anti-Methodist sermon, 'On

[13] See John K. Sheriff, *The Good-Natured Man: The Evolution of a Moral Ideal, 1660–1800* (Alabama: University of Alabama Press, 1982).
[14] See note to p. 190 below.

Enthusiasm', Sterne argues that we 'come not into the world equipt with virtues, as we do with talents', but act virtuously only 'by the endeavours of our own wills and concurrent influences of a gracious agent' (p. 217). Virtue has to vie with the 'stream of our affections and appetites [that] but too naturally carry us the other way' (pp. 217–18). Close as this comes to the Hobbesian assessment of human nature, it is ultimately distanced from it by the counterbalancing idea of the divine residue. None the less, the sermons regularly stress the divided nature of fallen man, and this understanding of human appetites and affections is a key element in Sterne's treatment of the mixed impulses that typically underlie Yorick's philanthropy in *A Sentimental Journey*.

Following the practice of favourite sermonists like Joseph Hall and John Norris,[15] Sterne's sermons address the hearts as well as heads of his listeners. Thus, as Griffiths' review of *A Sentimental Journey* suggests, it was as much the affective rhetoric of the sermons as the celebrated 'pathetic tales' of the fiction that informed Sterne's eighteenth-century reputation as a master of pathos. When the former slave, Ignatius Sancho, wrote to Sterne in 1766 declaring his adoration of 'Philanthropy', he thanked him for the character of *Tristram Shandy*'s 'amiable uncle Toby' and claimed: 'Your Sermons have touched me to the heart, and I hope have amended it'.[16] This willingness to be both moved and improved by what Sterne called stories 'painted to the heart'[17] is quite alien to modern sensibilities, but finds many echoes in the responses of contemporary readers to scenes of pathos in such novels as Richardson's *Clarissa* (1747–8). Modern readers are likely to discover bathos and mawkishness in the representations of tearful familial affection or pathetic spectacles of virtue in distress that are common currency in sermons and mid-eighteenth-century fiction alike. In a culture informed by Christian morality in which didacticism was not only expected but apparently enjoyed by readers, however, pathetic

[15] For a thorough discussion of Sterne's sources and theology see Melvyn New's introduction to Florida edn., vol. v: *The Notes to the Sermons* (Gainesville, Fla.: University Press of Florida, 1996), 1–55.

[16] *The Letters of Ignatius Sancho*, ed. Paul Edwards and Polly Rewt (Edinburgh: Edinburgh University Press, 1994), 85. For Sterne's correspondence with Sancho, see note to p. 60 below.

[17] *TS*, III. xx. 233.

rhetoric was understood differently.[18] As Sterne argues in his sermon, 'The Prodigal Son':

lessons of wisdom have never such power over us, as when they are wrought into the heart, through the ground-work of a story which engages the passions: Is it that we are like iron, and must first be heated before we can be wrought upon? or, Is the heart so in love with deceit, that where a true report will not reach it, we must cheat it with a fable, in order to come at truth?[19]

Accordingly, Sterne's sermons deploy pathos in the effort to persuade his fallible parishioners to live virtuously within the Christian scheme. The short sentimental tableaux, which punctuate such sermons as 'The House of Feasting' and 'Job's Account', aim to underscore the discourses' teachings about the shortness and troubles of life by imbuing them with the weight of emotional authenticity. Although the pathetic episodes of the fiction are more developed and more complex in their effects, the self-borrowings and echoes of 'Job's Account' in *A Sentimental Journey* are one of many indications that Sterne drew on his experience as a sermonist when he wanted to engage his readers' emotions.[20]

While the concerns of *A Sentimental Journey* are reflected in a number of Sterne's sermons, 'The Levite and his Concubine' is especially relevant to the novel's treatment of sexual desire. Written 'against rash judgment' (p. 211) of others' failings, the sermon uses the story of the Levite to argue for forgiveness of sins and a cultivation of the social virtues of pity and understanding 'that we might live with . . . kind intercourse in this world' (p. 213). In a series of passages that are echoed in *A Sentimental Journey*,[21] Sterne accounts for the Levite's relationship with his concubine in ways which seek to reconcile private passions with the demands of society. Desire for companionship with the opposite sex, and desire itself properly directed, are not only God given, Sterne contends, but belong to a more general and improving human yearning for

---

[18] For an illuminating discussion of the relationship between didacticism and readerly pleasure, see J. Paul Hunter, *Before Novels: The Cultural Contexts of Eighteenth-Century English Fiction* (New York: Norton and Company, 1990), ch. 9.

[19] Florida edn., vol. iv: *The Sermons*, ed. Melvyn New (Gainesville, Fla.: University Press of Florida,1996), 20. 186.

[20] For the echoes of 'Job's Account', see below, notes to pp. 60, 61.

[21] See below, notes to pp. 24, 45, and 78.

'society and friendship' (p. 208).[22] This view is fundamental to *A Sentimental Journey*, and it is no coincidence that Sterne reworks two passages from the sermon in the novel's most explicit defence of desire:

If nature has so wove her web of kindness, that some threads of love and desire are entangled with the piece—must the whole web be rent in drawing them out?—Whip me such stoics, great governor of nature! . . . Wherever thy providence shall place me for the trials of my virtue . . . let me feel the movements which rise out of it, and which belong to me as a man—and if I govern them as a good one—I will trust the issues to thy justice, for thou has made us—and not we ourselves. (p. 78)

A Sentimental Journey

When *The Sermons of Mr. Yorick* were printed in 1760, a number of reviewers took exception to 'the manner of their publication'. In attributing the sermons to *Tristram Shandy*'s Yorick, Sterne, according to the *Monthly Review* of May 1760, was shamefully associating 'the solemn dictates of religion' with 'Buffoons and ludicrous Romancers'.[23] Undeterred, Sterne retained the controversial title when he published two more volumes of sermons in 1766. This willingness to stick to his guns in the face of sometimes shrill criticism is especially noteworthy in the light of the suggestion that *A Sentimental Journey* represents Sterne's capitulation to the reviewers' demands that he exchange indecency for the '*innocently humorous*'.[24] Although he was clearly aware that readers willing to accept ribald satire from the laity had different expectations of Anglican ministers, he was secure enough in what he saw as the moral basis of his writing to characterise his critics as 'Hypocrites and Tartufes'[25] and to continue writing as he thought best. Had Sterne really been swayed by the criticisms of the periodical reviewers, his last work would surely have been quite different in

[22] For an insightful discussion of Sterne's understanding of desire and its parallels in the writing of John Norris, see Melvyn New, 'The Odd Couple: Laurence Sterne and John Norris of Bemerton', *Philological Quarterly*, 75 (1996), 361–85.

[23] *Monthly Review* (May 1760), 422–5, in Howes (ed.), *Laurence Sterne: The Critical Heritage*, 77.

[24] *Monthly Review* (Feb. 1765), in Howes (ed.), *Laurence Sterne: The Critical Heritage*, 167.

[25] *Letters*, 411.

character. As it is, *A Sentimental Journey* cocks a snook at prudish Tartuffes by boldly insisting that love and desire are integral to nature's 'web of kindness'. Rather than censoring out any hint of indelicacy, Sterne wrote a book replete with mischievously lewd wordplay, which frankly and comically explores Yorick's often questionable responses to the chance encounters with women that his journey throws up.

Although Sterne's belief in the integrity of his work enabled him to take many of the reviewers' strictures with a pinch of salt, he was sufficiently stung by the slights on his character to feel the need to mount something of a defence. Rather than a sop to his critics, *A Sentimental Journey* is intended, among other things, as a defiant riposte and vindication of Sterne's personal reputation. In presenting *A Sentimental Journey* as Mr Yorick's journey, Sterne was drawing on his readers' familiarity with his published sermons and Yorick's role as a witty, but none the less balanced and moral, presence in *Tristram Shandy*'s imagined world. In so doing, Sterne clearly hoped to convince his readers that he was much less like Tristram than his severest critics claimed. *A Sentimental Journey*, Sterne told the author Richard Griffith, was to be 'his *Work of Redemption*'.[26] As is clear from a letter written earlier in the year to Ignatius Sancho, the work of redemption was given an extra edge by Sterne's sense of impending mortality: 'I shall live this year at least, I hope, be it but to give the world, before I quit it, as good impressions of me, as you have, Sancho. I would only covenant for just so much health and spirits, as are sufficient to carry my pen thro' the task I have set it this summer'.[27] That such good impressions were meant to offer an alternative to an image tarnished by a bawdy book and gossip about the rumoured sexual indiscretions of a celebrity author is made clear in a letter written two months later to a friend: 'my Sentimental Journey will, I dare say, convince you that my feelings are from the heart, and that that heart is not of the worst molds— praised be God for my sensibility! Though it has often made me wretched, yet I would not exchange it for all the pleasures the grossest sensualist ever felt'.[28]

---

[26] Richard Griffith, *A Series of Genuine Letters, between Henry and Frances* (London, 1786), v. 86–7, quoted in *Letters*, 399.

[27] *Letters*, 370.

[28] Ibid. 395–6.

Apart from the desire to redeem his reputation, it is clear that *A Sentimental Journey* also grew out of Sterne's search for the kind of inspiration that *Tristram Shandy* was no longer providing. The first six volumes of the novel had been written and published in a burst of creative activity between the summer of 1759 and December 1761. Partly because ill health led him to make two lengthy trips to Europe, it was three years before the seventh and eighth volumes appeared and two more before the final single-volume instalment. Unsurprisingly, Sterne's enthusiasm and inspiration appear to have flagged during this time and the diminishing sales of the later volumes were hardly encouraging. Of the new ideas which came to him, some were furnished by his experiences of travelling in Europe, and in the seventh volume Sterne has Tristram fly from death by making his own journey across the Channel to France. Described by Sterne as 'a laughing good temperd Satyr against Traveling (as puppies travel)',[29] the volume is more centrally concerned with satirizing particular travel writers than *A Sentimental Journey*, but it shares with it an insistence that travel narrative should be about contact with people rather than the arid documentation of sights seen.

By the time Sterne came to write the final volume of *Tristram Shandy* in the summer and autumn of 1766, the embryonic plan for *A Sentimental Journey* was sufficiently developed for him to include in it an episode that is sometimes seen as an advertisement for the later work. Digressing briefly from the comic narrative of the amours of Uncle Toby and the Widow Wadman, Sterne takes his readers back to France to paint a picture of Tristram's encounter with 'poor Maria'. Different in emphasis from Yorick's later encounter with the beautiful and distracted young woman, the scene, none the less, has much in common with the pathetic episodes of *A Sentimental Journey*. Moved at first by the postillion's narrative of Maria's woes, Tristram is moved even more by her physical presence: 'she was beautiful; and if ever I felt the full force of an honest heart-ache, it was the moment I saw her'. Characteristically, Sterne complicates Tristram's seemingly innocent 'heart-ache' by comically revealing the lust that the language of feeling masks. Sitting down between Maria and her goat, Tristram is jolted out of his reverie: 'MARIA look'd wistfully for some time at me, and then at her

---

[29] Ibid. 231.

goat——and then at me——and then at her goat again, and so on, alternately——Well, Maria, said I softly——What resemblance do you find?'[30] Sterne's willingness to puncture moments of pathos in this way is now often read as a signal that he is parodying sentimental idioms and mocking emotional response *per se*. Yet this is surely to mistake Sterne's point. In the orthodox belief that human beings are 'not angels, but men cloathed with bodies',[31] Sterne often stages scenes of sympathetic response in his fiction in order to demonstrate that even compassion is seldom, if ever, unmixed with less worthy passions like desire. Tristram's desire for Maria does not negate his pity for her plight, but it does qualify it and prevent a complacent celebration of his angelic benevolence.

For modern readers, Yorick's response to his meeting with Maria in *A Sentimental Journey* is likely to appear as self-satisfied as it seemed moving to Sterne's contemporaries. Having wiped both Maria's tears of sorrow and his own tears of sympathy with his handkerchief, Yorick feels 'such undescribable emotions within' as to convince him, in spite of 'all the books with which materialists have pester'd the world' (p. 95), of the existence of his soul. While Sterne allows for the possibility that the parson's reaction is sexual as well as sympathetic, the allusion to materialism should warn us against the discovery of ironic hyperbole in Yorick's reading of his emotional responses. Outside the context of eighteenth-century thought, Yorick's reasoning can seem comically flawed, but in the light of the long-running controversy between atheistic materialists and Christian thinkers, his conclusion partakes of a logic that enabled theologians to hold on to the notion of the immateriality of the soul (without which there can be no afterlife).[32] Sterne takes the orthodox position that since matter cannot think, emotion, like other physical feelings and sensations, has its source in the immaterial soul. A kind of circular reasoning thus imbues Yorick's tearful sympathy for Maria with spiritual value. This understanding of compassion also illuminates the apostrophe to sensibility that he is moved to utter after the encounter: 'Dear sensibility! source inexhausted of all that's precious in our joys, or costly in our sorrows! . . . eternal

---

[30] *TS*, IX. xxiv. 783.

[31] *Sermons*, 43. 402. Sterne repeats the phrase in *TS*, v. vii. 431–2.

[32] See John W. Yolton, *Thinking Matter: Materialism in Eighteenth-Century Britain* (Minneapolis: University of Minnesota Press, 1983).

fountain of our feelings!—'tis here I trace thee—and this is thy divinity which stirs within me' (p. 98). Yorick's pity for Maria may, like Tristram's, be mingled with lust, but his sensibility—the source of disinterested fellow feeling *and* erotic response—partakes of the divine residue.

Responding to the characteristic intermingling of pathos and comedy in Sterne's fiction, Friedrich Nietzsche observed that the 'reader who demands to know . . . whether he is making a serious or a laughing face, must be given up for lost: for he knows how to encompass both in a *single* facial expression'.[33] The ambiguity Nietzsche so prized is typically produced by abrupt transitions of mood and tone. Thus the Maria episode in *Tristram Shandy* is introduced by bawdy allusions to the chances of catching venereal disease in Italy and concluded with Tristram's ejaculation: 'What an excellent inn at Moulins!'[34] Partly because of a modern suspicion of any explicit or overtly rhetorical address to the reader's emotions, we are apt to assume that comic realism will necessarily undercut pathos. Yet Sterne follows favourite writers such as Cervantes in a kind of sceptical balancing in which he presents not laughter *or* tears, but both. Significantly, the story of Maria in *Tristram Shandy* is prefaced by an 'Invocation' to the 'GENTLE Spirit of sweetest humour, who erst didst sit upon the easy pen of my beloved CERVANTES',[35] and *A Sentimental Journey* too acknowledges its Cervantic heritage in its several allusions to *Don Quixote*. Cervantes is the single most important precursor of eighteenth-century comic fiction, but in writers like Fielding, Smollett, and Sterne, his influence is also clearly seen in their handling of pathetic episodes. Alongside robust and sometimes scatological comedy, *Don Quixote* presents pathetic tales of pastoral romance and tearful scenes of sympathetic response. Like Sterne, Cervantes is unwilling to let either genuine feeling or satiric laughter stand alone: rather he presents both in their mutually qualifying integrity. Fittingly, an allusion to Sancho Panza's comic lamentation for his lost ass gently modifies the pathetic tableau of 'The Dead Ass' (pp. 33–5) in *A Sentimental Journey*. As one of

[33] Friedrich Nietzsche, *Human, All Too Human, A Book for Free Spirits*, trans. R. J. Hollingdale with an introduction by Erich Heller (Cambridge: Cambridge University Press, 1986), 238–9.

[34] *TS*, IX. xxiv. 784.

[35] Ibid. 780.

Yorick's key statements has it: 'there is nothing unmixt in this world' (p. 74).

That the design of *A Sentimental Journey* was already developing in Sterne's mind when he wrote the last volume of *Tristram Shandy* is further suggested by a veiled reference to Tobias Smollett's *Travels through France and Italy* (1766) in the prelude to Maria's story. 'I do not think', says Tristram, 'a journey through France and Italy, provided a man keeps his temper all the way, so bad a thing as some people would make you believe.'[36] The subtlety of the allusion is an indication of the relatively high profile of Smollett's *Travels* and its quickly acquired notoriety as an ill-tempered account of European travel. *A Sentimental Journey* is sometimes seen as Sterne's reply to Smollett, but it would be wrong to overstress the latter's role in Sterne's scheme. On a number of occasions, Sterne alludes to observations made in the *Travels* and implicitly asks his readers to contrast the reactions of the sentimental Yorick with those of the splenetic Smollett. The brief caricature of Smollett as the 'learned SMELFUNGUS' whose 'spleen and jaundice' distorted 'every object he pass'd by' (p. 24) similarly, if not altogether fairly, constructs the Scottish writer as the prejudiced and irascible other of the traveller who is open to the 'large volume of adventures [that] may be grasped ... by him who interests his heart in every thing' (p. 23). Nevertheless, Smelfungus, like the generalized figure of Mundungus, represents more a type of traveller than a particular satiric butt targeted on the grounds of profound ideological differences.

The relationship between Smollett's *Travels* and *A Sentimental Journey* is to some extent mirrored in the latter's relationship to the genre of travel writing. Because his own journeys to Europe had received some public notice, some of Sterne's first readers might well have expected to find authentic experience underpinning Yorick's ostensibly fictional journey. Nevertheless, few of Yorick's experiences bear any relation to his creator's, and Sterne's real interest is in the commonplaces and conventions of travel *writing* and not in the kind of detailed accounts of French and Italian culture that form the focus of genuine travel books like Smollett's. Like Swift's *Gulliver's Travels* (1726), *A Sentimental Journey* exploits the reader's appetite for travel narrative better to subvert their expectations. The

---

[36] *TS*, IX. xxiv. 780–1.

place names that head many of the sections of the novel seem to promise the reader predictable descriptions of the monuments and buildings of French towns and cities. Instead, Yorick offers his observations on such seeming trifles as a meeting with a mendicant monk, a Parisian barber's penchant for hyperbole or an encounter with 'a Chevalier de St. Louis selling *patès*' (p. 66). While this focus on the apparently banal is central to Yorick's contention that 'nonsensical *minutiæ*' (42) reveal more about French culture than the grander reports of traditional travel writers, it also belongs to the novel's larger strategy of defamiliarization. In this and other respects *A Sentimental Journey* is something of an anti-travel book, flouting generic conventions, at the level of both form and content, in order to disturb the reader's settled assumptions. Where English travellers typically condemned the idleness and greed of monks or expressed outrage at the French habit of urinating in public, Yorick learns lessons from both Father Lorenzo's humility and Madame de Rambouliet's candour. More centrally, Yorick's *sentimental* journey playfully indulges, before finally overturning, the commonplace association between European travel and sexual adventure. Time and again, Sterne places Yorick in circumstances that presage erotic liaisons only to have them culminate in comic anti-climax.

In his discussion of the impact of travel literature on the early novel, J. Paul Hunter suggests that in fiction the journey 'is usually . . . a structure of convenience' in which 'precise location is . . . less important than the fact that there *are* different locations and that people in different places actually differ from one another. The menu . . . of most novels may be human nature, but there are several courses, and the implication is that no single view of human nature will serve—that cultures alter people, people alter circumstances, and circumstances alter cases'.[37] The observation is clearly applicable to the way in which Sterne uses Yorick's journey as a means of weighing general 'truths' about human benevolence, affection, and desire in the modifying contexts encountered by the 'expatriated adventurer' (p. 8). Yorick describes his adventure in Calais as 'an assay upon human nature' (p. 24) and the idea of assaying, or testing, human nature might be extended to the novel as a whole. Indeed, the structure of a journey is particularly productive for Sterne because

[37] Hunter, *Before Novels*, 353.

of the opportunities it affords for testing Yorick's emotional responses and codes of conduct in a variety of unfamiliar situations. Behind Sterne's approach lies the Protestant emphasis on self-examination (leading ideally to self-knowledge) and the tradition of casuistry, which had migrated from conduct literature into fiction in the early eighteenth century.[38] Casuistry, according to the *Oxford English Dictionary*, is 'that part of Ethics which resolves cases of conscience, applying the general rules of religion and morality to particular instances in which "circumstances alter cases", or in which there appears to be a conflict of duties'. While the rigours of casuistry proper may seem alien to the comedy of *A Sentimental Journey*, Sterne alludes explicitly to this tradition in the headings of two episodes—'The Case of Conscience' (pp. 80–1) and 'The Case of Delicacy' (pp. 100–4)—and less overtly in such sections as 'The Temptation' and 'The Conquest' (pp. 76–9). Playful though these episodes are, the insistence of 'The Levite and his Concubine' that circumstances should qualify judgement of sexual transgression is especially germane to their message. More broadly, *A Sentimental Journey* regularly stages scenes of temptation in which either Yorick's 'base' (p. 13) or nobler passions—and sometimes both—are revealed. Perhaps one explanation of why eighteenth-century readers celebrated the book in spite of its frank treatment of Yorick's sexual impulses, lies in Sterne's candid acceptance of conflicted human nature. If Yorick is denied complete self-knowledge, the reader, it is hoped, can learn from his experiences. As Thomas Jefferson observed of Yorick's treatment of the Franciscan: 'we are sorrowful at the rebuke, and secretly resolve *we* will never do so: we are pleased with the subsequent atonement, and view with emulation a soul candidly acknowledging its faults, and making a just reparation'.

Interestingly, Jefferson refers to *A Sentimental Journey* to demonstrate his contention that fictional representations of acts of charity and 'atrocious' deeds have improving effects on the reader. To be moved by Sterne is, for Jefferson, a form of 'exercise . . . of the moral feelings, [which] produces a habit of thinking and acting virtuously'.[39] Like Sancho's delight that Sterne's sermons had touched

---

[38] Hunter, *Before Novels*, 285–94.
[39] Jefferson to Robert Skipworth, 3 Aug. 1771, in Howes (ed.), *Laurence Sterne: The Critical Heritage*, 215.

and amended his heart, Jefferson's understanding of the rhetorical functions of pathos helps us to recover the kind of reader response that informed Sterne's reputation as the progenitor of sentimental fiction in the 1770s and 80s. Not least among the lessons to be learnt from Jefferson's reading of Sterne is that modern connotations of 'sentimental' have little in common with the word's eighteenth-century resonances. While 'sentimental' still retains positive connotations in some usages, it now more typically denotes mawkish and indulgent emotionalism. Such pejorative connotations began to be current in the 1780s when a predictable backlash against the excesses of some of Sterne's imitators, and a growing sense that essentially private manifestations of sensibility were poor substitutes for active charity, contributed to a growing suspicion of the language of feeling. When Sterne described Yorick's journey as 'sentimental', however, his understanding of the word was quite different.

One of the significations of 'sentimental' available to Sterne derives from the noun 'sentiment', suggesting a moral reflection or opinion. Although such reflections need not have an emotional colouring, a 'sentiment' was often seen to proceed from an alliance of head and heart. Thus Adam Smith's *Theory of Moral Sentiments* (1759) focuses on compassionate sympathy and offers a theoretical analysis of morals understood to have an emotional basis. In this light, the 'sentimental' in Sterne's title might be read as an indication that Yorick's narrative is concerned with the reflections or moral sentiments—especially those relating to the social virtues of compassion and philanthropy—occasioned by his travels. When Sterne wrote *A Sentimental Journey*, however, key words in the lexicon of feeling had a variety of connotations and he clearly wanted to exploit some of this semantic instability. A sense of this instability can be gleaned from Sterne's own use of 'sentimental' in his letters, sermons, and fiction. In one instance, the word is used ironically to refer to its libidinous opposite—as in *Tristram Shandy*'s reference to the 'sentimental parts of . . . *French* Romances'.[40] It can mean emotionally touching—as in the 'most sentimental group' of 'The Levite and his Concubine' (p. 206)–and it can also signify platonic, non-sexual affection. Thus Sterne signs off a letter to David Garrick: 'I love you dearly—and Y^r Lady better.—not hobbi-horsically—but most

---

[40] *TS*, I. xviii. 57.

sentimentally & affectionately'.[41] Insofar as Yorick's erotic encounters are unconsummated (with the possible exception of the 'connection' (p. 48) with the Marquesina di F***), his journey is 'sentimental' in this non-sexual sense. Yorick's meetings with women are, none the less, often risqué enough to bring this purely chaste signification to the borders of irony. In a book intent on demonstrating the entanglements of 'love and desire' in nature's 'web of kindness' (p. 78), it is appropriate that Sterne's title should be deliberately ambiguous, hovering between 'pure' feeling and ironic suggestiveness, but settling on neither.

Following Richardson's influential example, the figure of virtue in distress in mid-century fiction is characteristically a woman whose virtue and chastity are more or less synonymous. In the novel, at least, wider cultural anxieties about human nature are often reduced to an equation of vice with male sexuality and virtue with chaste female sensibility. Although there were dissenting voices, sexuality is typically the rock upon which efforts to imagine both personal virtue and social being founder. Like Fielding, Sterne is concerned to contest this model and refuses, as Melvyn New puts it, 'to accept the Pauline trap of condemning the body so vociferously that the body becomes the site of all ethical conflict'.[42] Where the period's understanding of sensibility frequently involved a censoring out of sexuality, Sterne seeks to reconcile feeling and desire. The lesson of the letter La Fleur persuades Yorick to send to Mme de L*** is that desire is impoverished without feeling, while feeling is equally diminished without a love that includes desire. For Sterne, the traditional separation of love into two kinds—*agape* (non-sexual love) and *eros* (desire)—cannot be strictly maintained. The ambiguity of Sterne's title thus enacts the novel's central contention that the distinction between pure feeling and impure desire can only be sustained in defiance of the complex fabric of God-given human nature.

Missing Sterne's point and demonstrating a surprising insensitivity to the undercurrent of bawdy innuendo found throughout the novel, the *Monthly Review* objected that Sterne chose to end the second volume with a scene 'bordering rather on sensuality rather

---

[41] *Letters*, 237.
[42] Melvyn New, 'Sterne in the Future Tense', *The Shandean*, 11 (1999–2000), 68.

than sentiment'.[43] Given Sterne's effort to deconstruct the binary opposition between sensuality and feeling, however, it is altogether fitting that the completed portion of *A Sentimental Journey* should end by juxtaposing an idyllic 'feast of love'[44] (p. 99) with the mischievous 'Case of Delicacy', in which prudery paradoxically leads to Yorick inadvertently groping the Fille de Chambre. The episode is a fable of sorts which develops Sterne's contention that the '*extreams* of DELICACY, and the *beginnings* of CONCUPISCENCE'[45] are closely related. This view also seems to inform Sterne's plea in *A Sentimental Journey* for a more honest acceptance of human physicality. Living up to the type of the reserved Englishman, Yorick is at first embarrassed by the candour of the French, but by the second month of his stay, he can take Madame de Rambouliet's '*Rien que pisser*' (p. 52) in his stride. Similarly, his scruples about the Count de B****'s indelicacies are put into perspective by Bevoriskius' recognition of God's mercy in the urgent 'reiteration of' the cock-sparrow's 'caresses' (p. 74). Clearly Yorick's embarrassment is replete with the irony of his creator's reputation as a purveyor of bawdy, but it also represents a more serious challenge to those 'whose clay-cold heads and luke-warm hearts' enable them to 'argue down or mask' passions given to them by the 'father of spirits' (p. 78).

The Journal to Eliza

As Sterne worked on *A Sentimental Journey* in the summer of 1767, he was also keeping a journal addressed to a 22-year-old woman he had met in London five months earlier.[46] When the extant portion of the journal begins on 12 April, its addressee, Elizabeth Draper, was nine days into what would be a nine-month return voyage to her husband and home in Bombay. About eight weeks later, Sterne was writing the opening episode of his novel and, with a characteristic conflation of fiction and reality, self-consciously immortalizing Mrs Draper in the reference to the 'little picture' of 'Eliza' (p. 3) that

[43] *Monthly Review* (March 1768), 174–85, in Howes (ed.), *Laurence Sterne: The Critical Heritage*, 201.

[44] See note to p. 99 below.

[45] *TS*, V. 1. 415.

[46] For a detailed account of the genesis of the *Journal* and Sterne's relationship with Elizabeth Draper, see Arthur H. Cash, *Laurence Sterne: The Later Years* (London: Methuen, 1986), 283–304.

Yorick wears about his neck. Referring to the allusion in the journal entry for 17 June, Sterne offers his own succinct gloss on Yorick's and Eliza's relationship:

I have brought your name *Eliza!* and Picture into my work—where they will remain—when You and I are at rest for ever—Some Annotator or explainer of my works in this place will take occasion, to speak of the Friendship which Subsisted so long and faithfully betwixt Yorick and the Lady he speaks of . . . he will tell the world . . . [t]hat Yorick, (whether he made much Opposition is not known) from an acquaintance—soon became her Admirer—they caught fire at each other at the same time—and they would often say, without reserve to the world, and without any Idea of saying wrong in it, That their Affections for each other were *unbounded*—(p. 132)

Informative though it is, the gloss leaves much for the annotator to explain. Most obviously, 'Friendship' seems inadequate to describe feelings characterized as mutually unbounded and, on Sterne's part at least, strong enough to fuel a fantasy of a future marriage, in spite of his serious ill health, an age gap of over thirty years, and the fact that both parties were already married. In reality, Sterne's effort to annotate and explain what he saw as a key episode in his life is also an attempt to impose the clarity of his own hopes on the far less certain facts of his brief relationship with Elizabeth Draper. In the letters he sent to her before she sailed for India, Sterne's uncertainty, and even confusion, is similarly evident in the self-images he projects. Confessing that he is 'half in love'[47] in the first extant letter, the letters that follow find Sterne presenting himself less as a would-be lover and more as a disinterested friend, father, and mentor. This confusion about the nature of his love for 'Eliza' is evident too in the *Journal*'s less than convincing efforts to maintain the very distinction between *agape* and *eros* that *A Sentimental Journey* contests.

At once the strangest and least coherent of Sterne's writings, the *Journal*'s relationship to *A Sentimental Journey* remains a matter of debate. For Wilbur Cross, who first published the *Journal* in 1904, 'it completely reveals the pathological state of the emotions . . . whence sprang the *Sentimental Journey*'.[48] More recently, John Mullan has

---

[47] *Letters*, 298.
[48] Wilbur L. Cross, *The Life and Times of Laurence Sterne* (New Haven: Yale University Press, 1929), 460. *The Journal to Eliza* was so named by Cross after Swift's *Journal to Stella*.

argued that the *Journal*'s artifice and conventional expression tell us 'about a writer whom Sterne fabricated, not about [his] original emotional condition'.[49] Different as they are, both readings share a desire to distance Sterne from the often self-pitying and frequently lachrymose man of feeling who emerges from the pages of the *Journal*.

If we can discount Cross's mistaken notion that Sterne's frequent bouts of illness had reduced him to a pathological condition, Mullan's reading of the *Journal* as a form of idealized self-fashioning is more difficult to gainsay. Although it is unlikely that Sterne ever expected the *Journal* to find its way into print, it is perfectly possible that he hoped it would contribute in some way to his posthumous reputation. Even so, there is abundant evidence in the range of Sterne's public and private writings to indicate that he valued the ideals associated with the culture of sensibility—humanity, compassion, and the feeling heart—as highly as the majority of his contemporaries. The difference between real and rhetorical emotion is impossible to gauge through the medium of print, but it has to be acknowledged again that what is moving to one age can be simply mawkish to another. Conventions tend to become clichés when they have lost the power to speak and Sterne writes at a moment when the language of the heart was understood as the most sincere form of communication. When Sterne describes Mrs James's sympathetic response to the separation of Yorick and Eliza, her 'pathetick flood of Tears' is an index of 'kindly nature' (p. 117) and affecting evidence that the divide between self and other can be bridged.

For all their conventionality, the men of feeling who inhabit many novels of the period partake of a larger cultural response to the elevation of sensibility and its associations with a particular construction of chaste femininity. The gendering and desexualizing of virtuous sensibility had significant implications for traditional conceptions of masculinity, and the effort to rethink them is as apparent in the mid-century novel as it is in the period's wider concern with the reformation of male manners.[50] Although it is in some ways untypical, Mackenzie's *The Man of Feeling* is testimony to the real difficulties writers encountered in their attempts to imagine a good

[49] John Mullan, *Sentiment and Sociability: The Language of Feeling in the Eighteenth Century* (Oxford: Clarendon Press, 1990), 186.

[50] See Barker-Benfield, *The Culture of Sensibility*, chs. 2 and 5.

man. Mackenzie's hero is devoid of anti-social appetites and yet so sensitized to the suffering of the world that social being becomes an impossibility. In Fielding's Tom Jones, Richardson's Sir Charles Grandison, and the Yorick of *A Sentimental Journey*, the treatment of the relationship between male sensibility and sexuality is more complex, but the difficulty of reconciling the two is equally evident. For Sterne, as the *Journal* reveals, these difficulties were as much personal as intellectual.

In the 1740s, Sterne happily spent time in the traditionally masculine and the mildly libertine company of the club of friends— playfully known as the 'Demoniacs'—who gathered at the Yorkshire home of his college friend, John Hall-Stevenson. During the same period, he was able to reconcile his status as a married divine with evenings in York spent with women procured for him by his servant. The *Journal* and a number of the letters from his final months suggest, however, that Sterne had become genuinely uncomfortable with his rakish, sexual self. There are, of course, many reasons why he might want to persuade Elizabeth Draper that her suitor was a man of sensibility rather than a libertine. Yet the very logic of the construction of 'Eliza' as 'too good . . . to love aught but Virtue' (p. 113) almost compels him to deny his own sexual impulses. Eliza's sensibility is so refined that 'not one man out of 50' is 'informd with feelings—or endow'd either with heads or hearts able to possess and fill [her] mind' (p. 134). Similarly, having made the somewhat surprising decision to tell Eliza that he had been diagnosed with venereal disease, Sterne is forced to protest a little too much in presenting it as an extraordinary irony: 'thus Eliza is your Yorick . . . your friend with all his sensibilities, suffering the Chastisement of the grossest Sensualist' (pp. 112–13).

While parts of *A Sentimental Journey* and the *Journal* were written at the same time, most of the novel was composed after Sterne's commitment to the 'Diary of [his] miserable feelings' (p. 107) had waned, and when, in all probability, he realized the element of wishfulness and self-delusion in his idealized view of a brief relationship. It is sometimes therefore suggested that a post-infatuation Sterne mocked his own folly in *A Sentimental Journey*, but it is equally possible to see the novel as a serious response to ethical concerns that had been given a new edge by personal experience. In the *Journal*, Sterne follows the Richardsonian pattern of opposing virtue and feeling to sexuality, and consequently falls into the error that *A Sentimental Journey* is so concerned to avoid. Setting out on his travels wearing Eliza's image around his neck and convinced that he understands 'sentiment and fine feelings' (p. 3), the chance experiences of the journey regularly cause Yorick to revise his settled assumptions. Just as his theoretical benevolence is immediately tested by the meeting with the monk, so Yorick's belief in an impossibly rarefied love is challenged, and finally unravelled, by a succession of encounters with women whose pulses speak a more complicated language.

T. P.

NOTE ON THE TEXTS

The text of *A Sentimental Journey* is based on that of the first edition (*A*), which appeared about 27 February 1768. In the second edition, which appeared on 29 March (eleven days after the death of Sterne), a number of misprints and other obvious errors were corrected, but there are no signs of authorial revision. I depart from the text of the first edition only in the following instances:

Page and line
of present edition

9, 36–10, 2
The simple Traveller,	The simple Traveller,
and the last of all (if you please)	And last of all (if you please) The
The Sentimental Traveller	Sentimental Traveller (meaning
(meaning thereby myself)]	thereby myself) *A*

15, 5	attached] which attached *A*
27, 15	ill off] ill of *A*
31, 15	well be,] be well, *A*
38, 3	*fille de chambre*,] *fille dè chambre, A*
39, 5	angry:] angry *A*
42, 19	to think] of thinking *A*
54, 11	he loves] he love *A*
54, 27	if it is] if is *A*
55, 8	one] one one *A*
55, 19	together.] together *A*
57, 8	set out;] sat out; *A*
57, 19, 21, and 26	La Fleur] Le Fleur *A*
59, 7	I could not] that I could not *A*
60, 13–14	nor do I remember] or do I remember*A*
61, 7	multitude of] multitude of of *A*
62, 5	by myself] by himself *A*
62, 21	a livre] a a livre *A*
62, 35	Lord C's gentleman] Lord's C's gentleman *A*
65, 31	coachman] coachmen *A*
71, 28	*Me Voici!*] Me, *Voici! A*
72, 30	moments!—] moments!— —*A*
74, 33	*polis.*] *poli.s A*
75, 11	the heart] the the heart *A*
75, 16	refinements,] resentment, *A*
75, 27	rubbing] ribbing *A*
76, 17	When] Whey *A*

76, 32	the same colour as] the same colour of *A*
78, 3	into the left—] into into the left—*A*
83, 6	Montriul] Montreal *A*
87, 14	where am I] where I am *A*
87, 39	be read] me read *A*
88, 28	prithee,] pritheé, *A*
88, 29	see if you canst get] *see if you canst get A*
90, 36	the morning] the the morning *A*
94, 24	neighbourhood] neighbouthood *A*
96, 30	too much] to much *A*
97, 28	sufferings had] sufferings has *A*
101, 7	his road up.] his up road. *A*
101, 21	beds in it,] beds, in it *A*
101, 35	a look] alook *A*
103, 18	inasmuch as] inasmuch *A*
104, 12	by way of asseveration—] by way asseveration—*A*

In the first edition open inverted commas are renewed at the beginning of each new line of a speech or other quotation: no attempt has been made to follow this practice. Nor have the full-stops after the heading of each chapter been reproduced. A degree sign indicates a note at the end of the book.

The text of *The Journal to Eliza* is based on that in *Letters of Laurence Sterne*, edited by Lewis Perry Curtis, but it has been collated throughout with the manuscript in the British Museum. Fuller annotation may be found in Curtis. Whereas Curtis presents an exact transcript, I have omitted almost all the numerous deletions in the manuscript, and expanded most of the abbreviations. Like Curtis, I retain Sterne's spelling and punctuation. On several occasions Sterne's original doubling of words has been retained.

A Political Romance is reprinted from the copy in the Library of Trinity College, Cambridge, in strict observance of Sterne's injunction to the original printer: 'at your Peril, . . . do not presume to alter or transpose one Word, nor rectify one false Spelling, nor so much as add or diminish one Comma or Tittle, in or to my *Romance*.'

I.J.

The text of the sermons is based on the first editions (*A*) of the *Sermons of Mr. Yorick*, i–iv (1760, 1766) and the *Sermons of the late Rev. Mr. Sterne*, v–vii (1769). In the case of the sermons from volumes i and ii, a number of emendations have been made on the basis of what appear to be Sterne's corrections and stylistic changes in the second edition of 1760. In accordance with modern conventions, the long 's' has been modernized and running quotation marks have been omitted throughout the text. Otherwise, the text departs from the first editions only in the following instances:

T. P.

183, 31	exquisitely fitted for] exquisitely for *A*
187, 15	would not absolutely] would absolutely *A*
188, 19–20	look.—Under . . . heart, such] look—under . . . heart. Such *A*
188, 29	cast, how insensibly do the thoughts carry] cast, the thoughts insensibly carry *A*
188, 30	farther?] farther *A*
188, 31–2	it, how naturally do they] it, they *A*
188, 33	be?] be *A*
191, 18	that] that. *A*
193, 15	social;—yet] social.—Yet *A*
193, 20	warmly] warm *A*
194, 18	sacrificed] sacrified *A*
194, 22	misconduct, how] misconduct? How *A*
194, 39	incapable] capable *A*
195, 24	should most have wished] could most chuse *A*
196, 10	they are] it is *A*
196, 11	they are] it is *A*
201, 35	in such] in a such *A*
202, 27	comparison? 'Tis] comparison?' Tis *A*
203, 7	years.'] years. *A*
204, 20	¶ If] no ¶ *A*
205, 17	taken.'†] taken." *A*
205, 38	† N. B.] N. B. *A*
206, 11	wherever] whereever *A*
208, 32	unto] into *A*
216, 17	assistance] as- | tance *A*

SELECT BIBLIOGRAPHY

Editions

A Political Romance, ed. Kenneth Monkman (Menston: Scolar Press, 1971).

The Journal to Eliza, in *Letters of Laurence Sterne*, ed. Lewis Perry Curtis (Oxford: Clarendon Press, 1935).

A Sentimental Journey, ed. Gardner D. Stout, Jr. (Berkeley: University of California Press, 1967).

A Sentimental Journey and Other Writings, ed. Tom Keymer (London: J. M. Dent, 1994).

A Sentimental Journey and Bramine's Journal, *The Florida Edition of the Works of Laurence Sterne*, vol. vi, ed. Melvyn New and W. G. Day (Gainesville, Fla.: University Press of Florida, 2002).

The Sermons of Laurence Sterne, *The Florida Edition of the Works of Laurence Sterne*, vol. iv, ed. Melvyn New (Gainesville, Fla.: University Press of Florida, 1996).

Biographical Studies, Letters, and Early Reception

Cash, Arthur H., *Laurence Sterne: The Early and Middle Years* (London: Methuen, 1975).

—— *Laurence Sterne: The Later Years* (London: Methuen, 1986).

Curtis, Lewis Perry (ed.), *Letters of Laurence Sterne* (Oxford: Clarendon Press, 1935).

Howes, Alan B., *Yorick and the Critics: Sterne's Reputation in England 1760–1868* (New Haven: Yale University Press, 1958).

—— (ed.), *Laurence Sterne: The Critical Heritage* (London: Routledge, 1974).

Ross, Ian Campbell, *Laurence Sterne: A Life* (Oxford: Oxford University Press, 2001).

Studies of Sentimental Fiction and its Contexts

Barker-Benfield, G. J., *The Culture of Sensibility: Sex and Society in Eighteenth-Century Britain* (Chicago: University of Chicago Press, 1992).

Conger, Syndy McMillen, *Sensibility in Transformation: Creative Resistance to Sentiment from the Augustans to the Romantics* (London: Associated University Presses, 1990).

Crane, R. S., 'Suggestions towards a Genealogy of the "Man of Feeling" ', *ELH* 1 (1934), 205–30.

Erämetsä, Eric, *A Study of the Word 'Sentimental' and of Other Linguistic*

Characteristics of Eighteenth-Century Sentimentalism in England (Helsinki: Liikekirjapaino Oy, 1951).

Greene, Donald, 'Latitudinarianism and Sensibility: The Genealogy of the "Man of Feeling" Reconsidered', *Modern Philology*, 75 (1977), 159–83.

Mayo, R. D., *The English Novel in the Magazines 1740–1815* (Evanston, Ill.: Northwestern University Press, 1962).

Mullan, John, 'Sentimental Novels', in John Richetti (ed.), *The Cambridge Companion to the Eighteenth-Century Novel* (Cambridge: Cambridge University Press, 1996), 236–54.

Richetti, John, *The English Novel in History, 1700–1780* (London: Routledge, 1999), ch. 8.

Rousseau, G. S., 'Nerves, Spirits and Fibres: Towards Defining the Origin of Sensibility', in R. F. Brissenden and J. C. Eade (eds.), *Studies in the Eighteenth Century III* (Toronto: University of Toronto Press, 1976), 137–57.

Sheriff, John K., *The Good-Natured Man: The Evolution of a Moral Ideal, 1660–1800* (Alabama: University of Alabama, 1982).

Skinner, Gillian, *Sensibility and Economics in the Novel 1740–1800* (Basingstoke: Macmillan, 1999).

Tave, Stuart M., *The Amiable Humorist* (Chicago: University of Chicago Press, 1960).

Todd, Janet, *Sensibility: An Introduction* (London: Methuen, 1986).

Criticism on Sterne

Byrd, Max, *Tristram Shandy* (London: George Allen & Unwin, 1985).

Kraft, Elizabeth, *Laurence Sterne Revisited* (New York: Twayne Publishers, 1996).

Lamb, Jonathan, *Sterne's Fiction and the Double Principle* (Cambridge: Cambridge University Press, 1989).

Lanham, Richard, *Tristram Shandy: The Games of Pleasure* (Berkeley: University of California Press, 1973).

New, Melvyn, *Laurence Sterne as Satirist* (Gainesville, Fla.: University Presses of Florida, 1970).

—— 'Job's Wife and Sterne's Other Women', in Laura Claridge and Elizabeth Langland (eds.), *Out of Bounds: Male Writers and Gender(ed) Criticism* (Amherst, Mass.: University of Massachusetts Press, 1991), 55–74.

—— (ed.), *Tristram Shandy: Contemporary Critical Essays* (London: Macmillan, 1992).

—— *Tristram Shandy: A Book for Free Spirits* (New York: Twayne Publishers, 1994).

—— 'The Odd Couple: Laurence Sterne and John Norris of Bemerton', *Philological Quarterly*, 75 (1996), 361–85.

—— (ed.), *Critical Essays on Laurence Sterne* (New York: G. K. Hall, 1998).

Parnell, Tim, 'A Story Painted to the Heart? *Tristram Shandy* and Sentimentalism Reconsidered', *The Shandean*, 9 (1997), 122–35.

Rodgers, James, 'Sensibility, Sympathy, Benevolence: Physiology and Moral Philosophy in *Tristram Shandy*', in L. J. Jordanova (ed.), *Languages of Nature: Critical Essays on Science and Literature* (New Brunswick, NJ: Rutgers University Press, 1986), 117–58.

Stedmond, John M., *The Comic Art of Laurence Sterne: Convention and Innovation in 'Tristram Shandy' and 'A Sentimental Journey'* (Toronto: University of Toronto Press, 1967).

Traugott, John, *Tristram Shandy's World: Sterne's Philosophical Rhetoric* (Berkeley: University of California Press, 1954).

Studies of A Sentimental Journey

Battestin, Martin C., '*A Sentimental Journey* and the Syntax of Things', in J. C. Hilson, M. M. B. Jones, and J. R. Watson (eds.), *Augustan Worlds: New Essays in Eighteenth-Century Literature* (New York: Barnes and Noble, 1978), 223–39.

—— 'Sterne among the Philosophes: Body and Soul in *A Sentimental Journey*', *Eighteenth-Century Fiction*, 7 (1994), 17–36.

Berthoud, Jacques, 'The Beggar in *A Sentimental Journey*', *The Shandean*, 3 (1991), 37–48.

Brissenden, R. F., *Virtue in Distress: Studies in the Novel of Sentiment from Richardson to Sade* (London: Macmillan, 1974), pt. 2, ch. 3.

Cash, Arthur Hill, *Sterne's Comedy of Moral Sentiments: The Ethical Dimension of the Journey* (Pittsburgh: Duquesne University Press, 1966).

Chadwick, Joseph, 'Infinite Jest: Interpretation in Sterne's *A Sentimental Journey*', *Eighteenth-Century Studies*, 12 (1978–9), 190–205.

Dussinger, John A., 'The Sensorium in the World of *A Sentimental Journey*', *Ariel*, 13 (1982), 3–16.

Ellis, Markman, *The Politics of Sensibility: Race, Gender and Commerce in the Sentimental Novel* (Cambridge: Cambridge University Press, 1996), ch. 2.

Fairer, David, 'Sentimental Translation in Mackenzie and Sterne', *Essays in Criticism*, 49 (1999), 132–51.

Frank, Judith, ' "A Man Who Laughs is Never Dangerous": Character and Class in Sterne's *A Sentimental Journey*', *ELH* 56 (1989), 97–124.

Gould, Rebecca, 'Sterne's Sentimental Yorick as Male Hysteric', *Studies in English Literature*, 36 (1996), 641–53.

Kay, Carol, *Political Constructions: Defoe, Richardson & Sterne in Relation to Hobbes, Hume, & Burke* (Ithaca, NY: Cornell University Press, 1988), ch. 4.

Keymer, Tom, 'Marvell, Thomas Hollis, and Sterne's Maria: Parody in *A Sentimental Journey*', *The Shandean*, 5 (1993), 9–31.

Kraft, Elizabeth, 'The Pentecostal Moment in *A Sentimental Journey*', in New (ed.), *Critical Essays on Laurence Sterne*, 292–310.

Lamb, Jonathan, 'Language and Hartleian Associationism in *A Sentimental Journey*', *Eighteenth-Century Studies*, 13 (1980), 285–312.

Loveridge, Mark, *Laurence Sterne and the Argument about Design* (London: Macmillan, 1982), ch. 7.

McGlynn, Paul D., 'Sterne's Maria: Madness and Sentimentality', *Eighteenth-Century Life*, 3 (1976), 39–43.

MacLean, Kenneth, 'Imagination and Sympathy: Sterne and Adam Smith', *Journal of the History of Ideas*, 10 (1949), 399–410.

Markley, Robert, 'Sentimentality as Performance: Shaftesbury, Sterne, and the Theatrics of Virtue', in F. Nussbaum and L. Brown (eds.), *The New Eighteenth Century* (London: Methuen, 1987), 210–30.

Mullan, John, *Sentiment and Sociability: The Language of Feeling in the Eighteenth Century* (Oxford: Clarendon Press, 1990), ch. 4.

New, Melvyn, 'Proust's Influence on Sterne: Remembrance of Things to Come', *Modern Language Notes*, 103 (1988), 1031–55.

Putney, Rufus, 'The Evolution of *A Sentimental Journey*', *Philological Quarterly*, 19 (1940), 349–69.

Seidel, Michael, 'Narrative and Sterne's *A Sentimental Journey*', *Genre*, 18 (1985), 1–22.

Stout, Gardner D., 'Yorick's *Sentimental Journey*: A Comic "Pilgrim's Progress" for the Man of Feeling', *ELH* 30 (1963), 395–412.

Van Sant, Ann Jessie, *Eighteenth-Century Sensibility and the Novel: The Senses in Social Context* (Cambridge: Cambridge University Press, 1993), ch. 6.

Wehrs, Donald, 'Levinas and Sterne: From the Ethics of the Face to the Aesthetics of Unrepresentability', in New (ed.), *Critical Essays on Laurence Sterne*, 311–29.

Studies of the Sermons *and/or their Theological Contexts*

Downey, James, *The Eighteenth-Century Pulpit* (Oxford: Clarendon Press, 1969).

—— 'The Sermons of Mr. Yorick: A Reassessment of Hammond', *English Studies in Canada*, 4 (1978), 193–211.

Fanning, Christopher, ' "The Things Themselves": Origins and Originality in Sterne's Sermons', *The Eighteenth Century: Theory and Interpretation*, 40 (1999), 29–45.

Hammond, Lansing Van der Heyden, *Laurence Sterne's 'Sermons of Mr. Yorick'* (New Haven: Yale University Press, 1948).

New, Melvyn (ed.), *The Florida Edition of the Works of Laurence Sterne*, vol. v, *The Notes to the Sermons* (Gainesville, Fla.: University Presses of Florida, 1996).

Reedy, Gerard, *The Bible and Reason: Anglicans and Scripture in Late Seventeenth-Century England* (Philadelphia: University of Pennsylvania Press, 1985).

Rivers, Isabel, *Reason, Grace and Sentiment: A Study of the Language of Religion and Ethics in England 1660–1780*, vol. i, *Whichcote to Wesley* (Cambridge: Cambridge University Press, 1991), vol. ii, *Shaftesbury to Hume* (Cambridge: Cambridge University Press, 2000).

Spellman, W. H., *The Latitudinarians and the Church of England* (Athens, Ga.: University of Georgia Press, 1993).

Further Reading in Oxford World's Classics

Cervantes, Miguel de, *Don Quixote*, trans. Charles Jarvis, ed. M. C. Riley.

Fielding, Henry, *Joseph Andrews and Shamela*, ed. Douglas Brooks-Davies and Thomas Keymer.

—— *Tom Jones*, ed. John Bender and Simon Stern.

Goldsmith, Oliver, *The Vicar of Wakefield*, ed. Arthur Friedman.

Mackenzie, Henry, *The Man of Feeling*, ed. Brian Vickers.

Sheridan, Frances, *Memoirs of Miss Sidney Bidulph*, ed. Patricia Köster and Jean Coates Cleary.

Smollett, Tobias, *The Expedition of Humphry Clinker*, ed. Lewis M. Knapp and Paul-Gabriel Boucé.

—— *Travels through France and Italy*, ed. Frank Felsenstein.

Sterne, Laurence, *Tristram Shandy*, ed. Ian Campbell Ross.

A CHRONOLOGY OF LAURENCE STERNE

1713 24 November: LS born in Clonmel, Ireland. His father, Roger Sterne, though by birth and education a gentleman, is a poorly paid ensign in the army; his mother, Agnes, the stepdaughter of a sutler.

1713–23 Spends early childhood travelling between the Sterne family home in Yorkshire and various barracks in England and Ireland.

1724 Begins attending Hipperholme school near Halifax, leaving Ireland and his family for good.

1731 31 July: Roger Sterne dies at Port Antonio, Jamaica.

1733 11 November: enters Jesus College, Cambridge. The college's graduates typically enter the priesthood. Among LS's fellow students is John Hall, who will become a lifelong friend.

1737 January: awarded BA. 6 March: admitted to the Order of Deacons and licensed assistant curate of St Ives, Huntingdon. Takes up duties at St Ives on Easter Day.

1738 18 February: licensed assistant curate of Catton, Yorkshire. 20 August: with the help of the influence of his uncle, Jaques Sterne, LS is ordained priest and collated to the vicarage of Sutton-on-the-Forest, Yorkshire.

1740 July: awarded MA.

1741 19 January: admitted as prebendary of Givendale, Yorkshire. 30 March: marries Elizabeth Lumley in York Minster. Writes for the *York Gazetteer* on behalf of local pro-Walpole Whigs. 28 October: *Query upon Query*, an effective piece of by-election propaganda, published in the *Daily Gazetteer*.

1742 8 January: admitted as prebendary of North Newbald, Yorkshire. Walpole resigns as First Commissioner of the Treasury and Chancellor of the Exchequer.

1743 July: LS's poem, 'The Unknown World: Verses occasion'd by hearing a Pass-Bell', published in the *Gentleman's Magazine*.

1744 14 March: inducted into the living of Stillington (2 miles north of Sutton). 1 November: purchases the Tindal Farm, beginning an experiment with farming that is finally abandoned in 1758.

1745   1 October: the Sternes' first daughter, Lydia, is born and dies the next day.

1746   1 July: in the aftermath of the Jacobite rebellion of 1745–6, LS publishes a piece of anti-Catholic propaganda in the *York Journal: or Protestant Courant.*

1747   April: *The Case of Elijah and the Widow of Zerephath* preached as a charity sermon at St Michael le Belfry, York. The sermon is published in York in the summer. 1 December: birth of second daughter, Lydia, who survives.

1750   29 July: *The Abuses of Conscience* preached as an assize sermon at York Minster, and subsequently published in York.

1751   12 July: preferred to the Commissaryship of the Peculiar Court of Pickering and Pocklington.

1759   January: *A Political Romance* published in York and subsequently withdrawn. December: *Tristram Shandy*, I–II published in York.

1760   28 March: nominated by Lord Fauconberg to the living of Coxwold, Yorkshire. 2 April: publication of the London edition of *Tristram Shandy*, I–II. 22 May: *The Sermons of Mr. Yorick*, I–II. June: arrives in Coxwold, which is to be his Yorkshire home for the rest of his life.

1761   29 January: *Tristram Shandy*, III–IV. 22 December: *Tristram Shandy*, V–VI.

1762   January: travels to France in the hope of improving his health. In Paris, LS is a regular visitor to the house of the Baron d'Holbach, where he meets Diderot, d'Alembert, the abbé Morellet and Crébillon *fils*. 8 July: Elizabeth and Lydia join LS in Paris. July: the Sterne family set out for Toulouse, where they stay until June 1763.

1764   May: returns to England, leaving his family in the south of France.

1765   23 January: *Tristram Shandy*, VII–VIII. October: sets out for France and Italy. November–December: visits Turin, Milan, Florence, and Rome.

1766   January: visits Naples, where he stays until March. 18 April: *The Sermons of Mr. Yorick*, III–IV. June: returns to England.

1767   30 January: *Tristram Shandy*, IX. Meets Elizabeth Draper in London. April: Elizabeth Draper sails for India and LS begins the *Journal to Eliza*.

1768   27 February: *A Sentimental Journey*, I–II. 18 March: LS dies at
his London lodgings in Bond Street. 22 March: funeral held at
St George's Church, Hanover Square. LS's body is stolen and
taken to Cambridge where it is anatomized in front of medical
students.

1769   3 June: *Sermons by the Late Rev. Mr. Sterne*, V–VII.

1773   *Letters from Yorick to Eliza*, containing the ten letters LS is
known to have written to Elizabeth Draper before her return to
India.

1775   11 July: Elizabeth Sterne dies in France. 26 October: *Letters of
the Late Rev. Mr. Laurence Sterne, to His Most Intimate Friends*.
The edition sees the first publication of LS's 'Memoirs', 'An
Impromptu', and the 'Fragment in the Manner of Rabelais'.

A

SENTIMENTAL JOURNEY

THROUGH

FRANCE AND ITALY

BY

MR. YORICK

VOLUME I

A SENTIMENTAL JOURNEY &c. &c.

———They order, said I, this matter° better in France—

—You have been in France? said my gentleman,° turning quick upon me with the most civil triumph in the world.—Strange! quoth I, debating the matter with myself, That one and twenty miles sailing, for 'tis absolutely no further from Dover to Calais, should give a man these rights—I'll look into them: so giving up the argument—I went straight to my lodgings, put up half a dozen shirts and a black pair of silk breeches—'the coat I have on, said I, looking at the sleeve, will do'—took a place in the Dover stage;° and the packet° sailing at nine the next morning—by three I had got sat down to my dinner upon a fricassee'd chicken so incontestably in France, that had I died that night of an indigestion, the whole world could not have suspended the effects of the *Droits d'aubaine*—my shirts, and black pair of silk breeches—portmanteau and all must have gone to the King of France—even the little picture which I have so long worn, and so often have told thee, Eliza,° I would carry with me into my grave, would have been torn from my neck.—Ungenerous!—to seize upon the wreck of an unwary passenger, whom your subjects had beckon'd to their coast—by heaven! Sire, it is not well done; and much does it grieve me, 'tis the monarch of a people so civilized and courteous, and so renown'd for sentiment and fine feelings, that I have to reason with——

But I have scarce set foot in your dominions——

CALAIS

When I had finish'd my dinner, and drank the King of France's health, to satisfy my mind that I bore him no spleen, but, on the

---

* All the effects of strangers (Swiss and Scotch excepted) dying in France, are seized by virtue of this law, tho' the heir be upon the spot——the profit of these contingencies being farm'd, there is no redress.°

contrary, high honour for the humanity of his temper—I rose up an inch taller for the accommodation.°

—No—said I—the Bourbon is by no means a cruel race: they may be misled like other people; but there is a mildness in their blood. As I acknowledged this, I felt a suffusion of a finer kind upon my cheek—more warm and friendly to man, than what Burgundy (at least of two livres° a bottle, which was such as I had been drinking) could have produced.

—Just God! said I, kicking my portmanteau aside, what is there in this world's goods which should sharpen our spirits, and make so many kind-hearted brethren of us, fall out so cruelly as we do by the way?

When man is at peace with man, how much lighter than a feather is the heaviest of metals in his hand! he pulls out his purse, and holding it airily and uncompress'd, looks round him, as if he sought for an object to share it with—In doing this, I felt every vessel in my frame dilate—the arteries beat all chearily together, and every power which sustained life, perform'd it with so little friction, that 'twould have confounded the most *physical precieuse*° in France: with all her materialism, she could scarce have called me a machine—

I'm confident, said I to myself, I should have overset her creed.

The accession of that idea, carried nature, at that time, as high as she could go—I was at peace with the world before, and this finish'd the treaty with myself—

—Now, was I a King of France, cried I—what a moment for an orphan to have begg'd his father's portmanteau of me!

THE MONK
CALAIS

I HAD scarce utter'd the words, when a poor monk of the order of St. Francis came into the room to beg something for his convent. No man cares to have his virtues the sport of contingencies—or one man may be generous, as another man is puissant°—*sed non, quo ad hanc*°— or be it as it may—for there is no regular reasoning upon the ebbs and flows of our humours; they may depend upon the same causes, for ought I know, which influence the tides themselves—'twould oft be no discredit to us, to suppose it was so: I'm sure at least for myself, that in many a case I should be more highly satisfied, to have it said by the world, 'I had had an affair with the moon, in which there was neither sin nor shame,' than have it pass altogether as my own act and deed, wherein there was so much of both.

—But be this as it may. The moment I cast my eyes upon him, I was predetermined not to give him a single sous;° and accordingly I put my purse into my pocket—button'd it up—set myself a little more upon my centre, and advanced up gravely to him: there was something, I fear, forbidding in my look: I have his figure this moment before my eyes, and think there was that in it which deserved better.

The monk, as I judged from the break in his tonsure, a few scatter'd white hairs upon his temples, being all that remained of it, might be about seventy—but from his eyes, and that sort of fire which was in them, which seemed more temper'd by courtesy than years, could be no more than sixty—Truth might lie between—He was certainly sixty-five; and the general air of his countenance, notwithstanding something seem'd to have been planting wrinkles in it before their time, agreed to the account.

It was one of those heads, which Guido° has often painted—mild, pale—penetrating, free from all common-place ideas of fat contented ignorance° looking downwards upon the earth—it look'd forwards; but look'd, as if it look'd at something beyond this world. How one of his order came by it, heaven above, who let it fall upon a monk's shoulders, best knows: but it would have suited a Bramin,° and had I met it upon the plains of Indostan, I had reverenced it.

The rest of his outline may be given in a few strokes; one might put it into the hands of any one to design, for 'twas neither elegant or otherwise, but as character and expression made it so: it was a thin, spare form, something above the common size, if it lost not the distinction by a bend forwards in the figure—but it was the attitude of Intreaty;° and as it now stands presented to my imagination, it gain'd more than it lost by it.

When he had enter'd the room three paces, he stood still; and laying his left hand upon his breast, (a slender white staff with which he journey'd being in his right)—when I had got close up to him, he introduced himself with the little story of the wants of his convent, and the poverty of his order—and did it with so simple a grace—and such an air of deprecation was there in the whole cast of his look and figure—I was bewitch'd not to have been struck with it—

—A better reason was, I had predetermined not to give him a single sous.

THE MONK
CALAIS

—'TIS very true, said I, replying to a cast upwards with his eyes, with which he had concluded his address—'tis very true—and heaven be their resource who have no other but the charity of the world, the stock of which, I fear, is no way sufficient for the many *great claims* which are hourly made upon it.

As I pronounced the words *great claims*, he gave a slight glance with his eye downwards upon the sleeve of his tunick—I felt the full force of the appeal—I acknowledge it, said I—a coarse habit, and that but once in three years, with meagre diet—are no great matters; and the true point of pity is, as they can be earn'd in the world with so little industry, that your order should wish to procure them by pressing upon a fund which is the property of the lame, the blind, the aged and the infirm—the captive who lies down counting over and over again the days of his afflictions, languishes also for his share of it; and had you been of the *order of mercy*, instead of the order of St. Francis,° poor as I am, continued I, pointing at my portmanteau, full chearfully should it have been open'd to you, for the ransom of the unfortunate—The monk made me a bow—but of all others, resumed I, the unfortunate of our own country, surely, have the first rights; and I have left thousands in distress upon our own shore— The monk gave a cordial wave with his head—as much as to say, No doubt, there is misery enough in every corner of the world, as well as within our convent—But we distinguish, said I, laying my hand upon the sleeve of his tunick, in return for his appeal—we distinguish, my good Father! betwixt those who wish only to eat the bread of their own labour—and those who eat the bread of other people's, and have no other plan in life, but to get through it in sloth and ignorance, *for the love of God.*°

The poor Franciscan made no reply: a hectic° of a moment pass'd across his cheek, but could not tarry—Nature seemed to have had done with her resentments in him; he shewed none—but letting his staff fall within his arm, he press'd both his hands with resignation upon his breast, and retired.

THE MONK
CALAIS

My heart smote me the moment he shut the door—Psha! said I with an air of carelessness, three several times—but it would not do: every ungracious syllable I had utter'd, crouded back into my imagination: I reflected, I had no right over the poor Franciscan, but to deny him; and that the punishment of that was enough to the disappointed without the addition of unkind language—I consider'd his grey hairs—his courteous figure seem'd to re-enter and gently ask me what injury he had done me?—and why I could use him thus—I would have given twenty livres for an advocate—I have behaved very ill; said I within myself; but I have only just set out upon my travels; and shall learn better manners as I get along.

THE DESOBLIGEANT
CALAIS

When a man is discontented with himself, it has one advantage however, that it puts him into an excellent frame of mind for making a bargain. Now there being no travelling through France and Italy without a chaise°—and nature generally prompting us to the thing we are fittest for, I walk'd out into the coach yard to buy or hire something of that kind to my purpose: an old *Desobligeant in the furthest corner of the court, hit my fancy at first sight, so I instantly got into it, and finding it in tolerable harmony with my feelings, I ordered the waiter to call Monsieur Dessein° the master of the hôtel—but Monsieur Dessein being gone to vespers, and not caring to face the Franciscan whom I saw on the opposite side of

---

* A chaise, so called in France, from its holding but one person.

the court, in conference with a lady just arrived, at the inn—I drew the taffeta curtain betwixt us, and being determined to write my journey, I took out my pen and ink, and wrote the preface to it in the *Disobligeant*.

PREFACE
IN THE DESOBLIGEANT

IT must have been observed by many a peripatetic philosopher,° That nature has set up by her own unquestionable authority certain boundaries and fences to circumscribe the discontent of man: she has effected her purpose in the quietest and easiest manner by laying him under almost insuperable obligations to work out his ease, and to sustain his sufferings at home. It is there only that she has provided him with the most suitable objects to partake of his happiness, and bear a part of that burden which in all countries and ages, has ever been too heavy for one pair of shoulders. 'Tis true we are endued with an imperfect power of spreading our happiness sometimes beyond *her* limits, but 'tis so ordered, that from the want of languages, connections, and dependencies, and from the difference in education, customs and habits, we lie under so many impediments in communicating our sensations out of our own sphere, as often amount to a total impossibility.

It will always follow from hence, that the balance of sentimental commerce° is always against the expatriated adventurer: he must buy what he has little occasion for at their own price—his conversation will seldom be taken in exchange for theirs without a large discount—and this, by the by, eternally driving him into the hands of more equitable brokers for such conversation as he can find, it requires no great spirit of divination to guess at his party—

This brings me to my point; and naturally leads me (if the see-saw of this *Desobligeant* will but let me get on) into the efficient as well as the final causes° of travelling—

Your idle people that leave their native country and go abroad for some reason or reasons which may be derived from one of these general causes—

> Infirmity of body,
> Imbecility of mind, or
> Inevitable necessity.

The first two include all those who travel by land or by water, labouring with pride, curiosity, vanity or spleen, subdivided and combined *in infinitum*.

The third class includes the whole army of peregrine° martyrs; more especially those travellers who set out upon their travels with the benefit of the clergy,° either as delinquents travelling under the direction of governors recommended by the magistrate—or young gentlemen transported by the cruelty of parents and guardians, and travelling under the direction of governors recommended by Oxford, Aberdeen and Glasgow.

There is a fourth class, but their number is so small that they would not deserve a distinction, was it not necessary in a work of this nature to observe the greatest precision and nicety, to avoid a confusion of character.° And these men I speak of, are such as cross the seas and sojourn in a land of strangers with a view of saving money for various reasons and upon various pretences: but as they might also save themselves and others a great deal of unnecessary trouble by saving their money at home—and as their reasons for travelling are the least complex of any other species of emigrants, I shall distinguish these gentlemen by the name of

> Simple Travellers.

Thus the whole circle of travellers may be reduced to the following *Heads*.

> Idle Travellers,
> Inquisitive Travellers,
> Lying Travellers,
> Proud Travellers,
> Vain Travellers,
> Splenetic Travellers.

Then follow the Travellers of Necessity.

> The delinquent and felonious Traveller,
> The unfortunate and innocent Traveller,
> The simple Traveller,

and last of all (if you please) The Sentimental Traveller (meaning thereby myself) who have travell'd, and of which I am now sitting down to give an account—as much out of *Necessity*, and the *besoin de* Voyager,° as any one in the class.

I am well aware, at the same time, as both my travels and observations will be altogether of a different cast from any of my forerunners; that I might have insisted upon a whole nitch entirely to myself—but I should break in upon the confines of the *Vain* Traveller, in wishing to draw attention towards me, till I have some better grounds for it, than the mere *Novelty of my Vehicle*.°

It is sufficient for my reader, if he has been a traveller himself, that with study and reflection hereupon he may be able to determine his own place and rank in the catalogue—it will be one step towards knowing himself; as it is great odds, but he retains some tincture and resemblance, of what he imbibed or carried out, to the present hour.

The man who first transplanted the grape of Burgundy to the Cape of Good Hope (observe he was a Dutch man) never dreamt of drinking the same wine at the Cape, that the same grape produced upon the French mountains—he was too phlegmatic for that—but undoubtedly he expected to drink some sort of vinous liquor; but whether good, bad, or indifferent—he knew enough of this world to know, that it did not depend upon his choice, but that what is generally called *chance* was to decide his success: however, he hoped for the best; and in these hopes, by an intemperate confidence in the fortitude of his head, and the depth of his discretion, *Mynheer* might possibly overset both in his new vineyard; and by discovering his nakedness,° become a laughing-stock to his people.

Even so it fares with the poor Traveller, sailing and posting through the politer kingdoms of the globe in pursuit of knowledge and improvements.

Knowledge and improvements are to be got by sailing and posting for that purpose; but whether useful knowledge and real improvements, is all a lottery—and even where the adventurer is successful, the acquired stock must be used with caution and sobriety to turn to any profit—but as the chances run prodigiously the other way both as to the acquisition and application, I am of opinion, That a man would act as wisely, if he could prevail upon himself, to live contented without foreign knowledge or foreign improvements, especially if he lives in a country that has no absolute want of either—and indeed, much grief of heart has it oft and many a time cost me, when I have observed how many a foul step the inquisitive Traveller has measured to see sights and look into discoveries; all which, as Sancho Pança said to Don Quixote,° they might have seen dry-shod at home. It is an age so full of light, that there is scarce a country or corner of Europe whose beams are not crossed and interchanged with others—Knowledge in most of its branches, and in most affairs, is like music in an Italian street, whereof those may partake, who pay nothing—But there is no nation under heaven—and God is my record, (before whose tribunal I must one day come and give an account of this work)—that I do not speak it vauntingly—But there is no nation under heaven abounding with more variety of learning—where the sciences may be more fitly woo'd, or more surely won than here—where art is encouraged, and will so soon rise high—where Nature (take her all together) has so little to answer for—and, to close all, where there is more wit and variety of character to feed the mind with—Where then, my dear countrymen, are you going°—

—We are only looking at this chaise, said they—Your most obedient servant, said I, skipping out of it, and pulling off my hat—We were wondering, said one of them, who, I found, was an *inquisitive traveller*—what could occasion its motion.——'Twas the agitation, said I coolly, of writing a preface—I never heard, said the other, who was a *simple traveller*, of a preface wrote in a *Desobligeant*.—It would have been better, said I, in a *Vis a Vis.*°

—*As an English man does not travel to see English men*, I retired to my room.

CALAIS

I Perceived that something darken'd the passage more than myself, as I stepp'd along it to my room; it was effectually° Mons. Dessein, the master of the hôtel, who had just return'd from vespers, and, with his hat under his arm, was most complaisantly following me, to put me in mind of my wants. I had wrote myself pretty well out of conceit with° the *Desobligeant*; and Mons. Dessein speaking of it, with a shrug, as if it would no way suit me, it immediately struck my fancy that it belong'd to some *innocent traveller*, who, on his return home, had left it to Mons. Dessein's honour to make the most of. Four months had elapsed since it had finish'd its career of Europe in the corner of Mons. Dessein's coach-yard; and having sallied out from thence but a vampt-up° business at the first, though it had been twice taken to pieces on Mount Sennis,° it had not profited much by its adventures—but by none so little as the standing so many months unpitied in the corner of Mons. Dessein's coach-yard. Much indeed was not to be said for it—but something might—and when a few words will rescue misery out of her distress, I hate the man who can be a churl of them.

—Now was I the master of this hôtel, said I, laying the point of my fore-finger on Mons. Dessein's breast, I would inevitably make a point of getting rid of this unfortunate *Desobligeant*—it stands swinging reproaches at you every time you pass by it—

Mon Dieu!° said Mons. Dessein—I have no interest—Except the interest, said I, which men of a certain turn of mind take, Mons. Dessein, in their own sensations—I'm persuaded, to a man who feels for others as well as for himself, every rainy night, disguise it as you will, must cast a damp upon your spirits—You suffer, Mons. Dessein, as much as the machine—

I have always observed, when there is as much *sour* as *sweet* in a compliment, that an Englishman is eternally at a loss within himself, whether to take it, or let it alone: a Frenchman never is: Mons. Dessein made me a bow.

C'est bien vrai,° said he—But in this case I should only exchange one disquietude for another, and with loss: figure to yourself, my dear Sir, that in giving you a chaise which would fall to pieces before you had got half way to Paris—figure to yourself how much I should suffer, in giving an ill impression of myself to a man of honour, and lying at the mercy, as I must do, *d'un homme d'esprit.*°

The dose was made up exactly after my own prescription; so I could not help taking it—and returning Mons. Dessein his bow, without more casuistry° we walk'd together towards his Remise,° to take a view of his magazine° of chaises.

IN THE STREET
CALAIS

It must needs be a hostile kind of a world, when the buyer (if it be but of a sorry post-chaise) cannot go forth with the seller thereof into the street to terminate the difference betwixt them, but he instantly falls into the same frame of mind and views his conventionist° with the same sort of eye, as if he was going along with him to Hyde-park corner to fight a duel. For my own part, being but a poor sword's-man, and no way a match for Monsieur *Dessein*, I felt the rotation of all the movements within me, to which the situation is incident—I looked at Monsieur *Dessein* through and through—ey'd him as he walked along in profile—then, *en face°*—thought he look'd like a Jew—then a Turk—disliked his wig—cursed him by my gods—wished him at the devil—

—And is all this to be lighted up in the heart for a beggarly account of three or four louisd'ors,° which is the most I can be over-reach'd in?—Base passion! said I, turning myself about, as a man naturally does upon a sudden reverse of sentiment—base, ungentle passion! thy hand is against every man, and every man's hand against thee°—heaven forbid! said she, raising her hand up to her forehead, for I had turned full in front upon the lady whom I had seen in conference with the monk—she had followed us unperceived—Heaven forbid indeed! said I, offering her my own—she had a black pair of silk gloves open only at the thumb and two fore-fingers, so accepted it without reserve—and I led her up to the door of the Remise.

Monsieur *Dessein* had *diabled°* the key above fifty times before he found out he had come with a wrong one in his hand: we were as impatient as himself to have it open'd; and so attentive to the obs-tacle, that I continued holding her hand almost without knowing it; so that Monsieur *Dessein* left us together with her hand in mine, and with our faces turned towards the door of the Remise, and said he would be back in five minutes.

Now a colloquy of five minutes, in such a situation, is worth one of as many ages, with your faces turned towards the street: in the latter case, 'tis drawn from the objects and occurrences without—when your eyes are fixed upon a dead blank—you draw purely from yourselves. A silence of a single moment upon Monsieur *Dessein*'s leaving us, had been fatal to the situation—she had infallibly turned about—so I begun the conversation instantly.—

—But what were the temptations, (as I write not to apologize for the weaknesses of my heart in this tour,—but to give an account of them)—shall be described with the same simplicity, with which I felt them.

THE REMISE DOOR
CALAIS

WHEN I told the reader that I did not care to get out of the *Desobligeant*, because I saw the monk in close conference with a lady just arrived at the inn—I told him the truth; but I did not tell him the whole truth; for I was full as much restrained by the appearance and figure of the lady he was talking to. Suspicion crossed my brain, and said, he was telling her what had passed: something jarred upon it within me—I wished him at his convent.

When the heart flies out before the understanding, it saves the judgment a world of pains°—I was certain she was of a better order of beings—however, I thought no more of her, but went on and wrote my preface.

The impression returned, upon my encounter with her in the street; a guarded frankness with which she gave me her hand, shewed, I thought, her good education and her good sense; and as I led her on, I felt a pleasurable ductility° about her, which spread a calmness over all my spirits—

—Good God! how a man might lead such a creature as this round the world with him!—

I had not yet seen her face—'twas not material; for the drawing was instantly set about, and long before we had got to the door of the Remise, *Fancy* had finished the whole head, and pleased herself as much with its fitting her goddess, as if she had dived into the TIBER for it°—but thou art a seduced, and a seducing slut; and albeit thou cheatest us seven times a day with thy pictures and images, yet with so many charms dost thou do it, and thou deckest out thy pictures in the shapes of so many angels of light, 'tis a shame to break with thee.

When we had got to the door of the Remise, she withdrew her hand from across her forehead, and let me see the original—it was a face of about six and twenty—of a clear transparent brown, simply set off without rouge or powder°—it was not critically handsome, but there was that in it, which in the frame of mind I was in, attached me much more to it—it was interesting;° I fancied it wore the characters of a widow'd look, and in that state of its declension,° which had passed the two first paroxysms of sorrow, and was quietly beginning to reconcile itself to its loss—but a thousand other distresses might have traced the same lines; I wish'd to know what they had been— and was ready to enquire, (had the same *bon ton*° of conversation permitted, as in the days of Esdras)—'*What aileth thee? and why art thou disquieted? and why is thy understanding troubled?*'°—In a word, I felt benevolence for her;° and resolved some way or other to throw in my mite of courtesy—if not of service.°

Such were my temptations—and in this disposition to give way to them, was I left alone with the lady with her hand in mine, and with our faces both turned closer to the door of the Remise than what was absolutely necessary.

THE REMISE DOOR
CALAIS

THIS certainly, fair lady! said I, raising her hand up a little lightly as I began, must be one of Fortune's whimsical doings: to take two utter strangers by their hands—of different sexes, and perhaps from different corners of the globe, and in one moment place them together in such a cordial situation, as Friendship herself could scarce have atchieved for them, had she projected it for a month—

—And your reflection upon it, shews how much, Monsieur, she has embarrassed you by the adventure.—

When the situation is, what we would wish, nothing is so ill-timed as to hint at the circumstances which make it so: you thank Fortune, continued she—you had reason—the heart knew it, and was satisfied; and who but an English philosopher would have sent notices of it to the brain to reverse the judgment?

In saying this, she disengaged her hand with a look which I thought a sufficient commentary upon the text.

It is a miserable picture which I am going to give of the weakness of my heart, by owning, that it suffered a pain, which worthier occasions could not have inflicted.—I was mortified with the loss of her hand, and the manner in which I had lost it carried neither oil nor wine to the wound:° I never felt the pain of a sheepish inferiority so miserably in my life.

The triumphs of a true feminine heart are short upon these discomfitures. In a very few seconds she laid her hand upon the cuff of my coat, in order to finish her reply; so some way or other, God knows how, I regained my situation.

—She had nothing to add.

I forthwith began to model a different conversation for the lady, thinking from the spirit as well as moral of this, that I had been mistaken in her character; but upon turning her face towards me, the spirit which had animated the reply was fled—the muscles relaxed, and I beheld the same unprotected look of distress which first won me to her interest—melancholy! to see such sprightliness the prey of sorrow.—I pitied her from my soul; and though it may seem ridiculous enough to a torpid heart,—I could have taken her into my arms, and cherished her, though it was in the open street, without blushing.

The pulsations of the arteries along my fingers pressing across hers, told her what was passing within me:° she looked down—a silence of some moments followed.

I fear, in this interval, I must have made some slight efforts towards a closer compression of her hand, from a subtle sensation I felt in the palm of my own—not as if she was going to withdraw hers—but, as if she thought about it—and I had infallibly lost it a second time, had not instinct more than reason directed me to the last resource in these dangers—to hold it loosely, and in a manner as if I was every moment going to release it, of myself; so she let it continue, till Monsieur *Dessein* returned with the key; and in the mean time I set myself to consider how I should undo the ill impressions which the poor monk's story, in case he had told it her, must have planted in her breast against me.

THE SNUFF-BOX
CALAIS

THE good old monk was within six paces of us, as the idea of him cross'd my mind; and was advancing towards us a little out of the line, as if uncertain whether he should break in upon us or no.—He stopp'd, however, as soon as he came up to us, with a world of frankness; and having a horn snuff-box in his hand, he presented it open to me—You shall taste mine—said I, pulling out my box (which was a small tortoise one) and putting it into his hand—'Tis most excellent, said the monk; Then do me the favour, I replied, to accept of the box and all, and when you take a pinch out of it, sometimes recollect it was the peace-offering of a man who once used you unkindly, but not from his heart.

The poor monk blush'd as red as scarlet. *Mon Dieu!* said he, pressing his hands together—you never used me unkindly.—I should think, said the lady, he is not likely. I blush'd in my turn; but from what movements, I leave to the few who feel to analyse— Excuse me, Madame, replied I—I treated him most unkindly; and from no provocations—'Tis impossible, said the lady.—My God! cried the monk, with a warmth of asseveration which seemed not to belong to him—the fault was in me, and in the indiscretion of my zeal—the lady opposed it, and I joined with her in maintaining it was impossible, that a spirit so regulated as his, could give offence to any.

I knew not that contention could be rendered so sweet and pleasurable a thing to the nerves as I then felt it.—We remained silent, without any sensation of that foolish pain which takes place, when in such a circle you look for ten minutes in one another's faces without saying a word. Whilst this lasted, the monk rubb'd his horn box upon the sleeve of his tunick; and as soon as it had acquired a little air of brightness by the friction—he made a low bow, and said, 'twas too late to say whether it was the weakness or goodness of our tempers which had involved us in this contest—but be it as it would—he begg'd we might exchange boxes—In saying this, he presented his to me with one hand, as he took mine from me in the other; and having kiss'd it—with a stream of good nature in his eyes he put it into his bosom—and took his leave.

I guard this box, as I would the instrumental parts of my religion, to help my mind on to something better: in truth, I seldom go abroad without it; and oft and many a time have I called up by it the courteous spirit of its owner to regulate my own, in the justlings of the world; they had found full employment for his, as I learnt from his story, till about the forty-fifth year of his age, when upon some military services ill requited, and meeting at the same time with a disappointment in the tenderest of passions, he abandon'd the sword and the sex together, and took sanctuary, not so much in his convent as in himself.

I feel a damp upon my spirits, as I am going to add, that in my last return through Calais, upon inquiring after Father Lorenzo, I heard he had been dead near three months, and was buried, not in his convent, but, according to his desire, in a little cimetiery belonging to it, about two leagues off: I had a strong desire to see where they had laid him—when, upon pulling out his little horn box, as I sat by his grave, and plucking up a nettle or two at the head of it, which had no business to grow there, they all struck together so forcibly upon my affections, that I burst into a flood of tears—but I am as weak as a woman; and I beg the world not to smile, but pity me.

THE REMISE DOOR
CALAIS

I HAD never quitted the lady's hand all this time; and had held it so long, that it would have been indecent to have let it go, without first pressing it to my lips: the blood and spirits, which had suffer'd a revulsion° from her, crouded back to her, as I did it.

Now the two travellers who had spoke to me in the coach-yard, happening at that crisis to be passing by, and observing our communications, naturally took it into their heads that we must be *man and wife* at least; so stopping as soon as they came up to the door of the Remise, the one of them, who was the inquisitive traveller, ask'd us, if we set out for Paris the next morning?—I could only answer for myself, I said; and the lady added, she was for Amiens.—We dined there yesterday, said the simple traveller—You go directly through the town, added the other, in your road to Paris. I was going to return a thousand thanks for the intelligence, *that Amiens was in the road to*

Paris; but, upon pulling out my poor monk's little horn box to take a pinch of snuff—I made them a quiet bow, and wishing them a good passage to Dover—they left us alone—

—Now where would be the harm, said I to myself, if I was to beg of this distressed lady to accept of half of my chaise?—and what mighty mischief could ensue?

Every dirty passion, and bad propensity in my nature, took the alarm, as I stated the proposition—It will oblige you to have a third horse, said AVARICE, which will put twenty livres out of your pocket.—You know not who she is, said CAUTION—or what scrapes the affair may draw you into, whisper'd COWARDICE—

Depend upon it, Yorick! said DISCRETION, 'twill be said you went off with a mistress, and came by assignation to Calais for that purpose—

—You can never after, cried HYPOCRISY aloud, shew your face in the world—or rise, quoth MEANNESS, in the church—or be any thing in it, said PRIDE, but a lousy prebendary.°

—But 'tis a civil thing, said I—and as I generally act from the first impulse, and therefore seldom listen to these cabals, which serve no purpose, that I know of, but to encompass the heart with adamant—I turn'd instantly about to the lady—

—But she had glided off unperceived, as the cause was pleading, and had made ten or a dozen paces down the street, by the time I had made the determination; so I set off after her with a long stride, to make her the proposal with the best address I was master of; but observing she walk'd with her cheek half resting upon the palm of her hand—with the slow, short-measur'd step of thoughtfulness, and with her eyes, as she went step by step, fix'd upon the ground, it struck me, she was trying the same cause herself.—God help her! said I, she has some mother-in-law, or tartufish° aunt, or nonsensical old woman, to consult upon the occasion, as well as myself: so not caring to interrupt the processe, and deeming it more gallant to take her at discretion than by surprize, I faced about, and took a short turn or two before the door of the Remise, whilst she walk'd musing on one side.

IN THE STREET
CALAIS

HAVING, on first sight of the lady, settled the affair in my fancy, 'that she was of the better order of beings'—and then laid it down as a second axiom, as indisputable as the first, That she was a widow, and wore a character of distress—I went no further; I got ground enough for the situation which pleased me—and had she remained close beside my elbow till midnight, I should have held true to my system, and considered her only under that general idea.

She had scarce got twenty paces distant from me, ere something within me called out for a more particular inquiry—it brought on the idea of a further separation—I might possibly never see her more—the heart is for saving what it can; and I wanted the traces thro' which my wishes might find their way to her, in case I should never rejoin her myself: in a word, I wish'd to know her name—her family's—her condition; and as I knew the place to which she was going, I wanted to know from whence she came: but there was no coming at all this intelligence: a hundred little delicacies stood in the way. I form'd a score different plans—There was no such thing as a man's asking her directly—the thing was impossible.

A little French *debonaire* captain, who came dancing down the street, shewed me, it was the easiest thing in the world; for popping in betwixt us, just as the lady was returning back to the door of the Remise, he introduced himself to my acquaintance, and before he had well got announced, begg'd I would do him the honour to present him to the lady—I had not been presented myself—so turning about to her, he did it just as well by asking her, if she had come from Paris?—No: she was going that rout, she said.—*Vous n'etez pas de Londre?*—She was not, she replied.—Then Madame must have come thro' Flanders.—*Apparamment vous etez Flammande?* said the French captain.—The lady answered, she was.—*Peutetre, de Lisle?*° added he—She said, she was not of Lisle.—Nor Arras?—nor Cambray?—nor Ghent?—nor Brussels? She answered, she was of Brussels.

He had had the honour, he said, to be at the bombardment of it last war°—that it was finely situated, *pour cela*°—and full of noblesse when the Imperialists were driven out by the French (the lady made a slight curtsy)—so giving her an account of the affair, and of the share he had had in it—he begg'd the honour to know her name—so made his bow.

—*Et Madame a son Mari?*°—said he, looking back when he had made two steps—and without staying for an answer—danced down the street.

Had I served seven years apprenticeship to good breeding, I could not have done as much.

THE REMISE
CALAIS

As the little French captain left us, Mons. Dessein came up with the key of the Remise in his hand, and forthwith let us into his magazine of chaises.

The first object which caught my eye, as Mons. Dessein open'd the door of the Remise, was another old tatter'd *Desobligeant:* and notwithstanding it was the exact picture of that which had hit my fancy so much in the coach-yard but an hour before—the very sight of it stirr'd up a disagreeable sensation within me now; and I thought 'twas a churlish beast into whose heart the idea could first enter, to construct such a machine; nor had I much more charity for the man who could think of using it.

I observed the lady was as little taken with it as myself: so Mons. Dessein led us on to a couple of chaises which stood abreast, telling us as he recommended them, that they had been purchased by my Lord A. and B. to go the *grand tour*, but had gone no further than Paris, so were in all respects as good as new—They were too good—so I pass'd on to a third, which stood behind, and forthwith began to chaffer° for the price—But 'twill scarce hold two, said I, opening the door and getting in—Have the goodness, Madam, said Mons. Dessein, offering his arm, to step in—The lady hesitated half a second, and stepp'd in; and the waiter that moment beckoning to speak to Mons. Dessein, he shut the door of the chaise upon us, and left us.

THE REMISE
CALAIS

C'EST bien comique,° 'tis very droll, said the lady smiling, from the reflection that this was the second time we had been left together by a parcel of nonsensical contingencies—*c'est bien comique*, said she—

—There wants nothing, said I, to make it so, but the comick use which the gallantry of a Frenchman would put it to—to make love the first moment, and an offer of his person the second.

'Tis their *fort:*° replied the lady.

It is supposed so at least—and how it has come to pass, continued I, I know not; but they have certainly got the credit of understanding more of love, and making it better than any other nation upon earth: but for my own part I think them errant bunglers, and in truth the worst set of marksmen that ever tried Cupid's patience.

—To think of making love by *sentiments!*

I should as soon think of making a genteel suit of cloaths out of remnants:—and to do it—pop—at first sight by declaration—is submitting the offer and themselves with it, to be sifted, with all their *pours* and *contres,*° by an unheated mind.

The lady attended as if she expected I should go on.

Consider then, madam, continued I, laying my hand upon hers—

That grave people hate Love for the name's sake°—

That selfish people hate it for their own—

Hypocrites for heaven's—

And that all of us both old and young, being ten times worse frighten'd than hurt by the very *report*—What a want of knowledge in this branch of commerce a man betrays, whoever lets the word come out of his lips, till an hour or two at least after the time, that his silence upon it becomes tormenting. A course of small, quiet attentions, not so pointed as to alarm—nor so vague as to be misunderstood,—with now and then a look of kindness, and little or nothing said upon it—leaves Nature for your mistress, and she fashions it to her mind.—

Then I solemnly declare, said the lady, blushing—you have been making love to me all this while.

THE REMISE
CALAIS

MONSIEUR *Dessein* came back to let us out of the chaise, and acquaint the lady, the Count de L—— her brother was just arrived at the hotel. Though I had infinite good will for the lady, I cannot say, that I rejoiced in my heart at the event—and could not help telling her so—for it is fatal to a proposal, Madam, said I, that I was going to make you—

—You need not tell me what the proposal was, said she, laying her hand upon both mine, as she interrupted me.—A man, my good Sir, has seldom an offer of kindness to make to a woman, but she has a presentiment of it some moments before—

Nature arms her with it, said I, for immediate preservation—But I think, said she, looking in my face, I had no evil to apprehend—and to deal frankly with you, had determined to accept it.—If I had—(she stopped a moment)—I believe your good will would have drawn a story from me, which would have made pity the only dangerous thing in the journey.

In saying this, she suffered me to kiss her hand twice, and with a look of sensibility mixed with a concern she got out of the chaise—and bid adieu.

IN THE STREET
CALAIS

I NEVER finished a twelve-guinea bargain so expeditiously in my life: my time seemed heavy upon the loss of the lady, and knowing every moment of it would be as two, till I put myself into motion—I ordered post horses directly, and walked towards the hotel.

Lord! said I, hearing the town clock strike four, and recollecting that I had been little more than a single hour in Calais—

—What a large volume of adventures may be grasped within this little span of life by him who interests his heart in every thing, and who, having eyes to see,° what time and chance° are perpetually holding out to him as he journeyeth on his way, misses nothing he can *fairly* lay his hands on.—

—If this won't turn out something—another will—no matter— 'tis an assay° upon human nature—I get my labour for my pains—'tis enough—the pleasure of the experiment has kept my senses, and the best part of my blood awake, and laid the gross to sleep.°

I pity the man who can travel from *Dan* to *Beersheba*,° and cry, 'Tis all barren—and so it is; and so is all the world to him who will not cultivate the fruits it offers. I declare, said I, clapping my hands chearily together, that was I in a desart, I would find out wherewith in it to call forth my affections—If I could not do better, I would fasten them upon some sweet myrtle, or seek some melancholy cypress° to connect myself to—I would court their shade, and greet them kindly for their protection—I would cut my name upon them, and swear they were the loveliest trees throughout the desert: if their leaves wither'd, I would teach myself to mourn, and when they rejoiced, I would rejoice along with them.

The learned SMELFUNGUS° travelled from Boulogne to Paris— from Paris to Rome—and so on—but he set out with the spleen and jaundice, and every object he pass'd by was discoloured or distorted—He wrote an account of them, but 'twas nothing but the account of his miserable feelings.

I met Smelfungus in the grand portico of the Pantheon—he was just coming out of it—*'Tis nothing but a huge cock-pit**, said he—I wish you had said nothing worse of the Venus of Medicis, replied I—for in passing through Florence, I had heard he had fallen foul upon the goddess, and used her worse than a common strumpet, without the least provocation in nature.°

I popp'd upon Smelfungus again at Turin, in his return home; and a sad tale of sorrowful adventures had he to tell, 'wherein he spoke of moving accidents by flood and field, and of the cannibals which each other eat: the Anthropophagi'°—he had been flea'd alive, and bedevil'd, and used worse than St. Bartholomew, at every stage he had come at°—

—I'll tell it, cried Smelfungus, to the world. You had better tell it, said I, to your physician.

Mundungus,° with an immense fortune, made the whole tour;

---

* Vide S——'s Travels.

going on from Rome to Naples—from Naples to Venice—from Venice to Vienna—to Dresden, to Berlin, without one generous connection or pleasurable anecdote to tell of; but he had travell'd straight on looking neither to his right hand or his left, lest Love or Pity should seduce him out of his road.

Peace be to them! if it is to be found; but heaven itself, was it possible to get there with such tempers, would want objects to give it—every gentle spirit would come flying upon the wings of Love to hail their arrival—Nothing would the souls of Smelfungus and Mundungus hear of, but fresh anthems of joy, fresh raptures of love, and fresh congratulations of their common felicity—I heartily pity them: they have brought up no faculties for this work; and was the happiest mansion in heaven to be allotted to Smelfungus and Mundungus, they would be so far from being happy, that the souls of Smelfungus and Mundungus would do penance there to all eternity.°

MONTRIUL

I HAD once lost my portmanteau from behind my chaise, and twice got out in the rain, and one of the times up to the knees in dirt, to help the postilion° to tie it on, without being able to find out what was wanting—Nor was it till I got to Montriul, upon the landlord's asking me if I wanted not a servant, that it occurred to me, that that was the very thing.

A servant! That I do most sadly, quoth I—Because, Monsieur, said the landlord, there is a clever young fellow, who would be very proud of the honour to serve an Englishman—But why an English one, more than any other?—They are so generous, said the landlord—I'll be shot if this is not a livre out of my pocket, quoth I to myself, this very night—But they have wherewithal to be so, Monsieur, added he—Set down one livre more for that, quoth I—It was but last night, said the landlord, *qu'un my Lord Anglois presentoit un ecu a la fille de chambre—Tant pis, pour Mad^lle Janatone,*° said I.

Now Janatone being the landlord's daughter, and the landlord supposing I was young in French, took the liberty to inform me, I should not have said *tant pis*—but, *tant mieux. Tant mieux, toujours, Monsieur,*° said he, when there is any thing to be got—*tant pis*, when

there is nothing. It comes to the same thing, said I. *Pardonnez moi*,°
said the landlord.

I cannot take a fitter opportunity to observe once for all, that *tant
pis* and *tant mieux* being two of the great hinges in French conversation, a stranger would do well to set himself right in the use of them,
before he gets to Paris.

A prompt French Marquis at our ambassador's table demanded
of Mr. H——, if he was H—— the poet?° No, said H—— mildly—
Tant pis, replied the Marquis.

It is H—— the historian, said another—*Tant mieux*, said the Marquis. And Mr. H——, who is a man of an excellent heart, return'd
thanks for both.

When the landlord had set me right in this matter, he called in La
Fleur, which was the name of the young man he had spoke of—
saying only first, That as for his talents, he would presume to say
nothing—Monsieur was the best judge what would suit him; but for
the fidelity of La Fleur, he would stand responsible in all he was
worth.

The landlord deliver'd this in a manner which instantly set my
mind to the business I was upon—and La Fleur, who stood waiting
without, in that breathless expectation which every son of nature of
us have felt in our turns, came in.

MONTRIUL

I AM apt to be taken with all kinds of people at first sight; but never
more so, than when a poor devil comes to offer his service to so poor
a devil as myself; and as I know this weakness, I always suffer my
judgment to draw back something on that very account—and this
more or less, according to the mood I am in, and the case—and I may
add the gender too, of the person I am to govern.°

When La Fleur enter'd the room, after every discount I could
make for my soul, the genuine look and air of the fellow determined
the matter at once in his favour; so I hired him first—and then began
to inquire what he could do: But I shall find out his talents, quoth I,
as I want them—besides, a Frenchman can do every thing.

Now poor La Fleur could do nothing in the world but beat a

drum, and play a march or two upon the fife.° I was determined to make his talents do; and can't say my weakness was ever so insulted by my wisdom, as in the attempt.

La Fleur had set out early in life, as gallantly as most Frenchmen do, with *serving* for a few years; at the end of which, having satisfied the sentiment, and found moreover, That the honour of beating a drum was likely to be its own reward, as it open'd no further track of glory to him—he retired *a ses terres*,° and lived *comme il plaisoit a Dieu*°—that is to say, upon nothing.

—And so, quoth *Wisdome*, you have hired a drummer to attend you in this tour of your's thro' France and Italy! Psha! said I, and do not one half of our gentry go with a hum-drum *compagnon du voiage*° the same round, and have the piper and the devil and all to pay besides? When man can extricate himself with an *equivoque*° in such an unequal match—he is not ill off—But you can do something else, La Fleur? said I——O qu'oui!°—he could make spatterdashes,° and play a little upon the fiddle—Bravo! said Wisdome—Why, I play a bass myself,° said I—we shall do very well.—You can shave, and dress a wig a little, La Fleur?—He had all the dispositions in the world—It is enough for heaven! said I, interrupting him—and ought to be enough for me—So supper coming in, and having a frisky English spaniel on one side of my chair, and a French valet, with as much hilarity in his countenance as ever nature painted in one, on the other—I was satisfied to my heart's content with my empire; and if monarchs knew what they would be at, they might be as satisfied as I was.

MONTRIUL

As La Fleur went the whole tour of France and Italy with me, and will be often upon the stage, I must interest the reader a little further in his behalf, by saying, that I had never less reason to repent of the impulses which generally do determine me, than in regard to this fellow—he was a faithful, affectionate, simple soul as ever trudged after the heels of a philosopher; and notwithstanding his talents of drum-beating and spatterdash-making, which, tho' very good in themselves, happen'd to be of no great service to me, yet was I hourly recompenced by the festivity of his temper—it supplied all defects—I had a constant resource in his looks in all difficulties and distresses of my own—I was going to have added, of his too; but La Fleur was out of the reach of every thing; for whether 'twas hunger or thirst, or cold or nakedness, or watchings, or whatever stripes of ill luck La Fleur met with in our journeyings,° there was no index in his physiognomy to point them out by—he was eternally the same; so that if I am a piece of a philosopher, which Satan now and then puts it into my head I am—it always mortifies the pride of the conceit, by reflecting how much I owe to the complexional° philosophy of this poor fellow, for shaming me into one of a better kind. With all this, La Fleur had a small cast of the coxcomb°—but he seemed at first sight to be more a coxcomb of nature than of art; and before I had been three days in Paris with him—he seemed to be no coxcomb at all.

MONTRIUL

THE next morning La Fleur entering upon his employment, I delivered to him the key of my portmanteau with an inventory of my half a dozen shirts and silk pair of breeches; and bid him fasten all upon the chaise—get the horses put to—and desire the landlord to come in with his bill.

C'est un garçon de bonne fortune,° said the landlord, pointing through the window to half a dozen wenches who had got round about La Fleur, and were most kindly taking their leave of him, as the postilion was leading out the horses. La Fleur kissed all their hands round and round again, and thrice he wiped his eyes, and thrice he promised he would bring them all pardons from Rome.

The young fellow, said the landlord, is beloved by all the town, and there is scarce a corner in Montriul where the want of him will not be felt: he has but one misfortune in the world, continued he, 'He is always in love.'—I am heartily glad of it, said I,—'twill save me the trouble every night of putting my breeches under my head. In saying this, I was making not so much La Fleur's eloge,° as my own, having been in love with one princess or another almost all my life, and I hope I shall go on so, till I die, being firmly persuaded, that if ever I do a mean action, it must be in some interval betwixt one passion and another: whilst this interregnum lasts, I always perceive my heart locked up—I can scarce find in it, to give Misery a sixpence; and therefore I always get out of it as fast as I can, and the moment I am re-kindled, I am all generosity and good will again; and would do any thing in the world either for, or with any one, if they will but satisfy me there is no sin in it.°

—But in saying this—surely I am commending the passion—not myself.

A FRAGMENT°

——THE town of Abdera, notwithstanding Democritus lived there trying all the powers of irony and laughter to reclaim it, was the vilest and most profligate town in all Thrace.° What for poisons, conspiracies and assassinations—libels, pasquinades° and tumults, there was no going there by day—'twas worse by night.

Now, when things were at the worst, it came to pass, that the Andromeda of Euripides° being represented at Abdera, the whole orchestra° was delighted with it: but of all the passages which delighted them, nothing operated more upon their imaginations, than the tender strokes of nature which the poet had wrought up in that pathetic speech of Perseus,

O Cupid, prince of God and men, &c.

Every man almost spoke pure iambics° the next day, and talk'd of nothing but Perseus his pathetic address—'O Cupid! prince of God and men'—in every street of Abdera, in every house—'O Cupid! Cupid!'—in every mouth, like the natural notes of some sweet melody which drops from it whether it will or no—nothing but 'Cupid! Cupid! prince of God and men'—The fire caught—and the whole city, like the heart of one man, open'd itself to Love.

No pharmacopolist° could sell one grain of helebore°—not a single armourer had a heart to forge one instrument of death—Friendship and Virtue met together, and kiss'd each other in the street—the golden age return'd, and hung o'er the town of Abdera—every

Abderite took his oaten pipe, and every Abderitish woman left her purple web, and chastly sat her down and listen'd to the song—

'Twas only in the power, says the Fragment, of the God whose empire extendeth from heaven to earth, and even to the depths of the sea, to have done this.

MONTRIUL

WHEN all is ready, and every article is disputed and paid for in the inn, unless you are a little sour'd by the adventure, there is always a matter to compound at the door, before you can get into your chaise; and that is with the sons and daughters of poverty, who surround you. Let no man say, 'let them go to the devil'—'tis a cruel journey to send a few miserables, and they have had sufferings enow without it: I always think it better to take a few sous out in my hand; and I would counsel every gentle traveller to do so likewise: he need not be so exact in setting down his motives for giving them—they will be register'd elsewhere.

For my own part, there is no man gives so little as I do; for few that I know have so little to give: but as this was the first publick act of my charity in France, I took the more notice of it.

A well-a-way! said I. I have but eight sous in the world, shewing them in my hand, and there are eight poor men and eight poor women for 'em.

A poor tatter'd soul without a shirt on instantly withdrew his claim, by retiring two steps out of the circle, and making a disqualifying bow on his part. Had the whole parterre° cried out, *Place aux dames,*° with one voice, it would not have conveyed the sentiment of a deference for the sex with half the effect.

Just heaven! for what wise reasons hast thou order'd it, that beggary and urbanity, which are at such variance in other countries, should find a way to be at unity in this?

—I insisted upon presenting him with a single sous, merely for his *politesse.*°

A poor little dwarfish brisk fellow, who stood over-against° me in the circle, putting something first under his arm, which had once been a hat, took his snuff-box out of his pocket, and generously offer'd a pinch on both sides of him: it was a gift of consequence, and modestly declined—The poor little fellow press'd it upon them with a nod of welcomeness—*Prenez en—prenez*,° said he, looking another way; so they each took a pinch—Pity thy box should ever want one! said I to myself; so I put a couple of sous into it—taking a small pinch out of his box, to enhance their value, as I did it—He felt the weight of the second obligation more than that of the first—'twas doing him an honour—the other was only doing him a charity—and he made me a bow down to the ground for it.

—Here! said I to an old soldier with one hand, who had been campaign'd and worn out to death in the service—here's a couple of sous for thee—*Vive le Roi!*° said the old soldier.

I had then but three sous left: so I gave one, simply *pour l'amour de Dieu*,° which was the footing on which it was begg'd—The poor woman had a dislocated hip; so it could not well be, upon any other motive.

Mon cher et tres charitable Monsieur°—There's no opposing this, said I.

My Lord Anglois—the very sound was worth the money—so I gave *my last sous for it.* But in the eagerness of giving, I had over-look'd a *pauvre honteux*,° who had no one to ask a sous for him, and who, I believed, would have perish'd, ere he could have ask'd one for himself: he stood by the chaise a little without the circle, and wiped a tear from a face which I thought had seen better days—Good God! said I—and I have not one single sous left to give him—But you have a thousand! cried all the powers of nature, stirring within me—so I gave him—no matter what—I am ashamed to say *how much*, now—and was ashamed to think, how little, then: so if the reader can form any conjecture of my disposition, as these two fixed points are given him, he may judge within a livre or two what was the precise sum.

I could afford nothing for the rest, but, *Dieu vous benisse—Et le bon Dieu vous benisse encore*°—said the old soldier, the dwarf, &c. The *pauvre honteux* could say nothing—he pull'd out a little hand-kerchief, and wiped his face as he turned away—and I thought he thank'd me more than them all.

THE BIDET

HAVING settled all these little matters, I got into my post-chaise with more ease than ever I got into a post-chaise in my life; and La Fleur having got one large jack-boot on the far side of a little *bidet**,° and another on this (for I count nothing of his legs)—he canter'd away before me as happy and as perpendicular as a prince.—

—But what is happiness! what is grandeur in this painted scene of life! A dead ass, before we had got a league, put a sudden stop to La Fleur's career—his bidet would not pass by it—a contention arose betwixt them, and the poor fellow was kick'd out of his jack-boots the very first kick.

La Fleur bore his fall like a French christian, saying neither more or less upon it, than, Diable! so presently got up and came to the charge again astride his bidet, beating him up to it as he would have beat his drum.

The bidet flew from one side of the road to the other, then back again—then this way—then that way, and in short every way but by the dead ass.—La Fleur insisted upon the thing—and the bidet threw him.

What's the matter, La Fleur, said I, with this bidet of thine?

—*Monsieur*, said he, *c'est un cheval le plus opiniatré du monde*°— Nay, if he is a conceited beast, he must go his own way, replied I—so La Fleur got off him, and giving him a good sound lash, the bidet took me at my word, and away he scamper'd back to Montriul.— *Peste!*° said La Fleur.

It is not *mal a propos*° to take notice here, that tho' La Fleur availed himself but of two different terms of exclamation in this encounter—namely, *Diable!* and *Peste!* that there are nevertheless three, in the French language; like the positive, comparative, and superlative, one or the other of which serve for every unexpected throw of the dice in life.

Le Diable! which is the first, and positive degree, is generally used upon ordinary emotions of the mind, where small things only fall out contrary to your expectations—such as—the throwing once doublets°—La Fleur's being kick'd off his horse, and so forth— cuckoldom, for the same reason, is always—*Le Diable!*

---

* Post horse.

But in cases where the cast° has something provoking in it, as in that of the bidet's running away after, and leaving La Fleur aground in jack-boots—'tis the second degree.

'Tis then *Peste!*

And for the third°—

—But here my heart is wrung with pity and fellow-feeling, when I reflect what miseries must have been their lot, and how bitterly so refined a people must have smarted, to have forced them upon the use of it.—

Grant me, O ye powers which touch the tongue with eloquence in distress!°—whatever is my *cast*, Grant me but decent words to exclaim in, and I will give my nature way.

—But as these were not to be had in France, I resolved to take every evil just as it befell me without any exclamation at all.

La Fleur, who had made no such covenant with himself, followed the bidet with his eyes till it was got out of sight—and then, you may imagine, if you please, with what word he closed the whole affair.

As there was no hunting down a frighten'd horse in jack-boots, there remained no alternative but taking La Fleur either behind the chaise, or into it.—

I preferred the latter, and in half an hour we got to the post-house at Nampont.

NAMPONT
THE DEAD ASS

AND this, said he, putting the remains of a crust into his wallet°—and this, should have been thy portion, said he, hadst thou been alive to have shared it with me. I thought by the accent, it had been an apostrophe° to his child; but 'twas to his ass, and to the very ass we had seen dead in the road, which had occasioned La Fleur's misadventure. The man seemed to lament it much; and it instantly brought into my mind Sancho's lamentation° for his; but he did it with more true touches of nature.

The mourner was sitting upon a stone bench at the door, with the ass's pannel° and its bridle on one side, which he took up from time to time—then laid them down—look'd at them and shook his head. He then took his crust of bread out of his wallet again, as if to eat it; held it some time in his hand—then laid it upon the bit of his ass's bridle—looked wistfully at the little arrangement he had made—and then gave a sigh.

The simplicity of his grief drew numbers about him, and La Fleur amongst the rest, whilst the horses were getting ready; as I continued sitting in the post-chaise, I could see and hear over their heads.

—He said he had come last from Spain, where he had been from the furthest borders of Franconia; and had got so far on his return home, when his ass died. Every one seem'd desirous to know what business could have taken so old and poor a man so far a journey from his own home.

It had pleased heaven, he said, to bless him with three sons, the finest lads in all Germany; but having in one week lost two of the eldest of them by the small-pox, and the youngest falling ill of the same distemper, he was afraid of being bereft of them all; and made a vow, if Heaven would not take him from him also, he would go in gratitude to St. Iago in Spain.°

When the mourner got thus far on his story, he stopp'd to pay nature her tribute—and wept bitterly.

He said, Heaven had accepted the conditions; and that he had set out from his cottage with this poor creature, who had been a patient partner of his journey—that it had eat the same bread with him all the way, and was unto him as a friend.°

Every body who stood about, heard the poor fellow with concern—La Fleur offered him money.—The mourner said, he did not want it—it was not the value of the ass—but the loss of him.—The ass, he said, he was assured loved him—and upon this told them a long story of a mischance upon their passage over the Pyrenean mountains which had separated them from each other three days; during which time the ass had sought him as much as he had sought the ass, and that they had neither scarce eat or drank till they met.

Thou hast one comfort, friend, said I, at least in the loss of thy poor beast; I'm sure thou hast been a merciful master to him.—Alas! said the mourner, I thought so, when he was alive—but now that he is dead I think otherwise.—I fear the weight of myself and my afflictions together have been too much for him—they have shortened the poor creature's days, and I fear I have them to answer for.—Shame on the world! said I to myself—Did we love each other, as this poor soul but loved his ass—'twould be something.—

NAMPONT
THE POSTILLION

THE concern which the poor fellow's story threw me into, required some attention: the postillion paid not the least to it, but set off upon the *pavé*° in a full gallop.

The thirstiest soul in the most sandy desert of Arabia could not have wished more for a cup of cold water,° than mine did for grave and quiet movements; and I should have had an high opinion of the postillion had he but stolen off with me in something like a pensive pace.—On the contrary, as the mourner finished his lamentation, the fellow gave an unfeeling lash to each of his beasts, and set off clattering like a thousand devils.

I called to him as loud as I could, for heaven's sake to go slower— and the louder I called the more unmercifully he galloped.—The deuce take him and his galloping too—said I—he'll go on tearing my nerves to pieces till he has worked me into a foolish passion, and then he'll go slow, that I may enjoy the sweets of it.

The postillion managed the point to a miracle: by the time he had got to the foot of a steep hill about half a league from Nampont,—he had put me out of temper with him—and then with myself, for being so.

My case then required a different treatment; and a good rattling gallop would have been of real service to me.—

—Then, prithee get on—get on, my good lad, said I.

The postillion pointed to the hill—I then tried to return back to the story of the poor German and his ass—but I had broke the clue°—and could no more get into it again, than the postillion could into a trot.—

—The deuce go, said I, with it all! Here am I sitting as candidly disposed to make the best of the worst, as ever wight° was, and all runs counter.

There is one sweet lenitive at least for evils, which nature holds out to us; so I took it kindly at her hands, and fell asleep; and the first word which roused me was *Amiens.*

—Bless me! said I, rubbing my eyes—this is the very town where my poor lady is to come.

AMIENS

THE words were scarce out of my mouth, when the Count de L***'s post-chaise, with his sister in it, drove hastily by: she had just time to make me a bow of recognition—and of that particular kind of it, which told me she had not yet done with me. She was as good as her look; for, before I had quite finished my supper, her brother's servant came into the room with a billet,° in which she said, she had taken the liberty to charge me with a letter, which I was to present myself to Madame R*** the first morning I had nothing to do at Paris. There was only added, she was sorry, but from what *penchant* she had not considered, that she had been prevented telling me her story—that she still owed it me; and if my rout° should ever lay through Brussels, and I had not by then forgot the name of Madame de L***—that Madame de L*** would be glad to discharge her obligation.

Then I will meet thee, said I, fair spirit! at Brussels—'tis only returning from Italy through Germany to Holland, by the rout of Flanders, home—'twill scarce be ten posts out of my way; but were it ten thousand! with what a moral delight will it crown my journey, in sharing in the sickening incidents of a tale of misery told to me by such a sufferer? to see her weep! and though I cannot dry up the fountain of her tears, what an exquisite sensation is there still left, in wiping them away from off the cheeks° of the first and fairest of women, as I'm sitting with my handkerchief in my hand in silence the whole night besides her.

There was nothing wrong in the sentiment; and yet I instantly reproached my heart with it in the bitterest and most reprobate° of expressions.

It had ever, as I told the reader, been one of the singular blessings of my life, to be almost every hour of it miserably in love with some one; and my last flame happening to be blown out by a whiff of jealousy on the sudden turn of a corner, I had lighted it up afresh at the pure taper of Eliza but about three months before—swearing as I did it, that it should last me through the whole journey—Why should I dissemble the matter? I had sworn to her eternal fidelity—she had a right to my whole heart—to divide my affections was to lessen them—to expose them, was to risk them: where there is risk, there may be loss—and what wilt thou have, Yorick! to answer to a heart so full of trust and confidence—so good, so gentle and unreproaching?

—I will not go to Brussels, replied I, interrupting myself—but my imagination went on—I recall'd her looks at that crisis of our separation° when neither of us had power to say Adieu! I look'd at the picture she had tied in a black ribband about my neck—and blush'd as I look'd at it—I would have given the world to have kiss'd it,—but was ashamed—And shall this tender flower, said I, pressing it between my hands—shall it be smitten to its very root—and smitten, Yorick! by thee, who hast promised to shelter it in thy breast?

Eternal fountain of happiness! said I, kneeling down upon the ground—be thou my witness—and every pure spirit which tastes it, be my witness also, That I would not travel to Brussels, unless Eliza went along with me, did the road lead me towards heaven.

In transports of this kind, the heart, in spite of the understanding, will always say too much.°

THE LETTER
AMIENS

FORTUNE had not smiled upon La Fleur; for he had been unsuccessful in his feats of chivalry—and not one thing had offer'd to signalize° his zeal for my service from the time he had enter'd into it, which was almost four and twenty hours. The poor soul burn'd with impatience; and the Count de L***'s servant's coming with the letter, being the first practicable occasion which offered, La Fleur had laid hold of it; and in order to do honour to his master, had taken him into a back parlour in the Auberge,° and treated him with a cup or two of the best wine in Picardy; and the Count de L***'s servant in return, and not to be behind hand in politeness with La Fleur, had taken him back with him to the Count's hôtel.° La Fleur's *prevenancy*° (for there was a passport in his very looks) soon set every servant in the kitchen at ease with him; and as a Frenchman, whatever be his talents, has no sort of prudery in shewing them, La Fleur, in less than five minutes, had pull'd out his fife, and leading off the dance himself with the first note, set the *fille de chambre*, the *maitre d'hotel*,° the cook, the scullion, and all the household, dogs and cats, besides an old monkey, a-dancing: I suppose there never was a merrier kitchen since the flood.

Madame de L***, in passing from her brother's apartments to her own, hearing so much jollity below stairs, rung up her *fille de chambre* to ask about it; and hearing it was the English gentleman's servant who had set the whole house merry with his pipe, she order'd him up.

As the poor fellow could not present himself empty, he had loaden'd himself in going up stairs with a thousand compliments to Madame de L***, on the part of his master—added a long apocrypha of inquiries after Madame de L***'s health—told her, that Monsieur his master was *au desespoire*° for her re-establishment from the fatigues of her journey—and, to close all, that Monsieur had received the letter which Madame had done him the honour——And he has done me the honour, said Madame de L***, interrupting La Fleur, to send a billet in return.

Madame de L*** had said this with such a tone of reliance upon the fact, that La Fleur had not power to disappoint her expectations—he trembled for my honour—and possibly might not altogether be unconcerned for his own, as a man capable of being attach'd to a master who could be a wanting *en egards vis a vis d'une femme*;° so that when Madame de L*** asked La Fleur if he had brought a letter—*O qu'oui*,° said La Fleur: so laying down his hat upon the ground, and taking hold of the flap of his right side pocket with his left hand, he began to search for the letter with his right—then contrary-wise—*Diable!*—then sought every pocket—pocket by pocket, round, not forgetting his fob°—*Peste!*—then La Fleur emptied them upon the floor—pulled out a dirty cravat—a handkerchief—a comb—a whip lash—a night-cap—then gave a peep into his hat—*Quelle etourderie!*° He had left the letter upon the table in the Auberge—he would run for it, and be back with it in three minutes.

I had just finished my supper when La Fleur came in to give me an account of his adventure: he told the whole story simply as it was; and only added, that if Monsieur had forgot (*par hazard*)° to answer

Madame's letter, the arrangement gave him an opportunity to recover the *faux pas*—and if not, that things were only as they were.

Now I was not altogether sure of my *etiquette*, whether I ought to have wrote or no; but if I had—a devil himself could not have been angry: 'twas but the officious zeal of a well-meaning creature for my honour; and however he might have mistook the road—or embarrassed me in so doing—his heart was in no fault—I was under no necessity to write—and what weighed more than all—he did not look as if he had done amiss.

—'Tis all very well, La Fleur, said I.—'Twas sufficient. La Fleur flew out of the room like lightening, and return'd with pen, ink, and paper, in his hand; and coming up to the table, laid them close before me, with such a delight in his countenance, that I could not help taking up the pen.

I begun and begun again; and though I had nothing to say, and that nothing might have been express'd in half a dozen lines, I made half a dozen different beginnings, and could no way please myself.

In short, I was in no mood to write.

La Fleur stepp'd out and brought a little water in a glass to dilute my ink—then fetch'd sand and seal-wax—It was all one: I wrote, and blotted, and tore off, and burnt, and wrote again—*Le Diable l'emporte!*° said I half to myself—I cannot write this self-same letter; throwing the pen down despairingly as I said it.

As soon as I had cast down the pen, La Fleur advanced with the most respectful carriage up to the table, and making a thousand apologies for the liberty he was going to take, told me he had a letter in his pocket wrote by a drummer in his regiment to a corporal's wife, which, he durst say, would suit the occasion.

I had a mind to let the poor fellow have his humour—Then prithee, said I, let me see it.

La Fleur instantly pull'd out a little dirty pocket-book cramm'd full of small letters and billet-doux° in a sad condition, and laying it upon the table, and then untying the string which held them all together, run them over one by one, till he came to the letter in question—*La voila!*° said he, clapping his hands: so unfolding it first, he laid it before me, and retired three steps from the table whilst I read it.

THE LETTER

MADAME,

JE suis penetré de la douleur la plus vive, et reduit en même temps au desespoir par ce retour imprevû du Corporal qui rend notre entrevue de ce soir la chose du monde la plus impossible.

Mais vive la joie! et toute la mienne sera de penser a vous.

L'amour n'est *rien* sans sentiment.°

Et le sentiment est encore *moins* sans amour.

On dit qu'on ne doit jamais se desesperer.

On dit aussi que Monsieur le Corporal monte la garde Mercredi: alors ce sera mon tour.

Chacun a son tour.

En attendant—Vive l'amour! et vive la bagatelle!

Je suis, MADAME,

Avec toutes les sentiments les plus respecteux et les plus tendres tout a vous,°

JAQUES ROQUE.

It was but changing the Corporal into the Count—and saying nothing about mounting guard on Wednesday—and the letter was neither right or wrong—so to gratify the poor fellow, who stood trembling for my honour, his own, and the honour of his letter,—I took the cream gently off it, and whipping it up in my own way—I seal'd it up and sent him with it to Madame de L***—and the next morning we pursued our journey to Paris.

PARIS

WHEN a man can contest the point by dint of equipage, and carry all on floundering before him with half a dozen lackies and a couple of cooks—'tis very well in such a place as Paris—he may drive in at which end of a street he will.

A poor prince who is weak in cavalry, and whose whole infantry does not exceed a single man, had best quit the field; and singalize himself in the cabinet, if he can get up into it—I say *up into it*—for there is no descending perpendicular amongst 'em with a '*Me voici! mes enfans*'°—here I am—whatever many may think.

I own my first sensations, as soon as I was left solitary and alone in my own chamber in the hotel, were far from being so flattering as I had prefigured them. I walked up gravely to the window in my dusty black coat, and looking through the glass saw all the world in yellow, blue, and green, running at the ring of pleasure.—The old with broken lances, and in helmets which had lost their vizards—the young in armour bright which shone like gold, beplumed with each gay feather of the east—all—all tilting at it like fascinated knights in tournaments of yore for fame and love.°—

Alas, poor Yorick!° cried I, what art thou doing here? On the very first onset of all this glittering clatter, thou art reduced to an atom— seek—seek some winding alley, with a tourniquet° at the end of it, where chariot never rolled or flambeau° shot its rays—there thou mayest solace thy soul in converse sweet with some kind *grisset*° of a barber's wife, and get into such coteries!—

—May I perish! if I do, said I, pulling out the letter which I had to present to Madame de R***.—I'll wait upon this lady, the very first thing I do. So I called La Fleur to go seek me a barber directly—and come back and brush my coat.

THE WIG
PARIS

WHEN the barber came, he absolutely refused to have any thing to do with my wig: 'twas either above or below his art: I had nothing to do, but to take one ready made of his own recommendation.

—But I fear, friend! said I, this buckle° won't stand.—You may immerge° it, replied he, into the ocean, and it will stand—

What a great scale is every thing upon in this city! thought I— The utmost stretch of an English periwig-maker's ideas could have gone no further than to have 'dipped it into a pail of water'—What difference! 'tis like time to eternity.

I confess I do hate all cold conceptions, as I do the puny ideas which engender them; and am generally so struck with the great works of nature, that for my own part, if I could help it, I never would make a comparison less than a mountain at least. All that can be said against the French sublime in this instance of it, is this—that the grandeur is *more* in the *word*; and *less* in the *thing*.° No doubt the ocean fills the mind with vast ideas; but Paris being so far inland, it was not likely I should run post a hundred miles out of it, to try the experiment—the Parisian barber meant nothing.—

The pail of water standing besides the great deep, makes certainly but a sorry figure in speech—but 'twill be said—it has one advantage—'tis in the next room, and the truth of the buckle may be tried in it without more ado, in a single moment.

In honest truth, and upon a more candid revision of the matter, *The French expression professes more than it performs.*

I think I can see the precise and distinguishing marks of national characters more in these nonsensical *minutiæ*, than in the most important matters of state; where great men of all nations talk and stalk so much alike, that I would not give ninepence to chuse amongst them.

I was so long in getting from under my barber's hands, that it was too late to think of going with my letter to Madame R*** that night: but when a man is once dressed at all points for going out, his reflections turn to little account, so taking down the name of the Hotel de Modene where I lodged, I walked forth without any determination where to go—I shall consider of that, said I, as I walk along.

THE PULSE
PARIS

HAIL ye small sweet courtesies of life, for smooth do ye make the road of it! like grace and beauty which beget inclinations to love at first sight; 'tis ye who open this door and let the stranger in.

—Pray, Madame, said I, have the goodness to tell me which way I must turn to go to the Opera comique:°—Most willingly, Monsieur, said she, laying aside her work—

I had given a cast with my eye into half a dozen shops as I came along in search of a face not likely to be disordered by such an interruption; till at last, this hitting my fancy, I had walked in.

She was working a pair of ruffles° as she sat in a low chair on the far side of the shop facing the door—

—*Tres volentieres*; most willingly, said she, laying her work down upon a chair next her, and rising up from the low chair she was sitting in, with so chearful a movement and so chearful a look, that had I been laying out fifty louis d'ors with her, I should have said—'This woman is grateful.'

You must turn, Monsieur, said she, going with me to the door of the shop, and pointing the way down the street I was to take—you must turn first to your left hand—*mais prenez guarde*°—there are two turns; and be so good as to take the second—then go down a little way and you'll see a church, and when you are past it, give yourself the trouble to turn directly to the right, and that will lead you to the foot of the *pont neuf*, which you must cross—and there, any one will do himself the pleasure to shew you—

She repeated her instructions three times over to me with the same good natur'd patience the third time as the first;—and if *tones and manners* have a meaning, which certainly they have, unless to hearts which shut them out—she seem'd really interested, that I should not lose myself.

I will not suppose it was the woman's beauty, notwithstanding she was the handsomest grisset, I think, I ever saw, which had much to do with the sense I had of her courtesy; only I remember, when I told her how much I was obliged to her, that I looked very full in her eyes,—and that I repeated my thanks as often as she had done her instructions.

I had not got ten paces from the door, before I found I had forgot every tittle° of what she had said—so looking back, and seeing her still standing in the door of the shop as if to look whether I went right or not—I returned back, to ask her whether the first turn was to my right or left—for that I had absolutely forgot.—Is it possible! said she, half laughing.—'Tis very possible, replied I, when a man is thinking more of a woman, than of her good advice.

As this was the real truth—she took it, as every woman takes a matter of right, with a slight courtesy.°

—*Attendez!*° said she, laying her hand upon my arm to detain me, whilst she called a lad out of the back-shop to get ready a parcel of gloves. I am just going to send him, said she, with a packet into that quarter, and if you will have the complaisance to step in, it will be ready in a moment, and he shall attend you to the place.—So I walk'd in with her to the far side of the shop, and taking up the ruffle in my hand which she laid upon the chair, as if I had a mind to sit, she sat down herself in her low chair, and I instantly sat myself down besides her.

—He will be ready, Monsieur, said she, in a moment—And in that moment, replied I, most willingly would I say something very civil to you for all these courtesies. Any one may do a casual act of good nature, but a continuation of them shews it is a part of the temperature;° and certainly, added I, if it is the same blood which comes from the heart, which descends to the extremes (touching her wrist) I am sure you must have one of the best pulses of any woman in the world—Feel it, said she, holding out her arm. So laying down my hat, I took hold of her fingers in one hand, and applied the two forefingers of my other to the artery—

—Would to heaven! my dear Eugenius,° thou hadst passed by, and beheld me sitting in my black coat, and in my lack-a-day-sical manner, counting the throbs of it, one by one, with as much true devotion as if I had been watching the critical ebb or flow of her fever—How wouldst thou have laugh'd and moralized upon my new profession?—and thou shouldst have laugh'd and moralized on—Trust me, my dear Eugenius, I should have said, 'there are worse occupations in this world *than feeling a woman's pulse*.'—But a Grisset's! thou wouldst have said—and in an open shop! Yorick—

—So much the better: for when my views are direct, Eugenius, I care not if all the world saw me feel it.

THE HUSBAND
PARIS

I HAD counted twenty pulsations, and was going on fast towards the fortieth, when her husband coming unexpected from a back parlour into the shop, put me a little out in my reckoning—'Twas no body but her husband, she said—so I began a fresh score—Monsieur is so good, quoth she, as he pass'd by us, as to give himself the trouble of feeling my pulse—The husband took off his hat, and making me a bow, said, I did him too much honour—and having said that, he put on his hat and walk'd out.

Good God! said I to myself, as he went out—and can this man be the husband of this woman?

Let it not torment the few who know what must have been the grounds of this exclamation, if I explain it to those who do not.

In London a shopkeeper and a shopkeeper's wife seem to be one bone and one flesh: in the several endowments of mind and body, sometimes the one, sometimes the other has it, so as in general to be upon a par, and to tally with each other as nearly as man and wife need to do.

In Paris, there are scarce two orders of beings more different: for the legislative and executive powers of the shop not resting in the husband, he seldom comes there—in some dark and dismal room behind, he sits commerceless in his thrum° night-cap, the same rough son of Nature that Nature left him.

The genius of a people where nothing but the monarchy is *salique*,° having ceded this department, with sundry others, totally to the women°—by a continual higgling with customers of all ranks and sizes from morning to night, like so many rough pebbles shook long together in a bag, by amicable collisions, they have worn down their asperities and sharp angles, and not only become round and smooth, but will receive, some of them, a polish like a brilliant°—Monsieur *le Mari*° is little better than the stone under your foot—

—Surely—surely man! it is not good for thee to sit alone°—thou wast made for social intercourse and gentle greetings, and this improvement of our natures from it, I appeal to, as my evidence.

—And how does it beat, Monsieur? said she.—With all the benignity, said I, looking quietly in her eyes, that I expected—She was going to say something civil in return—but the lad came into the shop with the gloves—*A propos*, said I; I want a couple of pair myself.

THE GLOVES
PARIS

THE beautiful Grisset rose up when I said this, and going behind the counter, reach'd down a parcel and untied it: I advanced to the side over-against her: they were all too large. The beautiful Grisset measured them one by one across my hand—It would not alter the dimensions—She begg'd I would try a single pair, which seemed to be the least—She held it open—my hand slipp'd into it at once—It will not do, said I, shaking my head a little—No, said she, doing the same thing.

There are certain combined looks of simple subtlety—where whim, and sense, and seriousness, and nonsense, are so blended, that all the languages of Babel° set loose together could not express them—they are communicated and caught so instantaneously, that you can scarce say which party is the infecter. I leave it to your men of words to swell pages about it—it is enough in the present to say again, the gloves would not do; so folding our hands within our arms, we both loll'd upon the counter—it was narrow, and there was just room for the parcel to lay between us.

The beautiful Grisset look'd sometimes at the gloves, then sideways to the window, then at the gloves—and then at me. I was not disposed to break silence—I follow'd her example: so I look'd at the gloves, then to the window, then at the gloves, and then at her—and so on alternately.

I found I lost considerably in every attack—she had a quick black eye, and shot through two such long and silken eye-lashes with such penetration, that she look'd into my very heart and reins°—It may seem strange, but I could actually feel she did—°

—It is no matter, said I, taking up a couple of the pairs next me, and putting them into my pocket.

I was sensible the beautiful Grisset had not ask'd above a single livre above the price—I wish'd she had ask'd a livre more, and was puzzling my brains how to bring the matter about—Do you think, my dear Sir, said she, mistaking my embarrassment, that I could ask a *sous* too much of a stranger—and of a stranger whose politeness, more than his want of gloves, has done me the honour to lay himself at my mercy?—*M'en croyez capable?*°—Faith! not I, said I; and if you were, you are welcome—So counting the money into her hand, and with a lower bow than one generally makes to a shopkeeper's wife, I went out, and her lad with his parcel followed me.

THE TRANSLATION
PARIS

THERE was no body in the box I was let into but a kindly old French officer. I love the character, not only because I honour the man whose manners are softened by a profession which makes bad men worse; but that I once knew one—for he is no more—and why should I not rescue one page from violation by writing his name in it, and telling the world it was Captain Tobias Shandy, the dearest of my flock and friends, whose philanthropy I never think of at this long distance from his death—but my eyes gush out with tears.° For his sake, I have a predilection for the whole corps of veterans; and so I strode over the two back rows of benches, and placed myself beside him.

The old officer was reading attentively a small pamphlet, it might be the book of the opera, with a large pair of spectacles. As soon as I sat down, he took his spectacles off, and putting them into a shagreen° case, return'd them and the book into his pocket together. I half rose up, and made him a bow.

Translate this into any civilized language in the world—the sense is this:

'Here's a poor stranger come in to the box—he seems as if he knew no body; and is never likely, was he to be seven years in Paris, if every man he comes near keeps his spectacles upon his nose—'tis shutting the door of conversation absolutely in his face—and using him worse than a German.'°

The French officer might as well have said it all aloud; and if he had, I should in course have put the bow I made him into French too, and told him, 'I was sensible of his attention, and return'd him a thousand thanks for it.'

There is not a secret so aiding to the progress of sociality, as to get master of this *short hand*, and be quick in rendering the several turns of looks and limbs, with all their inflections and delineations, into plain words. For my own part, by long habitude, I do it so mechanic-ally, that when I walk the streets of London, I go translating all the way; and have more than once stood behind in the circle, where not three words have been said, and have brought off twenty different dialogues with me, which I could have fairly wrote down and sworn to.

I was going one evening to Martini's concert° at Milan, and was just entering the door of the hall, when the Marquesina di F***° was coming out in a sort of a hurry—she was almost upon me before I saw her; so I gave a spring to one side to let her pass—She had done the same, and on the same side too; so we ran our heads together: she instantly got to the other side to get out: I was just as unfortunate as she had been; for I had sprung to that side, and opposed her passage again—We both flew together to the other side, and then back—and so on—it was ridiculous; we both blush'd intolerably; so I did at last the thing I should have done at first—I stood stock still, and the Marquesina had no more difficulty. I had no power to go into the room, till I had made her so much reparation as to wait and follow her with my eye to the end of the passage—She look'd back twice, and walk'd along it rather side-ways, as if she would make room for any one coming up stairs to pass her—No, said I—that's a vile translation: the Marquesina has a right to the best apology I can make her; and that opening is left for me to do it in—so I ran and begg'd pardon for the embarrassment I had given her, saying it was my intention to have made her way. She answered, she was guided by the same intention towards me—so we reciprocally thank'd each other. She was at the top of the stairs; and seeing no *chichesbee*° near her, I begg'd to hand her to her coach—so we went down the stairs, stopping at every third step to talk of the concert and the adven-ture—Upon my word, Madame, said I when I had handed her in, I made six different efforts to let you go out—And I made six efforts, replied she, to let you enter—I wish to heaven you would make a seventh, said I—With all my heart, said she, making room—Life is too short to be long about the forms of it—so I instantly stepp'd in, and she carried me home with her—And what became of the con-cert, St. Cecilia,° who, I suppose, was at it, knows more than I.

I will only add, that the connection which arose out of that trans-lation, gave me more pleasure than any one I had the honour to make in Italy.

THE DWARF
PARIS

I HAD never heard the remark made by any one in my life, except by one; and who that was,° will probably come out in this chapter; so that being pretty much unprepossessed, there must have been grounds for what struck me the moment I cast my eyes over the *parterre*°—and that was, the unaccountable sport of nature in forming such numbers of dwarfs—No doubt, she sports at certain times in almost every corner of the world; but in Paris, there is no end to her amusements—The goddess seems almost as merry as she is wise.

As I carried my idea out of the *opera comique* with me, I measured every body I saw walking in the streets by it—Melancholy application! especially where the size was little—the face extremely dark—the eyes quick—the nose long—the teeth white—the jaw prominent—to see so many miserables, by force of accidents driven out of their own proper class into the very verge of another, which it gives me pain to write down—every third man a pigmy!—some by ricketty heads and hump backs—others by bandy legs—a third set arrested by the hand of Nature in the sixth and seventh years of their growth—a fourth, in their perfect and natural state, like dwarf apple-trees; from the first rudiments and stamina of their existence, never meant to grow higher.

A medical traveller might say, 'tis owing to undue bandages—a splenetic one, to want of air—and an inquisitive traveller, to fortify the system, may measure the height of their houses—the narrowness of their streets, and in how few feet square in the sixth and seventh stories such numbers of the *Bourgoisie* eat and sleep together; but I remember, Mr. Shandy the elder,° who accounted for nothing like any body else, in speaking one evening of these matters, averred, that children, like other animals, might be increased almost to any size, provided they came right into the world; but the misery was, the citizens of Paris were so coop'd up, that they had not actually room enough to get them—I do not call it getting any thing, said he—'tis getting nothing—Nay, continued he, rising in his argument, 'tis getting worse than nothing, when all you have got, after twenty or five and twenty years of the tenderest care and most nutritious aliment bestowed upon it, shall not at last be as high as my leg. Now,

Mr. Shandy being very short,° there could be nothing more said upon it.

As this is not a work of reasoning, I leave the solution as I found it, and content myself with the truth only of the remark, which is verified in every lane and by-lane of Paris. I was walking down that which leads from the Carousal to the Palais Royal, and observing a little boy in some distress at the side of the gutter, which ran down the middle of it, I took hold of his hand, and help'd him over. Upon turning up his face to look at him after, I perceived he was about forty—Never mind, said I; some good body will do as much for me when I am ninety.

I feel some little principles within me, which incline me to be merciful towards this poor blighted part of my species, who have neither size or strength to get on in the world—I cannot bear to see one of them trod upon; and had scarce got seated beside my old French officer, ere the disgust was exercised, by seeing the very thing happen under the box we sat in.

At the end of the orchestra,° and betwixt that and the first side-box, there is a small esplanade left, where, when the house is full, numbers of all ranks take sanctuary. Though you stand, as in the parterre, you pay the same price as in the orchestra. A poor defenceless being of this order had got thrust some how or other into this luckless place—the night was hot, and he was surrounded by beings two feet and a half higher than himself.° The dwarf suffered inexpressibly on all sides; but the thing which incommoded him most, was a tall corpulent German, near seven feet high, who stood directly betwixt him and all possibility of his seeing either the stage or the actors. The poor dwarf did all he could to get a peep at what was going forwards, by seeking for some little opening betwixt the German's arm and his body, trying first one side, then the other; but the German stood square in the most unaccommodating posture that can be imagined—the dwarf might as well have been placed at the bottom of the deepest draw-well in Paris; so he civilly reach'd up his hand to the German's sleeve, and told him his distress—The German turn'd his head back, look'd down upon him as Goliah did upon David—and unfeelingly resumed his posture.

I was just then taking a pinch of snuff out of my monk's little horn box—And how would thy meek and courteous spirit, my dear monk!

so temper'd to *bear and forbear!*—how sweetly would it have lent an ear to this poor soul's complaint!

The old French officer seeing me lift up my eyes with an emotion, as I made the apostrophe,° took the liberty to ask me what was the matter—I told him the story in three words; and added, how inhuman it was.

By this time the dwarf was driven to extremes, and in his first transports, which are generally unreasonable, had told the German he would cut off his long queue° with his knife—The German look'd back coolly, and told him he was welcome if he could reach it.

An injury sharpened by an insult, be it to who it will, makes every man of sentiment a party: I could have leaped out of the box to have redressed it.—The old French officer did it with much less confusion; for leaning a little over, and nodding to a centinel, and pointing at the same time with his finger to the distress—the centinel made his way up to it.—There was no occasion to tell the grievance—the thing told itself; so thrusting back the German instantly with his musket—he took the poor dwarf by the hand, and placed him before him.—This is noble! said I, clapping my hands together—And yet you would not permit this, said the old officer, in England.

—In England, dear Sir, said I, *we sit all at our ease.*°

The old French officer would have set me at unity with myself, in case I had been at variance,—by saying it was a *bon mot*°—and as a *bon mot* is always worth something at Paris, he offered me a pinch of snuff.

THE ROSE
PARIS

It was now my turn to ask the old French officer 'What was the matter?' for a cry of '*Haussez les mains, Monsieur l'Abbe,*'° re-echoed from a dozen different parts of the parterre, was as unintelligible to me, as my apostrophe to the monk had been to him.

He told me, it was some poor Abbe in one of the upper loges,° who he supposed had got planted perdu° behind a couple of grissets in order to see the opera, and that the parterre espying him, were insisting upon his holding up both his hands during the representation.—And can it be supposed, said I, that an ecclesiastick would pick the Grisset's pockets? The old French officer smiled, and whispering in my ear, open'd a door of knowledge which I had no idea of—

Good God! said I, turning pale with astonishment—is it possible, that a people so smit with sentiment should at the same time be so unclean, and so unlike themselves—*Quelle grossierte!*° added I.

The French officer told me, it was an illiberal sarcasm at the church, which had begun in the theatre about the time the Tartuffe was given in it, by Moliere—but, like other remains of Gothic manners, was declining—Every nation, continued he, have their refinements and *grossiertes*, in which they take the lead, and lose it of one another by turns—that he had been in most countries, but never in one where he found not some delicacies, which other seemed to want. *Le* POUR, *et le* CONTRE *se trouvent en chaque nation;*° there is a balance, said he, of good and bad every where; and nothing but the knowing it is so can emancipate one half of the world from the prepossessions which it holds against the other—that the advantage of travel, as it regarded the *sçavoir vivre,*° was by seeing a great deal both of men and manners; it taught us mutual toleration; and mutual toleration, concluded he, making me a bow, taught us mutual love.

The old French officer delivered this with an air of such candour and good sense, as coincided with my first favourable impressions of his character—I thought I loved the man; but I fear I mistook the object—'twas my own way of thinking—the difference was, I could not have expressed it half so well.

It is alike troublesome to both the rider and his beast—if the latter goes pricking up his ears, and starting all the way at every object which he never saw before—I have as little torment of this kind as any creature alive; and yet I honestly confess, that many a thing gave me pain, and that I blush'd at many a word the first month—which I found inconsequent and perfectly innocent the second.

Madame de Rambouliet,° after an acquaintance of about six weeks with her, had done me the honour to take me in her coach about two leagues out of town—Of all women, Madame de Rambouliet is the most correct; and I never wish to see one of more virtues and purity of heart—In our return back, Madame de Rambouliet desired me to pull the cord—I ask'd her if she wanted any thing—*Rien que pisser,*° said Madame de Rambouliet—

Grieve not, gentle traveller, to let Madame de Rambouliet p—ss on—And, ye fair mystic nymphs! go each one *pluck your rose*,° and scatter them in your path—for Madame de Rambouliet did no more—I handed Madame de Rambouliet out of the coach; and had I been the priest of the chaste CASTALIA,° I could not have served at her fountain with a more respectful decorum.

END OF VOL. I.

VOLUME II

THE FILLE DE CHAMBRE
PARIS

WHAT the old French officer had deliver'd upon travelling, bringing Polonius's advice to his son° upon the same subject into my head— and that bringing in Hamlet; and Hamlet, the rest of Shakespear's works, I stopp'd at the Quai de Conti in my return home, to purchase the whole set.

The bookseller said he had not a set in the world—*Comment!*° said I; taking one up out of a set which lay upon the counter betwixt us.——He said, they were sent him only to be got bound, and were to be sent back to Versailles in the morning to the Count de B****.°

—And does the Count de B**** said I, read Shakespear? *C'est un Esprit fort;*° replied the bookseller.—He loves English books; and what is more to his honour, Monsieur, he loves the English too. You speak this so civilly, said I, that 'tis enough to oblige an Englishman to lay out a Louis d'or or two at your shop—the bookseller made a bow, and was going to say something, when a young decent girl of about twenty, who by her air and dress, seemed to be *fille de chambre* to some devout woman of fashion, came into the shop and asked for *Les Egarments du Cœur & de l'Esprit:*° the bookseller gave her the book directly; she pulled out a little green sattin purse run round with a ribband of the same colour, and putting her finger and thumb into it, she took out the money, and paid for it. As I had nothing more to stay me in the shop, we both walked out at the door together.

——And what have you to do, my dear, said I, with *The Wander-ings of the Heart*, who scarce know yet you have one? nor till love has first told you it, or some faithless shepherd has made it ache, can'st thou ever be sure it is so.—*Le Dieu m'en guard!*° said the girl.—With reason, said I—for if it is a good one, 'tis pity it should be stolen: 'tis a little treasure to thee, and gives a better air to your face, than if it was dress'd out with pearls.

The young girl listened with a submissive attention, holding her sattin purse by its ribband in her hand all the time—'Tis a very small

one, said I, taking hold of the bottom of it—she held it towards me—
and there is very little in it, my dear, said I; but be but as good as
thou art handsome, and heaven will fill it: I had a parcel of crowns in
my hand to pay for Shakespear; and as she had let go the purse
intirely, I put a single one in;° and tying up the ribband in a bow-knot,
returned it to her.

The young girl made me more a humble courtesy than a low
one—'twas one of those quiet, thankful sinkings where the spirit
bows itself down—the body does no more than tell it. I never gave a
girl a crown in my life which gave me half the pleasure.

My advice, my dear, would not have been worth a pin to you, said
I, if I had not given this along with it: but now, when you see the
crown, you'll remember it—so don't, my dear, lay it out in ribbands.

Upon my word, Sir, said the girl, earnestly, I am incapable—in
saying which, as is usual in little bargains of honour, she gave me her
hand—*En verite, Monsieur, je mettrai cet argent apart*,° said she.

When a virtuous convention is made betwixt man and woman, it
sanctifies their most private walks: so notwithstanding it was dusky,
yet as both our roads lay the same way, we made no scruple of
walking along the Quai de Conti together.

She made me a second courtesy in setting off, and before we got
twenty yards from the door, as if she had not done enough before,
she made a sort of a little stop to tell me again,—she thank'd me.

It was a small tribute, I told her, which I could not avoid paying to
virtue, and would not be mistaken in the person I had been rendering it to for the world—but I see innocence, my dear, in your face—
and foul befal the man who ever lays a snare in its way!

The girl seem'd affected some way or other with what I said—she
gave a low sigh—I found I was not impowered to enquire at all after
it—so said nothing more till I got to the corner of the Rue de Nevers,
where we were to part.

—But is this the way, my dear, said I, to the hotel de Modene? she
told me it was—or, that I might go by the Rue de Guineygaude,
which was the next turn.—Then I'll go, my dear, by the Rue de
Guineygaude, said I, for two reasons; first I shall please myself, and
next I shall give you the protection of my company as far on your
way as I can. The girl was sensible I was civil—and said, she wish'd
the hotel de Modene was in the Rue de St. Pierre——You live there?
said I.—She told me she was *fille de chambre* to Madame *R****—*

Good God! said I, 'tis the very lady for whom I have brought a letter from Amiens—The girl told me that Madame *R*****, she believed expected a stranger with a letter, and was impatient to see him—so I desired the girl to present my compliments to Madame R****, and say I would certainly wait upon her in the morning.

We stood still at the corner of the Rue de Nevers whilst this pass'd—We then stopp'd a moment whilst she disposed of her *Egarments de Cœur*, &c. more commodiously than carrying them in her hand—they were two volumes; so I held the second for her whilst she put the first into her pocket; and then she held her pocket, and I put in the other after it.

'Tis sweet to feel by what fine-spun threads our affections are drawn together.

We set off a-fresh, and as she took her third step, the girl put her hand within my arm—I was just bidding her—but she did it of herself with that undeliberating simplicity, which shew'd it was out of her head that she had never seen me before. For my own part, I felt the conviction of consanguinity so strongly, that I could not help turning half round to look in her face, and see if I could trace out any thing in it of a family likeness—Tut! said I, are we not all relations?°

When we arrived at the turning up of the Rue de Guineygaude, I stopp'd to bid her adieu for good an all: the girl would thank me again for my company and kindness—She bid me adieu twice—I repeated it as often; and so cordial was the parting between us, that had it happen'd any where else, I'm not sure but I should have signed it with a kiss of charity, as warm and holy as an apostle.

But in Paris, as none kiss each other but the men—I did, what amounted to the same thing——

——I bid God bless her.

THE PASSPORT
PARIS

WHEN I got home to my hotel, La Fleur told me I had been enquired after by the Lieutenant de Police—The duce take it! said I——I know the reason. It is time the reader should know it, for in the order of things in which it happened, it was omitted; not that it was out of

my head; but that had I told it then, it might have been forgot now—
and now is the time I want it.

I had left London with so much precipitation, that it never enter'd
my mind that we were at war with France;° and had reach'd Dover,
and look'd through my glass at the hills beyond Boulogne, before the
idea presented itself; and with this in its train, that there was no
getting there without a passport. Go but to the end of a street, I have
a mortal aversion for returning back no wiser than I set out; and as
this was one of the greatest efforts I had ever made for knowledge, I
could less bear the thoughts of it: so hearing the Count de **** had
hired the packet,° I begg'd he would take me in his *suite*.° The Count
had some little knowledge of me, so made little or no difficulty—
only said, his inclination to serve me could reach no further than
Calais; as he was to return by way of Brussels to Paris: however,
when I had once pass'd there, I might get to Paris without interruption; but that in Paris I must make friends and shift for myself.—Let
me get to Paris, Monsieur le Count, said I—and I shall do very well.
So I embark'd, and never thought more of the matter.

When La Fleur told me the Lieutenant de Police had been enquiring after me—the thing instantly recurred—and by the time La
Fleur had well told me, the master of the hotel came into my room to
tell me the same thing, with this addition to it, that my passport had
been particularly ask'd after: the master of the hotel concluded with
saying, He hoped I had one.—Not I, faith! said I.

The master of the hotel retired three steps from me, as from an
infected person, as I declared this—and poor La Fleur advanced
three steps towards me, and with that sort of movement which a
good soul makes to succour a distress'd one—the fellow won my
heart by it; and from that single *trait*,° I knew his character as perfectly, and could rely upon it as firmly, as if he had served me with
fidelity for seven years.

Mon seignior! cried the master of the hotel—but recollecting
himself as he made the exclamation, he instantly changed the tone of
it—If Monsieur, said he, has not a passport (*apparament*°) in all likeli-
hood he has friends in Paris who can procure him one.—Not that I
know of, quoth I, with an air of indifference.—Then *certes*,° replied
he, you'll be sent to the Bastile or the Chatelet, *au moins*.° Poo! said I,
the king of France is a good natured soul—he'll hurt no body.—*Cela
n'empeche pas*,° said he—you will certainly be sent to the Bastile

to-morrow morning.—But I've taken your lodgings for a month, answer'd I, and I'll not quit them a day before the time for all the kings of France in the world. La Fleur whisper'd in my ear, That no body could oppose the king of France.

Pardi! said my host, *ces Messieurs Anglois sont des gens tres extra-ordinaires*°—and having both said and sworn it—he went out.

THE PASSPORT
The Hotel at Paris

I COULD not find in my heart to torture La Fleur's with a serious look upon the subject of my embarrassment, which was the reason I had treated it so cavalierly: and to shew him how light it lay upon my mind, I dropt the subject entirely; and whilst he waited upon me at supper, talk'd to him with more than usual gaiety about Paris, and of the opera comique.—La Fleur had been there himself, and had fol-lowed me through the streets as far as the bookseller's shop; but seeing me come out with the young *fille de chambre*, and that we walk'd down the Quai de Conti together, La Fleur deem'd it unnecessary to follow me a step further—so making his own reflec-tions upon it, he took a shorter cut——and got to the hotel in time to be inform'd of the affair of the Police against my arrival.

As soon as the honest creature had taken away, and gone down to sup himself, I then began to think a little seriously about my situ-ation.—

—And here, I know, Eugenius, thou wilt smile at the remem-brance of a short dialogue which pass'd betwixt us the moment I was going to set out——I must tell it here.

Eugenius, knowing that I was as little subject to be overburthen'd with money as thought, had drawn me aside to interrogate me how much I had taken care for; upon telling him the exact sum, Eugenius shook his head, and said it would not do; so pull'd out his purse in order to empty it into mine.—I've enough in conscience, Eugenius, said I.——Indeed, Yorick, you have not, replied Eugenius—I know France and Italy better than you.——But you don't consider, Eugenius, said I, refusing his offer, that before I have been three days in Paris, I shall take care to say or do something or other for which I shall get clapp'd up into the Bastile, and that I shall live there a couple of months entirely at the king of France's expence.—I beg pardon, said Eugenius, drily: really, I had forgot that resource.

Now the event I treated gaily came seriously to my door.

Is it folly, or nonchalance, or philosophy, or pertinacity—or what is it in me, that, after all, when La Fleur had gone down stairs, and I was quite alone, I could not bring down my mind to think of it otherwise than I had then spoken of it to Eugenius?

—And as for the Bastile! the terror is in the word—Make the most of it you can, said I to myself, the Bastile is but another word for a tower—and a tower is but another word for a house you can't get out of—Mercy on the gouty! for they are in it twice a year—but with nine livres a day, and pen and ink and paper and patience, albeit a man can't get out, he may do very well within—at least for a month or six weeks; at the end of which, if he is a harmless fellow his innocence appears, and he comes out a better and wiser man than he went in.

I had some occasion (I forget what) to step into the courtyard, as I settled this account; and remember I walk'd down stairs in no small triumph with the conceit of my reasoning—Beshrew the *sombre* pencil!° said I vauntingly—for I envy not its powers, which paints the evils of life with so hard and deadly a colouring. The mind sits terrified at the objects she has magnified herself, and blackened: reduce them to their proper size and hue she overlooks them—'Tis true, said I, correcting the proposition—the Bastile is not an evil to be despised—but strip it of its towers—fill up the fossè°— unbarricade the doors—call it simply a confinement, and suppose 'tis some tyrant of a distemper—and not of a man which holds you in it—the evil vanishes, and you bear the other half without complaint.

I was interrupted in the hey-day of this soliloquy, with a voice which I took to be of a child, which complained 'it could not get out.'—I look'd up and down the passage, and seeing neither man, woman, or child, I went out without further attention.

In my return back through the passage, I heard the same words repeated twice over; and looking up, I saw it was a starling hung in a little cage.—'I can't get out—I can't get out,'° said the starling.

I stood looking at the bird: and to every person who came through the passage it ran fluttering to the side towards which they approach'd it, with the same lamentation of its captivity—'I can't get out', said the starling—God help thee! said I, but I'll let thee out, cost what it will; so I turn'd about the cage to get to the door; it was twisted and double twisted so fast with wire, there was no getting it open without pulling the cage to pieces—I took both hands to it.

The bird flew to the place where I was attempting his deliverance, and thrusting his head through the trellis,° press'd his breast against it, as if impatient—I fear, poor creature! said I, I cannot set thee at liberty—'No,' said the starling—'I can't get out—I can't get out,' said the starling.

I vow, I never had my affections more tenderly awakened; nor do I remember an incident in my life, where the dissipated spirits, to which my reason had been a bubble, were so suddenly call'd home. Mechanical as the notes were, yet so true in tune to nature were they chanted, that in one moment they overthrew all my systematic reasonings upon the Bastile; and I heavily walk'd up stairs, unsaying every word I had said in going down them.

Disguise thyself as thou wilt, still slavery! said I—still thou art a bitter draught; and though thousands in all ages have been made to drink of thee, thou art no less bitter on that account.°—'tis thou, thrice sweet and gracious goddess, addressing myself to LIBERTY, whom all in public or in private worship, whose taste is grateful, and ever wilt be so, till NATURE herself shall change—no *tint* of words can spot thy snowy mantle, or chymic power turn thy sceptre into iron—with thee to smile upon him as he eats his crust, the swain is happier than his monarch, from whose court thou art exiled— Gracious heaven! cried I, kneeling down upon the last step but one in my ascent—grant me but health, thou great Bestower of it, and give me but this fair goddess as my companion—and shower down thy mitres,° if it seems good unto thy divine providence, upon those heads which are aching for them.

THE CAPTIVE
PARIS

THE bird in his cage pursued me into my room; I sat down close to my table, and leaning my head upon my hand, I begun to figure to myself the miseries of confinement. I was in a right frame for it, and so I gave full scope to my imagination.

I was going to begin with the millions of my fellow creatures born to no inheritance but slavery;° but finding, however affecting the picture was, that I could not bring it near me, and that the multitude of sad groups in it did but distract me.—

—I took a single captive,° and having first shut him up in his dungeon, I then look'd through the twilight of his grated door to take his picture.

I beheld his body half wasted away with long expectation and confinement, and felt what kind of sickness of the heart it was which arises from hope deferr'd.° Upon looking nearer I saw him pale and feverish: in thirty years the western breeze had not once fann'd his blood—he had seen no sun, no moon in all that time—nor had the voice of friend or kinsman breathed through his lattice—his children—

—But here my heart began to bleed—and I was forced to go on with another part of the portrait.

He was sitting upon the ground upon a little straw, in the furthest corner of his dungeon, which was alternately his chair and bed: a little calender of small sticks were laid at the head notch'd all over with the dismal days and nights he had pass'd there—he had one of these little sticks in his hand, and with a rusty nail he was etching another day of misery to add to the heap. As I darkened the little light he had, he lifted up a hopeless eye towards the door, then cast it down—shook his head, and went on with his work of affliction. I heard his chains upon his legs, as he turn'd his body to lay his little stick upon the bundle—He gave a deep sigh— I saw the iron enter into his soul°—I burst into tears—I could not sustain the picture of confinement which my fancy had drawn—I startled up from my chair, and calling La Fleur, I bid him bespeak me a *remise*, and have it ready at the door of the hotel by nine in the morning.

—I'll go directly, said I, myself to Monsieur Le Duke de Choiseul.°

La Fleur would have put me to bed; but not willing he should see any thing upon my cheek, which would cost the honest fellow a heart ache—I told him I would go to bed by myself—and bid him go do the same.

THE STARLING
ROAD to VERSAILLES

I GOT into my *remise* the hour I proposed: La Fleur got up behind, and I bid the coachman make the best of his way to Versailles.

As there was nothing in this road, or rather nothing which I look for in travelling, I cannot fill up the blank better than with a short history of this self-same bird, which became the subject of the last chapter.

Whilst the Honourable Mr. **** was waiting for a wind at Dover it had been caught upon the cliffs before it could well fly, by an English lad who was his groom; who not caring to destroy it, had taken it in his breast into the packet—and by course of feeding it, and taking it once under his protection, in a day or two grew fond of it, and got it safe along with him to Paris.

At Paris the lad had laid out a livre in a little cage for the starling, and as he had little to do better the five months his master stay'd there, he taught it in his mother's tongue the four simple words—(and no more)—to which I own'd myself so much it's debtor.

Upon his master's going on for Italy—the lad had given it to the master of the hotel—But his little song for liberty, being in an *unknown* language at Paris—the bird had little or no store set by him—so La Fleur bought both him and his cage for me for a bottle of Burgundy.

In my return from Italy I brought him with me to the country in whose language he had learn'd his notes—and telling the story of him to Lord A—Lord A begg'd the bird of me—in a week Lord A gave him to Lord B—Lord B made a present of him to Lord C—and Lord C's gentleman sold him to Lord D's for a shilling—Lord D gave him to Lord E—and so on—half round the alphabet—From that rank he pass'd into the lower house, and pass'd the hands of as many commoners——But as all these wanted to *get in*°—and my bird wanted to get out—he had almost as little store set by him in London as in Paris.

It is impossible but many of my readers must have heard of him; and if any by mere chance have ever seen him—I beg leave to inform them, that that bird was my bird—or some vile copy set up to represent him.

I have nothing further to add upon him, but that from that time to this, I have borne this poor starling as the crest to my arms.°— Thus:

——And let the heralds officers twist his neck about if they dare.

THE ADDRESS
VERSAILLES

I SHOULD not like to have my enemy take a view of my mind, when I am going to ask protection of any man: for which reason I generally endeavour to protect myself; but this going to Monsieur Le Duc de C***** was an act of compulsion—had it been an act of choice, I should have done it, I suppose, like other people.

How many mean plans of dirty address, as I went along, did my servile heart form! I deserved the Bastile for every one of them.

Then nothing would serve me, when I got within sight of Versailles, but putting words and sentences together, and conceiving attitudes and tones to wreath myself into Monsieur Le Duc de C*****'s good graces—This will do——said I—Just as well, retorted I again, as a coat carried up to him by an adventurous taylor, without taking his measure—Fool! continued I—see Monsieur Le Duc's face first—observe what character is written in it; take notice in what posture he stands to hear you—mark the turns and expressions of his body and limbs—And for the tone—the first sound which comes from his lips will give it you; and from all these together you'll compound an address at once upon the spot, which cannot disgust the Duke—the ingredients are his own, and most likely to go down.

Well! said I, I wish it well over—Coward again! as if man to man was not equal, throughout the whole surface of the globe; and if in the field—why not face to face in the cabinet° too? And trust me, Yorick, whenever it is not so, man is false to himself; and betrays his own succours° ten times, where nature does it once. Go to the Duc de C**** with the Bastile in thy looks—My life for it, thou wilt be sent back to Paris in half an hour, with an escort.

I believe so, said I—Then I'll go to the Duke, by heaven! with all the gaity and debonairness in the world.—

—And there you are wrong again, replied I—A heart at ease, Yorick, flies into no extremes—'tis ever on its center.—Well! well! cried I, as the coachman turn'd in at the gates—I find I shall do very well: and by the time he had wheel'd round the court, and brought me up to the door, I found myself so much the better for my own lecture, that I neither ascended the steps like a victim to justice, who was to part with life upon the topmost,—nor did I mount them with a skip and a couple of strides, as I do when I fly up, Eliza! to thee, to meet it.°

As I enter'd the door of the saloon, I was met by a person who possibly might be the maitre d'hotel,° but had more the air of one of the under secretaries, who told me the Duc de C**** was busy—I am utterly ignorant, said I, of the forms of obtaining an audience, being an absolute stranger, and what is worse in the present conjuncture of affairs, being an Englishman too.——He replied, that did not increase the difficulty.—I made him a slight bow, and told him, I had something of importance to say to Monsieur Le Duc. The secretary look'd towards the stairs, as if he was about to leave me to carry up this account to some one—But I must not mislead you, said I—for what I have to say is of no manner of importance to Monsieur Le Duc de C****—but of great importance to myself.—*C'est une autre affaire,*° replied he——Not at all, said I, to a man of gallantry.—But pray, good sir, continued I, when can a stranger hope to have *accesse?* In not less than two hours, said he, looking at his watch. The number of equipages in the court-yard seem'd to justify the calculation, that I could have no nearer a prospect—and as walking backwards and forwards in the saloon, without a soul to commune with, was for the time as bad as being in the Bastile itself, I instantly went back to my *remise*, and bid the coachman drive me to the *cordon bleu*, which was the nearest hotel.

I think there is a fatality in it—I seldom go to the place I set out for.

LE PATISSER°
VERSAILLES

BEFORE I had got half-way down the street, I changed my mind: as I am at Versailles, thought I, I might as well take a view of the town; so I pull'd the cord, and ordered the coachman to drive round some of the principal streets—I suppose the town is not very large, said I.—The coachman begg'd pardon for setting me right, and told me it was very superb, and that numbers of the first dukes and marquises and counts had hotels°—The Count de B****, of whom the bookseller at the Quai de Conti had spoke so handsomely the night before, came instantly into my mind.—And why should I not go, thought I, to the Count de B****, who has so high an idea of English books, and Englishmen—and tell him my story? so I changed my mind a second time—In truth it was the third; for I had intended that day for Madame de R**** in the Rue St. Pierre, and had devoutly sent her word by her *fille de chambre* that I would assuredly wait upon her—but I am govern'd by circumstances—I cannot govern them: so seeing a man standing with a basket on the other side of the street, as if he had something to sell, I bid La Fleur go up to him and enquire for the Count's hotel.

La Fleur return'd a little pale; and told me it was a Chevalier de St. Louis° selling *patès°*—It is impossible, La Fleur! said I.—La Fleur could no more account for the phenomenon than myself; but persisted in his story: he had seen the croix set in gold, with its red ribband, he said, tied to his button-hole—and had look'd into the basket and seen the *patès* which the Chevalier was selling; so could not be mistaken in that.

Such a reverse in man's life awakens a better principle than curiosity: I could not help looking for some time at him as I sat in the *remise*—the more I look'd at him—his croix and his basket, the stronger they wove themselves into my brain—I got out of the *remise* and went towards him.

He was begirt with a clean linen apron which fell below his knees, and with a sort of a bib went half way up his breast; upon the top of this, but a little below the hem, hung his croix. His basket of little *patès* was cover'd over with a white damask° napkin; another of the same kind was spread at the bottom; and there was a look of *propreté°* and neatness throughout; that one might have bought his *patès* of him, as much from appetite as sentiment.

He made an offer of them to neither; but stood still with them at the corner of a hotel, for those to buy who chose it, without solicitation.

He was about forty-eight—of a sedate look, something approaching to gravity. I did not wonder.—I went up rather to the basket than him, and having lifted up the napkin and taken one of his *patès* into my hand—I begg'd he would explain the appearance which affected me.

He told me in a few words, that the best part of his life had pass'd in the service, in which, after spending a small patrimony, he had obtain'd a company and the croix with it; but that at the conclusion of the last peace,° his regiment being reformed, and the whole corps, with those of some other regiments, left without any provision—he found himself in a wide world without friends, without a livre—and indeed, said he, without any thing but this—(pointing, as he said it, to his croix)—The poor chevalier won my pity, and he finish'd the scene, with winning my esteem too.

The king, he said, was the most generous of princes, but his generosity could neither relieve or reward every one, and it was only his misfortune to be amongst the number. He had a little wife, he said, whom he loved, who did the *patisserie*;° and added, he felt no dishonour in defending her and himself from want in this way— unless Providence had offer'd him a better.

It would be wicked to with-hold a pleasure from the good, in passing over what happen'd to this poor Chevalier of St. Louis about nine months after.

It seems he usually took his stand near the iron gates which lead up to the palace, and as his croix had caught the eye of numbers, numbers had made the same enquiry which I had done—He had told them the same story, and always with so much modesty and good sense, that it had reach'd at last the king's ears—who hearing the Chevalier had been a gallant officer, and respected by the whole regiment as a man of honour and integrity—he broke up his little trade by a pension of fifteen hundred livres a year.

As I have told this to please the reader, I beg he will allow me to relate another out of its order, to please myself—the two stories reflect light upon each other,—and 'tis a pity they should be parted.

THE SWORD
RENNES

WHEN states and empires have their periods of declension,° and feel in their turns what distress and poverty is—I stop not to tell the causes which gradually brought the house d'E**** in Britany into decay. The Marquis d'E**** had fought up against his condition with great firmness; wishing to preserve, and still shew to the world some little fragments of what his ancestors had been—their indiscretions had put it out of his power. There was enough left for the little exigencies of *obscurity*—But he had two boys who look'd up to him for *light*—he thought they deserved it. He had tried his sword—it could not open the way—the *mounting*° was too expensive—and simple œconomy was not a match for it—there was no resource but commerce.

In any other province in France, save Britany, this was smiting the root for ever of the little tree his pride and affection wish'd to see reblossom—But in Britany, there being a provision for this,° he avail'd himself of it; and taking an occasion when the states were assembled at Rennes, the Marquis, attended with his two boys, enter'd the court; and having pleaded the right of an ancient law of the duchy, which, though seldom claim'd, he said, was no less in force; he took his sword from his side—Here—said he—take it; and be trusty guardians of it, till better times put me in condition to reclaim it.

The president accepted the Marquis's sword—he stay'd a few minutes to see it deposited in the archives of his house—and departed.

The Marquis and his whole family embarked the next day for Martinico, and in about nineteen or twenty years of successful application to business, with some unlook'd for bequests from distant branches of his house—return'd home to reclaim his nobility and to support it.

It was an incident of good fortune which will never happen to any traveller, but a sentimental one, that I should be at Rennes at the very time of this solemn requisition: I call it solemn—it was so to me.

The Marquis enter'd the court with his whole family: he supported his lady—his eldest son supported his sister, and his youngest was at the other extreme of the line next his mother.—he put his handkerchief to his face twice—

—There was a dead silence. When the Marquis had approach'd within six paces of the tribunal, he gave the Marchioness to his youngest son, and advancing three steps before his family—he reclaim'd his sword. His sword was given him, and the moment he got it into his hand he drew it almost out of the scabbard—'twas the shining face of a friend he had once given up—he look'd attentively along it, beginning at the hilt, as if to see whether it was the same—when observing a little rust which it had contracted near the point, he brought it near his eye, and bending his head down over it—I think I saw a tear fall upon the place: I could not be deceived by what followed.

'I shall find, said he, some *other way*, to get it off.'

When the Marquis had said this, he return'd his sword into its scabbard, made a bow to the guardians of it—and, with his wife and daughter and his two sons following him, walk'd out.

O how I envied him his feelings!

THE PASSPORT
VERSAILLES

I FOUND no difficulty in getting admittance to Monsieur Le Count de B****. The set of Shakespears was laid upon the table, and he was tumbling them over.° I walk'd up close to the table, and giving first such a look at the books as to make him conceive I knew what they were—I told him I had come without any one to present me, knowing I should meet with a friend in his apartment who, I trusted, would do it for me—it is my countryman the great Shakespear, said I, pointing to his works—*et ayez la bontè, mon cher ami*, apostrophizing his spirit, added I, *de me faire cet honneur la.*°——

The Count smil'd at the singularity of the introduction; and seeing I look'd a little pale and sickly,° insisted upon my taking an armchair: so I sat down; and to save him conjectures upon a visit so out of all rule, I told him simply of the incident in the bookseller's shop, and how that had impell'd me rather to go to him with the story of a little embarrassment I was under, than to any other man in France—And what is your embarrassment? let me hear it, said the Count. So I told him the story just as I have told it the reader—

—And the master of my hotel, said I, as I concluded it, will needs have it, Monsieur le Count, that I shall be sent to the Bastile—but I have no apprehensions, continued I—for in falling into the hands of the most polish'd people in the world, and being conscious I was a true man, and not come to spy the nakedness of the land,° I scarce thought I laid at their mercy.—It does not suit the gallantry of the French, Monsieur le Count, said I, to shew it against invalids.

An animated blush came into the Count de B****'s cheeks, as I spoke this—*Ne craignez rien*—Don't fear, said he—Indeed I don't, replied I again—besides, continued I a little sportingly—I have come laughing all the way from London to Paris, and I do not think Monsieur le Duc de Choiseul is such an enemy to mirth, as to send me back crying for my pains.

——My application to you, Monsieur le Compte de B**** (making him a low bow) is to desire he will not.

The Count heard me with great good nature, or I had not said half as much—and once or twice said—*C'est bien dit.*° So I rested my cause there—and determined to say no more about it.

The Count led the discourse: we talk'd of indifferent things;—of books and politicks, and men—and then of women—God bless them all! said I, after much discourse about them—there is not a man upon earth who loves them so much as I do: after all the foibles I have seen, and all the satires I have read against them, still I love them; being firmly persuaded that a man who has not a sort of an affection for the whole sex, is incapable of ever loving a single one as he ought.

Hèh bien! Monsieur l'Anglois,° said the Count, gaily—You are not come to spy the nakedness of the land—I believe you—*ni encore,*° I dare say, *that* of our women—But permit me to conjecture—if, *par hazard,*° they fell in your way—that the prospect would not affect you.

I have something within me which cannot bear the shock of the least indecent insinuation: in the sportability of chit-chat I have often endeavoured to conquer it, and with infinite pain have hazarded a thousand things to a dozen of the sex together—the least of which I could not venture to a single one, to gain heaven.

Excuse me, Monsieur Le Count, said I—as for the nakedness of your land, if I saw it, I should cast my eyes over it with tears in them—and for that of your women (blushing at the idea he had excited in me) I am so evangelical in this, and have such a fellow-feeling for what ever is *weak* about them, that I would cover it with a garment, if I knew how to throw it on—But I could wish, continued I, to spy the *nakedness* of their hearts, and through the different disguises of customs, climates, and religion, find out what is good in them, to fashion my own by—and therefore am I come.

It is for this reason, Monsieur le Compte, continued I, that I have not seen the Palais royal—nor the Luxembourg—nor the Façade of the Louvre—nor have attempted to swell the catalogues we have of pictures, statues, and churches—I conceive every fair being as a temple,° and would rather enter in, and see the original drawings and loose sketches hung up in it, than the transfiguration of Raphael° itself.

The thirst of this, continued I, as impatient as that which inflames the breast of the connoisseur, has led me from my own home into France—and from France will lead me through Italy—'tis a quiet journey of the heart in pursuit of NATURE, and those affections which rise out of her, which make us love each other—and the world, better than we do.°

The Count said a great many civil things to me upon the occasion; and added very politely how much he stood obliged to Shakespear for making me known to him—but, *a-propos*, said he—Shakespear is full of great things—He forgot a small punctillio of announcing your name—it puts you under a necessity of doing it yourself.

THE PASSPORT
VERSAILLES

THERE is not a more perplexing affair in life to me, than to set about telling any one who I am°—for there is scarce any body I cannot give a better account of than of myself; and I have often wish'd I could do it in a single word—and have an end of it. It was the only time and occasion in my life, I could accomplish this to any purpose—for Shakespear lying upon the table, and recollecting I was in his books, I took up Hamlet, and turning immediately to the grave-diggers scene in the fifth act, I lay'd my finger upon YORICK, and advancing the book to the Count, with my finger all the way over the name— *Me Voici!*° said I.

Now whether the idea of poor Yorick's skull was put out of the Count's mind, by the reality of my own, or by what magic he could drop a period of seven or eight hundred years, makes nothing in this account—'tis certain the French conceive better than they combine—I wonder at nothing in this world, and the less at this; inasmuch as one of the first of our own church, for whose candour and paternal sentiments I have the highest veneration, fell into the same mistake in the very same case.—'He could not bear, he said, to look into sermons wrote by the king of Denmark's jester.'°—Good, my lord! said I—but there are two Yorick's. The Yorick your lordship thinks of, has been dead and buried eight hundred years ago; he flourish'd in Horwendillus's° court—the other Yorick is myself, who have flourish'd my lord in no court—He shook his head—Good God! said I, you might as well confound Alexander the Great, with Alexander the Copper-smith,° my lord——'Twas all one, he replied—

—If Alexander king of Macedon could have translated° your lordship, said I—I'm sure your Lordship would not have said so.

The poor Count de B**** fell but into the same *error*——

—*Et, Monsieur, est il Yorick?* cried the Count.—*Je le suis,* said I.— *Vous?—Moi—moi qui ai l'honneur de vous parler, Monsieur le Compte—Mon Dieu!* said he, embracing me——*Vous etes Yorick.*°

The Count instantly put the Shakespear into his pocket—and left me alone in his room.

THE PASSPORT
VERSAILLES

I COULD not conceive why the Count de B**** had gone so abruptly out of the room, any more than I could conceive why he had put the Shakespear into his pocket—*Mysteries which must explain themselves, are not worth the loss of time, which a conjecture about them takes up*: 'twas better to read Shakespear; so taking up, '*Much Ado about Nothing,*' I transported myself instantly from the chair I sat in to Messina in Sicily, and got so busy with Don Pedro and Benedick and Beatrice, that I thought not of Versailles, the Count, or the Passport.

Sweet pliability of man's spirit, that can at once surrender itself to illusions, which cheat expectation and sorrow of their weary moments!—long—long since had ye number'd out my days,° had I not trod so great a part of them upon this enchanted ground: when my way is too rough for my feet, or too steep for my strength, I get off it, to some smooth velvet path which fancy has scattered over with rose-buds of delights; and having taken a few turns in it, come back strengthen'd and refresh'd—When evils press sore upon me, and there is no retreat from them in this world, then I take a new course—I leave it—and as I have a clearer idea of the elysian fields than I have of heaven, I force myself, like Eneas, into them—I see him meet the pensive shade of his forsaken Dido—and wish to recognize it—I see the injured spirit wave her head, and turn off silent from the author of her miseries and dishonours°—I lose the feelings for myself in hers—and in those affections which were wont to make me mourn for her when I was at school.

Surely this is not walking in a vain shadow—nor does man disquiet himself in vain,° *by it*—he oftener does so in trusting the issue of his commotions° to reason only.—I can safely say for myself, I was never able to conquer any one single bad sensation in my heart so decisively, as by beating up° as fast as I could for some kindly and gentle sensation, to fight it upon its own ground.

When I had got to the end of the third act, the Count de B**** entered with my Passport in his hand. Mons. le Duc de C****, said the Count, is as good a prophet, I dare say, as he is a statesman—*Un homme qui rit*, said the duke, *ne sera jamais dangereuz.*°—Had it been for any one but the king's jester, added the Count, I could not have got it these two hours.—*Pardonnez moi*, Mons. Le Compte, said I—I am not the king's jester.—But you are Yorick?—Yes.—*Et vous plaisantez?*°—I answered, Indeed I did jest—but was not paid for it—'twas entirely at my own expence.°

We have no jester at court, Mons. Le Compte, said I, the last we had was in the licentious reign of Charles the IId°—since which time our manners have been so gradually refining, that our court at present is so full of patriots,° who wish for *nothing* but the honours and wealth of their country—and our ladies are all so chaste, so spotless, so good, so devout—there is nothing for a jester to make a jest of—

Voila un persiflage!° cried the Count.

THE PASSPORT
VERSAILLES

As the Passport was directed to all lieutenant governors, governors, and commandants of cities, generals of armies, justiciaries, and all officers of justice, to let Mr. Yorick, the king's jester, and his baggage, travel quietly along—I own the triumph of obtaining the Passport was not a little tarnish'd by the figure I cut in it—But there is nothing unmixt in this world; and some of the gravest of our divines have carried it so far as to affirm, that enjoyment itself was attended even with a sigh—and that the greatest *they knew of*, terminated *in a general way*, in little better than a convulsion.°

I remember the grave and learned Bevoriskius,° in his commentary upon the generations from Adam, very naturally breaks off in the middle of a note to give an account to the world of a couple of sparrows upon the out-edge of his window, which had incommoded him all the time he wrote, and at last had entirely taken him off from his genealogy.

—'Tis strange! writes Bevoriskius; but the facts are certain, for I have had the curiosity to mark them down one by one with my pen—but the cock-sparrow during the little time that I could have finished the other half this note, has actually interrupted me with the reiteration of his caresses three and twenty times and a half.

How merciful, adds Bevoriskius, is heaven to his creatures!

Ill fated Yorick! that the gravest of thy brethren should be able to write that to the world, which stains thy face with crimson, to copy in even thy study.

But this is nothing to my travels—So I twice—twice beg pardon for it.

CHARACTER
VERSAILLES

AND how do you find the French? said the Count de B****, after he had given me the Passport.

The reader may suppose that after so obliging a proof of courtesy, I could not be at a loss to say something handsome to the enquiry.

—*Mais passe, pour cela*°—Speak frankly, said he; do you find all the urbanity in the French which the world give us the honour of?—I had found every thing, I said, which confirmed it—*Vraiment*, said the count.—*Les Francois sont polis.*°—To an excess, replied I.

The count took notice of the word *excesse*; and would have it I meant more than I said. I defended myself a long time as well as I could against it—he insisted I had a reserve, and that I would speak my opinion frankly.

I believe, Mons. Le Compte, said I, that man has a certain compass,° as well as an instrument; and that the social and other calls have occasion by turns for every key in him; so that if you begin a note too high or too low, there must be a want either in the upper or under part, to fill up the system of harmony.—The Count de B**** did not understand music, so desired me to explain it some other way. A polish'd nation, my dear Count, said I, makes every one its debtor; and besides urbanity itself, like the fair sex, has so many charms; it goes against the heart to say it can do ill; and yet, I believe, there is but a certain line of perfection, that man, take him altogether, is empower'd to arrive at—if he gets beyond, he rather exchanges changes qualities, than gets them. I must not presume to say, how far this has affected the French in the subject we are speaking of—but should it ever be the case of the English, in the progress of their refinements, to arrive at the same polish which distinguishes the French, if we did not lose the *politesse de cœur*,° which inclines men more to human actions, than courteous ones—we should at least lose that distinct variety and originality of character, which distinguishes them, not only from each other, but from all the world besides.°

I had a few king William's shillings° as smooth as glass in my pocket; and foreseeing they would be of use in the illustration of my hypothesis, I had got them into my hand, when I had proceeded so far—

See, Mons. Le Compte, said I, rising up, and laying them before him upon the table—by jingling and rubbing one against another for seventy years together in one body's pocket or another's, they are become so much alike, you can scarce distinguish one shilling from another.°

The English, like antient medals, kept more apart, and passing but few peoples hands, preserve the first sharpnesses which the fine hand of nature has given them—they are not so pleasant to feel—but in return, the legend is so visible, that at the first look you see whose image and superscription they bear.—But the French, Mons. Le Compte, added I, wishing to soften what I had said, have so many excellencies, they can the better spare this—they are a loyal, a gallant, a generous, an ingenious, and good temper'd people as is under heaven—if they have a fault—they are too *serious*.°

Mon Dieu! cried the Count, rising out of his chair.

Mais vous plaisantez,° said he, correcting his exclamation.—I laid my hand upon my breast, and with earnest gravity assured him, it was my most settled opinion.

The Count said he was mortified, he could not stay to hear my reasons, being engaged to go that moment to dine with the Duc de C****.

But if it is not too far to come to Versailles to eat your soup with me, I beg, before you leave France, I may have the pleasure of knowing you retract your opinion—or, in what manner you support it.—But if you do support it, Mons. Anglois, said he, you must do it with all your powers, because you have the whole world against you.—I promised the Count I would do myself the honour of dining with him before I set out for Italy—so took my leave.

THE TEMPTATION
PARIS

When I alighted at the hotel, the porter told me a young woman with a band-box° had been that moment enquiring for me.—I do not know, said the porter, whether she is gone away or no. I took the key of my chamber of him, and went up stairs; and when I had got within ten steps of the top of the landing before my door, I met her coming easily down.

It was the fair *fille de chambre* I had walked along the Quai de Conti with: Madame de R**** had sent her upon some commissions to a *merchande de modes*° within a step or two of the hotel de Modene; and as I had fail'd in waiting upon her, had bid her enquire if I had left Paris; and if so, whether I had not left a letter address'd to her.

As the fair *fille de chambre* was so near my door she turned back, and went into the room with me for a moment or two whilst I wrote a card.

It was a fine still evening in the latter end of the month of May—the crimson window curtains (which were of the same colour as those of the bed) were drawn close—the sun was setting and reflected through them so warm a tint into the fair *fille de chambre*'s face—I thought she blush'd—the idea of it made me blush myself—

we were quite alone; and that super-induced° a second blush before the first could get off.

There is a sort of a pleasing half guilty blush, where the blood is more in fault than the man—'tis sent impetuous from the heart, and virtue flies after it—not to call it back, but to make the sensation of it more delicious to the nerves—'tis associated.—

But I'll not describe it.—I felt something at first within me which was not in strict unison with the lesson of virtue I had given her the night before—I sought five minutes for a card—I knew I had not one.—I took up a pen—I laid it down again—my hand trembled—the devil was in me.

I know as well as any one, he is an adversary, whom if we resist, he will fly from us—but I seldom resist him at all; from a terror, that though I may conquer, I may still get a hurt in the combat—so I give up the triumph, for security; and instead of thinking to make him fly, I generally fly myself.

The fair *fille de chambre* came close up to the bureau where I was looking for a card—took up first the pen I cast down, then offered to hold me the ink: she offer'd it so sweetly, I was going to accept it—but I durst not—I have nothing, my dear, said I, to write upon.—Write it, said she, simply, upon any thing.—

I was just going to cry out, Then I will write it, fair girl! upon thy lips.—

If I do, said I, I shall perish—so I took her by the hand, and led her to the door, and begg'd she would not forget the lesson I had given her—She said, Indeed she would not—and as she utter'd it with some earnestness, she turned about, and gave me both her hands, closed together, into mine—it was impossible not to compress them in that situation—I wish'd to let them go; and all the time I held them, I kept arguing within myself against it—and still I held them on.—In two minutes I found I had all the battle to fight over again—and I felt my legs and every limb about me tremble at the idea.

The foot of the bed was within a yard and a half of the place where we were standing—I had still hold of her hands—and how it happened I can give no account, but I neither ask'd her—nor drew her—nor did I think of the bed—but so it did happen, we both sat down.

I'll just shew you, said the fair *fille de chambre*, the little purse I have been making to-day to hold your crown. So she put her hand into her right pocket, which was next me, and felt for it for some time—then into the left—'She had lost it.'—I never bore expectation more quietly—it was in her right pocket at last—she pulled it out; it was of green taffeta, lined with a little bit of white quilted sattin, and just big enough to hold the crown—she put it into my hand—it was pretty; and I held it ten minutes with the back of my hand resting upon her lap—looking sometimes at the purse, sometimes on one side of it.°

A stitch or two had broke out in the gathers of my stock°—the fair *fille de chambre*, without saying a word, took out her little hussive,° threaded a small needle, and sew'd it up—I foresaw it would hazard the glory of the day; and as she passed her hand in silence across and across my neck in the manœuvre, I felt the laurels shake which fancy had wreath'd about my head.

A strap had given way in her walk, and the buckle of her shoe was just falling off—See, said the *fille de chambre*, holding up her foot—I could not for my soul but fasten the buckle in return, and putting in the strap—and lifting up the other foot with it, when I had done, to see both were right—in doing it too suddenly—it unavoidably threw the fair *fille de chambre* off her center—and then—

THE CONQUEST

YES——and then—Ye whose clay-cold heads and luke-warm hearts can argue down or mask your passions—tell me, what trespass is it that man should have them? or how his spirit stands answerable, to the father of spirits, but for his conduct under them?

If nature has so wove her web of kindness, that some threads of love and desire are entangled with the piece—must the whole web be rent in drawing them out?—Whip me such stoics, great governor of nature! said I to myself—Wherever thy providence shall place me for the trials of my virtue—whatever is my danger—whatever is my situation—let me feel the movements which rise out of it, and which belong to me as a man°—and if I govern them as a good one—I will trust the issues to thy justice, for thou hast made us—and not we ourselves.°

As I finish'd my address, I raised the fair *fille de chambre* up by the hand, and led her out of the room—she stood by me till I lock'd the door and put the key in my pocket—*and then*—the victory being quite decisive—and not till then, I press'd my lips to her cheek, and, taking her by the hand again, led her safe to the gate of the hotel.

THE MYSTERY
PARIS

IF a man knows the heart, he will know it was impossible to go back instantly to my chamber—it was touching a cold key with a flat third to it, upon the close of a piece of musick,° which had call'd forth my affections—therefore, when I let go the hand of the *fille de chambre*, I remain'd at the gate of the hotel for some time, looking at every one who pass'd by, and forming conjectures upon them, till my attention got fix'd upon a single object which confounded all kind of reasoning upon him.

It was a tall figure of a philosophic serious, adust° look, which pass'd and repass'd sedately along the street, making a turn of about sixty paces on each side of the gate of the hotel—the man was about fifty-two—had a small cane under his arm—was dress'd in a dark drab-colour'd coat, waistcoat, and breeches, which seem'd to have seen some years service—they were still clean, and there was a little air of frugal *propreté*° throughout him. By his pulling off his hat, and his attitude of accosting a good many in his way, I saw he was asking charity; so I got a sous or two out of my pocket ready to give him, as he took me in his turn—he pass'd by me without asking any thing— and yet did not go five steps further before he ask'd charity of a little woman—I was much more likely to have given of the two—He had scarce done with the woman, when he pull'd off his hat to another who was coming the same way.—An ancient gentleman came slowly—and, after him, a young smart one—He let them both pass, and ask'd nothing: I stood observing him half an hour, in which time he had made a dozen turns backwards and forwards, and found that he invariably pursued the same plan.

There were two things very singular in this, which set my brain to work, and to no purpose—the first was, why the man should *only* tell his story to the sex—and secondly—what kind of story it was, and what species of eloquence it could be, which soften'd the hearts of the women, which he knew 'twas to no purpose to practise upon the men.

There were two other circumstances which entangled this mystery—the one was, he told every woman what he had to say in her ear, and in a way which had much more the air of a secret than a petition—the other was, it was always successful—he never stopp'd a woman, but she pull'd out her purse, and immediately gave him something.

I could form no system to explain the phenomenon.

I had got a riddle to amuse me for the rest of the evening, so I walk'd up stairs to my chamber.

THE CASE OF CONSCIENCE
PARIS

I WAS immediately followed up by the master of the hotel, who came into my room to tell me I must provide lodgings else where.—How so, friend? said I.—He answer'd, I had had a young woman lock'd up with me two hours that evening in my bed-chamber, and 'twas against the rules of his house.—Very well, said I, we'll all part friends then—for the girl is no worse—and I am no worse—and you will be just as I found you.——It was enough, he said, to overthrow the credit of his hotel.—*Voyez vous, Monsieur,*° said he, pointing to the foot of the bed we had been sitting upon.—I own it had something of the appearance of an evidence; but my pride not suffering me to enter into any detail of the case, I exhorted him to let his soul sleep in peace, as I resolved to let mine do that night, and that I would discharge what I owed him at breakfast.

I should not have minded, *Monsieur*, said he, if you had had twenty girls—'Tis a score more, replied I, interrupting him, than I ever reckon'd upon—Provided, added he, it had been but in a morning.—And does the difference of the time of the day at Paris make a difference in the sin?—It made a difference, he said, in the scandal.—I like a good distinction in my heart; and cannot say I was intolerably out of temper with the man.—I own it is necessary, re-assumed the master of the hotel, that a stranger at Paris should have the opportunities presented to him of buying lace and silk stockings and ruffles,° *et tout cela*°—and 'tis nothing if a woman comes with a band box.——O' my conscience, said I, she had one; but I never look'd into it.—Then, *Monsieur*, said he, has bought nothing.—Not one earthly thing, replied I.—Because, said he, I could recommend one to you who would use you *en conscience.*°—But I must see her this night, said I.—He made me a low bow and walk'd down.

Now shall I triumph over this *maitre d'hotel*, cried I—and what then?—Then I shall let him see I know he is a dirty fellow.—And what then?—What then!—I was too near myself to say it was for the sake of others.—I had no good answer left—there was more of spleen than principle in my project, and I was sick of it before the execution.

In a few minutes the Grisset came in with her box of lace—I'll buy nothing however, said I, within myself.

The Grisset would shew me every thing—I was hard to please: she would not seem to see it; she open'd her little magazine,° laid all her laces one after another before me—unfolded and folded them up again one by one with the most patient sweetness—I might buy—or not—she would let me have every thing at my own price—the poor creature seem'd anxious to get a penny; and laid herself out to win me, and not so much in a manner which seem'd artful, as in one I felt simple and caressing.

If there is not a fund of honest cullibility° in man, so much the worse—my heart relented, and I gave up my second resolution as quietly as the first—Why should I chastise one for the trespass of another? if thou art tributary to this tyrant of an host, thought I, looking up in her face, so much harder is thy bread.

If I had not had more than four *Louis d'ors* in my purse, there was no such thing as rising up and shewing her the door, till I had first laid three of them out in a pair of ruffles.

—The master of the hotel will share the profit with her—no matter—then I have only paid as many a poor soul has *paid* before me for an act he *could* not do, or think of.

THE RIDDLE
PARIS

WHEN La Fleur came up to wait upon me at supper, he told me how sorry the master of the hotel was for his affront to me in bidding me change my lodgings.

A man who values a good night's rest will not lay down with enmity in his heart if he can help it—So I bid La Fleur tell the master of the hotel, that I was sorry on my side for the occasion I had given him—and you may tell him, if you will, La Fleur, added I, that if the young woman should call again, I shall not see her.

This was a sacrifice not to him, but myself, having resolved, after so narrow an escape, to run no more risks, but to leave Paris, if it was possible, with all the virtue I enter'd in.

C'est deroger à noblesse, Monsieur, said La Fleur, making me a bow down to the ground as he said it—*Et encore Monsieur*,° said he, may change his sentiments—and if (*par hazard*) he should like to amuse himself—I find no amusement in it, said I, interrupting him—

Mon Dieu! said La Fleur—and took away.°

In an hour's time he came to put me to bed, and was more than commonly officious—something hung upon his lips to say to me, or ask me, which he could not get off: I could not conceive what it was; and indeed gave myself little trouble to find it out, as I had another riddle so much more interesting upon my mind, which was that of the man's asking charity before the door of the hotel—I would have given any thing to have got to the bottom of it; and that, not out of curiosity—'tis so low a principle of enquiry, in general, I would not purchase the gratification of it with a two-sous piece—but a secret, I thought, which so soon and so certainly soften'd the heart of every woman you came near, was a secret at least equal to the philosopher's stone:° had I had both the Indies,° I would have given up one to have been master of it.

I toss'd and turn'd it almost all night long in my brains to no manner of purpose; and when I awoke in the morning, I found my spirit as much troubled with my *dreams*, as ever the king of Babylon had been with his; and I will not hesitate to affirm, it would have puzzled all the wise men of Paris, as much as those of Chaldea, to have given its interpretation.°

LE DIMANCHE
PARIS

It was Sunday; and when La Fleur came in, in the morning, with my coffee and role and butter, he had got himself so gallantly array'd, I scarce knew him.

I had covenanted at Montriul to give him a new hat with a silver button and loop, and four Louis d'ors *pour s'adoniser*,° when we got to Paris; and the poor fellow, to do him justice, had done wonders with it.

He had bought a bright, clean, good scarlet coat and a pair of breeches of the same—They were not a crown worse, he said, for the wearing—I wish'd him hang'd for telling me—they look'd so fresh, that tho' I knew the thing could not be done, yet I would rather have imposed upon my fancy with thinking I had bought them new for the fellow, than that they had come out of the *Rue de friperie*.°

This is a nicety which makes not the heart sore at Paris.

He had purchased moreover a handsome blue sattin waistcoat, fancifully enough embroidered—this was indeed something the worse for the services it had done, but 'twas clean scour'd—the gold had been touch'd up, and upon the whole was rather showy than otherwise—and as the blue was not violent, it suited with the coat and breeches very well: he had squeez'd out of the money, moreover, a new bag and a solitaire;° and had insisted with the *fripier*, upon a gold pair of garters to his breeches knees—He had purchased muslin ruffles, *bien brodées*,° with four livres of his own money—and a pair of white silk stockings for five more—and, to top all, nature had given him a handsome figure, without costing him a sous.

He enter'd the room thus set off, with his hair dress'd in the first stile, and with a handsome *bouquet* in his breast—in a word, there was that look of festivity in every thing about him, which at once put me in mind it was Sunday—and by combining both together, it instantly struck me, that the favour he wish'd to ask of me the night before, was to spend the day, as every body in Paris spent it, besides. I had scarce made the conjecture, when La Fleur, with infinite humility, but with a look of trust, as if I should not refuse him, begg'd I would grant him the day, *pour faire le galant vis à vis de sa maitresse*.°

Now it was the very thing I intended to do myself *vis à vis* Madame de R****—I had retain'd the *remise* on purpose for it, and it would not have mortified my vanity to have had a servant so well dress'd as La Fleur was to have got up behind it: I never could have worse spared him.

But we must *feel*, not argue in these embarrassments—the sons and daughters of service part with liberty, but not with Nature in their contracts; they are flesh and blood, and have their little vanities and wishes in the midst of the house of bondage,° as well as their task-masters—no doubt, they have set their self-denials at a price— and their expectations are so unreasonable, that I would often disap- point them, but that their condition puts it so much in my power to do it.

Behold!—Behold, I am thy servant°—disarms me at once of the powers of a master—

—Thou shalt go, La Fleur! said I.

—And what mistress, La Fleur, said I, canst thou have pick'd up in so little a time at Paris? La Fleur laid his hand upon his breast, and said 'twas a *petite demoiselle*° at Monsieur Le Compte de B****'s.—La Fleur had a heart made for society; and, to speak the truth of him let as few occasions slip him as his master—so that some how or other; but how—heaven knows—he had connected himself with the *demoiselle* upon the landing of the stair-case, during the time I was taken up with my Passport; and as there was time enough for me to win the Count to my interest, La Fleur had contrived to make it do to win the maid to his—the family, it seems, was to be at Paris that day, and he had made a party with her, and two or three more of the Count's houshold, upon the *boulevards*.

Happy people! that once a week at least are sure to lay down all your cares together; and dance and sing and sport away the weights of grievance, which bow down the spirit of other nations to the earth.°

THE FRAGMENT
PARIS

LA FLEUR had left me something to amuse myself with for the day more than I had bargain'd for, or could have enter'd either into his head or mine.

He had brought the little print of butter° upon a currant leaf; and as the morning was warm, and he had a good step to bring it, he had begg'd a sheet of waste paper to put betwixt the currant leaf and his hand—As that was plate sufficient, I bad him lay it upon the table as it was, and as I resolved to stay within all day I ordered him to call upon the *traiteur*° to bespeak my dinner, and leave me to breakfast by myself.

When I had finish'd the butter, I threw the currant leaf out of the window, and was going to do the same by the waste paper—but stopping to read a line first, and that drawing me on to a second and third—I thought it better worth; so I shut the window, and drawing a chair up to it, I sat down to read it.

It was in the old French of Rabelais's time,° and for ought I know might have been wrote by him—it was moreover in a Gothic letter, and that so faded and gone off by damps and length of time, it cost me infinite trouble to make any thing of it—I threw it down; and then wrote a letter to Eugenius—then I took it up again, and embroiled my patience with it afresh—and then to cure that, I wrote a letter to Eliza.—Still it kept hold of me; and the difficulty of understanding it increased but the desire.

I got my dinner; and after I had enlightened my mind with a bottle of Burgundy, I at it again°—and after two or three hours poring upon it, with almost as deep attention as ever Gruter or Jacob Spon° did upon a nonsensical inscription, I thought I made sense of it; but to make sure of it, the best way, I imagined, was to turn it into English, and see how it would look then—so I went on leisurely, as a trifling man does, sometimes writing a sentence—then taking a turn or two—and then looking how the world went, out of the window; so that it was nine o'clock at night before I had done it—I then begun and read it as follows.

THE FRAGMENT
PARIS

——Now as the notary's wife disputed the point with the notary° with too much heat—I wish, said the notary, throwing down the parchment, that there was another notary here only to set down and attest all this——

—And what would you do then, Monsieur? said she, rising hastily up—the notary's wife was a little fume of a woman,° and the notary thought it well to avoid a hurricane by a mild reply—I would go, answer'd he, to bed.——You may go to the devil, answer'd the notary's wife.

Now there happening to be but one bed in the house, the other two rooms being unfurnish'd, as is the custom at Paris, and the notary not caring to lie in the same bed with a woman who had but that moment sent him pell-mell to the devil, went forth with his hat and cane and short cloak, the night being very windy, and walk'd out ill at ease towards the *pont neuf*.

Of all the bridges which ever were built, the whole world who have pass'd over the *pont neuf*, must own, that it is the noblest—the finest—the grandest—the lightest—the longest—the broadest that ever conjoin'd land and land together upon the face of the terraqueous globe——

> *By this, it seems, as if the author of the fragment had not been a*
> *Frenchman.*°

The worst fault which divines and the doctors of the Sorbonne can allege against it, is, that if there is but a cap-full of wind in or about Paris, 'tis more blasphemously *sacre Dieu*'d° there than in any other aperture of the whole city—and with reason, good and cogent Messieurs; for it comes against you without crying *garde d'eau*,° and with such unpremeditable puffs, that of the few who cross it with their hats on, not one in fifty but hazards two livres and a half, which is its full worth.

The poor notary, just as he was passing by the sentry, instinctively clapp'd his cane to the side of it, but in raising it up the point of his cane catching hold of the loop of the sentinel's hat hoisted it over the spikes of the ballustrade clear into the Seine—

—*'Tis an ill wind*, said a boatman, who catch'd it, *which blows no body any good.*

The sentry being a gascon° incontinently twirl'd up his whiskers, and levell'd his harquebuss.°

Harquebusses in those days went off with matches; and an old woman's paper lanthorn° at the end of the bridge happening to be blown out, she had borrow'd the sentry's match to light it—it gave a moment's time for the gascon's blood to run cool, and turn the accident better to his advantage—*'Tis an ill wind*, said he, catching off the notary's castor,° and legitimating the capture with the boat-man's adage.

The poor notary cross'd the bridge, and passing along the rue de Dauphine into the fauxbourgs of St. Germain, lamented himself as he walk'd along in this manner:

Luckless man! that I am, said the notary, to be the sport of hurri-canes all my days——to be born to have the storm of ill language levell'd against me and my profession wherever I go—to be forced into marriage by the thunder of the church to a tempest of a woman—to be driven forth out of my house by domestic winds, and despoil'd of my castor by pontific° ones—to be here, bare-headed, in a windy night at the mercy of the ebbs and flows of accidents—where am I to lay my head?—miserable man! what wind in the two-and-thirty points of the whole compass can blow unto thee, as it does to the rest of thy fellow creatures, good!

As the notary was passing on by a dark passage, complaining in this sort, a voice call'd out to a girl, to bid her run for the next notary—now the notary being the next, and availing himself of his situation, walk'd up the passage to the door, and passing through an old sort of a saloon, was usher'd into a large chamber dismantled of every thing but a long military pike—a breast plate—a rusty old sword, and bandoleer,° hung up equi-distant in four different places against the wall.

An old personage, who had heretofore been a gentleman, and unless decay of fortune taints the blood along with it was a gentle-man at that time, lay supporting his head upon his hand in his bed; a little table with a taper burning was set close beside it, and close by the table was placed a chair—the notary sat him down in it; and pulling out his ink-horn and a sheet or two of paper which he had in his pocket, he placed them before him, and dipping his pen in his ink, and leaning his breast over the table, he disposed every thing to make the gentleman's last will and testament.

Alas! Monsieur le Notaire,° said the gentleman, raising himself up a little, I have nothing to bequeath which will pay the expence of bequeathing, except the history of myself, which, I could not die in peace unless I left it as a legacy to the world; the profits arising out of it, I bequeath to you for the pains of taking it from me—it is a story so uncommon, it must be read by all mankind—it will make the fortunes of your house—the notary dipp'd his pen into his ink-horn—Almighty director of every event in my life! said the old gentleman, looking up earnestly and raising his hands towards heaven—thou whose hand has led me on through such a labyrinth of strange passages down into this scene of desolation, assist the decaying memory of an old, infirm, and broken-hearted man—direct my tongue, by the spirit of thy eternal truth, that this stranger may set down naught but what is written in that Book,° from whose records, said he, clasping his hands together, I am to be condemn'd or acquitted!——the notary held up the point of his pen betwixt the taper and his eye—

—It is a story, Monsieur le Notaire, said the gentleman, which will rouse up every affection in nature—it will kill the humane, and touch the heart of cruelty herself with pity—

—The notary was inflamed with a desire to begin, and put his pen a third time into his ink-horn—and the old gentleman turning a little more towards the notary, began to dictate his story in these words—

—And where is the rest of it, La Fleur? said I, as he just then enter'd the room.

THE FRAGMENT
AND the *BOUQUET
PARIS

When La Fleur came up close to the table, and was made to comprehend what I wanted, he told me there were only two other sheets of it which he had wrapt round the stalks of a *bouquet* to keep it together, which he had presented to the *demoiselle* upon the *boulevards*—Then, prithee, La Fleur, said I, step back to her to the Count de B****'s hotel, and see if you canst get°—There is no doubt of it, said La Fleur—and away he flew.

In a very little time the poor fellow came back quite out of breath, with deeper marks of disappointment in his looks than could arise from the simple irreparability of the fragment—*Juste ciel!*° in less

---

* Nosegay.

than two minutes that the poor fellow had taken his last tender farewel of her—his faithless mistress had given his *gage d'amour*° to one of the Count's footmen—the footman to a young sempstress— and the sempstress to a fiddler, with my fragment at the end of it— Our misfortunes were involved together—I gave a sigh—and La Fleur echo'd it back again to my ear—

—How perfidious! cried La Fleur—How unlucky! said I.—

—I should not have been mortified, Monsieur, quoth La Fleur, if she had lost it—Nor I, La Fleur, said I, had I found it.

Whether I did or no, will be seen hereafter.

THE ACT OF CHARITY

PARIS

THE man who either disdains or fears to walk up a dark entry may be an excellent good man, and fit for a hundred things; but he will not do to make a good sentimental traveller. I count little of the many things I see pass at broad noon day, in large and open streets.— Nature is shy, and hates to act before spectators; but in such an unobserved corner, you sometimes see a single short scene of her's worth all the sentiments of a dozen French plays compounded together°—and yet they are *absolutely* fine;—and whenever I have a more brilliant affair upon my hands than common, as they suit a preacher just as well as a hero, I generally make my sermon out of 'em—and for the text—'Capadosia, Pontus and Asia, Phrygia and Pamphilia'°—is as good as any one in the Bible.

There is a long dark passage issuing out from the opera comique into a narrow street; 'tis trod by a few who humbly wait for a *fiacre**, or wish to get off quietly o'foot when the opera is done. At the end of it, towards the theatre, 'tis lighted by a small candle, the light of which is almost lost before you get half-way down, but near the door—'tis more for ornament than use: you see it as a fix'd star of the least magnitude; it burns—but does little good to the world, that we know of.

In returning along this passage, I discern'd, as I approach'd

* Hackney-coach.

within five or six paces of the door, two ladies standing arm in arm, with their backs against the wall, waiting, as I imagined, for a *fiacre*—as they were next the door, I thought they had a prior right; so edged myself up within a yard or little more of them, and quietly took my stand—I was in black, and scarce seen.

The lady next me was a tall lean figure of a woman of about thirty-six; the other of the same size and make, of about forty; there was no mark of wife or widow in any one part of either of them—they seem'd to be two upright vestal sisters,° unsapp'd by caresses, unbroke in upon by tender salutations: I could have wish'd to have made them happy—their happiness was destin'd, that night, to come from another quarter.

A low voice, with a good turn of expression, and sweet cadence at the end of it, begg'd for a twelve-sous piece betwixt them, for the love of heaven. I thought it singular, that a beggar should fix the quota of an alms—and that the sum should be twelve times as much as what is usually given in the dark. They both seemed astonish'd at it as much as myself.—Twelve sous! said one—a twelve-sous piece! said the other—and made no reply.

The poor man said, He knew not how to ask less of ladies of their rank; and bow'd down his head to the ground.

Poo! said they—we have no money.

The beggar remained silent for a moment or two, and renew'd his supplication.

Do not, my fair young ladies, said he, stop your good ears against me—Upon my word, honest man! said the younger, we have no change—Then God bless you, said the poor man, and multiply those joys which you can give to others without change!—I observed the elder sister put her hand into her pocket—I'll see, said she, if I have a sous.—A sous! give twelve, said the suppli-cant; Nature has been bountiful to you, be bountiful to a poor man.

I would, friend, with all my heart, said the younger, if I had it.

My fair charitable! said he, addressing himself to the elder—What is it but your goodness and humanity which makes your bright eyes so sweet, that they outshine the morning even in this dark passage? and what was it which made the Marquis de Santerre and his brother say so much of you both as they just pass'd by?

The two ladies seemed much affected; and impulsively at the same time they both put their hands into their pocket, and each took out a twelve-sous piece.

The contest betwixt them and the poor supplicant was no more—it was continued betwixt themselves, which of the two should give the twelve-sous piece in charity—and to end the dispute, they both gave it together, and the man went away.

THE RIDDLE EXPLAINED
PARIS

I STEPP'D hastily after him: it was the very man whose success in asking charity of the women before the door of the hotel had so puzzled me—and I found at once his secret, or at least the basis of it—'twas flattery.

Delicious essence! how refreshing art thou to nature! how strongly are all its powers and all its weaknesses on thy side! how sweetly dost thou mix with the blood, and help it through the most difficult and tortuous passages to the heart!

The poor man, as he was not straighten'd for time, had given it here in a larger dose: 'tis certain he had a way of bringing it into less form, for the many sudden cases he had to do with in the streets; but how he contrived to correct, sweeten, concentre,° and qualify it—I vex not my spirit with the inquiry—it is enough, the beggar gain'd two twelve-sous pieces—and they can best tell the rest, who have gain'd much greater matters by it.

PARIS

WE get forwards in the world not so much by doing services, as receiving them: you take a withering twig, and put it in the ground; and then you water it, because you have planted it.

Mons. Le Compte de B****, merely because he had done me one kindness in the affair of my passport, would go on and do me another, the few days he was at Paris, in making me known to a few people of rank; and they were to present me to others, and so on.

I had got master of my *secret*, just in time to turn these honours to some little account; otherwise, as is commonly the case, I should have din'd or supp'd a single time or two round, and then by *translating* French looks and attitudes into plain English, I should presently have seen, that I had got hold of the *couvert** of some more entertaining guest; and in course, should have resigned all my places one after another, merely upon the principle that I could not keep them.—As it was, things did not go much amiss.

I had the honour of being introduced to the old Marquis de B****: in days of yore he had signaliz'd himself by some small feats of chivalry in the *Cour d'amour*,° and had dress'd himself out to the idea of tilts and tournaments ever since—the Marquis de B**** wish'd to have it thought the affair was somewhere else than in his brain. 'He could like to take a trip to England,' and ask'd much of the English ladies. Stay where you are, I beseech you, Mons. le Marquise, said I—Les Messrs. Angloise can scarce get a kind look from them as it is.—The Marquis invited me to supper.

Mons. P**** the farmer-general° was just as inquisitive about our taxes.—They were very considerable, he heard—If we knew but how to collect them, said I, making him a low bow.

I could never have been invited to Mons. P****'s concerts upon any other terms.

I had been misrepresented to Madame de Q*** as an *esprit*°— Madam de Q*** was an *esprit* herself; she burnt with impatience to see me, and hear me talk. I had not taken my seat, before I saw she did not care a sous whether I had any wit or no—I was let in, to be convinced she had.—I call heaven to witness I never once open'd the door of my lips.

Madame de Q*** vow'd to every creature she met, 'She had never had a more improving conversation with a man in her life.'

There are three epochas in the empire of a French-woman—She is coquette—then deist—then *devôte:*° the empire during these is never lost—she only changes her subjects: when thirty-five years and more have unpeopled her dominions of the slaves of love, she re-peoples it with slaves of infidelity—and then with the slaves of the Church.

Madame de V*** was vibrating betwixt the first of these epochas:

---

* Plate, napkin, knife, fork, and spoon.

the colour of the rose was shading fast away—she ought to have been a deist five years before the time I had the honour to pay my first visit.

She placed me upon the same sopha with her, for the sake of disputing the point of religion more closely.—In short, Madame de V*** told me she believed nothing.

I told Madame de V*** it might be her principle; but I was sure it could not be her interest to level the outworks, without which I could not conceive how such a citadel as hers could be defended—that there was not a more dangerous thing in the world, than for a beauty to be a deist—that it was a debt I owed my creed, not to conceal it from her—that I had not been five minutes sat upon the sopha besides her, but I had begun to form designs—and what is it, but the sentiments of religion, and the persuasion they had existed in her breast, which could have check'd them as they rose up.

We are not adamant,° said I, taking hold of her hand—and there is need of all restraints, till age in her own time steals in and lays them on us—but, my dear lady, said I, kissing her hand—'tis too—too soon—

I declare I had the credit all over Paris of unperverting Madame de V***.—She affirmed to Mons. D*** and the Abbe M***, that in one half hour I had said more for revealed religion than all their Encyclopedia had said against it°—I was listed directly into Madame de V***'s *Coterie*—and she put off the epocha of deism for two years.

I remember it was in this *Coterie*, in the middle of a discourse, in which I was shewing the necessity of a *first cause*,° that the young Count de Faineant° took me by the hand to the furthest corner of the room, to tell me my *solitaire*° was pinn'd too strait about my neck—It should be *plus badinant*,° said the Count, looking down upon his own—but a word, Mons. Yorick, to *the wise*—

—And from the wise, Mons. Le Compte, replied I, making him a bow—*is enough*.

The Count de Faineant embraced me with more ardour than ever I was embraced by mortal man.

For three weeks together, I was of every man's opinion I met.— *Pardi! ce Mons. Yorick a autant d'esprit que nous autres.*——*Il raisonne bien*, said another.—*C'est un bon enfant*,° said a third.—And at this price I could have eaten and drank and been merry all the days of my

life at Paris; but 'twas a dishonest *reckoning*—I grew ashamed of it—
it was the gain of a slave—every sentiment of honour revolted
against it—the higher I got, the more was I forced upon my *beggarly
system*—the better the *Coterie*—the more children of Art—I languish'd for those of Nature:° and one night, after a most vile prostitu-
tion of myself to half a dozen different people, I grew sick—went to
bed—order'd La Fleur to get me horses in the morning to set out for
Italy.

MARIA
MOULINES

I NEVER felt what the distress of plenty was in any one shape till
now—to travel it through the Bourbonnois, the sweetest part of
France—in the hey-day of the vintage, when Nature is pouring her
abundance into every one's lap, and every eye is lifted up—a journey
through each step of which music beats time to *Labour*, and all her
children are rejoicing as they carry in their clusters—to pass through
this with my affections flying out, and kindling at every group before
me—and every one of 'em was pregnant with adventures.

Just heaven!—it would fill up twenty volumes—and alas! I have
but a few small pages left of this to croud it into—and half of these
must be taken up with the poor Maria my friend, Mr. Shandy, met
with near Moulines.°

The story he had told of that disorder'd maid affect'd me not a
little in the reading; but when I got within the neighbourhood where
she lived, it returned so strong into my mind, that I could not resist
an impulse which prompted me to go half a league out of the road to
the village where her parents dwelt to enquire after her.

'Tis going, I own, like the Knight of the Woeful Countenance,° in
quest of melancholy adventures—but I know not how it is, but I am
never so perfectly conscious of the existence of a soul within me, as
when I am entangled in them.

The old mother came to the door, her looks told me the story
before she open'd her mouth—She had lost her husband; he had
died, she said, of anguish, for the loss of Maria's senses about a
month before.—She had feared at first, she added, that it would have

plunder'd her poor girl of what little understanding was left—but, on the contrary, it had brought her more to herself—still she could not rest—her poor daughter, she said, crying, was wandering somewhere about the road—

—Why does my pulse beat languid as I write this? and what made La Fleur, whose heart seem'd only to be tuned to joy, to pass the back of his hand twice across his eyes, as the woman stood and told it? I beckon'd to the postilion to turn back into the road.

When we had got within half a league of Moulines, at a little opening in the road leading to a thicket, I discovered poor Maria sitting under a poplar—she was sitting with her elbow in her lap, and her head leaning on one side within her hand—a small brook ran at the foot of the tree.

I bid the postilion go on with the chaise to Moulines—and La Fleur to bespeak my supper—and that I would walk after him.

She was dress'd in white, and much as my friend described her, except that her hair hung loose, which before was twisted within a silk net.—She had, superadded likewise to her jacket, a pale green ribband which fell across her shoulder to the waist; at the end of which hung her pipe.—Her goat had been as faithless as her lover; and she had got a little dog in lieu of him, which she had kept tied by a string to her girdle; as I look'd at her dog, she drew him towards her with the string.—'Thou shalt not leave me, Sylvio,'° said she. I look'd in Maria's eyes, and saw she was thinking more of her father than of her lover or her little goat; for as she utter'd them the tears trickled down her cheeks.

I sat down close by her; and Maria let me wipe them away as they fell with my handkerchief.—I then steep'd it in my own—and then in hers—and then in mine—and then I wiped hers again—and as I did it, I felt such undescribable emotions within me, as I am sure could not be accounted for from any combinations of matter and motion.

I am positive I have a soul; nor can all the books with which materialists have pester'd the world ever convince me of the contrary.

MARIA

WHEN Maria had come a little to herself, I ask'd her if she remember'd a pale thin person of a man who had sat down betwixt her and her goat about two years before? She said, she was unsettled much at that time, but remember'd it upon two accounts—that ill as she was she saw the person pitied her; and next, that her goat had stolen his handkerchief, and she had beat him for the theft—she had wash'd it, she said, in the brook, and kept it ever since in her pocket to restore it to him in case she should ever see him again, which, she added, he had half promised her. As she told me this, she took the handkerchief out of her pocket to let me see it; she had folded it up neatly in a couple of vine leaves, tied round with a tendril—on opening it, I saw an S mark'd in one of the corners.

She had since that, she told me, stray'd as far as Rome, and walk'd round St Peter's once—and return'd back—that she found her way alone across the Apennines—had travell'd over all Lombardy without money—and through the flinty roads of Savoy without shoes—how she had borne it, and how she had got supported, she could not tell—but *God tempers the wind*, said Maria, to the shorn lamb.°

Shorn indeed! and to the quick, said I; and wast thou in my own land, where I have a cottage, I would take thee to it and shelter thee:° thou shouldst eat of my own bread, and drink of my own cup°—I would be kind to thy Sylvio—in all thy weaknesses and wanderings I would seek after thee and bring thee back—when the sun went down I would say my prayers, and when I had done thou shouldst play thy evening song upon thy pipe, nor would the incense of my sacrifice be worse accepted for entering heaven along with that of a broken heart.

Nature melted within me, as I utter'd this; and Maria observing, as I took out my handkerchief, that it was steep'd too much already to be of use, would needs go wash it in the stream.—And where will you dry it, Maria? said I—I'll dry it in my bosom, said she—'twill do me good.

And is your heart still so warm, Maria? said I.

I touch'd upon the string on which hung all her sorrows—she look'd with wistful disorder for some time in my face; and then, without saying any thing, took her pipe, and play'd her service to the

Virgin—The string I had touch'd ceased to vibrate—in a moment or two Maria returned to herself—let her pipe fall—and rose up.

And where art you going, Maria? said I.—She said to Moulines.—Let us go, said I, together.—Maria put her arm within mine, and lengthening the string, to let the dog follow—in that order we entered Moulines.

MARIA
MOULINES

THO' I hate salutations and greetings in the market-place,° yet when we got into the middle of this, I stopp'd to take my last look and last farewel of Maria.

Maria, tho' not tall, was nevertheless of the first order of fine forms—affliction had touch'd her looks with something that was scarce earthly—still she was feminine—and so much was there about her of all that the heart wishes, or the eye looks for in woman, that could the traces be ever worn out of her brain, and those of Eliza's out of mine, she should *not only eat of my bread and drink of my own cup*, but Maria should lay in my bosom, and be unto me as a daughter.°

Adieu, poor luckless maiden!—imbibe the oil and wine which the compassion of a stranger, as he journieth on his way, now pours into thy wounds—the being who has twice bruised thee can only bind them up for ever.°

THE BOURBONNOIS

THERE was nothing from which I had painted out for myself so joyous a riot of the affections, as in this journey in the vintage, through this part of France; but pressing through this gate of sorrow to it, my sufferings had totally unfitted me: in every scene of festivity I saw Maria in the back-ground of the piece, sitting pensive under her poplar; and I had got almost to Lyons before I was able to cast a shade across her—

—Dear sensibility! source inexhausted of all that's precious in our joys, or costly in our sorrows!° thou chainest thy martyr down upon his bed of straw—and 'tis thou who lifts him up to HEAVEN— eternal fountain of our feelings!—'tis here I trace thee—and this is thy divinity which stirs within me——not, that in some sad and sickening moments, '*my soul shrinks back upon herself, and startles at destruction*'°—mere pomp of words!—but that I feel some generous joys and generous cares beyond myself—all comes from thee, great—great SENSORIUM° of the world! which vibrates, if a hair of our heads but falls upon the ground,° in the remotest desert of thy creation.—Touch'd with thee, Eugenius draws my curtain when I languish°—hears my tale of symptoms, and blames the weather for the disorder of his nerves. Thou giv'st a portion of it sometimes to the roughest peasant who traverses the bleakest mountains—he finds the lacerated lamb of another's flock—This moment I beheld him leaning with his head against his crook, with piteous inclination looking down upon it—Oh! had I come one moment sooner!—it bleeds to death—his gentle heart bleeds with it—

Peace to thee, generous swain!—I see thou walkest off with anguish—but thy joys shall balance it—for happy is thy cottage— and happy is the sharer of it—and happy are the lambs which sport about you.

THE SUPPER

A SHOE coming loose from the fore-foot of the thill-horse,° at the beginning of the ascent of mount Taurira, the postilion dismounted, twisted the shoe off, and put it in his pocket; as the ascent was of five or six miles, and that horse our main dependence, I made a point of having the shoe fasten'd on again, as well as we could; but the postilion had thrown away the nails, and the hammer in the chaise-box, being of no great use without them, I submitted to go on.

He had not mounted half a mile higher, when coming to a flinty piece of road, the poor devil lost a second shoe, and from off his other fore-foot; I then got out of the chaise in good earnest; and seeing a house about a quarter of a mile to the left-hand, with a great deal to do, I prevailed upon the postilion to turn up to it. The look of the house, and of every thing about it, as we drew nearer, soon reconciled me to the disaster.—It was a little farm-house surrounded with about twenty acres of vineyard, about as much corn—and close to the house, on one side, was a *potagerie*° of an acre and a half, full of every thing which could make plenty in a French peasant's house— and on the other side was a little wood which furnished wherewithal to dress it. It was about eight in the evening when I got to the house—so I left the postilion to manage his point as he could—and for mine, I walk'd directly into the house.

The family consisted of an old grey-headed man and his wife, with five or six sons and sons-in-law and their several wives, and a joyous genealogy out of 'em.

They were all sitting down together to their lentil-soup; a large wheaten loaf was in the middle of the table; and a flaggon of wine at each end of it promised joy thro' the stages of the repast—'twas a feast of love.°

The old man rose up to meet me, and with a respectful cordiality would have me sit down at the table; my heart was sat down the moment I enter'd the room; so I sat down at once like a son of the family; and to invest myself in the character as speedily as I could, I instantly borrowed the old man's knife, and taking up the loaf cut myself a hearty luncheon;° and as I did it I saw a testimony in every eye, not only of an honest welcome, but of a welcome mix'd with thanks that I had not seem'd to doubt it.

Was it this; or tell me, Nature, what else it was which made this morsel so sweet—and to what magick I owe it, that the draught I took of their flaggon was so delicious with it, that they remain upon my palate to this hour?

If the supper was to my taste—the grace which follow'd it was much more so.

THE GRACE

WHEN supper was over, the old man gave a knock upon the table with the haft of his knife—to bid them prepare for the dance: the moment the signal was given, the women and girls ran all together into a back apartment to tye up their hair—and the young men to the door to wash their faces, and change their sabots;° and in three minutes every soul was ready upon a little esplanade before the house to begin—The old man and his wife came out last, and, placing me betwixt them, sat down upon a sopha of turf by the door.

The old man had some fifty years ago been no mean performer upon the vielle°—and at the age he was then of, touch'd it well enough for the purpose. His wife sung now-and-then a little to the tune—then intermitted—and joined her old man again as their children and grand-children danced before them.

It was not till the middle of the second dance, when, from some pauses in the movement wherein they all seemed to look up, I fancied I could distinguish an elevation of spirit different from that which is the cause or the effect of simple jollity.—In a word, I thought I beheld *Religion* mixing in the dance°—but as I had never seen her so engaged, I should have look'd upon it now, as one of the illusions of an imagination which is eternally misleading me, had not the old man, as soon as the dance ended, said, that this was their constant way; and that all his life long he had made it a rule, after supper was over, to call out his family to dance and rejoice; believing, he said, that a chearful and contented mind was the best sort of thanks to heaven that an illiterate peasant could pay—

——Or a learned prelate either, said I.

THE CASE OF DELICACY

WHEN you have gained the top of mount Taurira, you run presently down to Lyons—adieu then to all rapid movements! 'Tis a journey of caution; and it fares better with sentiments, not to be in a hurry with them; so I contracted with a Voiturin° to take his time with a couple of mules, and convey me in my own chaise safe to Turin through Savoy.

Poor, patient, quiet, honest people! fear not; your poverty, the treasury of your simple virtues, will not be envied you by the world, nor will your vallies be invaded by it.—Nature! in the midst of thy disorders, thou art still friendly to the scantiness thou hast created— with all thy great works about thee, little hast thou left to give, either to the scithe or to the sickle—but to that little, thou grantest safety and protection; and sweet are the dwellings which stand so shelter'd.

Let the way-worn traveller vent his complaints upon the sudden turns and dangers of your roads—your rocks—your precipices—the difficulties of getting up—the horrors of getting down—mountains impracticable—and cataracts, which roll down great stones from their summits, and block his road up.—The peasants had been all day at work in removing a fragment of this kind between St. Michael and Madane; and by the time my Voiturin got to the place, it wanted full two hours of compleating before a passage could any how be gain'd: there was nothing but to wait with patience—'twas a wet and tempestuous night; so that by the delay, and that together, the Voiturin found himself obliged to take up five miles short of his stage at a little decent kind of an inn by the road side.

I forthwith took possession of my bed-chamber—got a good fire—order'd supper; and was thanking heaven it was no worse—when a voiture arrived with a lady in it and her servant-maid.°

As there was no other bed-chamber in the house, the hostess, without much nicety,° led them into mine, telling them, as she usher'd them in, that there was no body in it but an English gentleman—that there were two good beds in it, and a closet within the room which held another—the accent in which she spoke of this third bed did not say much for it—however, she said, there were three beds, and but three people—and she durst say, the gentleman would do any thing to accommodate matters.—I left not the lady a moment to make a conjecture about it—so instantly made a declaration I would do any thing in my power.

As this did not amount to an absolute surrender of my bed-chamber, I still felt myself so much the proprietor, as to have a right to do the honours of it—so I desired the lady to sit down—pressed her into the warmest seat—call'd for more wood—desired the hostess to enlarge the plan of the supper, and to favour us with the very best wine.

The lady had scarce warm'd herself five minutes at the fire, before she began to turn her head back, and give a look at the beds; and the oftener she cast her eyes that way, the more they return'd perplex'd—I felt for her—and for myself; for in a few minutes, what by her looks, and the case itself, I found myself as much embarrassed as it was possible the lady could be herself.

That the beds we were to lay in were in one and the same room, was enough simply by itself to have excited all this—but the position of them, for they stood parallel, and so very close to each other as only to allow space for a small wicker chair betwixt them, render'd the affair still more oppressive to us—they were fixed up moreover near the fire, and the projection of the chimney on one side, and a large beam which cross'd the room on the other, form'd a kind of recess for them that was no way favourable to the nicety of our sensations—if any thing could have added to it, it was, that the two beds were both of 'em so very small, as to cut us off from every idea of the lady and the maid lying together; which in either of them, could it have been feasible, my lying besides them, tho' a thing not to be wish'd, yet there was nothing in it so terrible which the imagination might not have pass'd over without torment.

As for the little room within, it offer'd little or no consolation to us; 'twas a damp cold closet, with a half dismantled window shutter, and with a window which had neither glass or oil paper in it to keep out the tempest of the night. I did not endeavour to stifle my cough when the lady gave a peep into it; so it reduced the case in course to this alternative—that the lady should sacrifice her health to her feelings, and take up with the closet herself, and abandon the bed next mine to her maid—or that the girl should take the closet, &c. &c.

The lady was a Piedmontese of about thirty, with a glow of health in her cheeks.—The maid was a Lyonoise of twenty, and as brisk and lively a French girl as ever moved.—There were difficulties every way—and the obstacle of the stone in the road, which brought us into the distress, great as it appeared whilst the peasants were removing it, was but a pebble to what lay in our ways now—I have only to add, that it did not lessen the weight which hung upon our spirits, that we were both too delicate to communicate what we felt to each other upon the occasion.

We sat down to supper; and had we not had more generous wine to it than a little inn in Savoy could have furnish'd, our tongues had been tied up, till necessity herself had set them at liberty—but the lady having a few bottles of Burgundy in her voiture sent down her Fille de Chambre for a couple of them; so that by the time supper was over, and we were left alone, we felt ourselves inspired with a strength of mind sufficient to talk, at least, without reserve upon our situation. We turn'd it every way, and debated and considered it in all kind of lights in the course of a two hours negociation; at the end of which the articles were settled finally betwixt us, and stipulated for in form and manner of a treaty of peace—and I believe with as much religion and good faith on both sides, as in any treaty which as yet had the honour of being handed down to posterity.

They were as follows:

First. As the right of the bed-chamber is in Monsieur—and he thinking the bed next to the fire to be the warmest, he insists upon the concession on the lady's side of taking up with it.

Granted, on the part of Madame; with a proviso, That as the curtains of that bed are of a flimsy transparent cotton, and appear likewise too scanty to draw close, that the Fille de Chambre, shall fasten up the opening, either by corking pins,° or needle and thread, in such manner as shall be deemed a sufficient barrier on the side of Monsieur.

2dly. It is required on the part of Madame, that Monsieur shall lay the whole night through in his robe de chambre.°

Rejected: inasmuch as Monsieur is not worth a robe de chambre; he having nothing in his portmanteau but six shirts and a black silk pair of breeches.

The mentioning the silk pair of breeches made an entire change of the article—for the breeches were accepted as an equivalent for the robe de chambre, and so it was stipulated and agreed upon that I should lay in my black silk breeches all night.

3dly. It was insisted upon, and stipulated for by the lady, that after Monsieur was got to bed, and the candle and fire extinguished, that Monsieur should not speak one single word the whole night.

Granted; provided Monsieur's saying his prayers might not be deem'd an infraction of the treaty.

There was but one point forgot in this treaty, and that was the manner in which the lady and myself should be obliged to undress and get to bed—there was but one way of doing it, and that I leave to the reader to devise; protesting as I do it, that if it is not the most delicate in nature, 'tis the fault of his own imagination°—against which this is not my first complaint.

Now when we were got to bed, whether it was the novelty of the situation, or what it was, I know not; but so it was, I could not shut my eyes; I tried this side and that, and turn'd and turn'd again, till a full hour after midnight; when Nature and patience both wearing out—O my God! said I——

—You have broke the treaty, Monsieur, said the lady, who had no more slept than myself.—I begg'd a thousand pardons—but insisted it was no more than an ejaculation°—she maintain'd 'twas an entire infraction of the treaty—I maintain'd it was provided for in the clause of the third article.

The lady would by no means give up her point, tho' she weakened her barrier by it; for in the warmth of the dispute, I could hear two or three corking pins fall out of the curtain to the ground.

Upon my word and honour, Madame, said I—stretching my arm out of bed, by way of asseveration—

—(I was going to have added, that I would not have trespass'd against the remotest idea of decorum for the world)—

—But the Fille de Chambre hearing there were words between us, and fearing that hostilities would ensue in course, had crept silently out of her closet, and it being totally dark, had stolen so close to our beds, that she had got herself into the narrow passage which separated them, and had advanc'd so far up as to be in a line betwixt her mistress and me—

So that when I stretch'd out my hand, I caught hold of the Fille de Chambre's

THE JOURNAL TO
ELIZA

THE JOURNAL TO ELIZA

THIS Journal wrote under the fictitious Names of Yorick and Draper—and sometimes of the Bramin and Bramine°—but tis a Diary of the miserable feelings of a person separated from a Lady for whose Society he languish'd—

The real Names—are foreigne—and the Account a Copy from a french Manuscript in M^r S——s hands—but wrote as it is, to cast a Viel over them—There is a Counterpart—which is the Lady's Account° what transactions dayly happend—and what Sentiments occupied her mind, during this Separation from her Admirer—these are worth reading—the translator cannot say so much in favour of Yoricks—which seem to have little Merit beyond their honesty and truth—

Continuation of the Bramines Journal.°

Sunday April 13.°

wrote the last farewel to Eliza by Mr Wats* who sails this day for Bombay—inclosed her likewise the Journal kept from the day we parted, to this—so from hence continue it till the time we meet again—Eliza does the same, so we shall have mutual testimonies to deliver hereafter to each other, That the Sun has not more constantly rose and set upon the earth, than We have thought of and remember'd, what is more chearing than Light itself—eternal Sun-shine! Eliza!—dark to me is all this world without thee! and most heavily will every hour pass over my head, till that is come which brings thee, dear Woman back to Albion. dined with Hall &c—at the brawn's head—the whole Pandamonium° assembled—supp'd together at Halls—worn out both in body and mind, and paid a severe reckoning all the night.

April 14. got up tottering and feeble—then is it, Eliza, that I feel the want of thy friendly hand and friendly Council—and yet, with thee beside Me, thy Bramin would lose the merit of his virtue—he could not err—I will take thee upon any terms, Eliza! I shall be happy here—and I will be so just, so kind to thee, I will deserve not to be miserable hereafter—a Day dedicated to Abstinence and

* *(he saild 23)*

reflection—and what Object will employ the greatest part of mine—
full well does my Eliza know—

Munday. April 15.

worn out with fevers of all kinds but most, by that fever of the
heart with which I'm eternally wasting, and shall waste till I see Eliza
again°—dreadful Suffering of 15 Months!—it may be more—great
Controuler of Events! surely thou wilt proportion this, to my
Strength, and to that of my Eliza. pass'd the whole afternoon in
reading her Letters, and reducing them to the order in which they
were wrote to me—staid the whole evening at home—no pleasure or
Interest in either Society or Diversions—What a change, my dear
Girl, hast thou made in me!—but the Truth is, thou hast only turn'd
the tide of my passions a new way—they flow, Eliza to thee—and
ebb from every other Object in this world—and Reason tells me they
do right—for my heart has rated thee at a Price, that all the world is
not rich enough to purchase thee from me, at.   In a high fever all
the night.

April 16. and got up so ill, I could not go to Mrs James° as I had
promised her—took James's Powder° however—and leand the whole
day with my head upon My hand; sitting most dejectedly at the
Table with my Eliza's Picture before me—sympathizing and soothing me—O my Bramine! my Friend! my—Help-mate!°—for that, (if
I'm a prophet) is the Lot mark'd out for thee,—and such I consider
thee now, and thence it is, Eliza, I Share so righteously with thee, in
all the evil or good which befalls thee—But all our portion is Evil
now, and all our hours grief—I look forwards towards the Elysium°
we have so often and rapturously talk'd of—Cordelia's Spirit° will fly
to tell thee in some sweet Slumber, the moment the door is opend
for thee—and The Bramin of the Vally, shall follow the track wherever it leads him, to get to his Eliza, and invite her to his Cottage.°—

5 in the afternoon—I have just been eating my Chicking, sitting
over my repast upon it, with Tears—a bitter Sause—Eliza! but I
could eat it with no other—when Molly spread the Table Cloath, my
heart fainted with in me—one solitary plate—one knife—one fork—
one Glass!—O Eliza! twas painfully distressing°—I gave a thousand
pensive penetrating Looks at the Arm chair thou so often graced on
these quiet, sentimental Repasts—and Sighed and laid down my
knife and fork,—and took out my handkerchiff, clap'd it across my
face, and wept like a child—I shall read the same affecting Account

of many a sad Dinner which Eliza has had no power to taste of, from the same feelings and recollections, how She and her Bramin have eat their bread in peace and Love together.

April 17. with my friend Mrs James in Gerard street, with a present of Colours and apparatus for painting:—Long Conversation about thee my Eliza—sunk my heart with an infamous Account of Draper and his detested Character at Bombay—for What a Wretch art thou thou hazarding thy life, my dear friend, and what thanks is his nature capable of returning?—thou wilt be repaid with Injuries and Insults! Still there is a blessing in store for the meek and gentle, and Eliza will not be disinherited of it:° her Bramin is kept alive by this hope only—otherwise he is so sunk both in Spirits and looks, Eliza would scarse know him again. dined alone again to day; and begin to feel a pleasure in this kind of resigned Misery arising from this Situation, of heart unsupported by aught but its own tenderness—Thou owest me much Eliza!—and I will have patience; for thou wilt pay me all—But the Demand is equal;—much I owe thee, and with much shalt thou be requited.——Sent for a Chart of the Atlantic Ocean, to make conjectures upon what part of it my Treasure was floating—O! tis but a little way off—and I could venture after it in a Boat, methinks—I'm sure I could, was I to know Eliza was in distress—but fate has chalk'd out other roads. for us—We must go on with many a weary step, each in our separate heartless track, till Nature——

April 18.

This day, set up my Carriage,—new Subject of heartache, That Eliza is not here to share it with me.

Bought Orm's account of India°—why?—Let not my Bramine ask me—her heart will tell her Why I do this, and every Thing—

April 19. poor Sick-headed, sick hearted Yorick! Eliza has made a Shadow of thee—I am absolutely good for nothing, as every mortal is who can think and talk but upon one thing!—how I shall rally my powers, alarms me; for Eliza thou has melted them all into one—the power of loving thee°—and with such ardent affection as triumphs over all other feelings—was with our faithful friend all the morning; and dined with her and James—What is the Cause, that I can never talk about my Eliza to her, but I am rent in pieces—I burst into tears a dozen different times after dinner, and such affectionate gusts of passion, That She was ready to leave the room,—and sympathize in private for us—I weep for You both, said she (in a whisper,) for Elizas Anguish is as sharp as yours—her heart as tender—her constancy as great—heaven join Your hands I'm sure together!—James was occupied in reading a pamphlet upon the East India affairs—so I answerd her with a kind look, a heavy sigh, and a stream of tears—What was passing in Eliza's breast, at this affecting Crisis?—something kind, and pathetic! I will lay my Life.

8 o'clock—retired to my room, to tell my dear this—to run back the hours of Joy I have pass'd with her—and meditate upon those which are still in reserve for Us.—By this time Mr James tells me, You will have got as far from me, as the Maderas—and that in two months more, you will have doubled the Cape of good hope—I shall trace thy track every day in the Map, and not allow one hour for contrary Winds, or Currents—every engine of nature shall work together for us—Tis the Language of Love—and I can speak no other. And so, good night, to thee, and may the gentlest delusions of love impose upon thy dreams, as I forbode they will, this night, on those of thy Bramine.

April 20. Easter Sunday.

was not disappointed—yet awoke in the most acute pain—Something Eliza is wrong with me—you should be ill out of Sympathy—and yet you are too ill already—my dear friend—all day at home—in extream dejection.

April 21. The Loss of Eliza, and attention to that one Idea, brought on a fever—a consequence, I have for some time, forseen—but had not a sufficient Stock of cold philosophy to remedy—to satisfy my friends, call'd in a Physician—Alas! alas! the only Physician, and who carries the Balm of my Life along with her,—is Eliza.—why did I suffer thee to go from me?—surely thou hast more than once call'd thyself, my Eliza, to the same Account.—twil cost us both dear! but it could not be otherwise—We have submitted—we shall be rewarded.

Twas a prophetic Spirit, which dictated the Account of Corporal Trim's uneasy night when the fair Beguin ran in his head,°—for every night and almost every Slumber of mine, since the day We parted, is a repe[ti]tion of the same description—dear Eliza! I am very ill—very ill for thee—but I could still give thee greater proofs of my Affection. parted with 12 Ounces of blood, in order to quiet what was left in me—tis a vain experiment,—physicians cannot understand this; tis enough for me that Eliza does.—I am worn down my dear Girl to a Shadow, and but that I'm certain thou wilt not read this, till I'm restored—thy Yorick would not let the Winds hear his Complaints—4 o'clock—sorrowful Meal! for twas upon our old dish.—We shall liv[e] to eat it, my Dear Bramine, with comfort.

8. at night, our dear friend Mrs James, from the forbodings of a good heart, thinking I was ill; sent her Maid to enquire after me—I had alarm'd her on Saturday; and not being with her on sunday,—her friendship supposed the Condition, I was in—She suffers most tenderly for Us, my Eliza!—and We owe her more than all the Sex—or indeed both Sexes if not, all the world put together—adieu! my sweet Eliza! for this night—thy Yorick is going to waste himself on a restless bed, where he will turn from side to Side a thousand times—and dream by Intervals of things terrible and impossible—That Eliza is false to Yorick, or Yorick is false to Eliza——

April 22^d—rose with utmost difficulty—my Physician order'd me back to bed as soon as I had got a dish of Tea—was bled again; my arm broke loose and I half bled to death in bed before I felt it. O Eliza! how did thy Bramine mourn the want of thee to tye up his wounds, and comfort his dejected heart—still something bids me hope—and hope, I will—and it shall be the last pleasurable Sensation I part with.

4 o'clock They are making my bed—how shall I be able to continue my Journal, in it?—If there remains a chasm here—think Eliza, how ill thy Yorick must have been.—this moment received a Card from our dear friend, beging me to take [care] of a Life so valuable to my friends—but most so—She adds, to my poor dear Eliza.—not a word from the Newnhams!° but they had no such exhortation in their harts, to send thy Bramine—adieu to em!—

April 23.—a poor night. and am only able to quit my bed at 4 this afternoon—to say a word to my dear—and fulfill my engagement to her, 'of letting no day pass over my head without some kind communication with thee—faint resemblance, my dear girl, of *x* and how our days are to pass, when one kingdom holds us—visited in bed by 40 friends, in the Course of the Day—is not one warm affectionate call, of that friend, for whom I sustain Life, worth 'em all?—What thinkest thou my Eliza.—

April 24.

So ill, I could not write a word all this morning—not so much, as Eliza! farewell to thee;—I'm going——am a little better.—

So Shall not depart, as I apprehended—being this morning something better—and my Symptoms become milder, by a tolerable easy night.—and now, if I have strength and Spirits to trail my pen down to the bottom of the page, I have as whimsical a Story to tell you, and as comically disastrous as ever befell one of our family—Shandy's Nose—his *name*—his Sash-Window are fools to it.° It will serve at *least* to amuse You. The Injury I did myself in catching cold upon James's pouder, fell, you must know, upon the worst part it could,—the most painful, and most dangerous of any in the human Body—It was on this Crisis, I call'd in an able Surgeon and with him an able physician (both my friends) to inspect my disaster—tis a venerial Case, cried my two Scientifick friends.—'tis impossible. at least to be that, replied I—for I have had no commerce whatever with the Sex—not even with my wife, added I, these 15 Years—You are ***** however my good friend, said the Surgeon, or there is no such Case in the world—what the Devil! said I without knowing Woman—we will not reason about it, said the Physician, but you must undergo a course of Mercury,—I'll lose my life first, said I,—and trust to Nature, to Time—or at the worst—to Death,—so I put an end with some Indignation to the Conference; and determined to bear all the torments I underwent, and ten times more rather than, submit to be treated as a *Sinner*, in a point where I had acted like a *Saint*.° Now as the father of mischief° would have it, who has no pleasure like that of dishonouring the righteous—it so fell out, That from The moment I dismiss'd my Doctors—my pains began to rage with a violence not to be express'd, or supported. every hour became more intollerable—I was got to bed—cried out and raved the whole night—and was got up so near dead, That my friends insisted upon my sending again for my Physician and Surgeon—I told them upon the word of a man of Strict honour, They were both mistaken as to my case—but tho' they had reason'd wrong—they might act right—but that sharp as my sufferings were, I felt them not so sharp as the Imputation, which a venerial treatment of my case, laid me under—They answerd that these taints of the blood laid dormant 20 Years—but that they would not reason with me in a matter wherein I was so delicate—but Would do all the Office for which they were call'd in—namely, to put an end to my torment, which otherwise would put an end to me.—and so have I been compell'd. to surrender myself—and thus Eliza is your Yorick, your Bramine—your friend with all his

sensibilities, suffering the Chastisement of the grossest Sensualist°—
Is it not a most ridiculous Embarassment, as ever Yorick's Spirit
could be involved in—

Tis needless to tell Eliza, that nothing but the purest conscious-
ness of Virtue, could have tempted Eliza's friend to have told her this
Story—Thou art too good my Eliza to love aught but Virtue—and
too discerning not to distinguish the open Character which bears it,
from the artful and double one which affects it—This, by the way,
would make no bad anecdote in T. Shandy's Life—however I
thought at least it would amuse you, in a Country where *less Matters*
serve.—This has taken me three Sittings—it ought to be a good picture—I'm more proud, That it is a true one. In ten Days, I shall be
able to get out—my room allways full of friendly Visiters—and my
rapper eternally going with Cards and enquiries after me. I should be
glad of the Testimonies—without the Tax.

Every thing convinces me, Eliza, We shall live to meet again—
So—Take care of your health, to add to the comfort of it.

April 25. after a tolerable night, I am able, Eliza, to sit up and hold
a discourse with the sweet Picture thou hast left behind thee of
thyself, and tell it how much I had dreaded the catastrophe, of never
seeing its dear Original more in this world—never did that Look of
sweet resignation appear so eloquent as now; it has said more to my
heart—and cheard it up more effectually above little fears and *may
be's*—Than all the Lectures of philosophy I have strength to apply to
it, in my present Debility of mind and body.—as for the latter—my
men of Science, will set it properly a going again—tho' upon what
principles—the Wise Men of Gotham° know as much as they—If
they *act right*—What is it to me, how *wrong they think*; for finding my
machine a much less tormenting one to me than before, I become
reconciled to my Situation, and to their Ideas of it——but don't You
pity me, after all, my dearest and my best of friends? I know to what
an amount thou wilt Shed over Me, this tender Tax—and tis the
Consolation springing out of that, of what a good heart it is which
pours this friendly balm on mine, That has already, and will for ever
heal every evil of my Life.   and What is becoming, of my Eliza,
all this time!—where is she sailing?—What Sickness or other evils
have befallen her? I weep often my dear Girl, for those my Imagination surrounds thee with—What would be the measure of my
Sorrow, did I know thou wast distressd?—adieu—adieu. and trust

my dear friend—my dear Bramine, that there still wants nothing to kill me in a few days, but the certainty, That thou wast suffering, what I am—and yet I know thou art ill—but when thou returnest back to England, all shall be set right.—so heaven waft thee to us upon the wings of Mercy—that is, as speedily as the winds and tides can do thee this friendly office. This is the 7th day That I have tasted nothing better than Water gruel—am going, at the solicitation of Hall, to eat of a boild fowl—so he dines with me on it—and a dish of Macaruls—

7 o'clock—I have drank to thy Name Eliza! everlasting peace and happiness (for my Toast) in the first glass of Wine I have adventured to drink. my friend has left me—and I am alone,—like thee in thy solitary Cabbin after thy return from a tastless meal in the round house° and like thee I fly to my Journal, to tell thee, I never prized thy friendship so high, or loved thee more—or wish'd so ardently to be a sharer of all the weights which Providence has laid upon thy tender frame—Than this moment—when upon taking up my pen, my poor pulse quickend—my pale face glowed—and tears stood ready in my Eyes to fall upon the paper, as I traced the word Eliza. O Eliza! Eliza! ever best and blessed of all thy Sex! blessed in thyself and in thy Virtues—and blessed and endearing to all who know thee—to Me, Eliza, most so; because I *know more* of thee than any other—This is the true philtre° by which Thou hast charm'd me and wilt for ever charm and hold me thine, whilst Virtue and faith hold this world together; tis the simple Magick, by which I trust, I have won a place in that heart of thine on which I depend so satisfied, That Time and distance, or change of every thing which might allarm the little hearts of little men, create no uneasy suspence in mine—It scorns to doubt—and scorns to be doubted—tis the only exception—When Security is not the parent of Danger.

My Illness will keep me three weeks longer in town.—but a Journey in less time would be hazardous, unless a short one across the Desert which I should set out upon to morrow, could I carry a Medcine with me which I was sure would prolong one Month of Your Life—or should it happen——

but why make Suppositions?—when Situations happen—tis time enough to shew thee That thy Bramin is the truest and most friendly of mortal Spirits, and capable of doing more for his Eliza, than his pen will suffer him to promise.

April 26. Slept not till three this morning—was in too delicious Society to think of it; for I was all the time with thee besides me, talking over the projess of our friendship, and turning the world into a thousand Shapes to enjoy it. got up much better for the Conversation—found myself improved in body and mind and recruited° beyond any thing I lookd for; My Doctors, stroked their beards, and look'd ten per Cent wiser upon feeling my pulse, and enquiring after my Symptoms—am still to run thro' a course of Van Sweetens corrosive Mercury, or rather Van Sweeten's° Course of Mercury is to run thro' me—I shall be sublimated to an etherial Substance° by the time my Eliza sees me—she must be sublimated and uncorporated too, to be able to see me—but I was always transparent and a Being easy to be seen thro', or Eliza had never loved me nor had Eliza been of any other *Cast°* herself, could her Bramine have held *Communion°* with her. hear every day from our worthy sentimental friend—who rejoyces to think that the Name of Eliza is still to vibrate upon Yoricks ear—this, my dear Girl, many who loved me dispair'd off—poor Molly who is all attention to me—and every day brings in the name of poor Mrs Draper, told me last night, that She and her Mistress had observed, I had never held up my head, since the Day you last dined with me—That I had seldome laughd or smiled—had gone to no Diversions—but twice or thrice at the most, dined out—That they thought I was broken hearted, for She never enterd the room or passd by the door, but she heard me sigh heavily—That I neither eat or slept or took pleasure in any Thing as before, except writing——

The Observation will draw a Sigh, Eliza, from thy feeling heart—and yet, so thy heart would wish to have it—tis fit in truth We suffer equally—nor can it be otherwise—when the Causes of Anguish in two hearts are so proportion'd, as in ours.—Surely—Surely—Thou art mine Eliza! for dear have have I bought thee!

April 27. Things go better with me, Eliza! and I shall be reestablish'd soon, except in bodily weakness; not yet being able to rise from my arm chair, and walk to the other corner of my room, and back to it again, without fatigue—I shall double my Journey to morrow, and if the day is warm the day after be got into my Carriage and be transported into Hyde park for the advantage of air and exercise—wast thou but besides me, I could go to Salt hill,° Im sure, and feel the Journey short and pleasant.—another Time!—the present, alas! is not ours. I pore so much on thy Picture—I have it *off by heart*—dear

Girl—oh tis sweet! tis kind! tis reflecting! tis affectionate! tis—thine my Bramine—I say my matins and Vespers° to it—I quiet my Murmurs, by the Spirit which speaks in it—'all will end Well my Yorick.'—I declare my dear Bramine I am so secured and wrapt up in this Belief, That I would not part with the Imagination, of how happy I am to be with thee, for all the Offers of present Interest or Happiness the whole world could tempt me with; in the loneliest Cottage that Love and Humility ever dwelt in, with thee along with me, I could possess more refined Content, Than in the most glittering Court; and with thy Love and fidelity, taste truer joys, my Eliza! and make thee also partake of more, than all the senseless parade of this silly world could compensate to either of us—with this, I bound all my desires and worldly views—what are they worth without Eliza? Jesus! grant me but this, I will deserve it—I will make My Bramine, as Happy, as thy goodness wills her—I will be the Instrument of her recompense for the sorrows and disappointments thou has suffer'd her to undergo; and if ever I am false, unkind or ungentle to her; so let me be dealt with by thy Justice.

9 o'clock, I am preparing to go to bed my dear Girl, and first pray for thee, and then to Idolize thee for two wakeful hours upon my pillow—I shall after that, I find dream all night of thee, for all the day have I done nothing but think of thee—something tells, that thou hast this day, been employd exactly in the same Way. good night, fair Soul—and may the sweet God of sleep close gently thy eyelids—and govern and direct thy Slumbers—adieu—adieu, adieu!

April 28. I was not deceived Eliza! by my presentiment that I should find thee out in my dreams; for I have been with thee almost the whole night, alternately soothing thee, or telling thee my sorrows—I have rose up comforted and strengthend—and found myself so much better, that I orderd my Carriage, to carry me to our mutual friend°—Tears ran down her cheeks when She saw how pale and wan I was—and never gentle Creature sympathiz'd more tenderly—I beseech you, cried the good Soul, not to regard either difficulties or expences but fly to Eliza directly—I see you will dye without her—save yourself for her—how shall I look her in the face? What can I say to her, when on her return, I have to tell her, That her Yorick is no more!—Tell her my dear friend, said I, That I will meet her in a better world—and that I have left this, because I could not live without her; tell Eliza, my dear friend added I—That I died broken hearted—and that you were a Witness to it—as I said this, She burst into the most pathetick flood of Tears—that ever kindly nature shed   you never beheld so affecting a Scene—! 'twas too much for Nature! Oh! she is good—I love her as my Sister!—and could Eliza have been a witness, hers would have melted down to Death and scarse have been brought back, from an Extacy so celestial, and savouring of another world.—I had like to have fainted, and to that Degree was my heart and Soul affected, it was with difficulty I could reach the Street door; I have got home, and shall lay all day upon my Sopha—and to morrow morning my dear Girl write again to thee; for I have not strength to drag my pen—

April 29.

I am so ill to day, my dear, I can only tell you so—I wish I was put into a Ship for Bombay—I wish I may otherwise hold out till the hour We might otherwise have met—I have too many evils upon me at once—and yet I will not faint under them—Come!—Come to me soon my Eliza and save me!

April 30. Better to day—but am too much visited and find my Strength wasted by the attention I must give to all concern'd for me—I will go Eliza, be it but by ten mile Journeys, home to my thatchd Cottage°—and there I shall have no respit—for I shall do nothing but think of thee—and burn out this weak Taper of Life. by the flame thou hast superadded to it—fare well My dear **** to morrow begins a new month—and I hope to give thee in it, a more sunshiny Side of myself—Heaven! how is it with my Eliza—

May I. got out into the park to day—Sheba° there on Horseback; pass'd twice by her without knowing her—She stop'd the third time—to ask me how I did—I would not have askd you, Solomon! said She, but your Looks affected me—for you'r half dead I fear—I thank'd Sheba, very kindly, but without any emotion but what sprung from gratitude—Love alas! was fled with thee Eliza!—I did not think Sheba could have changed so much in grace and beauty— Thou hadst shrunk poor Sheba away into Nothing,—but a good natured girl, without powers or charms—I *fear* your Wife is dead, quoth Sheba—no, you don't *fear* it Sheba said I—Upon my Word Solomon! I would quarrel with You, was you not so ill—If you knew the Cause of my Illness, Sheba, replied I, you would quarrel but the more with me—You lie, Solomon! answered Sheba, for I know the Cause already—and am so little out of Charity with You upon it—

That I give You leave to come and drink Tea with me before You leave Town—you're a good honest Creature Sheba—no! you Rascal, I am not—but I'm in Love, as much as you can be for your Life— I'm glad of it Sheba! said I—You Lie. said Sheba, and so canter'd away.—O My Eliza, had I ever truely loved another (which I never did) Thou hast long ago, cut the Root of all Affection in me—and planted and waterd and nourish'd it, to bear fruit only for thyself— Continue to give me proofs I have had and shall preserve the same rights over thee my Eliza! and if I ever murmur at the sufferings of Life, after that, Let me be numberd with the ungrateful.—I look now forwards with Impatience for the day thou art to get to Madras—and from thence shall I want to hasten thee to Bombay— where heaven will make all things Conspire to lay the Basis of thy health and future happiness—be true my dear girl, to thy self—and the rights of Self preservation which Nature has given thee!—per- severe—be firm—be pliant be placid—be courteous—but still be true to thy self—and never give up your Life,—or suffer the dis- quieting altercations, or small outrages you may undergo in this momentous point, to weigh a Scruple in the Ballance—Firmness— and fortitude and perseverance gain almost impossibilities—and *Skin* for *Skin*, saith *Job, nay all that a Man has, will he give* for his Life'°—oh My Eliza! That I could take the Wings of the Morning,° and fly to aid thee in *this* virtuous Struggle.   went to Ranelagh° at 8 this night, and sat still till ten—came home ill.

    May 2nd

    I fear I have relapsed—sent afresh for my Doctor—who has con- fined me to my Sopha—being able neither able to walk, stand or sit upright, without aggravating my Symptoms—I'm still to be treated as if I was a Sinner—and in truth have some appearances so strongly implying it, That was I not conscious I had had no Commerce with the Sex these 15 Years, I would decamp to morrow for Montpellier in the South of France, where Maladies of this sort are better treated and all taints more radically driven out of the Blood—than in this Country; but If I continue long ill—I am still determined to repair there—not to undergo a Cure of a distemper I cannot have, but for the bettering my Constitution by a better Climate.—I write this as I lie upon my back—in which posture I must continue, I fear some days—If I am able—will take up my pen again before night—

    4 o'clock.—an hour dedicated to Eliza! for I have dined alone—

and ever since the Cloath has been laid, have done nothing but call upon thy dear Name—and ask why tis not permitted thou shouldst sit down, and share my Macarel and foul—there would be enough, said Molly as she place'd it upon the Table to have served both You and poor Mrs Draper—I never bring in the Knives and forks, added She, but I think of her°—There was no more trouble with you both, than with one of You—I never heard a high or a hasty word from either of You—You were surely made, added Molly, for one another, You are both so kind so quiet and so friendly—Molly furnished me with Sause to my Meat—for I wept my plate full, Eliza! and now I have begun, could shed tears till Supper again—and then go to bed weeping for thy absence till morning. Thou hast bewitch'd me with powers, my dear Girl, from which no power shall unlose me—and if fate can put this Journal of my Love into thy hands, before we meet, I know with what warmth it will inflame the kindest of hearts, to receive me. peace be with thee, my Eliza, till that happy moment!—

9 at night I shall never get possession of myself, Eliza! at this rate—I want to Call off my Thoughts from thee, that I may now and then, apply them to some con[c]erns which require both my attention and genius; but to no purpose—I had a Letter to write to Lord Shelburn°—and had got my apparatus in order to begin—when a Map of India coming in my Way—I begun to study the length and dangers of my Eliza's Voiage to it, and have been amusing and frightening myself by turns, as I traced the path-way of the Earl of Chatham,° the whole Afternoon—good god! what a voiage for any one!—but for the poor relax'd frame of my tender Bramine to cross the Line° twice! and be subject to the Intolerant heats, and the hazards which must be the consequence of em to such an unsupported Being!—O Eliza! 'tis too much—and if thou conquerest these, and all the other difficulties of so tremendous an alienation from thy Country, thy Children and thy friends, tis the hand of Providence which watches over thee for most merciful purposes—Let this persuasion, my dear Eliza! stick close to thee in all thy tryals—as it shall in those thy faithful Bramin is put to—till the mark'd hour of deliverance comes. I'm going to sleep upon this religious Elixir—may the Infusion of it distil into the gentlest of hearts—for that Eliza! is thine—sweet, dear, faithful Girl, most kindly does thy Yorick greet thee with the wishes of a good night. and—of Millions yet to come—

May 3rd Sunday What can be the matter with me! Some thing is wrong, Eliza! in every part of me—I do not gain strength; nor have I the feelings of health returning back to me; even my best moments seem merely the efforts of my mind to get well again, because I cannot reconcile myself to the thoughts of never seeing thee Eliza more.—for something is out of tune in every Chord of me—still with thee to nurse and sooth me, I should soon do well—The Want of thee is half my distemper—but not the whole of it—I must see Mrs James tonight, tho' I know not how to get there—but I shall not sleep, if I don't talk of You to her—so shall finish this Days Journal on my return—/May 4th—

Directed by Mrs James how to write Over-Land to thee, my Eliza!—would gladly tear out thus much of my Journal to send to thee—but the Chances are too many against it's getting to Bombay—or of being deliverd into your own hands—shall write a long long Letter—and trust it to fate and thee. was not able to say three words at Mrs James, thro' utter weakness of body and mind; and when I got home—could not get up stairs with Molly's aid—have rose a little better, my dear girl—and will live for thee—do the same for thy Bramin, I beseech thee. a Line from thee now, in this state of my Dejection,—would be worth a Kingdome to me!—

May 4. Writing by way of Vienna and Bussorah° to My Eliza.— this and Company took up the day.

5th writing to Eliza.—and trying l'*Extraite de* Saturne upon myself.—(a french Nostrum)°—

6th Dined out for the first time—came home to enjoy a More harmonious evening with my Eliza, than I could expect at Soho Con[c]ert°—every Thing my dear Girl, has lost its former relish to me—and for thee eternally does it quicken! writing to thee over Land—all day.

7. continue poorly, my dear!—but my blood warms, every moment I think of our future Scenes.—so must grow strong, upon the Idea—what shall I do upon the Reality?—O God!—

8th employ'd in writing to my Dear all day—and in projecting happiness for her—tho in misery myself. O! I have undergone Eliza!—but the worst is over—(I hope)—so adieu to those Evils, and let me hail the happiness to come.

9th, 10th and 11th so unaccountably disorder'd—I cannot Say

more—but that I would suffer ten times more with Smiles for my Eliza—adieu bless'd Woman!—

12th O Eliza! That my weary head was now laid upon thy Lap—(tis all that's left for it)—or that I had thine, reclining upon my bosome, and there resting all its disquietudes;—my Bramine—the world or Yorick must perish, before that foundation shall fail thee!—I continue poorly—but I turn my Eyes *Eastward* the oftener, and with more earnestness for it—

Great God of Mercy! shorten the Space betwixt us,—Shorten the space of our miseries!

13th Could not get the General post Office to take charg[e] of my Letters to You—so gave thirty shillings to a Merchant to further them to Aleppo° and from thence to Bassorah—so you will receive 'em, (I hope in god) sa[fe] by Christmas—Surely 'tis not impossible, but [I] may be made happy as my Eliza, by so[me] transcript from her, by that time—If not I shall hope—and hope, every week, and every hour of it, for Tidings of Comfort—we taste not of it *now*, my dear Bramine—but we will make full meals upon it hereafter.—Cards from 7 or 8 of our Grandies to dine with them before I leave Town—shall go like a Lamb to the Slaughter°—'*Man delights not me—nor Woman*'°

14. a little better to day—and would look pert, if my heart would but let me—dined with Lord and Lady Bellasis.°—so beset with Company—not a moment to write.

15—Undone with too much Society yesterday,—You scarse can Conceive my dear Eliza what a poor Soul I am—how I shall be got down to Coxwould—heaven knows—for I am as weak as a Child—You would not like me the worse for it, Eliza, if you was here—My friends like me, the more,—and Swear I shew more true fortitude and eveness of temper in my Suffering than Seneca, or Socrates°—I am, My Bramin, resigned.

16—Taken up all day with wor[l]dly matters, just as my Eliza was, the week before her departure—breakfasted with Lady Spencer°—[c]aught her with the Character of your Portrait—caught her passions still more with that of yourself—and my Attachment to the most amiable of Beings.—drove at night to Ranalagh°—staid an hour—returnd to my Lodgings, dissatisfied.

17. At Court°—every thing in this world seems in Masquerade, but thee dear Woman—and therefore I am sick of all the world b[ut]

thee—one Evening *so spent*, *as the [S]aturday's which preceeded our*
Separation—would sicken all the Conversation of the world—I relish no
Converse since—when will the like return?—tis hidden from us both,
for the wisest ends—and the hour will come my Eliza! when We shall
be convinced, that every event has been order'd for the best for Us—
Our fruit is not ripend—the accidents of time and Seasons will ripen
every Thing *together* for Us—a little better to day—or could not
have wrote this. dear Bramine rest thy Sweet Soul in peace!.

18. Laid sleepless all the night, with thinking of the many dangers
and sufferings, my dear Girl! that thou art exposed to—from thy
Voiage and thy sad state of health—but I find I must think no more
upon them—I have rose wan and trembling with the Havock they
have made upon my Nerves—tis death to me to apprehend° for
you—I must flatter my Imagination, That every Thing goes well
with You—Surely no evil can have befallen You—for if it had—I
had felt some monitory° sympathetic Shock within me, which would
have spoke like Revelation.—So farewell to all tormenting *May be's*,
in regard to my Eliza—She is well—she thinks of her Yorick with as
much Affection and true esteem as ever—and values him as much
above the World, as he values his Bramine—

19—Packing up, or rather Molly for me, the whole day—
tormenting! had not Molly all the time talk'd of poor Mrs Draper—
and recounted every Visit She had made me, and every repast She
had shared with me—how good a Lady!—How sweet a temper!—
how beautiful!—how genteel!—how gentle a Carriage—and how
soft and engaging a look!.—the poor girl is bewitch'd with us both—
infinitely interested in our Story, tho' She knows nothing of it but
from her penetration and Conjectures—She says however tis Impossible not to be in Love with her—

—In heart felt truth, Eliza! I'm of Molly's Opinion—

20—Taking Leave of all the Town, before my departure to
morrow.

21. detaind by Lord and Lady Spence[r] who had made a party to
dine and sup on my Account. Impatient to set out for my Solitude—
there the Mind, Eliza! gains strength, and learns to lean upon herself,—and seeks refuge in its own Constancy and Virtue—in the
world it seeks or accepts of a few treacherous supports—the feign'd
Compassion of one—the flattery of a second—the Civilities of a
third—the friendship of a fourth—they all decieve—and bring the

Mind back to where mine is retreating—that is Eliza! to itself—to thee (who art my second self) to retirement, reflection & Books°—When The Stream of Things, dear Bramine, Brings Us both together to this Haven—will not your heart take up its rest for ever? and will not your head Leave the world to those who can make a better thing of it—if there are any who know how.—Heaven take thee Eliza! under it's Wing—adieu! adieu.——

22nd Left Bond Street and London with it, this Morning—What a Creature I am! my heart has ached this week to get away—and still was ready to bleed in quiting a Place where my Connection with my dear dear Eliza began—Adieu to it! till I am summon'd up to the Downs° by a Message, to fly to her—for I think I shall not be able to support Town without you—and would chuse rather to sit solitary here, till the End of the next Summer—to be made happy altogether,—then seek for happiness,—or even suppose I can have it, but in Eliza's Society.

—23d bear my Journey badly—ill—and dispirited all the Way [? 28 May]—staid two days on the road at the Archbishops of Yorks°—shewd his Grace and his Lady and Sister your portrait—with a short but interesting Story of my friendship for the Original—kindly nursed and honourd both—arrived at my Thatched Cottage the 28th of May

29th and 30th confined to my bed—so emaciated, and unlike what I was, I could scarse be angry with thee Eliza, if thou Coulds not remember me, did heaven send me across thy way—Alas! poor Yorick!—'*remember thee! Pale Ghost—remember thee—whilst Memory holds a seat in this* distracted World—Remember thee,—Yes, from the Table of her Memory, shall just Eliz[a] wipe away all trivial men°—and leave a thron[e] for Yorick—adieu dear constant Girl—adieu—adieu.—and Remember my Truth and eternal fidelity—Remember how I Love—remember What I suffer.—Thou art mine Eliza by Purchace—had I not earn'd thee with a better price.—

31 Going this day upon a long course of Corrosive Mercury—which in itself, is deadly poyson, but given in a certain preparation, not very dangerous—I was forced to give it up in Town, from the terrible Cholicks° both in Stomach and Bowels—but the Faculty° thrust it down my Throat again—These Gentry have got it into their Noddles, That mine is an Ecclesiastick Rhum° as the french call it—god help em! I submit as my Uncle Toby did, in drinking Water,

upon the wound he received in his Groin—*Merely for quietness sake.*°

June 1 The Faculty, my dear Eliza! have mistaken my Case—why not Yours? I wish I could fly to you and attend You but one month as a physician—You'l Languish and dye where you are,—(if not by the climate)—most certainly by their *Ignorance of your Case*, and the unskilful Treatment you must be a martyr for in such a place as Bombay.—I'm Languishing here myself with every Aid and help—and tho' I shall conquer it—yet have had a cruel Struggle—Would my dear friend, I could ease yours, either by my advice—my attention—my Labour—my purse—They are all at Your Service, such as they are—and that You know Eliza—or my friendship for you is not worth a rush.

June 2^d

This morning surpriz'd with a Letter from my Lydia—that She and her Mama,° are coming to pay me a Visit—but on Condition I promise not to detain them in England beyond next April—when, they purpose, by my Consent, to retire into France, and establish themselves for Life—To all which I have freely given my parole° of Honour—and so shall have them with me for the Summer—from October to April—they take Lodgings in York—When they Leave me for good and all I suppose. ☞—Every thing for the best! Eliza.

This unexpected visit, is neither a visit of friendship or form—but tis a visit, such as I know you will never make me,—of pure Interest—to pillage What they can from me. In the first place to sell a small estate I have of sixty pounds a year—and lay out the purchase money in joint annuitys for them in the french Funds; by this they will obtain 200 pounds a year, to be continued to the longer Liver—and as it rids me of all future care—and moreover transfers their In[c]ome to the Kingdom where they purpose to live—I'm truely acquiescent—tho' I lose the Contingency of surviving them—but 'tis no matter—I shall have enough—and a hundred or two hundred Pounds for Eliza whenever She will honour me with putting her hand into my Purse—In the main time, I am not sorry for this Visit, as every Thing will be finally settled between us by it—only as their Annuity will be too strait°—I shall engage to remit them a 100 Guineas a year more, during my Wife's Life—and then, I will think, Eliza, of living for myself and the Being I love as much!—But I shall be pillaged in a hundred small Item's by them—which I have a Spirit above saying, *no*-to; as Provisions of all sorts of Linnens—for house

use—Body Use—printed Linnens for Gowns—Magazeens° of Teas—Plate, all I have (but 6 Silver Spoons)—In short I shall be pluck'd bare—all but of your Portrait and Snuff Box and your other dear Presents—and the neat furniture of my thatch'd Palace—and upon those I set up Stock again; Eliza What Say You, Eliza! shall we join our little *Capitals*° together?—will Mr Draper give us leave?—he may safely—if your Virtue and Honour are only concernd,— 'twould be safe in Yoricks hands, as in a Brothers—I would not wish Mr Draper to allow you above half I allow Mrs Sterne—Our Capital would be too great, and tempt us from the Society of poor Cordelia —who begins to wish for You.

By this time, I trust You have doubled the Cape of good hope— and sat down to your writing Drawer, and look'd in Yoricks face, as you took out your Journal; to tell him so—I hope he seems to smile as kindly upon You Eliza, as ever—Your Attachment and Love for me, will make him do so to eternity—if ever he should change his Air, Eliza!—I charge you catechize° your own Heart.—Oh! twil never happen!—

June 3^d—Cannot write my Travels, or give one half hours close attention to them, upon Thy Account, my dearest friend—Yet write I must, and what to do with You, whilst I write—I declare I know not—I want to have you ever before my Imagination—and cannot keep You out of my heart or head—In short thou enterst my Library, Eliza! (as thou one day shalt) without tapping—or sending for—by thy own Right of ever being close to thy Bramine—now I must shut you out out sometimes—or meet you Eliza! with an empty purse upon the Beach—pity my entanglements from other passions—my Wife with me every moment of the Summer—think what restraint upon a Fancy that should Sport and be in all points at its ease—O had I, my dear Bramine this Summer, to soften—and modulate my feelings—to enrich my fancy, and fill my heart brim full with bounty—my Book would be worth the reading—

It will be by stealth if I am able to go on with my Journal at all—It will have many Interruptions—and Hey ho's! most sentimentally utter'd—Thou must take it as it pleases God.—as thou must take the Writer—eternal Blessings be about You, Eliza! I am a little better, and now find I shall be set right in all points—my only anxiety is about You—I want to prescribe for you. My Eliza—for I think I understand your *Case* better than all the Faculty. adieu. adieu.

June 4. Hussy!°—I have employ'd a full hour upon your sweet sentimental Picture—and a couple of hours upon yourself—and with as much kind friendship, as the hour You left me—I deny it— Time lessens no Affections which honour and merit have planted—I would give more, and hazard more now for your happiness than in any one period, since I first learn'd to esteem you—is it so with thee my friend? has absence weakend my Interest—has time worn out any Impression—or is Yoricks Name less Musical in Eliza's ears?—my heart smites me, for asking the question—tis Treason against thee Eliza and Truth—Ye are dear Sisters, and your Brother Bramin Can never live to see a Separation amongst us.—What a similitude in our Trials, Whilst asunder!—Providence has order'd every Step better, than we could have order'd them, for the particular good we wish each other—This you will comment upon and find the Sense of without my explanation.

I wish this Summer and Winter with all I am to go through with in them, in business and Labour and Sorrow, well over—I have much to compose—and much to discompose me—have my Wife's pro-jects—and my own Views arising out of them, to harmonize and turn to account—I have Millions of heart aches to suffer and reason with—and in all this Storm of Passions, I have but one small anchor, Eliza! to keep this weak Vessel of mine from perishing—I trust all I have to it—as I trust Heaven, which cannot leave me, without a fault, to perish.—may the same just Heaven my Eliza, be that eternal Canopy which shall shelter thy head from evil till we meet— Adieu—adieu. adieu.—

June 5.

I Sit down to write this day, in good earnest—so read Eliza! quietly besides me—I'll not give you a Look—except one of kind-ness.—dear Girl! if thou lookest so bewitching once more—I'll turn thee out of my Study—You may bid me defiance, Eliza.—You can-not conceive how much and how universally I'm pitied, upon the Score of this unexpected Visit from france—my friends think it will kill me—If I find myself in danger I'll fly to You to Bombay—will Mr Draper receive me?—he ought—but he will never know What reasons make it his *Interest* and *Duty*—We must leave all all to that Being—who is infinitely removed above all Straitness° of heart . . . and is a friend to the friendly, as well as to the friendless.

June 6.—am quite alone in the depth of that sweet Recesse, I have so often described to You—tis sweet in itself—but You never come across me—but the perspective brightens up—and every Tree and Hill and Vale and Ruin about me—smiles as if you was amidst 'em—delusive moments!—how pensive a price do I pay for you—fancy sustains the Vision, whilst She has Strength—but Eliza! Eliza is not with me!—I sit down upon the first Hillock Solitary as a sequester'd Bramin—I wake from my delusion to a thousand Disquietudes, which many talk of—my Eliza!—but few feel°—then weary my Spirit with thinking, plotting, and projecting—and when Ive brought my System to my mind—am only Doubly miserable, That I cannot execute it—

Thus—Thus my dear Bramine are we tost at present in this tempest—Some Haven of rest will open to us. assuredly—God made us not for Misery and Ruin—he has orderd all our Steps°—and influenced our Attachments for what is worthy of them—It must end well—Eliza!—

June 7.

I have this week finish'd a sweet little apartment which all the time it was doing, I flatter'd the most delicious of Ideas, in thinking I was making it for you—Tis a neat little simple elegant room, overlook'd only by the Sun—just big enough to hold a Sopha,—for us—a Table, four Chairs, a Bureau—and a Book case.—They are to be all yours, Room and all—and there Eliza! shall I enter ten times a day to give thee Testimonies of my Devotion—Was't thou this moment sat down, it would be the sweetest of earthly Tabernacles°—I shall enrich it, from time to time, for thee—till Fate lets me lead thee by the hand into it—and then it can want no Ornament.—tis a little oblong room—with a large Sash° at the end—a little elegant fire-place—with as much room to dine around it, as in Bond street.—But in sweetness and Simplicity, and silence beyond any thing—Oh my Eliza!—I shall see thee surely Goddesse of this Temple,—and the most sovereign one, of all I have—and of all the powers heaven has trusted me with—They were lent me, Eliza! only for thee—and for thee my dear Girl shall be kept and employ'd.—You know *What rights* You have over me—wish to heaven I could Convey the Grant more amply than I have *done*—but 'tis the same—tis register'd where it will longest last—and that is in the feeling and most sincere of human hearts—You know I mean this reciprocally—and when-ever I mention the Word Fidelity and Truth, in Speaking of your

Reliance on mine—I always Imply the same Reliance upon the same Virtues in my Eliza.—I love thee Eliza! and will love thee for ever. Adieu.—

June 8.

Begin to recover, and sensibly to gain strength every day—and have such an appetite as I have not had for some Years—I prophecy I shall be the better, for the very Accident which has occasiond my Illness, and that the Medcines and Regimen I have submitted to, will make A thorough Regeneration of me, and that I shall have more health and Strength, than I have enjoy'd these ten Years—Send me such an Account of thy self Eliza, by the first sweet Gale—but tis impossible You should from Bombay—twil be as fatal to You, as it has been to thousands of your Sex—England and Retirement in it, can only save you—Come!—Come away—

June 9th I keep a post Chaise and a couple of fine horses, and take the Air every day in it—I go out—and return to my Cottage Eliza! alone—'tis melancholly, what should be matter of enjoyment; and the more so for that reason—I have a thousand things to remark and say as I roll along—but I want You to say them to—I could sometimes be wise—and often Witty—but I feel it a reproach to be the latter whilst Eliza is so far from hearing me—and What is Wisdome to a foolish weak heart like mine!—Tis like the Song of Melody to a broken Spirit—You must teach me fortitude my dear Bramine—for with all the tender qualities which make you the most precious of Women—and most wanting of all other Women of a kind protector—yet you have a passive kind of sweet Courage which bears You up—more than any one Virtue I can summon up in my own Case—We were made with Tempers for each other, Eliza! and You are blessd with such a certain turn of Mind and reflection—that if Self love does not blind me—I resemble no Being in the world so nearly as I do You—do you wonder tha[t] I have such friendship for you?—for my own part, I should not be astonish'd, Eliza, if you was to declare, 'You was up to the ears in Love with Me'.

June 10th—You are stretching over now in the Trade Winds from the Cape to Madrass—(I hope)—but I know it not. some friendly Ship You possibly have met with, and I never read an Account of an India Man° arrived—but I expect that it is the Messenger of the news my heart is upon the rack for.—I calculate, That you will arrive at Bombay by the beginning of October—by February, I shall surely

hear from you thence—but from Madrass sooner.—I expect you
Eliza in person, by September—and shall scarse go to London till
March—for what have I to do there, when (expect printing my
Book) I have no Interest or Passion to gratify—I shall return in June
to Coxwould—and there wait for the glad Tidings of your arrival in
the Downs—won't You write to me Eliza! by the first Boat?—would
not you wish to be greeted by your Yorick upon the Beech?—or be
met by him to hand you out of your postchaise, to pay him for the
Anguish he underwent, in handing you in to it?—I know your
answers—my Spirit is with You. farewel dear friend—

June 11. I am every day negociating to sell my little Estate besides
me—to send the money into France, to purchace peace to myself—
and a certainty of never having it interrupted by Mrs Sterne—who
when She is sensible I have given her all I can part with—will be at
rest herself—Indeed her plan to purchace annuities in france—is a
pledge of Security to me—That She will live her days out there—
otherwise She could have no end in transporting this two thousand
pounds out of England——nor would I consent but upon that
plan—but I may be at rest!—if my imagination will but let me—Hall
says tis no matter where she lives; If we are but separate, tis as good
as if the Ocean rolld between us—and so I should Argue to another
Man—but, tis an Idea which won't do so well for me—and tho'
nonsensical enough—Yet I shall be most at rest when there is that
Bar between Us—was I never so sure, I should never be interrupted
by her, in England—but I may be at rest I say, on that head—for they
have left all their Cloaths and plate and Linnen behind them in
france—and have joind in the most earnest Entreaty, That they may
return and fix in france—to which I have give[n] my word and honour—You will be bound with me Eliza! I hope, for performance of
my promise—I never yet broke it, in cases where Interest or pleasure
could have tempted me,—and shall hardly do it, now, when tempted
only by misery.—In Truth Eliza! thou art the Object to which every
act of mine is directed—You interfere in every Project—I rise—I go
to sleep with this in my Brain—how will my dear Bramine approve
of this?—which way will it conduce to make her happy? and how will
it be a proof of my Affection to her? are all the Enquiries I make.—
Your Honour, your Conduct, your Truth and regard for my
esteem—I know will equally direct every Step—and movement of
your Desires—and with that Assurance, is it, my dear Girl, That I

sustain Life,—But when will those Sweet eyes of thine, run over these Declarations?—how—and with Whom are they to be entrusted; to be conveyd to You?—unless Mrs James's friendship to us, finds some expedient—I must wait—till the first evening I'm with You—when I shall present You with—them as a better Picture of me, than Cosway° Could do for You. .—have been dismally ill all day—oweing to my course of Medecines which are too strong and forcing for this gawsy° Constitution of mine—I mend with them however—good God! how is it with You?—

June 12. I have return'd from a delicious Walk of Romance, my Bramine, which I am to tread a thousand times over with You swinging upon my arm—tis to my Convent°—and I have pluckd up a score Bryars by the roots which grew near the edge of the foot way, that they might not scratch or incommode you—had I been sure of your taking that walk with me the very next day, I could not have been more serious in my employment—dear Enthusiasm!°—thou bringst things forwards in a moment, which Time keeps for Ages back—I have you ten times a day besides me—I talk to You Eliza, for hours together—I take your Council—I hear your reasons—I admire you for them!—to this magic of a warm Mind, I owe all that's worth living for, during this State of our Trial—Every Trincket you gave or exchanged with me, has its force—Your Picture is Yourself—all Sentiment, Softness, and Truth—It speaks—it listens—'tis convincd—it resignes—Dearest Original! how like unto thee does it seem—and will seem—till thou makest it vanish, by thy presence—I'm but so, so—but advancing in health—to meet you.—to nurse you, to nourish you against° you come—for I fear, You will not arrive, but in a State that calls out to Yorick for support—Thou art Mistress, Eliza, of all the powers he has to sooth and protect thee—for thou art Mistress of his heart; his affections; and his reason—and beyond that, except a paltry purse, he has nothing worth giving thee—.

June 13.

This has been a year of presents to me—my Bramine—How many presents have I received from You, in the first place?—Lord Spencer has loaded me with a grand Ecritoire° of 40 Guineas—I am to receive this week a fourty Guinea-present of a gold Snuff Box, as fine as Paris can fabricate one—with an Inscription on it, more valuable, than the Box itself—I have a present of a portrait, (which by the by, I have immortalized in my Sentimental Journey)° worth them both—I say nothing of a gold Stock° buccle and Buttons—tho' I rate them above rubies, because they were Consecrated by the hand of Friendship, as She fitted them to me.—I have a present of the Sculptures upon poor Ovid's Tomb,° who died in Exile, tho' he wrote so well upon the Art of Love—These are in six beautiful Pictures executed on Marble at Rome°—and these Eliza, I keep sacred as Ornaments for your Cabinet, on Condition I hang them up.—and last of all, I have had a present, Eliza! this Year, of a Heart so finely set—with such rich materials—and Workmanship—That Nature must have had the chief hand in it—If I am able to keep it—I shall be a rich Man; If I lose it—I shall be poor indeed—so poor! I shall stand begging at your gates.—But what can all these presents portend—That it will turn out a fortunate earnest, of what is to be given me hereafter—

June 14.

I want you to comfort me my dear Bramine—and reconcile my mind to 3 Months misery—some days I think lightly of it—on others—my heart sinks down to the earth—but tis the last Trial of conjugal Misery—and I wish it was to begin this moment, That it might run its period the faster—for sitting as I do, expecting sorrow—is suffering it—I am going to Hall to be philosophizd with for a Week or ten Days on this point—but one hour with you would calm me more and furnish me with stronger Supports, under this weight upon my Spirits, than all the world—put together—Heaven! to what distressful Encountres hast thou thought fit to expose me—and was it not, that thou hast blessd me with a chearfulness of disposition—and thrown an Object in my Way, That is to render that Sun Shine perpetual—Thy dealings with me, would be a mystery.—

June 15—from morning to night every moment of this day held in Bondage at my friend Lord ffauconberg's°—so have but a moment. left to close the day, as I do every one—with wishing thee a sweet nights rest—would I was at the feet of your Bed—fanning breezes to You, in your Slumbers—Mark!—you will dream of me this night—and if it is not recorded in your Journal—Ill say, you could not recollect it the day following—adieu.—

June 16.

My Chaise is so large—so high—so long—so wide—so Crawford's like,°—That I am building a coach house on purpose for it—do you dislike it for this gigantick Size?—now I remember, I heard You once say—You hated a small post Chaise—which you must know determined my Choice to this—because I hope to make you a present of it—and if you are squeamish I shall be as squeamish as You, and return you all your presents—but one—which I cannot part with—and what that is—I defy you to guess. I have bought a milch Asse this Afternoon—and purpose to live by Suction, to save the expences of houskeeping—and have a Score or two guineas in my purse, next September——

June 17

I have brought your name *Eliza!* and Picture into my work— where they will remain—when You and I are at rest for ever—Some Annotator or explainer of my works in this place will take occasion, to speak of the Friendship which Subsisted so long and faithfully betwixt Yorick and the Lady he speaks of—Her Name he will tell the world was Draper—a Native of India—married there to a gentleman in the India Service of that Name—, who brought her over to England for the recovery of her health in the Year 65—where She continued to April the Year 1767. It was about three months before her Return to India, That our Author's acquaintance and hers began. Mrs Draper had a great thirst for Knowledge—was handsome—genteel—engaging—and of such gentle dispositions and so enlightend an understanding,—That Yorick, (whether he made much Opposition is not known) from an acquaintance—soon became her Admirer—they caught fire at each other at the same time—and they would often say, without reserve to the world, and without any Idea of saying wrong in it, That their Affections for each other were *unbounded*—Mr Draper dying in the Year *****—This Lady return'd to England, and Yorick the year after becoming a Widower—They were married—and retiring to one of his Livings in Yorkshire, where was a most romantic Situation—they lived and died happily.—and are spoke of with honour in the parish to this day—

June 18

How do you like the History, of this couple, Eliza?—is it to your mind?—or shall it be written better some sentimental Evening after your return—tis a rough Sketch—but I could make it a pretty picture, as the outlines are just—we'll put our heads together and try what we can do. This last Sheet° has put it out of my power, ever to send you this Journal to India—I had been more guarded—but that

You have often told me, 'twas in vain to think of writing by Ships which sail in March,—as you hoped to be upon your return again by their Arrival at Bombay—If I can write a Letter, I will—but this Journal must be put into Eliza's hands by Yorick only—God grant you to read it soon.—

June. 19. I never was so well and alert, as I find myself this day— tho' with a face as pale and clear as a Lady after her Lying in,° Yet you never saw me so Young by 5 Years If You do not leave Bombay soon—You'l find me as young as Yourself—at this rate of going on——Summon'd from home. adieu.

June 20

I think my dear Bramine—That nature is turn'd upside down— for Wives go to visit Husbands, at greater perils, and take longer journies to pay them this Civility now a days out of ill Will—than good—Mine is flying post° a Journey of a thousand Miles—with as many Miles to go back—merely to see how I do, and whether I am fat or lean—and how far are you going to see your Helpmate—and at such hazards to your Life, as few Wives' best affections would be able to surmount—But Duty and Submission Eliza govern thee—by what impulses my Rib° is bent towards me—I have told you—and yet I would to God, Draper but received and treated you with half the courtesy and good nature—I wish you was with him—for the same reason I wish my Wife at Coxwould—That She might the sooner depart in peace.°—She is ill—of a Diarhea which she has from a weakness on her bowels ever since her paralitic Stroke.—Travelling post in hot weather, is not the best remedy for her—but my girl says—she is determined to venture—She wrote me word in Winter, She would not leave france, till her end approach'd—surely this journey is not prophetick! but twould invert the order of Things on the other side of this *Leaf*°—and what is to be on the next Leaf—The Fates, Eliza only can tell us—rest satisfied.

June 21.

have left off all medcines—not caring to tear my frame to pieces with 'em—as I feel perfectly well.—set out for Crasy Castle° to morrow morning—where I stay ten days—take my sentimental Voyage—and this Journal with me, as certain as the two first Wheels of my Chariot—I cannot go on without them—I long to see Yours—I shall read it a thousand times over If I get it before your Arrival— What would I now give for it—tho' I know there are *circumstances* in it, That will make my heart bleed and waste within me—*but if all blows over*—tis enough—we will not recount our Sorrows, but to shed tears of Joy over them—O Eliza! Eliza!—Heaven nor any Being it created, ever so possessd a Man's heart—as thou possessest mine—use it kindly—Hussy—that is, eternally be true to it.—

June 22. Ive been as far as York to day with no Soul with me in my Chase, but your Picture—for it has a *Soul*, I think—or something like one which has talk'd to me, and been the best Company I ever took a Jou[r]ney with (always excepting a Journey I once took with a friend of Yours to Salt hill, and Enfield Wash°—The pleasure I had in those Journies, have left *Impressions* upon my Mind, which will last my Life—You may tell her as much when You see her—she will not take it ill—I set out early to morrow morning to see Mr Hall—but take my Journal along with me.

June 24th
as pleasant a Journey as I am capable of taking Eliza! without thee—Thou shalt take it with me, when time and tide serve here-after, and every other Journey which ever gave me pleasure, shall be rolled over again with thee besides me.—Arno's Vale shall look gay again upon Eliza's Visit.°—and the Companion of her Journey, will grow young again as he sits upon her Banks with Eliza seated besides him—I have this and a thousand little parties of pleasure—and sys-tems of living out of the common high road; of Life, hourly working in my fancy for you—there wants only the *Dramatis Pers*onee for the performance—the play is wrote—the Scenes are painted—and the Curtain ready to be drawn up.—the whole Piece waits for thee, my Eliza—

June 25.—In a course of continual visits and Invitations here°— *Bombay-Lascelles*° dined here to day—(his Wife yesterday brought to bed)—(he is a poor sorry soul! but has taken a house two miles from Crasy Castle—What a stupid, selfish, unsentimental set of Beings are the Bulk of our Sex! by Heaven! not one man out of 50, informd with feelings—or endow'd either with heads or hearts able to possess and fill the mind of such a Being as thee, with one Vibration like its own—I never See or converse with one of my Sex—but I give this point a reflection—how would such a creature please my Bramine? I assure thee Eliza I have not been able to find one, whom I thought could please You—the turn of Sentiment, with which I left your Character possess'd—must improve, hourly upon You—Truth, fidelity, honour and Love mix'd up with Delicacy, garrantee one another—and a taste so improved as Yours, by so delicious fare, can never degenerate—I shall find you, my Bramine, if possible, more valuable and lovely, than when You first caught my esteem and kindness for You—and tho' I see not this change—I give you so much Credit for it—that at this moment, my heart glowes more warmly as I think of you—and I find myself more your Husband than contracts can make us—I stay here till the 29th—had intended a longer Stay—but much company and Dissipation rob me of the only comfort my mind takes, which is in retirement, where I can think of You Eliza! and enjoy you quietly and without Interruption—tis the Way We must expect all that is to be had of *real* enjoyment in this vile world—which being miserable itself—seems so confederated against the happiness of the Happy,—that they are forced to secure it in private—Variety must still be had;—and that, Eliza! and every thing with it which Yorick's sense, or generosity has to furnish to one he loves so much as thee—need I tell thee—Thou wilt be as much a Mistress of—as thou art eternally of thy Yorick—adieu adieu.—

June 26. el[e]ven at night—out all the day—dined with a large Party—shewd your Picture from the fullness of my heart—highly admired—alas! said I—did You but see the Original!—good night.—

June 27.

Ten in the morning, with my Snuff open at the Top of this sheet,—and your gentle sweet face opposite to mine,° and saying 'what I write will be cordially read'—possibly you may be precisely engaged at this very hour, the same way—and telling me some interesting Story about your health, Your sufferings—your heartarches—and other Sensations which friendship—absence and Uncertainty create within You. for my own part, my dear Eliza, I am a prey to every thing in its turn—and was it not for that sweet clew° of hope which is perpetual[ly] opening me a Way which is to lead me to thee thro' all this Labyrinth—was it not for this, my Eliza! how could I find rest for this bewilderd heart of mine?—I should wait for you till September came—and if you did not arrive with it—should sicken and die.—but I will live for thee—so count me Immortal—3 India Men arrived within ten days—will none of 'em bring me Tidings of You?—but I am foolish—but ever thine—my dear, dear Bramine.—

June 28.

O What a tormenting night have my dreams led me about You Eliza—Mrs Draper a Widow!—with a hand at Liberty to give!—and gave it to another!—She told me—I must acquiesce—it could not be otherwise—Acquies[c]e! cried I, waking in agonies—God be prais'd cried I—tis a dream—fell asleep after—dreamd You was married to the Captain of the Ship—I waked in a fever—but 'twas the Fever in my blood which brought on this painful chain of Ideas—for I am ill to day—and for want of more cheary Ideas, I torment my Eliza with these—whose Sensibility will suffer, if Yorick could dream but of her Infidelity! and I suffer Eliza in my turn, and think my self at present little better than an old Woman or a Dreamer of Dreams in the Scripture Language°—I am going to ride myself into better health and better fancies, with Hall—whose Castle lying near the Sea—We have a Beach as even as a mirrour of 5 miles in Length, before it, where we dayly run races in our Chaises, with one wheel in the Sea, and the other on the Sand°—O Eliza, with what fresh ardour and impatience when I'm viewing this element, do I sigh for thy return—But I need no *memento*'s of my Destitution and misery, for want of thee—I carry them about me,—and shall not lay them down—(for I worship and Idolize these tender sorrows) till I meet thee upon the Beech and present the handkerchiefs staind with blood which broke out, from my heart upon your departure—This token of What I felt at that Crisis,° Eliza, shall never, never be wash'd out. Adieu my dear Wife—you are still mine—notwithstanding all the Dreams and Dreamers in the World.—Mr Lascells dined with us—Mem^d I have to tell you a Conversation—I will not write, it—.

June 29. am got home from Halls—to Coxwould—O 'tis a delicious retreat! both from its beauty, and air of Solitude; and so sweetly does every thing about it invite the mind to rest from its Labours and be at peace with itself and the world—That tis the only place, Eliza, I could live in at this juncture—I hope one day, you will like it as much as your Bramine—It shall be decorated and made more worthy of You—by the time, fate encourages me to look for you—I have made you, a sweet Sitting Room (as I told You) already—and am projecting a good Bed-chamber adjoi[ni]ng it, with a pretty dressing room for You, which connects them together—and when they are finishd, will be as sweet a set of romantic Apartments, as You ever beheld—the Sleeping room will be very large—The dressing room, thro' which You pass into your Temple, will be little—but Big enough to hold a dressing Table—a couple of chairs, with room for your Nymph° to stand at her ease both behind and on either side of you—with spare Room to hang a dozen petticoats—gowns, &c—and Shelves for as many Bandboxes°—Your little Temple I have described—and what it will hold—but if it ever it holds You and I, my Eliza—the Room will not be too little for us—but We shall be *too big* for the Room.—

June 30—Tis now a quarter of a year (wanting 3 days) since You sail'd from the Downs—in one month more—You will be (I trust,) at Madras—and there you will stay I suppose 2 long long months, before you set out for Bombay—Tis there I shall want to hear from you,—most impatiently—because the most interesting Letters, must come from Eliza when she is there—at present, I can hear of your health, and tho' that of all Accounts affects me most—yet still I have hopes taking their Rise from that—and those are—What Impression you can make upon Mr Draper, towards setting You at Liberty—and leaving you to pursue the best measures for Your preservation—and these are points, I would go to Aleppo,° to know certainly: I have been possess'd all day and night with an opinion, That Draper will change his behaviour totally towards you—That he will grow friendly and caressing—and as he know[s] your Nature is easily to be won with gentleness, he will practice it to turn you from your purpose of quitting him—In short when it comes to the point of your going from him to England—it will have so much the face, if not the reality, of an alienation on your side from India for-ever, as a place you cannot live at—that he will part with You by no means, he can prevent—You will be cajolled my dear Eliza thus out of your Life—but what serves it to write this, unless means can be found for You to read it—If you come not—I will take the Safest Cautions I can, to have it got to You—and risk every thing, rather than You should not know how much I think of You—and how much stronger hold You have got of me, than ever.—Dillon° has obtain'd his fair Indian—and has this post wrote a kind Letter of enquiry after Yorick and his Bramine—he is a good Soul—and interests himself much in our fate—I have wrote him a whole Sheet of paper about us—it ought to have been copied into this Journal—but the uncertainty of your ever reading it, makes me omit that, with a thousand other things, which when we meet, shall beguile us of many a long winters night.—*those precious Nights!*—my Eliza!—You rate them as high as I do.—and look back upon the manner the hours glided over our heads in them, with the same Interest and Delight as the man you *spent them with*—They are all that remains to us—except the *Expectation* of their return—the Space between is a dismal Void—full of doubts, and suspence——Heaven and its kindest Spirits, my dear, rest over your thoughts by day—and free them from all disturbance at night adieu. adieu Eliza!—I have got over this Month—so fare wel to it, and the Sorrows it has brought with it—the next month, I prophecy will be worse—

July 1.—But who can foretell what a a month may produce—Eliza—I have no less than seven different chances—not one of which is improbable—and any one of [which] would set me much at Liberty—and some of 'em render me compleatly happy—as they would facilitate and open the road to thee—What these chances are I leave thee to conjecture, my Eliza—some of them You cannot divine—tho' I once hinted them to You—but those are pecuniary chances arising out of my Prebend°—and so not likely to stick in thy brain—nor could they occupy mine a moment, but on thy account . . .: I hope before I meet thee Eliza on the Beach, to have every thing plann'd; that depends on me properly—and for what depends upon him who orders every Event for us, to him I leave and trust it—We shall be happy at last. I know—tis the Corner Stone of all my Castles—and tis all I bargain for. I am perfectly recoverd—or more than recover'd—for never did I feel such Indications of health or Strength and promptness of mind—notwithstanding the Cloud hanging over me, of a Visit—and all its tormenting consequences—Hall has wrote an affecting little poem upon it—the next time I see him, I will get it, and trans[cr]ibe it in this Journal, for You... He has persuaded me to trust her with no more than fifteen hundred pounds into—Franc—twil purchase 150 pounds a year—and to let the rest come annually from myself. the advice is wise enough, If I can get her Off with it—Ill summon up the Husband a little (if I can)—and keep the 500 pounds remaining for emergencies—Who knows, Eliza, what sort of Emergencies may cry out for it—I conceive some—and you Eliza are not backward in Conception—so may conceive others. *I wish I was in Arno's Vale!°*

July 2ᵈ—But I am in the Vale of Coxwould and wish You saw in how princely a manner I live in it—tis a Land of Plenty—I sit down

alone to Venison, fish or Wild foul—or a couple of dishes of fouls—
with Curds, and strawberrys and Cream, and all the simple clean
plenty which a rich Vally can produce—with a Bottle of wine on my
right hand (as in Bond street) to drink your health—I have a hundred hens and chickens about my yard—and not a parishoner
catches a hare a rabbit or a Trout—but he brings it as an Offering°—
In short tis a golden Vally—and will be the golden Age when You
govern the rural feast, my Bramine, and are the Mistress of my table
and spread it with elegancy and that natural grace and bounty with
which heaven has disti[n]guish'd You.

—Time goes on slowly—every thing stands still—hours seem
days and days seem years whilst you lengthen the Distance between
us—from Madras to Bombay—I shall think it shortening—and then
desire and expectation will be upon the rack again—come—come—
    July 3^{d}
Hail! Hail! my dear Eliza—I steal something every day from my
sentimental Journey—to obey a more sentimental impulse in writing
to you—and giving you the present Picture of myself—my wishes—
my Love, my sincerity—my hopes—my fears—tell me, have I varied
in any one Lineament, from the first Sitting—to this last—have I
been less warm—less tender and affectionate than you expected or
could have wish'd me in any one of 'em—or, however varied in the
expressions of what I was and what I felt, have I not still presented
the same air and face towards thee?—take it as a Sample of what I
ever shall be—My dear Bramine—and that is—such as my honour,
my Engagements and promisses and desires have fix'd me—I want
You to be on the other side of my little table, to hear how sweetly
your Voice will be in Unison to all this—I want to hear what You
have to say to Your Yorick upon this Text.—what heavenly Consolation would drop from your Lips and how pathetically you would
enforce your Truth and Love upon my heart to free it from every
Aching doubt—Doubt! did I say—but I have none—and as soon
would I doubt the Scripture I have preach'd on—as question thy
promisses, or Suppose one Thought in thy heart during thy absence
from me, unworthy of my Eliza.—for if thou art false, my
Bramine—the whole world—and Nature itself are lyars—and—I
will trust to nothing on this side of heaven—but turn aside from all
Commerce with expectation, and go quietly on my way alone
towards a State where no disappointments can follow me—you are

grieved when I talk thus; it implies what does not exist in either of us—so cross it out, if thou wilt—or leave it as a part of the picture of a heart that *again* Languishes for Possession—and is disturbed at every Idea of its Uncertainty.—So heaven bless thee—and ballance thy passions better than I have power to regulate mine—farewel my dear Girl—I sit in dread of tomorrows post which is to bring me an Account when *Madame* is to arrive.—

July 4th—Hear nothing of her—so am tortured from post to post, for I want to know certainly *the day and hour of this Judgment*—She is moreover ill, as my Lydia writes me word—and I'm impatient to know whether tis that—or what other Cause detains her, and keeps me in this vile state of Ignorance—I'm pitied by every Soul, in proportion as her Character is detested—and her Errand known— She is coming, every one says, to flea° poor Yorick or slay him—and I am spirited up by every friend I have to sell my Life dear, and fight valiantly in defence both of my property and Life—Now my Maxim, Eliza, is quietly in three [words]—'Spare my Life, and take all I have°—If She is not content to decamp with that—One kingdome shall not hold us—for If she will not betake herself to France—I will. but these, I verily believe my fears and nothing more—for she will be as impatient to quit England—as I could wish her—but of this—you will know more, before I have gone thro' this month's Journal.—I get 2000 pounds for my Estate—that is, I had the Offer this morning of it—and think tis enough.—when that is gone—I will begin saving for thee—but in Saving myself for thee, That and every other kind Act is implied.

—get on slowly with my Work—but my head is too full of other Matters—yet will I finish it before I see London—for I am of too scrupulous honour to break faith with the world°—great Authors make no scruple of it—but if they are great Authors—I'm sure they are little Men.—and I'm sure also of another Point which concerns yourself—and that is Eliza, that You shall never find me one hair breadth a less Man than you [*illegible deletion*]—farewell—I love thee eternally—

July 5. Two Letters from the South of France by this post, by which by some fatality, I find not one of my Letters have got to them this month—This gives me concern—because it has the Aspect of an unseasonable unkindness in me—to take no notice of what has the appearance at least of a Civility in desiring to pay me a Visit—my daughter besides has not deserved ill of me—and tho' her mother has, I would not ungenerously take that Opportunity, which would most overwhelm her, to give any mark of my resentment—I have besides long since forgiven her—and am the more inclined now as she proposes a plan, by which I shall never more be disquieted—in these 2 last, she renews her request to have leave to live where she has transfer'd her fortune—and purposes, with my leave she says, to end her days in the South of france—to all which I have just been writing her a Letter of Consolation and good will—and to crown my professions, entreat her to take post with my girl to be here time enough to enjoy York races—and so having done my duty to them—I continue writing, to do it to thee Eliza who art the *Woman of my heart*, and for whom I am ordering and planning this, and every thing else—be assured my Bramine that ere every thing is ripe for our Drama,—I shall work hard to fit out and decorate a little Theatre for us to act on—but not before a crouded house—no Eliza—it shall be as secluded as the elysian fields—retirement is the nurse of Love and kindness—and I will Woo and caress thee in it in such sort, that every thicket and grotto we pass by, *shall* sollicit the remembrance of the mutual pledges We have exchanged of Affection with one another—Oh! these expectations—make me sigh, as I recite them—and many a heart-felt Interjection! do they cost me, as I saunter alone in the tracks we are to tread together hereafter—still I think thy heart is with me—and whilst I think so, I prefer it to all the Society this world can offer—and tis in truth my dear oweing to this—That tho I've received half a dozen Letters to press me to join my friends at Scarborough—that I've found pretences not to quit You *here*—and sacrifice the many sweet Occasions I have of giving my thoughts up to You—, for Company I cannot rellish *since* I *have tasted* my dear Girl, the *sweets of thine.*—

July 6

Three long Months and three long days are pass'd and gone, since my Eliza sighed on taking her leave of Albions cliffs, and of all in Albion,° which was dear to her—How oft have I smarted at the Idea, of that last longing Look by which thou badest adieu to all thy heart Sufferd at that dismal Crisis°—twas the Separation of Soul and Body—and equal to nothing but what passes on that tremendous Moment.—and like it in one Consequence, that thou art in another World; where I would give a world, to follow thee, or hear even an

Account of thee—for this I shall write in a few days to our dear
friend Mrs James—she possibly may have heard a single Syllable or
two about You—but it cannot be; the same must have been directed
towards Yoricks ear, to whom you would have wrote the name of
Eliza, had there been no time for more. I would almost now compound with Fate,—and was I sure Eliza only breathd—I would
thank heaven and acquiesce. I kiss your Picture—your Shawl—and
every trinket I exchanged with You—every day I live—alas! I shall
soon be debarrd of that—in a fortnight I must lock them up and clap
my seal and yours upon them in the most secret Cabinet of my
Bureau—You may divine the reason, Eliza! adieu—adieu!

   July 7.

—But not Yet—for I will find means to write to you every night
whilst my people are here—if I sit up till midnight, till they are
asleep.—I should not dare to face you, if I was worse than my word
in the smallest Item—and this Journal I promised You Eliza should
be kept without a chasm of a day in it. and had I my time to myself
and nothing to do, but gratify my propensity—I should write from
sun rise to Sun set to thee—But a Book to write—a Wife to receive
and make Treaties with—an estate to sell—a Parish to super-
intend—and a disquieted heart perpetually to reason with, are
eternal calls upon me—and yet I have you more in my mind than
ever—and in proportion as I am thus torn from your embraces—*I
cling the closer to the Idea of you*—Your Figure is ever before my
eyes—the sound of your voice vibrates with its sweetest tones the
live long day in my ear—I can see and hear nothing but my Eliza.
remember this, when You think my Journal too short, and compare it
not with thine, which tho' it will exceed it in length, can do no more
than equal it in Love and truth of esteem—for esteem thee I do
beyond all the powers of eloquence to tell thee how much—and I
love thee my dear Girl, and prefer thy Love to me, more than the
whole world—

   night.—have not eat or drunk all day thro' vexation of heart at a
couple of ungrateful unfeeling Letters from that Quarter, from
whence, had it pleas'd God, I should have lookd for all my Comforts—but he has will'd they should come from the east—and he
knows how I am satisfyed with all his Dispensations—but with none,
my dear Bramine, so much as this—with which Cordial upon my
Spirits—I go to bed, in hopes of seeing thee in my Dreams.

July 8ᵗʰ

eating my fowl, and my trouts and my cream and my strawberries, as melancholly and sad as a Cat;° for want of you—by the by, I have got one which sits quietly besides me, purring all day to my sorrows—and looking up gravely from time to time in my face, as if she knew my Situation.—how soothable my heart is Eliza, when such little things sooth it! for in some pathetic sinkings I feel even some support from this poor Cat—I attend to her purrings—and think, they harmonize me—they are *pianissimo*° at least, and do not disturb me.—poor Yorick! to be driven, with all his sensibilities, to these resources—all powerful Eliza, that has had this Magical authority over him; to bend him thus to the dust—But I'll have my revenge, Hussy!

July 9. I have been all day making a sweet Pavillion in a retired Corner of my garden—but my Partner and Companion and friend for whom I make it, is fled from me, and when she return[s] to me again, Heaven who first brought us together, best knows—When that hour is foreknown What a Paradice will I plant for thee—till then I walk as Adam did whilst there was no help-meet found for it, and could almost wish a deep Sleep would come upon me till that Moment When I can say as he did—'*Behold the Woman Thou has given me for Wife*'° She shall be call'd La Bramine. Indeed Indeed Eliza! my Life will be little better than a dream, till we approach nearer to each other—I live scarse conscious of my existence—or as if I wanted a vital part; and could not live above a few hours. and yet I live, and live, and live on, for thy Sake, and the sake of thy truth to me; which I measure by my own,—and I fight against every evil and every danger, that I may be able to support and shelter thee from danger and evil also.—upon my word, dear Girl, thou owest me much—but tis cruel to dun° thee when thou art not in a condition to pay—I think Eliza has not run off in her Yoricks debt—

July 10.

I cannot suffer you to be longer upon the Water—in 10 days time, You shall be at Madrass—the element roles in my head as much as yours, and I am sick at the sight and smell of it—for all this, my Eliza, I feel in Imagination and so strongly—I can bear it no longer—on the 20ᵗʰ therefore Instant I begin to write to you as a terrestrial Being—I must deceive myself—and think so I will notwithstanding all that Lascelles has told me°—but there is no truth in him.—I have just kiss'd your picture—even that sooths many an anxiety—I have found out the Body is too little for the head—it shall not be rectified, till I sit by the Original, and direct the Painter's Pencil, and that done, will take a Scamper to *Enfield* and see your dear Children—if You tire by the Way, there are *one or two* places to rest at.—I never stand out. God bless thee. I am thine as *ever*

July 11.

Sooth me—calm me—pour thy healing Balm Eliza, into the sorest of hearts—I'm pierced with the Ingratitude and unquiet Spirit of a restless unreasonable Wife whom neither gentleness or generosity can conquer—She has now enterd upon a new plan of waging War with me, a thousand miles off—thrice a week this last month, has the quietest man under heaven been outraged by her Letters—I have offer'd to give her every Shilling I was worth, except my preferment, to be let alone and left in peace by her—Bad Woman! nothing must now purchase this, unless I borrow 400 pounds to give her and carry into france more—I would perish first, my Eliza! e're I would give her a shilling of another man's, which I must do if I give her a Shilling more than I am worth.

—How I now feel the want of thee! my dear Bramine—my generous unworldly honest Creature—I shall die for want of thee for a thousand reasons—every emergency and every Sorrow each day brings along with it—tells me what a Treasure I am bereft off,—whilst I want thy friendship and Love to keep my head up from sinking—Gods will be done. but I think she will send me to my grave.—She will now keep me in torture till the end of September——and writing me word to day—she will delay her Journey two Months beyond her first Intention—it keeps me in eternal Suspence all the while—for she will come unawars at last upon me—and then adieu to the dear sweets of my retirement.

How cruelly are our Lots drawn, my dear—both made for happiness—and neither of us made to taste it! In feeling so acutely for my own disappointment I drop blood for thine, I call thee in, to my Aid—and thou wantest mine as much—Were we together we should recover—but never, never till then *nor by any other Recipe*.—

July 12.

am ill all day with the Impressions of Yesterdays account.—can neither eat or drink or sit still and write or read—I walk like a disturbed Spirit about my Garden—calling upon heaven and thee, to come to my Succour—couldst thou but write one word to me, it would be worth the world to me—my friends write me millions— and every one invites me to flee from my Solitude and come to them—I obey the commands of my friend Hall who has sent over on purpose to fetch me—or he will come himself for me—so I set off to morrow morning to take Sanctuary in Crasy Castle—The news papers have sent me there already by putting in the following paragraph.

'We hear from Yorkshire, That Skelton Castle is the present Rendevouz, of the most brilliant Wits of the Age—the admired Author of Tristram—Mr Garrick &c. been ing there, and Mr Coleman and many other men of Wit and Learning being every day expected'°—when I get there, which will be to morrow night, My Eliza will hear from her Yorick—her Yorick—who loves her more than ever.

July 13. Skelton Castle. Your picture has gone round the Table after supper—and your health after it, my invaluable friend!—even the Ladies, who hate grace in another, seemd struck with it in You— but Alas! you are as a dead Person—and Justice, (as in all such Cases,) is paid you in course—when thou returnest it will be render'd more Sparingly—but I'll make up all deficiencies—by honouring You more than ever Woman was honourd by man—every good Quality That ever good heart possess'd—thou possessest my dear Girl, and so sovereignly does thy temper and sweet sociability, which harmonize all thy other properties make me thine, that whilst thou art true to thyself and thy Bramin—he thinks thee worth a world—and would give a World was he master of it, for the undisturbed possession of thee—Time and Chance° are busy throwing this Die° for me—a fortunate Cast, or two, at the most, makes our fortune—it gives us each other—and then for the World—I will not give a pinch of Snuff.—Do take care of thyself—keep this prospect before thy eyes—have a view to it in all your Transactions, Eliza,— In a word Remember You are mine—and stand answerable for all you say and do to me—I govern myself by the same Rule—and such a History of myself can I lay before you, as shall create no blushes, but those of pleasure—tis midnight—and so sweet Sleep to thee the remai[ni]ng hours of it. I am more thine, my dear Eliza! than ever— but that cannot be—

July 14.

dining and feasting all day at Mr Turner's—his Lady a fine
Woman herself,° in love with your picture—O my dear Lady, cried I,
did you but know the Original—but what is she to you, Tristram—
nothing; but that I am in Love with her—et caetera°——said She—
no I have given over dashes—replied I——I verily think my Eliza I
shall get this Picture set, so as to wear it, as I first purposed—about
my neck—I do not like the place tis in°—it shall be nearer my heart—
Thou art ever in its centre—good night—

July 15. From home. (Skelton Castle) from 8 in the morning till
late at Supper—I seldom have put thee so off, my dear Girl—and yet
to morrow will be as bad—.

July 16. for Mr Hall has this Day left his Crasy Castle to come and
sojourn with me at Shandy Hall° for a few days—for so they have
long christend our retired Cottage—we are just arrived at it—and
whilst he is admiring the premisses—I have stole away to converse a
few minutes with thee, and in thy own dressing room—for I make
every thing thine and call it so, before hand, that thou art to be
mistress of hereafter. This *Hereafter*, Eliza, is but a melancholly
term—but the Certainty of its coming to us, brightens it up—pray
do not forget my prophecy in the Dedication of the Almanack—I
have the utmost faith in it myself—but by what impulse my mind
was struck with 3 Years—heaven, whom I believe it's author, best
knows—but I shall see your face before—but that I leave to You—
and to the Influence such a Being must have over all inferior ones—
We are going to dine with the Arch Bishop to morrow—and from
thence to Harrogate for three days, whilst thou dear Soul art pent up
in sultry Nastiness—without Variety or change of face or Conversation—Thou shalt have enough of both when I cater for thy happiness Eliza—and if an Affectionate husband and 400 pounds a year in
a sweeter Vally than that of Jehosophat° will do—less thou shalt never
have—but I hope more—and were it millions, tis the same—twould
be laid at thy feet—Hall is come in in raptures with every thing—
and so I shut up my Journal for to day and tomorrow for I shall not
be able to open it where I go—adieu my dear Girl—

18—was yesterday all the day with our Archbishop°—this good
Prelate, who is one of our most refined Wits—and the most of a
gentleman of our order—oppresses me with his kindness—he shews
in his treatment of me, what he told me upon taking my Leave—that

he loves me, and has a high Value for me—his Chaplains tell me, he is perpetually talking of me—and has such an Opinion of my head and heart that he begs to stand Godfather for my next Literary production—so has done me the honour of putting his name in a List° which I am most proud of because my Eliza's name is in it—I have just a moment to scrawl this to thee, being at York—where I want to be employd in taking you a little house, where the prophet may be accommodated with a '*Chamber in the Wall apart, with a stool and a Candlestick*'°—where his Soul can be at rest from the distractions of the world, and lean only upon his kind hostesse, and repose all his Cares, and melt them *along with hers* in her sympathetic bosom.

July 19. Harrogate Spaws.—drinking the waters here° till the 26th—to no effect, but a cold dislike of every one of your sex.—I did nothing, but make comparisons betwixt thee my Eliza, and every woman I saw and talk'd to—thou has made me so unfit for every one else—than I am thine as much from necessity, as Love—I am thine by a thousand sweet ties, the least of which shall never be relax'd— be assured my dear Bramine of this—and repay me in so doing, the Confidence I repose in thee—your Absence, your distresses, your sufferings; your conflicts; all make me rely but the more upon that fund in you, which is able to sustain so much weight—Providence I know will relieve you from one part of it—and it shall be the pleasure of my days to ease my dear friend of the other—I Love thee Eliza, more than the heart of Man ever loved Woman's—I even love thee more than I did, the day thou badest me farewel!—Farewell!— Farewell! to thee again—I'm going from hence to York. Races.°—

July 27. arrived at York.—where I had not been 2 hours before My heart was overset with a pleasure, which beggard every other, that fate could give me—save thyself—It was thy dear Packets from Iago°—I cannot give vent to all the emotions I felt even before I opend them—for I knew thy hand—and my seal,—which was only in thy possession.—O tis from my Eliza, said I.—I instantly shut the door of my Bed-Chamber, and orderd myself to be denied—and spent the whole evening, and till dinner the next day, in reading over and over again the most interesting Account—and the most endearing one, that ever tried the tenderness of man—I read and wept— and wept and read till I was blind—then grew sick, and went to bed—and in an hour calld again for the Candle—to read it once more—as for my dear Girls pains and her dangers I cannot write about them—because I cannot write my feelings or express them any how to my mind—O Eliza! but I will talk them over with thee with a sympathy that shall woo thee, so much better than I have ever done—That we will both be gainers in the end—'*Ill love thee for the dangers thou hast past*°—and thy Affection shall go hand in hand with me, because I'll pity thee—as no man ever pitied Woman—but Love like mine is never satisfied—else your second Letter from Iago—is a Letter so warm, so simple, so tender! I defy the world to produce such another—by all thats kind and gracious! I will so entreat thee Eliza! so k[i]ndly—that thou shalt say, I merit much of it—nay all—for my merit to thee, is my truth.

I now want to have this week of nonsensical Festivity over°—that I may get back, with thy picture which I ever carry about me—to my retreat and to Cordelia—when the days of our Afflictions are over, I oft amuse my fancy, with an Idea, that thou wilt come down to me by Stealth, and hearing where I have walk'd out to—surprize me some sweet moon Shiney Night at Cordelia's grave, and catch me in thy Arms over it—O My Bramin! my Bramin!—

July 31. am tired to death with the hurrying pleasures of these Races—I want still and *silent* ones—so return home tomorrow, in search of them—I shall find them as I sit contemplating over thy passive picture; sweet Shadow! of what is to come! for tis all I can now grasp—first and best of Woman kind! remember me, as I remember thee—tis asking a great deal, my Bramine!—but I cannot be satisfied with less—farwell—fare—happy till fate will let me cherish thee myself.—O my Eliza! thou writest to me with an Angels pen—and thou wouldst win me by thy Letters, had I never seen thy face, or known thy heart.

August 1. what a sad Story thou hast told me of thy Sufferings and Despondences, from St Iago, till thy meeting with the Dutch Ship°—twas a sympathy above Tears—I trembled every Nerve as I went from line to line—and every moment the Account comes across me—I suffer all I felt, over and over again—will providence suffer all this anguish without end—and without pity?—'*it no can be*'°—I am tried my dear Bramine in the furnace of Affliction° as much as thou—by the time we meet, We shall be fit only for each other—and should cast away upon any other Harbour.

August 2. my wife—uses me most unmercifully—every Soul advises me to fly from her—but where can I fly If I fly not to thee?

The Bishop of Cork and Ross° has made me great Offers in Ireland—but I will take no step without thee—and till heaven opens us some track—He is the best of feeling tender hearted men—knows our Story—sends You his Blessing—and says if the Ship you return in touches at Cork (which many India men do)—he will take you to his palace, till he can send for me to join You—he only hopes, he says, to join us together for ever—but more of this good Man, and his attachment to me—hereafter and of a couple of Ladies in the family &c. &c.

August 3rd

I have had an offer of exchanging two pieces of preferment I hold here (but sweet Cordelia's Parish is not one of 'em) for a living of 350 pounds a year in Surry about 30 miles from London—and retaining Coxwould and my Prebendaryship—which are half as much more—the Country also is sweet—but I will not—I cannot take any step unless I had thee my Eliza for whose sake I live, to consult with—and till the road is open for me as my heart wishes to advance—with thy sweet light Burden in my Arms, I could get up fast the hill of preferment, if I chose it—but without thee I feel Lifeless—and if a Mitre was offer'd me, I would not have it, till I could have thee too, to make it sit easy upon my brow°—I want kindly to smooth thine, and not only wipe away thy tears but dry up the Sourse of them for ever°—

—August 4°—Hurried backwards and forwards about the arrival of Madame, this whole week—and then farewel I fear to this journal—till I get up to London—and can pursue it as I wish. at present all I can write would be but the History of my miserable feelings—She will be ever present—and if I take up my pen for thee—something will jarr within me as I do it—that I must lay it down again—I will give you one general Account of all my sufferings together—but not in Journals—I shall set my wounds a-bleeding every day afresh by it—and the Story cannot be too short.—so worthiest, best, kindest and [most] affectionate of Souls farewell—every Moment will I have thee present—and sooth my sufferings with the looks my fancy shall cloath thee in.—Thou shalt lye down and rise up with me—about my bed and about my paths, and shalt see out all my Ways.—adieu—adieu—and remember one eternal truth, My dear Bramine, which is not the worse, because I have told it thee a thousand times before—That I am thine—and thine only, and for ever.

L. Sterne

November 1st.° All my dearest Eliza has turnd out more favourable than my hopes—M^rs S—— and my dear Girl have been 2 Months° with me and they have this day left me to go to spend the Winter at York, after having settled every thing to their hearts content—Mrs Sterne retired into france, whence she purposes not to stir, till her death—and never, has she vow'd, will give me another sorrowful or discontented hour—I have conquerd her, as I would every one else, by humanity and Generosity—and she leaves me, more than half in Love with me—She goes into the South of france, her health being insupportable in England—and her age, as she now confesses ten Years more, than I thought—being on the edge of sixty°—so God bless—and make the remainder of her Life happy— in order to which I am to remit her three hundred guineas a year— and give my dear Girl two thousand pounds—which with all Joy, I agree to,—but tis to be sunk into an annuity in the french Loans—

—And now Eliza! Let me talk to thee—But What can I say, What can I write—But the Yearnings of heart wasted with looking and wishing for thy Return—Return—Return! my dear Eliza! May heaven smooth the Way for thee to send thee safely to us, and soj[ourn] for Ever

A Political Romance,

Addressed

To ——— ———, *Esq ;*

OF *YORK*.

To which is subjoined a
KEY.

Ridiculum acri
Fortius et melius magnas plerumque secat Res.°

A POLITICAL ROMANCE, &c.

SIR,

IN my last, for want of something better to write about, I told you what a World of Fending and Proving° we have had of late, in this little Village of ours, about an *old-cast-Pair-of-black-Plush-Breeches*,° which *John*, our Parish-Clerk, about ten Years ago, it seems, had made a Promise of to one *Trim*,° who is our Sexton and Dog-Whipper.——To this you write me Word, that you have had more than either one or two Occasions to know a good deal of the shifty Behaviour of this said Master *Trim*,—and that you are astonished, nor can you for your Soul conceive, how so worthless a Fellow, and so worthless a Thing into the Bargain, could become the Occasion of such a Racket as I have represented.

Now, though you do not say expressly, you could wish to hear any more about it, yet I see plain enough that I have raised your Curiosity; and therefore, from the same Motive, that I slightly mentioned it at all in my last Letter, I will, in this, give you a full and very circumstantial Account of the whole Affair.

But, before I begin, I must first set you right in one very material Point, in which I have missled you, as to the true Cause of all this Uproar amongst us;——which does not take its Rise, as I then told you, from the Affair of the *Breeches*;—but, on the contrary, the whole Affair of the *Breeches* has taken its Rise from it:——To understand which, you must know, that the first Beginning of the Squabble was not between *John* the Parish-Clerk and *Trim* the Sexton, but betwixt the Parson of the Parish and the said Master *Trim*, about an old *Watch-Coat*,° which had many Years hung up in the Church, which *Trim* had set his Heart upon; and nothing would serve *Trim* but he must take it home, in order to have it converted into a *warm Under-Petticoat* for his Wife, and a *Jerkin* for himself, against Winter; which, in a plaintive Tone, he most humbly begg'd his Reverence would consent to.

I need not tell you, Sir, who have so often felt it, that a Principle of strong Compassion transports a generous Mind sometimes beyond what is strictly right,—the Parson was within an Ace of being an honourable Example of this very Crime;—for no sooner

did the distinct Words—*Petticoat*——*poor Wife*——*warm*——
Winter strike upon his Ear,——but his Heart warmed,—and,
before *Trim* had well got to the End of his Petition, (being a
Gentleman of a frank and open Temper) he told him he was
welcome to it, with all his Heart and Soul. But, *Trim*, says he, as
you see I am but just got down to my Living, and am an utter
Stranger to all Parish-Matters, know nothing about this old Watch-
Coat you beg of me, having never seen it in my Life, and therefore
cannot be a Judge whether 'tis fit for such a Purpose; or, if it is, in
Truth, know not whether 'tis mine to bestow upon you or not;——
you must have a Week or ten Days Patience, till I can make some
Inquiries about it;—and, if I find it is in my Power, I tell you again,
Man, your Wife is heartily welcome to an Under-Petticoat out
of it, and you to a Jerkin, was the Thing as good again as you
represent it.

It is necessary to inform you, Sir, in this Place, That the Parson
was earnestly bent to serve *Trim* in this Affair, not only from the
Motive of Generosity, which I have justly ascribed to him, but likewise from another Motive; and that was by way of making some Sort
of Recompence for a Multitude of small Services which *Trim* had
occasionally done, and indeed was continually doing, (as he was
much about the House) when his own Man was out of the Way. For
all these Reasons together, I say, the Parson of the Parish intended to
serve *Trim* in this Matter to the utmost of his Power: All that was
wanting was previously to inquire, if any one had a *Claim* to it;—or
whether, as it had, Time immemorial, hung up in the Church, the
taking it down might not raise a Clamour in the Parish. These
Inquiries were the very Thing that *Trim* dreaded in his Heart.—He
knew very well that if the Parson should but say one Word to the
Church-Wardens about it, there would be an End of the whole
Affair. For this, and some other Reasons not necessary to be told you,
at present, *Trim* was for allowing no Time in this Matter;—but, on
the contrary, doubled his Diligence and Importunity at the Vicarage-
House;—plagued the whole Family to Death;—pressed his Suit
Morning, Noon, and Night; and, to shorten my Story, teazed the
poor Gentleman, who was but in an ill State of Health, almost out of
his Life about it.

You will not wonder, when I tell you, that all this Hurry and
Precipitation, on the Side of Master *Trim*, produced its natural

Effect on the Side of the Parson, and that was, a Suspicion that all was not right at the Bottom.

He was one Evening sitting alone in his Study, weighing and turning this Doubt every Way in his Mind; and, after an Hour and a half's serious Deliberation upon the Affair, and running over *Trim*'s Behaviour throughout,—he was just saying to himself, *It must be so*;—when a sudden Rap at the Door put an End to his Soliloquy,—and, in a few Minutes, to his Doubts too; for a Labourer in the Town, who deem'd himself past his fifty-second Year, had been returned by the Constable in the Militia-List,°—and he had come, with a Groat° in his Hand, to search the Parish Register for his Age.—The Parson bid the poor Fellow put the Groat into his Pocket, and go into the Kitchen:—Then shutting the Study Door, and taking down the Parish Register,—*Who knows*, says he, *but I may find something here about this self-same Watch-Coat?*—He had scarce unclasped the Book, in saying this, when he popp'd upon the very Thing he wanted, fairly wrote on the first Page, pasted to the Inside of one of the Covers, whereon was a Memorandum about the very Thing in Question, in these express Words:

MEMORANDUM

The great Watch-Coat was purchased and given above two hundred Years ago, by the Lord of the Manor,° to this Parish-Church, to the sole Use and Behoof of the poor Sextons thereof, and their Successors, for ever, to be worn by them respectively in winterly cold Nights, in ringing Complines, Passing-Bells,° &c. **which the said Lord of the Manor had done, in Piety, to keep the poor Wretches warm, and for the good of his own Soul, for which they were directed to pray,** &c. &c. &c. &c. *Just Heaven!* said the Parson to himself, looking upwards, *What an Escape have I had! Give this for an Under-Petticoat to* Trim'*s Wife! I would not have consented to such a Desecration to be Primate of all* England; *nay, I would not have disturb'd a single Button of it for half my Tythes!*°

Scarce were the Words out of his Mouth, when in pops *Trim* with the whole Subject of the Exclamation under both his Arms.—I say, under both his Arms;—for he had actually got it ripp'd and cut out ready, his own Jerkin under one Arm, and the Petticoat under the other, in order to be carried to the Taylor to be made up,—and had just stepp'd in, in high Spirits, to shew the Parson how cleverly it had held out.

There are many good Similies now subsisting in the World, but which I have neither Time to recollect or look for, which would give you a strong Conception of the Astonishment and honest Indignation which this unexpected Stroke of *Trim*'s Impudence impress'd upon the Parson's Looks.—Let it suffice to say, That it exceeded all fair Description,—as well as all Power of proper Resentment,—— except this, that *Trim* was ordered, in a stern Voice, to lay the Bundles down upon the Table,—to go about his Business, and wait upon him, at his Peril, the next Morning at Eleven precisely:—Against° this Hour, like a wise Man, the Parson had sent to desire *John* the Parish-Clerk, who bore an exceeding good Character as a Man of Truth, and who having, moreover, a pretty Freehold of about eighteen Pounds a Year in the Township, was a leading Man in it; and, upon the whole, was such a one of whom it might be said,—That he rather did Honour to his Office,—than that his Office did Honour to him.—Him he sends for, with the Church-Wardens, and one of the Sides-Men, a grave, knowing, old Man,° to be present:—For as *Trim* had with-held the whole Truth from the Parson, touching the Watch-Coat, he thought it probable he would as certainly do the same Thing to others; though this, I said, was wise, the Trouble of the Precaution might have been spared,—because the Parson's Character was unblemish'd,—and he had ever been held by the World in the Estimation of a Man of Honour and Integrity.—*Trim*'s Character, on the contrary, was as well known, if not in the World, yet, at least, in all the Parish, to be that of a little, dirty, pimping, pettifogging, ambidextrous° Fellow,—who neither cared what he did or said of any, provided he could get a Penny by it.—This might, I say, have made any Precaution needless;—but you must know, as the Parson had in a Manner but just got down to his Living,° he dreaded the Consequences of the least ill Impression on his first Entrance amongst his Parishioners, which would have disabled him from doing them the Good he wished;—so that, out of Regard to his Flock, more than the necessary Care due to himself,—he was resolv'd not to lie at the Mercy of what Resentment might vent, or Malice lend an Ear to.—Accordingly the whole Matter was rehearsed from first to last by the Parson, in the Manner I've told you, in the Hearing of *John* the Parish-Clerk, and in the Presence of *Trim*.

Trim had little to say for himself, except 'That the Parson had absolutely promised to befriend him and his Wife in the Affair, to the utmost of his Power: That the Watch-Coat was certainly in his Power, and that he might still give it him if he pleased.'

To this, the Parson's Reply was short, but strong, 'That nothing was in his *Power* to do, but what he could do *honestly*:—That in giving the Coat to him and his Wife, he should do a manifest Wrong to the *next* Sexton; the great Watch-Coat being the most comfortable Part of the Place:—That he should, moreover, injure the Right of his own Successor, who would be just so much a worse Patron, as the Worth of the Coat amounted to;—and, in a Word, he declared, that his whole Intent in promising that Coat, was Charity to *Trim*; but *Wrong* to no Man; that was a Reserve, he said, made in all Cases of this Kind:—and he declared solemnly, *in Verbo Sacerdotis*,° That this was his Meaning, and was so understood by *Trim* himself.'

With the Weight of this Truth, and the great good Sense and strong Reason which accompanied all the Parson said upon the Subject,—poor *Trim* was driven to his last Shift,—and begg'd he might be suffered to plead his Right and Title to the Watch-Coat, if not by *Promise*, at least by *Services*.—It was well known how much he was entitled to it upon these Scores: That he had black'd the Parson's Shoes without Count, and greased his Boots above fifty Times:— That he had run for Eggs into the Town upon all Occasions;—— whetted° the Knives at all Hours;—catched his Horse and rubbed him down:——That for his Wife she had been ready upon all Occasions to charr° for them;—and neither he nor she, to the best of his Remembrance, ever took a Farthing, or any thing beyond a Mug of Ale.—To this Account of his Services he begg'd Leave to add those of his Wishes, which, he said, had been equally great.—He affirmed, and was ready, he said, to make it appear, by Numbers of Witnesses, 'He had drank his Reverence's Health a thousand Times, (by the bye, he did not add out of the Parson's own Ale): That he not only drank his Health, but wish'd it; and never came to the House, but ask'd his Man kindly how he did; that in particular, about half a Year ago, when his Reverence cut his Finger in paring an Apple, he went half a Mile to ask a cunning Woman, what was good to stanch Blood, and actually returned with a Cob-web in his Breeches Pocket:——

Nay, says *Trim*, it was not a Fortnight ago, when your Reverence took that violent Purge, that I went to the far End of the whole Town to borrow you a Close-stool,°—and came back, as my Neighbours, who flouted me, will all bear witness, with the Pan upon my Head, and never thought it too much.'

Trim concluded his pathetick Remonstrance with saying, 'He hoped his Reverence's Heart would not suffer him to requite so many faithful Services by so unkind a Return:—That if it was so, as he was the first, so he hoped he should be the last, Example of a Man of his Condition so treated.'——This Plan of *Trim*'s Defence, which *Trim* had put himself upon,—could admit of no other Reply but a general Smile.

Upon the whole, let me inform you, That all that could be said, *pro* and *con*, on both Sides, being fairly heard, it was plain, That *Trim*, in every Part of this Affair, had behaved very ill;——and *one* Thing, which was never expected to be known of him, happening in the Course of this Debate to come out against him;—namely, That he had gone and told the Parson, before he had ever set Foot in his Parish, That *John* his Parish-Clerk,—his Church-Wardens, and some of the Heads of the Parish, were a Parcel of Scoundrels.—Upon the Upshot, *Trim* was kick'd out of Doors; and told, at his Peril, never to come there again.

At first *Trim* huff'd and bounced most terribly;—swore he would get a Warrant;—then nothing would serve him but he would call° a Bye-Law, and tell the whole Parish how the Parson had misused him;—but cooling of that, as fearing the Parson might possibly bind him over to his good Behaviour, and, for aught he knew, might send him to the House of Correction,—he let the Parson alone; and, to revenge himself, falls foul upon his Clerk, who had no more to do in the Quarrel than you or I;—rips up the Promise of the old-cast-Pair-of-black-Plush-Breeches, and raises an Uproar in the Town about it,° notwithstanding it had slept ten Years.—But all this, you must know, is look'd upon in no other Light, but as an artful Stroke of Generalship in *Trim*, to raise a Dust, and cover himself under the disgraceful Chastisement he has undergone.

If your Curiosity is not yet satisfied,—I will now proceed to relate the *Battle* of the Breeches,° in the same exact Manner I have done *that* of the Watch-Coat.

Be it known then, that, about ten Years ago, when *John* was appointed Parish-Clerk of this Church, this said Master *Trim* took no small Pains to get into *John*'s good Graces; in order, as it afterwards appeared, to coax a Promise out of him of a Pair of Breeches, which *John* had then by him, of black Plush, not much the worse for wearing;—*Trim* only begging for God's Sake to have them bestowed upon him when *John* should think fit to cast them.

Trim was one of those kind of Men who loved a Bit of Finery in his Heart, and would rather have a tatter'd Rag of a Better Body's, than the best plain whole Thing his Wife could spin him.

John, who was naturally unsuspicious, made no more Difficulty of promising the Breeches, than the Parson had done in promising the Great Coat; and, indeed, with something less Reserve,——because the Breeches were *John*'s *own*, and he could give them, without Wrong, to whom he thought fit.

It happened, I was going to say unluckily, but, I should rather say, most luckily, for *Trim*, for he was the only Gainer by it,—that a Quarrel, about some six or eight Weeks after this, broke out between *the late* Parson of the Parish° and *John* the Clerk. Somebody (and it was thought to be Nobody but *Trim*) had put it into the Parson's Head, 'That *John*'s Desk in the Church was, at the least, four Inches higher than it should be:°——That the Thing gave Offence, and was indecorous, inasmuch as it approach'd too near upon a Level with the Parson's Desk itself. This Hardship the Parson complained of loudly,—and told *John* one Day after Prayers,—'He could bear it no longer:—And would have it alter'd and brought down as it should be.' *John* made no other Reply, but, 'That the Desk was not of his raising:——That 'twas not one Hair Breadth higher than he found it;—and that as he found it, so would he leave it:——In short, he would neither make an Encroachment, nor would he suffer one.'

The *late* Parson might have his Virtues, but the leading Part of his Character was not *Humility*; so that *John*'s Stiffness in this Point was not likely to reconcile Matters.—This was *Trim*'s Harvest.

After a friendly Hint to *John* to stand his Ground,—away hies *Trim* to make his Market° at the Vicarage:——What pass'd there, I will not say, intending not to be uncharitable; so shall content myself with only guessing at it, from the sudden Change that appeared in *Trim*'s Dress for the better;—for he had left his old ragged Coat, Hat and Wig, in the Stable, and was come forth strutting across the Church-yard, y'clad in a good creditable cast Coat,° large Hat and

Wig, which the Parson had just given him.——Ho! Ho! Hollo! *John!* cries *Trim*, in an insolent Bravo, as loud as ever he could bawl—See here, my Lad! how fine I am.——The more Shame for you, answered *John*, seriously.—Do you think, *Trim*, says he, such Finery, gain'd by such Services, becomes you, or can wear well?—Fye upon it, *Trim*;—I could not have expected this from you, considering what Friendship you pretended, and how kind I have ever been to you:—How many Shillings and Sixpences I have generously lent you in your Distresses?—Nay, it was but t'other Day that I promised you these black Plush Breeches I have on.——Rot your Breeches, quoth *Trim*; for *Trim*'s Brain was half turn'd with his new Finery:—Rot your Breeches, says he,—I would not take them up, were they laid at my Door;—give 'em, and be d——d to you, to whom you like;——I would have you to know I can have a better Pair at the Parson's any Day in the Week:——*John* told him plainly, as his Word had once pass'd him, he had a Spirit above taking Advantage of his Insolence, in giving them away to another:—But, to tell him his Mind freely, he thought he had got so many Favours of that Kind, and was so likely to get many more for the same Services, of the Parson, that he had better give up the Breeches, with good Nature, to some one who would be more thankful for them.

Here *John* mentioned *Mark Slender*,° (who, it seems, the Day before, had ask'd *John* for 'em) not knowing they were under Promise to *Trim*.——'Come, *Trim*, says he, let poor *Mark* have 'em,——You know he has not a Pair to his A——: Besides, you see he is just of my Size, and they will fit him to a T; whereas, if I give 'em to you,—look ye, they are not worth much; and, besides, you could not get your Backside into them, if you had them, without tearing them all to Pieces.'

Every Tittle of this was most undoubtedly true; for *Trim*, you must know, by foul Feeding, and playing the good Fellow at the Parson's, was grown somewhat gross about the lower Parts, *if not higher:* So that, as all *John* said upon the Occasion was fact, *Trim*, with much ado, and after a hundred Hum's and Hah's, at last, out of mere Compassion to *Mark, signs, seals, and delivers up* **all Right, Interest, and Pretensions whatsoever, in and to the said Breeches; thereby binding his Heirs, Executors, Administrators and Assignes, never more to call the said Claim in Question.**

All this Renunciation was set forth in an ample Manner, to be in pure Pity to *Mark*'s Nakedness;—but the Secret was, *Trim* had an Eye to, and firmly expected in his own Mind, the great Green Pulpit-Cloth and old Velvet Cushion,° which were that very Year to be taken down;—which, by the Bye, could he have wheedled *John* a second Time out of 'em, as he hoped, he had made up the Loss of his Breeches Seven-fold.

Now, you must know, this Pulpit-Cloth and Cushion were not in *John*'s Gift, but in the Church-Wardens, &c.—However, as I said above, that *John* was a leading Man in the Parish, *Trim* knew he could help him to them if he would:—But *John* had got a Surfeit of him;—so, when the Pulpit-Cloth, &c. were taken down, they were immediately given (*John* having a great Say in it) to *William Doe*,° who understood very well what Use to make of them.

As for the old Breeches, poor *Mark Slender* lived to wear them but a short Time, and they got into the Possession of *Lorry Slim*,° an unlucky Wight, by whom they are still worn;——in Truth, as you will guess, they are very thin by this Time:—But *Lorry* has a light Heart; and what recommends them to him, is this, that, as thin as they are, he knows that *Trim*, let him say what he will to the contrary, still envies the *Possessor* of them,—and, with all his Pride, would be very glad to wear them after *him*.

Upon this Footing have these Affairs slept quietly for near ten Years,——and would have slept for ever, but for the unlucky Kicking-Bout; which, as I said, has ripp'd this Squabble up afresh: So that it was no longer ago than last Week, that *Trim* met and insulted *John* in the public Town-Way, before a hundred People;—tax'd him with the Promise of the old-cast-Pair-of-black-Breeches, notwithstanding *Trim*'s solemn Renunciation; twitted him with the Pulpit-Cloth and Velvet Cushion,—as good as told him, he was ignorant of the common Duties of his Clerkship; adding, very insolently, That he knew not so much as to give out a common Psalm in Tune.——

John contented himself with giving a plain Answer to every Article that *Trim* had laid to his Charge, and appealed to his Neighbours who remembered the whole Affair;—and as he knew there was never any Thing to be got in wrestling with a Chimney-Sweeper,—he was going to take Leave of *Trim* for ever.——But, hold,—the Mob by this Time had got round them, and their High Mightinesses insisted upon having *Trim* tried upon the Spot.—*Trim* was accordingly tried;

and, after a full Hearing, was convicted a second Time, and handled more roughly by one or more of them, than even at the Parson's.

Trim, says one, are you not ashamed of yourself, to make all this Rout and Disturbance in the Town, and set Neighbours together by the Ears, about an old-worn-out-Pair-of-cast-Breeches, not worth Half a Crown?——Is there a cast-Coat, or a Place in the whole Town, that will bring you in a Shilling, but what you have snapp'd up, like a greedy Hound as you are?

In the first Place, are you not Sexton and Dog-Whipper, worth Three Pounds a Year?——Then you begg'd the Church-Wardens to let your Wife have the Washing and Darning of the Surplice and Church-Linen, which brings you in Thirteen Shillings and Four Pence.——Then you have Six Shillings and Eight Pence for oiling and winding up the Clock, both paid you at *Easter*.——The Pinder's Place,° which is worth Forty Shillings a Year,—you have got that too.——You are the Bailiff, which the late Parson got you, which brings you in Forty Shillings more.——Besides all this, you have Six Pounds a Year, paid you Quarterly for being Mole-Catcher to the Parish.——Aye, says the luckless Wight above-mentioned, (who was standing close to him with his Plush Breeches on) 'You are not only Mole-Catcher, *Trim*, but you catch STRAY CONIES° too in the *Dark*; and you pretend a *Licence* for it, which, I trow, will be look'd into at the next Quarter Sessions.' I maintain it, I have a Licence, says *Trim*, blushing as red as Scarlet:——I have a Licence,—and as I farm a Warren in the next Parish, I will catch Conies every Hour of the Night.—— *You catch Conies!* cries a toothless old Woman, who was just passing by.——

This set the Mob a laughing, and sent every Man home in perfect good Humour, except *Trim*, who waddled very slowly off with that Kind of inflexible Gravity only to be equalled by one Animal in the whole Creation,—and surpassed by none. I am,

SIR,

Yours, &c. &c.

FINIS.

POSTSCRIPT.

I HAVE broke open my Letter to inform you, that I miss'd the Opportunity of sending it by the Messenger, who I expected would have called upon me in his Return through this Village to *York*, so it has laid a Week or ten Days by me.

——I am not sorry for the Disappointment, because something has since happened, in Continuation of this Affair, which I am thereby enabled to transmit to you, all under one Trouble.

When I finished the above Account, I thought (as did every Soul in the Parish) *Trim* had met with so thorough a Rebuff from *John* the Parish-Clerk and the Town's Folks, who all took against him, that *Trim* would be glad to be quiet, and let the Matter rest.

But, it seems, it is not half an Hour ago since *Trim* sallied forth again; and, having borrowed a Sow-Gelder's Horn,° with hard Blowing he got the whole Town round him, and endeavoured to raise a Disturbance, and fight the whole Battle over again:°—That he had been used in the last Fray worse than a Dog;—not by *John* the Parish-Clerk,—for I shou'd not, quoth *Trim*, have valued him a Rush single Hands:—But all the Town sided with him, and twelve Men in *Buckram* set upon me all at once, and kept me in Play at Sword's Point for three Hours together.—Besides, quoth *Trim*, there were two misbegotten Knaves in *Kendal Green*,° who lay all the while in Ambush in *John*'s own House, and they all *sixteen* came upon my Back, and let drive at me together.—A Plague, says *Trim*, of all Cowards!—*Trim* repeated this Story above a Dozen Times;—which made some of the Neighbours pity him, thinking the poor Fellow crack-brain'd, and that he actually believed what he said. After this *Trim* dropp'd the Affair of the *Breeches*, and begun a fresh Dispute about the *Reading-Desk*, which I told you had occasioned some small Dispute between the *late* Parson and *John*, some Years ago.

This *Reading-Desk*, as you will observe, was but an Episode wove into the main Story by the Bye;—for the main Affair was the *Battle of the Breeches* and *Great Watch-Coat*.——However, *Trim* being at last driven out of these two Citadels,—he has seized hold, in his Retreat, of this *Reading-Desk*, with a View, as it seems, to take Shelter behind it.

I cannot say but the Man has fought it out obstinately enough;——and, had his Cause been good, I should have really pitied him. For when he was driven out of the *Great Watch-Coat*,——you see, he did not run away;—no,—he retreated behind the *Breeches*;—and, when he could make nothing of it behind the *Breeches*,—he got behind the *Reading-Desk*.—To what other Hold° *Trim* will next retreat, the Politicians of this Village are not agreed.—Some think his next Move will be towards the Rear of the Parson's Boot;—but, as it is thought he cannot make a long Stand there,—others are of Opinion, That *Trim* will once more in his Life get hold of the Parson's Horse, and charge upon him, or perhaps behind him.——But as the Horse is not easy to be caught, the more general Opinion is, That, when he is driven out of the *Reading-Desk*, he will make his last Retreat in such a Manner, as, if possible, to gain the *Close-Stool*,° and defend himself behind it to the very last Drop. If *Trim* should make this Movement, by my Advice he should be left besides his Citadel, in full Possession of the Field of Battle;—where, 'tis certain, he will keep every Body a League off, and may pop by himself till he is weary: Besides, as *Trim* seems bent upon *purging* himself, and may have Abundance of foul Humours to work off, I think he cannot be better placed.

But this is all Matter of Speculation.—Let me carry you back to Matter of Fact, and tell you what Kind of a Stand *Trim* has actually made behind the said *Desk*.

'Neighbours and Townsmen all, I will be sworn before my Lord Mayor, That *John* and his nineteen Men in *Buckram*, have abused me worse than a Dog; for they told you that I play'd fast and go-loose with the *late* Parson and him, in that old Dispute of theirs about the *Reading-Desk*; and that I made Matters worse between them, and not better.'

Of this Charge, *Trim* declared he was as innocent as the Child that was unborn: That he would be Book-sworn° he had no Hand in it. He produced a strong Witness;—and, moreover, insinuated, that *John* himself, instead of being angry for what he had done in it, had actually thank'd him. Aye, *Trim*, says the Wight in the Plush Breeches, but that was, *Trim*, the Day before *John* found thee out.—Besides, *Trim*, there is nothing in that:——For, the very Year that thou wast made Town's Pinder, thou knowest well, that I both thank'd thee myself; and, moreover, gave thee a good warm Supper for turning *John Lund*'s Cows and Horses out of my Hard-Corn Close; which if thou had'st not done, (as thou told'st me) I should have lost my whole Crop: Whereas, *John Lund* and *Thomas Patt*, who are both here to testify, and will take their Oaths on't, That thou thyself wast the very Man who set the Gate open; and, after all,—it was not thee, *Trim*,—'twas the Blacksmith's poor Lad who turn'd them out: So that a Man may be thank'd and rewarded too for a good Turn which he never did, nor ever did intend.

Trim could not sustain this unexpected Stroke;—so *Trim* march'd off the Field, without Colours flying, or his Horn sounding, or any other Ensigns of Honour whatever.

Whether after this *Trim* intends to rally a second Time,——or whether *Trim* may not take it into his Head to claim the Victory,—no one but *Trim* himself can inform you:—However, the general Opinion, upon the whole, is this,——That, in three several pitch'd Battles, *Trim* has been so *trimm'd*,° as never disastrous Hero was trimm'd before him.

The KEY.

This *Romance* was, by some Mischance or other, dropp'd in the *Minster-Yard, York,* and pick'd up by a Member of a small Political Club in that City; where it was carried, and publickly read to the Members the last Club Night.

It was instantly agreed to, by a great Majority, That it was a *Political Romance*; but concerning what State or Potentate, could not so easily be settled amongst them.

The President of the Night, who is thought to be as clear and quick-sighted as any one of the whole Club in Things of this Nature, discovered plainly, That the Disturbances therein set forth, related to those on the *Continent:*—That *Trim* could be Nobody but the King of *France,* by whose shifting and intriguing Behaviour, all *Europe* was set together by the Ears:—That *Trim's* Wife was certainly the *Empress,* who are as kind together, says he, as any Man and Wife can be for their Lives.—The more Shame for 'em, says an Alderman, low to himself.—Agreeable to this Key, continues the President,—The *Parson,* who I think is a most excellent Character,—is His Most Excellent Majesty King *George*;——*John,* the Parish-Clerk, is the King of *Prussia*; who, by the Manner of his first entering *Saxony,* shew'd the World most evidently,—That he did know how to lead out the Psalm, and in Tune and Time too, notwithstanding *Trim's* vile Insult upon him in that Particular.—But who do you think, says a Surgeon and Man-Midwife, who sat next him, (whose Coat-Button the President, in the Earnestness of this Explanation, had got fast hold of, and had thereby partly drawn him over to his Opinion) Who do you think, Mr. President, says he, are meant by the *Church-Wardens, Sides-Men, Mark Slender, Lorry Slim, &c.*—Who do I think? says he, Why,—Why, Sir, as I take the Thing,——the *Church-Wardens* and *Sides-Men,* are the *Electors* and the other *Princes* who form the *Germanick Body.*—And as for the other subordinate Characters of *Mark Slim,*—the *unlucky Wight* in the Plush Breeches,—the *Parson's Man* who was so often out of the Way, *&c. &c.*—these, to be sure, are the several *Marshals* and *Generals,* who fought, or should have fought, under them the last Campaign.—The Men in *Buckram,* continued the President, are the

Gross° of the King of *Prussia*'s Army, who are as *stiff* a Body of Men as are in the World:—And *Trim*'s saying they were twelve, and then nineteen, is a Wipe° for the *Brussels Gazetteer*, who, to my Knowledge, was never two Weeks in the same Story, about that or any thing else.

As for the rest of the *Romance*, continued the President, it sufficiently explains itself,—*The Old-cast-Pair-of-Black-Plush-Breeches* must be *Saxony*, which the *Elector*, you see, *has left off wearing*:—And as for the *Great Watch-Coat*, which, you know, covers all, it signifies all *Europe*; comprehending, at least, so many of its different States and Dominions, as we have any Concern with in the present War.

I protest, says a Gentleman who sat next but one to the President, and who, it seems, was the Parson of the Parish, a Member not only of the Political, but also of a Musical Club in the next Street;——I protest, says he, if this Explanation is right, which I think it is,—— That the whole makes a very fine Symbol.—You have always some Musical Instrument or other in your Head, I think, says the Alderman.——Musical Instrument! replies the Parson, in Astonishment,—Mr. Alderman, I mean an Allegory; and I think the greedy Disposition of *Trim* and his Wife, in ripping the *Great Watch-Coat* to Pieces, in order to convert it into a Petticoat for the one, and a Jerkin for the other, is one of the most beautiful of the Kind I ever met with; and will shew all the World what have been the true Views and Intentions of the Houses of *Bourbon* and *Austria* in this abominable Coalition,—I might have called it Whoredom:—Nay, says the Alderman, 'tis downright Adulterydom, or nothing.

This Hypothesis of the President's explain'd every Thing in the *Romance* extreamly well; and, withall, was delivered with so much Readiness and Air of Certainty, as begot an Opinion in two Thirds of the Club, that Mr. President was actually the Author of the *Romance* himself: But a Gentleman who sat on the opposite Side of the Table, who had come piping-hot from reading the History of King *William*'s and Queen *Anne*'s Wars, and who was thought, at the Bottom, to envy the President the Honour both of the *Romance* and Explanation too, gave an entire new Turn to it all. He acquainted the Club, That Mr. President was altogether wrong in every Supposition he had made, except that one, where the *Great Watch-Coat* was said by him to represent *Europe*, or at least a great Part of it:—So far he acknowledged he was pretty right; but that he had not gone far enough backwards into our History to come at the Truth. He then acquainted them, that the dividing the *Great Watch-Coat* did, and could, allude to nothing else in the World but the *Partition-Treaty*;° which, by the Bye, he told them, was the most unhappy and scandalous Transaction in all King *William*'s Life: It was that false Step, and that only, says he, rising from his Chair, and striking his Hand upon the Table with great Violence; it was that false Step, says he, knitting his Brows and throwing his Pipe down upon the Ground, that has laid the Foundation of all the Disturbances and Sorrows we feel and lament at this very Hour; and as for *Trim*'s giving up the *Breeches*, look ye, it is almost Word for Word copied from the *French* King and *Dauphin*'s Renunciation of *Spain* and the *West-Indies*, which all the World knew (as was the very Case of the *Breeches*) were renounced by them on purpose to be reclaim'd when Time should serve.

This Explanation had too much Ingenuity in it to be altogether slighted; and, in Truth, the worst Fault it had, seem'd to be the prodigious Heat of it; which (as an Apothecary, who sat next the Fire, observ'd, in a very low Whisper to his next Neighbour) was so much incorporated into every Particle of it, that it was impossible, under such Fermentation, it should work its desired Effect.

This, however, no way intimidated a little valiant Gentleman, though he sat the very next Man, from giving an Opinion as diametrically opposite as *East* is from *West*.

This Gentleman, who was by much the best Geographer in the whole Club, and, moreover, second Cousin to an Engineer, was positive the *Breeches* meant *Gibraltar*; for, if you remember, Gentlemen, says he, tho' possibly you don't, the Ichnography° and Plan of that Town and Fortress, it exactly resembles a Pair of Trunk-Hose, the two Promontories forming the two Slops,° &c. &c.—Now we all know, continued he, that King *George* the First made a Promise of that important Pass to the King of *Spain:*——So that the whole Drift of the *Romance*, according to my Sense of Things, is merely to vindicate the King and the Parliament in that Transaction, which made so much Noise in the World.

A Wholesale Taylor, who from the Beginning had resolved not to speak at all in the Debate,—was at last drawn into it, by something very unexpected in the last Person's Argument.

He told the Company, frankly, he did not understand what

Ichnography meant:°——But as for the Shape of a *Pair of Breeches*, as he had had the Advantage of cutting out so many hundred Pairs in his Life-Time, he hoped he might be allowed to know as much of the Matter as another Man.

Now, to my Mind, says he, there is nothing in all the Terraqueous Globe (a Map of which, it seems, hung up in his Work-Shop) so like a *Pair of Breeches* unmade up, as the Island of *Sicily:*—Nor is there any thing, if you go to that, quoth an honest Shoe-maker, who had the Honour to be a Member of the Club, so much like a *Jack-Boot*, to my Fancy, as the Kingdom of *Italy.*—What the Duce has either *Italy* or *Sicily* to do in the Affair? cries the President, who, by this Time, began to tremble for his Hypothesis,——What have they to do?—Why, answered the *Partition-Treaty* Gentleman, with great Spirit and Joy sparkling in his Eyes,—They have just so much, Sir, to do in the Debate as to overthrow your Suppositions, and to estab-lish the Certainty of mine beyond the Possibility of a Doubt: For, says he, (with an Air of Sovereign Triumph over the President's Poli-ticks)——By the *Partition-Treaty*, Sir, both *Naples* and *Sicily* were the very Kingdoms made to devolve upon the *Dauphin*;—and *Trim*'s *greasing the Parson*'s *Boots*, is a Devilish Satyrical Stroke;—for it exposes the Corruption and Bribery made Use of at that Juncture, in bringing over the several States and Princes of *Italy* to use their Interests at *Rome*, to stop the Pope from giving the Investitures of those Kingdoms to any Body else.—The Pope has not the Investi-ture° of *Sicily*, cries another Gentleman.—I care not, says he, for that.

Almost every one apprehended the Debate to be now ended, and that no one Member would venture any new Conjecture upon the *Romance*, after so many clear and decisive Interpretations had been given. But, hold,——Close to the Fire, and opposite to where the Apothecary sat, there sat also a Gentleman of the Law, who, from the Beginning to the End of the Hearing of this Cause, seem'd no way satisfied in his Conscience with any one Proceeding in it. This Gentleman had not yet opened his Mouth, but had waited patiently till they had all gone thro' their several Evidences on the other Side;—reserving himself, like an expert Practitioner, for the last Word in the Debate. When the *Partition-Treaty*-Gentleman had fin-ish'd what he had to say,——He got up,—and, advancing towards the Table, told them, That the Error they had all gone upon thus far, in making out the several Facts in the *Romance*,—was in looking too high;° which, with great Candor, he said, was a very natural Thing, and very excusable withall, in such a Political Club as theirs: For Instance, continues he, you have been searching the *Registers*, and looking into the *Deeds* of *Kings* and *Emperors*,——as if Nobody had any *Deeds* to shew or compare the *Romance* to but themselves.—— This, continued the Attorney, is just as much out of the Way of good Practice, as if I should carry a Thing slap-dash into the House of Lords, which was under forty Shillings, and might be decided in the next County-Court for six Shillings and Eight-pence.—He then took the *Romance* in his Left Hand, and pointing with the Fore-Finger of his Right towards the second Page, he humbly begg'd Leave to observe, (and, to do him Justice, he did it in somewhat of a *forensic Air*) That the *Parson, John*, and *Sexton*, shewed incontestably the Thing to be *Tripartite*; now, if you will take Notice, Gentlemen, says he, these several Persons, who are Parties to this Instrument, are merely Ecclesiastical; that the *Reading-Desk, Pulpit-Cloth*, and *Velvet Cushion*, are tripartite too; and are, by Intendment of Law, Goods and Chattles merely of an Ecclesiastick Nature, belonging and appertaining 'only unto them,' *and to them only.*—So that it appears very plain to me, That the *Romance*, neither directly nor indirectly, goes upon Temporal, but altogether upon Church-Matters.—And do not you think, says he, softening his Voice a little, and addressing himself to the Parson with a forced Smile,——Do not you think Doctor, says he, That the Dispute in the *Romance*, between the *Parson* of the Parish and *John*, about the Height of *John*'s Desk, is a very fine Panegyrick upon the *Humility* of *Church-Men?*——I think, says the Parson, it is much of the same Fineness with that which your Profession is complimented with, in the pimping, dirty, petty-fogging Character of *Trim*,—which, in my Opinion, Sir, is just such another Panegyrick upon the *Honesty* of *Attornies.*

Nothing whets the Spirits like an Insult:—Therefore the Parson went on with a visible Superiority and an uncommon Acuteness.——As you are so happy, Sir, continues he, in making Applications,—pray turn over a Page or two to the black Law-Letters in the *Romance*.—What do you think of them, Sir?——Nay,—pray read the Grant of the *Great Watch-Coat*—and *Trim*'s Renunciation of the *Breeches*.—Why, there is downright **Lease** and **Release** for you,— 'tis the very Thing, Man;——only with this small Difference,—and in which consists the whole Strength of the Panegyric,°——That the Author of the *Romance* has convey'd and reconvey'd, in about ten Lines,—what you, with the glorious Prolixity of the Law, could not have crowded into as many Skins of Parchment.

The Apothecary, who had paid the Attorney, the same Afternoon, a Demand of Three Pounds Six Shillings and Eight-Pence, for much such another Jobb,——was so highly tickled with the Parson's Repartee in that particular Point,—that he rubb'd his Hands together most fervently,—and laugh'd most triumphantly thereupon.

This could not escape the Attorney's Notice, any more than the Cause of it did escape his Penetration.

I think, Sir, says he, (dropping his Voice a Third)° you might well have spared this immoderate Mirth, since you and your Profession have the least Reason to triumph here of any of us.——I beg, quoth he, that you would reflect a Moment upon the *Cob-Web* which *Trim* went so far for, and brought back with an Air of so much Importance, in his Breeches Pocket, to lay upon the Parson's cut Finger.——This said Cob-Web, Sir, is a fine-spun Satyre, upon the flimsy Nature of one Half of the Shop-Medicines, with which you make a Property of the Sick, the Ignorant, and the Unsuspecting.——And as for the Moral of the *Close-Stool-Pan*, Sir, 'tis too plain,——Does not nine Parts in ten of the whole Practice, and of all you vend under *its Colours*, pass into and concenter° in that one nasty Utensil?——And let me tell you, Sir, says he, raising his Voice,—had not your unseasonable Mirth blinded you, you might have seen that *Trim*'s carrying the Close-Stool-Pan upon his Head the whole Length of the Town, without blushing, is a pointed Raillery,°—and one of the sharpest Sarcasms, Sir, that ever was thrown out upon you;—for it unveils the solemn Impudence of the whole Profession, who, I see, are ashamed of nothing which brings in Money.

There were two Apothecaries in the Club, besides the Surgeon mentioned before, with a Chemist and an Undertaker, who all felt themselves equally hurt and aggrieved by this discourteous Retort:—And they were all five rising up together from their Chairs, with full Intent of Heart, as it was thought, to return the *Reproof Valiant*° thereupon.—But the President, fearing it would end in a general Engagement, he instantly call'd out, *To Order*;—and gave Notice, That if there was any Member in the Club, who had not yet spoke, and yet did desire to speak upon the main Subject of the Debate,—that he should immediately be heard.

This was a happy Invitation for a stammering Member, who, it seems, had but a weak Voice at the best; and having often attempted to speak in the Debate, but to no Purpose, had sat down in utter Despair of an Opportunity.

This Member, you must know, had got a sad Crush upon his Hip, in the late *Election*, which gave him intolerable Anguish;—so that, in short, he could think of nothing else:—For which Cause, and others, he was strongly of Opinion, That the whole *Romance* was a just Gird° at the late *York* Election; and I think, says he, that the *Promise* of the *Breeches* broke, may well and truly signify *Somebody's else Promise*, which was broke, and occasion'd so much Disturbance amongst us.

——Thus every Man turn'd the Story to what was swimming uppermost in his own Brain;—so that, before all was over, there were full as many Satyres spun out of it,—and as great a Variety of Personages, Opinions, Transactions, and Truths, found to lay hid under the dark Veil of its Allegory, as ever were discovered in the thrice-renowned History of the Acts of *Gargantua* and *Pantagruel*.°

At the Close of all, and just before the Club was going to break up,—Mr. President rose from his Chair, and begg'd Leave to make the two following Motions, which were instantly agreed to, without any Division.

First, Gentlemen, says he, as *Trim*'s Character in the *Romance*, of a shuffling intriguing Fellow,—whoever it was drawn for, is, in Truth, as like the *French King* as it can stare,——I move, That the *Romance* be forthwith *printed:*—For, continues he, if we can but once turn the Laugh against him, and make him asham'd of what he has done, it may be a great Means, with the Blessing of God upon our Fleets and Armies, to save the Liberties of *Europe*.

In the *second* Place, I move, That Mr. Attorney, our worthy Member, be desired to take Minutes, upon the Spot, of every Conjecture which has been made upon the *Romance*, by the several Members who have spoke; which, I think, says he, will answer two good Ends:

1*st*, It will establish the Political Knowledge of our Club for ever, and place it in a respectable Light to all the World.

In the *next* Place, it will furnish what will be wanted; that is, a *Key* to the *Romance*.——In troth you might have said a whole Bunch of *Keys*, quoth a Whitesmith,° who was the only Member in the Club who had not said something in the Debate: But let me tell you, Mr. President, says he, That the *Right Key*, if it could but be found, would be worth the whole Bunch put together.

SIR,

YOU write me Word that the Letter I wrote to you, and now stiled *The Political Romance* is printing; and that, as it was drop'd by Carelessness, to make some Amends, you will overlook the Printing of it yourself, and take Care to see that it comes right into the World.

I was just going to return you Thanks, and to beg, withal, you would take Care That the Child be not laid at my Door.—But having, this Moment, perused the *Reply* to the *Dean* of *York*'s *Answer*,— it has made me alter my Mind in that respect; so that, instead of making you the Request I intended, I do here desire That the Child be filiated upon me, *Laurence Sterne*, Prebendary of *York*, &c. &c. And I do, accordingly, own it for my own true and lawful Offspring.

My Reason for this is plain;——for as, you see, the *Writer* of that *Reply*, has taken upon him to invade this *incontested Right* of another Man's in a Thing of this Kind, it is high Time for every Man to look to his own—Since, upon the *same Grounds*, and with half the Degree of Anger, that he affirms the Production of that very Reverend Gentleman's, to be the Child of many Fathers,° some one in his Spight (for I am not without my Friends of that Stamp) may run headlong into the other Extream, and swear, That mine had no Father at all:—And therefore, to make use of *Bays*'s Plea in the *Rehearsal*, for *Prince Pretty-Man*; I merely do it, as he says, 'for fear it should be said to be no Body's Child at all.'°

I have only to add two Things:—First, That, at your Peril, you do not presume to alter or transpose one Word, nor rectify one false Spelling, nor so much as add or diminish one Comma or Tittle, in or to my *Romance:*—For if you do,—In case any of the Descendents of *Curl*° should think fit to invade my Copy-Right, and print it over again in my Teeth, I may not be able, in a Court of Justice, to swear strictly to my own Child, after you had *so large a Share* in the begetting it.

In the next Place, I do not approve of your *quaint Conceit*° at the Foot of the Title Page of my *Romance*,——It would only set People on smiling a Page or two before I give them Leave;—and besides, all Attempts either at Wit or Humour, in that Place, are a Forestalling of what slender Entertainment of those Kinds are prepared within: Therefore I would have it stand thus:

YORK:

Printed in the Year 1759.

(*Price One Shilling.*)

I know you will tell me, That it is set too high; and as a Proof, you will say, That this last *Reply* to the *Dean's Answer* does consist of near as many Pages as mine; and yet is all sold for Six-pence.——— But mine, my dear Friend, is quite a *different Story:*—It is a Web wrought out of my own Brain, of twice the Fineness of this which he has spun out of his; and besides, I maintain it, it is of a more curious Pattern, and could not be afforded at the Price that his is sold at, by any *honest* Workman in *Great-Britain.*

Moreover, Sir, you do not consider, That the Writer is interested in his *Story*, and that it is his Business to set it a-going at *any Price:* And indeed, from the Information of Persons conversant in Paper and Print, I have very good Reason to believe, if he should sell every Pamphlet of them, he would inevitably be a *Great Loser* by it. This I believe verily, and am,

Dear Sir,

Your obliged Friend

Sutton on the Forest,
Jan. 20, 1759.

and humble Servant,

LAURENCE STERNE.

To Dr. TOPHAM.

SIR,

THOUGH the *Reply* to the *Dean* of *York* is not declared, in the *Title-Page*, or elsewhere, to be wrote by you,—Yet I take that Point for granted; and therefore beg Leave, in this public Manner, to write to you in Behalf of myself; with Intent to set you right in two Points where I stand concerned in this Affair; and which I find you have misapprehended, and consequently (as I hope) misrepresented.

The *First* is, in respect of some Words, made use of in the Instrument,° signed by Dr. *Herring*, Mr. *Berdmore*° and myself.—Namely, *to the best of our Remembrance and Belief*, which Words you have caught hold of, as implying some Abatement of our Certainty as to the Facts therein attested. Whether it was so with the other two Gentlemen who signed that Attestation with me, it is not for me to say; they are able to answer for themselves, and I desire to do so for myself; and therefore I declare to you, and to all Mankind, 'That the Words in the first Paragraph, *to the best of our Remembrance and Belief*, implied no Doubt remaining upon my Mind, nor any Distrust whatever of my Memory, from the Distance of Time;—Nor, in short, was it my Intention to attest the several Facts therein, as Matters of Belief—— But as Matters of as much Certainty as a Man was capable of having, or giving Evidence to. In Consequence of this Explanation of myself, I do declare myself ready to attest the same Instrument over again, striking out the Words *to the best of our Remembrance and Belief*, which I see, have raised this Exception to it.

Whether I was mistaken or no, I leave to better Judges; but I understood those Words were a very common Preamble to Attestations of Things, to which we bore the clearest Evidence:—— However, Dr. *Topham*, as you have claimed just such another Indulgence yourself, in the Case of begging the *Dean*'s Authority to say, what, as you affirm, you had sufficient Authority to say without, as a modest and Gentleman-like Way of Affirmation;—I wish you had spared either the one or the other of your Remarks upon these two Passages:

——*Veniam petimus, demusque vicissim.*°

There is another Observation relating to this Instrument, which I perceive has escaped your Notice; which I take the Liberty to point out to you, namely, That the Words, *To the best of our Remembrance and Belief*, if they imply any Abatement of Certainty, seem only confined to that Paragraph, and to what is immediately attested after them in it:—For in the second Paragraph, wherein the main Points are minutely attested, and upon which the whole Dispute, and main Charge against the *Dean*, turns, it is introduced thus:

'*We do particularly remember*, That as soon as Dinner was over, *&c.*'

In the second Place you affirm, 'That it is not said, That Mr. *Sterne* could affirm he had heard you charge the *Dean* with a Promise, in its own Nature so very extraordinary, as of the Commissaryship of the Dean and Chapter:'——To this I answer, That my true Intent in subscribing that very Instrument, and I suppose of others, was to attest this *very Thing*; and I have just now read that Part of the Instrument over; and cannot, for my Life, affirm it either more directly or expresly, than in the Words as they there stand;—— therefore please to let me transcribe them.

——'But being press'd by Mr. *Sterne* with an undeniable Proof, That he, (Dr. *Topham*) did propagate the said Story, (viz. *of a Promise from the Dean to Dr.* Topham *of the Dean and Chapter's Commissaryship*)—Dr. *Topham* did at last acknowledge it; adding, as his Reason or Excuse for so doing, That he apprehended (or Words to that Effect) he had a *Promise* under the *Dean's own Hand*, of the *Dean and Chapter's Commissaryship*.'

This I have attested, and what Weight the Sanction of an Oath will add to it, I am willing and ready to give.

As for Mr. *Ricard's*° feeble Attestation, brought to shake the Credit of this firm and solemn one, I have nothing to say to it, as it is only an Attestation of Mr *Ricard's* Conjectures upon the Subject.—But this I can say, That I had the Honour to be at the Deanery with the learned Counsel, when Mr. *Ricard* underwent that *most formidable* Examination you speak of;——and I solemnly affirm, That he then said, He knew nothing at all about the Matter, one Way or the other; and the Reasons he gave for his utter Ignorance, were, first, That he was then so full of Concern, at the Difference which arose between two Gentlemen, both his Friends, that he did not attend to the Subject Matter of it,——and of which he declared again he knew nothing at all. And secondly, If he had understood it then, the Distance would have put it out of his Head by this Time.

He has since scower'd his Memory, I ween; for now he says, That he apprehended the Dispute regarded something in the Dean's Gift, as he could not *naturally* suppose, *&c.* 'Tis certain, at the Deanery, he had *naturally* no Suppositions in his Head about this Affair; so that I wish this may not prove one of the After-Thoughts you speak of, and not so much a *natural* as an *artificial* Supposition of my good Friend's.

As for the *formidable* Enquiry you represent him as undergoing,— let me intreat you to give me Credit in what I say upon it,—— namely,——That it was as much the Reverse to every Idea that ever was couch'd under that Word, as Words can represent it to you. As for the learned Counsel and myself, who were in the Room all the Time, I do not remember that we, either of us, spoke ten Words. The Dean was the only one that ask'd Mr. *Ricard* what he remembered about the Affair of the Sessions Dinner; which he did in the most Gentleman-like and candid Manner,—and with an Air of as much Calmness and seeming Indifference, as if he had been questioning him about the News in the last *Brussels Gazette.*

What Mr. *Ricard* saw to terrify him so sadly, I cannot apprehend, unless the Dean's *Gothic* Book-Case,—which own has an odd Appearance to a Stranger; so that if he came terrified in his Mind there, and with a Resolution not to *plead*, he might *naturally suppose* it to be a great Engine brought there on purpose to exercise the *Peine fort et dure*° upon him.——But to be serious; if Mr. *Ricard* told you, That this Enquiry was *most formidable*, *He* was much to blame;—and if you have said it, without his express Information, then *You* are much to blame.

This is all, I think, in your *Reply*, which concerns me to answer:— As for the many coarse and unchristian Insinuations scatter'd throughout your *Reply*,—as it is my Duty to beg God to forgive you, so I do from my Heart: Believe me, Dr. *Topham*, they hurt yourself more than the Person they are aimed at; and when the *first Transport* of Rage is a little over, they will grieve you more too.

——prima est hæc Ultio.°

But these I hold to be no answerable Part of a Controversy;—and for the little that remains unanswered in yours,—I believe I could, in another half Hour, set it right in the Eyes of the World:——But this is not my Business.——And if it is thought worth the while, which I hope it never will, I know no one more able to do it than the very Reverend and Worthy Gentleman whom you have so unhandsomely insulted upon that Score.

SERMONS

The House of Feasting AND The House of Mourning Described.°

ECCLESIASTES vii. 2, 3.

It is better to go to the house of mourning, than to the house of feasting. ——

THAT I deny—but let us hear the wise man's reasoning upon it—*for that* is *the end of all men, and the living* will *lay it to* his *heart: sorrow is better than laughter*—for a crack'd-brain'd order of Carthusian monks,° I grant, but not for men of the world: For what purpose do you imagine, has GOD made us? for the social sweets of the well watered vallies where he has planted us, or for the dry and dismal deserts of a *Sierra Morena?*° are the sad accidents of life, and the uncheery hours which perpetually overtake us, are they not enough, but we must sally forth in quest of them,—belie our own hearts, and say, as your text would have us, that they are better than those of joy? did the Best of Beings send us into the world for this end—to go weeping through it,—to vex and shorten a life short and vexatious enough already? do you think my good preacher, that he who is infinitely happy, can envy us our enjoyments? or that a being so infinitely kind would grudge a mournful traveller, the short rest and refreshments necessary to support his spirits through the stages of a weary pilgrimage? or that he would call him to a severe reckoning, because in his way he had hastily snatch'd at some little fugacious° pleasures, merely to sweeten this uneasy journey of life, and recon- cile him to the ruggedness of the road, and the many hard justlings he is sure to meet with? Consider, I beseech you, what provision and accommodation, the Author of our being has prepared for us, that we might not go on our way sorrowing—how many caravansera's° of rest—what powers and faculties he has given us for taking it—what apt objects he has placed in our way to entertain us;—some of which he has made so fair, so exquisitely fitted for this end, that they have power over us for a time to charm away the sense of pain, to cheer up the dejected heart under poverty and sickness, and make it go and remember its miseries no more.

I will not contend at present against this rhetorick; I would choose rather for a moment to go on with the allegory, and say we are travellers, and, in the most affecting sense of that idea, that like travellers, though upon business of the last and nearest concern to us, may surely be allowed to amuse ourselves with the natural or artificial beauties of the country we are passing through, without reproach of forgetting the main errand we are sent upon; and if we can so order it, as not to be led out of the way, by the variety of prospects, edifices, and ruins which sollicit us, it would be a nonsensical piece of saint errantry° to shut our eyes.

But let us not lose sight of the argument in pursuit of the simile.

Let us remember various as our excursions are,—that we have still set our faces towards Jerusalem—that we have a place of rest and happiness, towards which we hasten, and that the way to get there is not so much to please our hearts, as to improve them in virtue;—that mirth and feasting are usually no friends to atchievements of this kind—but that a season of affliction is in some sort a season of piety—not only because our sufferings are apt to put us in mind of our sins, but that by the check and interruption which they give to our pursuits, they allow us what the hurry and bustle of the world too often deny us,—and that is a little time for reflection, which is all that most of us want to make us wiser and better men;—that at certain times it is so necessary a man's mind should be turned towards itself, that rather than want occasions, he had better purchase them at the expence of his present happiness.—He had better, as the text expresses it, *go to the house of mourning*, where he will meet with something to subdue his passions, than to the house of feasting, where the joy and gaity of the place is likely to excite them—That whereas the entertainments and caresses of the one place, expose his heart and lay it open to temptations—the sorrows of the other defend it, and as naturally shut them from it. So strange and unaccountable a creature is man! he is so framed, that he cannot but pursue happiness—and yet unless he is made sometimes miserable, how apt is he to mistake the way which can only lead him to the accomplishment of his own wishes!

This is the full force of the wise man's declaration.—But to do further justice to his words, I would endeavour to bring the subject still nearer.—For which purpose, it will be necessary to stop here, and take a transient view of the two places here referred to,—the house of mourning, and the house of feasting. Give me leave therefore, I beseech you, to recall both of them for a moment, to your imaginations, that from thence I may appeal to your hearts, how faithfully, and upon what good grounds, the effects and natural operations of each upon our minds are intimated in the text.

And first, let us look into the house of feasting.

And here, to be as fair and candid as possible in the description of this, we will not take it from the worst originals,° such as are opened merely for the sale of virtue, and so calculated for the end, that the disguise each is under not only gives power safely to drive on the bargain, but safely to carry it into execution too.

This, we will not suppose to be the case—nor let us even imagine, the house of feasting, to be such a scene of intemperance and excess, as the house of feasting does often exhibit;—but let us take it from one, as little exceptionable as we can—where there is, or at least appears nothing really criminal,—but where every thing seems to be kept within the visible bounds of moderation and sobriety.

Imagine then, such a house of feasting, where either by consent or invitation a number of each sex is drawn together for no other purpose but the enjoyment and mutual entertainment of each other, which we will suppose shall arise from no other pleasures but what custom authorises, and religion does not absolutely forbid.

Before we enter—let us examine, what must be the sentiments of each individual previous to his arrival, and we shall find that however they may differ from one another in tempers and opinions, that every one seems to agree in this—that as he is going to a house dedicated to joy and mirth, it was fit he should divest himself of whatever was likely to contradict that intention, or be inconsistent with it.—That for this purpose, he had left his cares—his serious thoughts—and his moral reflections behind him, and was come forth from home with only such dispositions and gaiety of heart as suited the occasion, and promoted the intended mirth and jollity of the place. With this preparation of mind, which is as little as can be supposed, since it will amount to no more than a desire in each to render himself an acceptable guest,—let us conceive them entering into the house of feasting, with hearts set loose from grave restraints, and open to the expectations of receiving pleasure. It is not necessary, as I premised, to bring intemperance into this scene—or to suppose such an excess in the gratification of the appetites as shall ferment the blood and set the desires in a flame:—Let us admit no more of it therefore, than will gently stir them, and fit them for the impressions which so benevolent a commerce° will naturally excite. In this disposition thus wrought upon beforehand and already improved to this purpose,—take notice, how mechanically° the thoughts and spirits rise—how soon, and insensibly, they are got above the pitch and first bounds which cooler hours would have marked.

When the gay and smiling aspect of things has begun to leave the passages to a man's heart thus thoughtlessly unguarded—when kind and caressing looks of every object without that can flatter his senses, have conspired with the enemy within to betray him, and put him off his defence—when music likewise has lent her aid, and tried her power upon his passions—when the voice of singing men, and the voice of singing women° with the sound of the viol and the lute have broke in upon his soul, and in some tender notes have touched the secret springs of rapture—that moment let us dissect and look into his heart—see how vain! how weak! how empty a thing it is! Look through its several recesses,—those pure mansions formed for the reception of innocence and virtue—sad spectacle! Behold those fair inhabitants now dispossessed—turned out of their sacred dwellings to make room—for what?—at the best for levity and indiscretion— perhaps for folly—it may be for more impure guests, which possibly in so general a riot of the mind and senses may take occasion to enter unsuspected at the same time.

In a scene and disposition thus described—can the most cautious say—thus far shall my desires go—and no farther? or will the coolest and most circumspect say, when pleasure has taken full possession of his heart, that no thought nor purpose shall arise there, which he would have concealed?—In those loose and unguarded moments the imagination is not always at command—in spite of reason and reflection, it will forceably carry him sometimes whither he would not— like the unclean spirit, in the parent's sad description of his child's case, which took him, and oft times cast him into the fire to destroy him, and wheresoever it taketh him, it teareth him, and hardly departeth from him.°

But this, you'll say, is the worst account of what the mind may suffer here.

Why may we not make more favourable suppositions?—that numbers by exercise and custom to such encounters, learn gradually to despise and triumph over them;—that the minds of many are not so susceptible of warm impressions, or so badly fortified against them, that pleasure should easily corrupt or soften them;—that it would be hard to suppose, of the great multitudes which daily throng and press into this house of feasting, but that numbers come out of it again, with *all* the innocence with which they entered;—and that if both sexes are included in the computation, what *fair* examples shall we see of many of so pure and chaste a turn of mind—that the house of feasting, with all its charms and temptations, was never able to excite a thought, or awaken an inclination which virtue need to blush at—or which the most scrupulous conscience might not support. God forbid we should say otherwise:—no doubt, numbers of all ages escape unhurt, and get off this dangerous sea without shipwreck. Yet, are they not to be reckoned amongst the more fortunate adventurers?—and though one would not absolutely prohibit the attempt, or be so cynical as to condemn every one who tries it, since there are so many I suppose who cannot well do otherwise, and whose condition and situation in life unavoidably force them upon it—yet we may be allowed to describe this fair and flattering coast—we may point out the unsuspected dangers of it, and warn the unwary passenger, where they lay. We may shew him what hazards his youth and inexperience will run, how little he can gain by the venture, and how much wiser and better it would be [as is implied in the text] to seek occasions rather to improve his little stock of virtue than incautiously expose it to so unequal a chance, where the best he can hope is to return safe with what treasure he carried out—but where probably, he may be so unfortunate as to lose it all—be lost himself, and undone for ever.

Thus much for the house of feasting; which, by the way, though generally open at other times of the year throughout the world, is supposed in christian countries, now every where to be universally shut up. And, in truth, I have been more full in my cautions against it, not only as reason requires,—but in reverence to this season* wherein our church exacts a more particular forbearance and self-denial in this point, and thereby adds to the restraints upon pleasure and entertainments which this representation of things has suggested against them already.

---

* Preached in *Lent*.

Here then, let us turn aside, from this gay scene; and suffer me to take you with me for a moment to one much fitter for your meditation. Let us go into the house of mourning, made so, by such afflictions as have been brought in, merely by the common cross accidents and disasters to which our condition is exposed,—where perhaps, the aged parents sit broken hearted, pierced to their souls with the folly and indiscretion of a thankless child—the child of their prayers, in whom all their hopes and expectations centred:—perhaps a more affecting scene—a virtuous family lying pinched with want, where the unfortunate support of it, having long struggled with a train of misfortunes, and bravely fought up against them—is now piteously borne down at the last—overwhelmed with a cruel blow which no forecast or frugality could have prevented.—O GOD! look upon his afflictions.—Behold him distracted with many sorrows, surrounded with the tender pledges of his love, and the partner of his cares— without bread to give them,—unable, from the remembrance of better days, to dig;—to beg, ashamed.

When we enter into the house of mourning such as this,—it is impossible to insult the unfortunate even with an improper look.— Under whatever levity and dissipation of heart, such objects catch our eyes,—they catch likewise our attentions, collect and call home our scattered thoughts, and exercise them with wisdom. A transient scene of distress, such as is here sketch'd, how soon does it furnish materials to set the mind at work? how necessarily does it engage it to the consideration of the miseries and misfortunes, the dangers and calamities to which the life of man is subject. By holding up such a glass° before it, it forces the mind to see and reflect upon the vanity,— the perishing condition and uncertain tenure of every thing in this world. From reflections of this serious cast, how insensibly do the thoughts carry us farther?—and from considering, what we are— what kind of world we live in, and what evils befall us in it, how naturally do they set us to look forwards at what possibly we shall be?—for what kind of world we are intended—what evils may befall us there—and what provision we should make against them, here, whilst we have time and opportunity.

If these lessons are so inseparable from the house of mourning here supposed—we shall find it a still more instructive school of wisdom when we take a view of the place in that more affecting light in which the wise man° seems to confine it in the text, in which, by the house of mourning, I believe, he means that particular scene of sorrow where there is lamentation and mourning for the dead.

Turn in hither, I beseech you, for a moment. Behold a dead man ready to be carried out, the only son of his mother, and she a widow. Perhaps a more affecting spectacle—a kind and an indulgent father of a numerous family, lies breathless—snatch'd away in the strength of his age—torn in an evil hour from his children and the bosom of a disconsolate wife.

Behold much people of the city gathered together to mix their tears, with settled sorrow in their looks, going heavily along to the house of mourning, to perform that last melancholy office, which when the debt of nature° is payed, we are called upon to pay each other.

If this sad occasion which leads him there, has not done it already, take notice, to what a serious and devout frame of mind every man is reduced, the moment he enters this gate of affliction. The busy and fluttering spirits, which in the house of mirth° were wont to transport him from one diverting object to another—see how they are fallen! how peaceably they are laid! in this gloomy mansion full of shades and uncomfortable damps to seize the soul—see, the light and easy heart, which never knew what it was to think before, how pensive it is now, how soft, how susceptible, how full of religious impressions, how deeply it is smitten with sense and with a love of virtue. Could we, in this crisis, whilst this empire of reason and religion lasts, and the heart is thus exercised with wisdom and busied with heavenly contemplations—could we see it naked as it is°—stripped of all its passions, unspotted by the world, and regardless of its pleasures— we might then safely rest our cause, upon this single evidence, and appeal to the most sensual, whether Solomon has not made a just determination here, in favour of the house of mourning?—not for its own sake, but as it is fruitful in virtue, and becomes the occasion of so much good. Without this end, sorrow I own has no use, but to shorten a man's days—nor can gravity, with all its studied solemnity of look and carriage, serve any end but to make one half of the world merry, and impose upon the other.°

Consider what has been said, and may GOD of his mercy bless you. Amen.

Vindication of Human Nature.°

ROMANS xiv. 7.

For none of us liveth to himself.°

THERE is not a sentence in scripture, which strikes a narrow soul with greater astonishment—and one might as easily engage to clear up the darkest problem in geometry to an ignorant mind, as make a sordid one comprehend the truth and reasonableness of this plain proposition.—No man liveth to himself! Why——Does any man live to any thing else?—In the whole compass of human life can a prudent man steer to a safer point?—Not live to himself!—To whom then?—Can any interests or concerns which are foreign to a man's self have such a claim over him, that he must serve under them—suspend his own pursuits—step out of his right course, till others have pass'd by him, and attain'd the several ends and purposes of living before him?

If, with a selfish heart, such an enquirer° should happen to have a speculating head too, he will proceed, and ask you whether this same principle which the apostle here throws out of the life of man, is not in fact the grand bias of his nature?——That however we may flatter ourselves with fine-spun notions of disinterestedness and heroism in what we do; that were the most popular of our actions strip'd naked; and the true motives and intentions of them search'd to the bottom; we should find little reason for triumph upon that score.——

In a word, he will say, that a man is altogether a bubble° to himself in this matter, and that after all that can be said in his behalf, the truest definition that can be given of him is this, that he is a selfish animal; and that all his actions have so strong a tincture of that character, as to shew (to whomever else he was intended to live) that in fact, he lives only to himself.

Before I reply directly to this accusation, I cannot help observing by the way, that there is scarce any thing which has done more disservice to social virtue, than the frequent representations of human nature, under this hideous picture of deformity, which by leaving out all that is generous and friendly in the heart of man, has sunk him below the level of a brute, as if he was a composition of all

that was mean-spirited and selfish. Surely, 'tis one step towards acting well, to think worthily of our nature; and as in common life, the
way to make a man honest, is, to suppose him so, and treat him as
such;—so here, to set some value upon ourselves, enables us to support the character, and even inspires and adds sentiments of generosity and virtue to those which we have already preconceived. The
scripture tells, That GOD made man in his own image,°—not surely
in the sensitive° and corporeal part of him, that could bear no resemblance with a pure and infinite spirit,—but what resemblance he
bore was undoubtedly in the moral rectitude, and the kind and
benevolent affections of his nature. And tho' the brightness of this
image has been sullied greatly by the fall of man, in our first parents,°
and the characters of it rendered still less legible, by the many super-
inductions° of his own depraved appetites since—yet 'tis a laudable
pride and a true greatness of mind to cherish a belief, that there is so
much of that glorious image still left upon it, as shall restrain him
from base and disgraceful actions; to answer which end, what
thought can be more conducive than that of our being made in the
likeness of the greatest and best of beings? This is a plain consequence. And the consideration of it should have in some measure
been a protection to human nature, from the rough usage she has
met with from the satirical pens of so many of the French writers,° as
well as of our own country, who with more wit than well-meaning
have desperately fallen foul upon the whole species, as a set of creatures incapable either of private friendship or public spirit, but just
as the case suited their own interest and advantage.

That there is selfishness, and meanness enough in the souls of one
part of the world, to hurt the credit of the other part of it, is what I
shall not dispute against; but to judge of the whole, from this bad
sample,° and because one man is plotting and artful in his nature—or,
a second openly makes his pleasure or his profit the sole centre of all
his designs—or because a third strait-hearted° wretch sits confined
within himself,——feels no misfortunes, but those which touch
himself; to involve the whole race without mercy under such
detested characters, is a conclusion as false, as it is pernicious; and
was it in general to gain credit, could serve no end, but the rooting
out of our nature all that is generous, and planting in the stead of it
such an aversion to each other, as must untie the bands of society,
and rob us of one of the greatest pleasures of it, the mutual

communications of kind offices; and by poisoning the fountain, rendering every thing suspected that flows through it.

To the honor of human nature, the scripture teaches us, that God made man upright°—and though he has since found out many inventions, which have much dishonoured this noble structure, yet the foundation of it stands as it was,——the whole frame and design of it carried on upon social virtue and public spirit, and every member of us so evidently supported by this strong cement, that we may say with the apostle, *that no man liveth to himself*. In whatsoever light we view him, we shall see evidently, that there is no station or condition of his life,—no office or relation, or circumstance, but there arises from it so many ties, so many indispensible claims upon him, as must perpetually carry him beyond any selfish consideration, and shew plainly, that was a man foolishly wicked enough to design to live to himself alone, he would either find it impracticable, or he would lose, at least, the very thing which made life itself desirable. We know that our creator, like an all-wise contriver in this, as in all other of his works has implanted in mankind such appetites and inclinations as were suitable for their state; that is, such as would naturally lead him to the love of society and friendship, without which he would have been found in a worse condition than the very beasts of the field. No one therefore who lives in society, can be said to live to himself,—he lives to his GOD,—to his king, and his country.——He lives to his family, to his friends, to all under his trust, and in a word, he lives to the whole race of mankind; whatsoever has the character of man, and wears the same image of GOD that he does, is truly his brother, and has a just claim to his kindness.——That this is the case in fact, as well as in theory, may be made plain to any one, who has made any observations upon human life.——When we have traced it through all its connections,—view'd it under the several obligations which succeed each other in a perpetual rotation through the different stages of a hasty pilgrimage, we shall find that these do operate so strongly upon it, and lay us justly under so many restraints, that we are every hour sacrificing something to society, in return for the benefits we receive from it.

To illustrate this, let us take a short survey of the life of any one man, (not liable to great exceptions, but such a life as is common to most) let us examine it merely to this point, and try how far it will answer such a representation.

If we begin with him in that early age, wherein the strongest marks of undisguised tenderness and disinterested compassion shew themselves,—I might previously observe, with what impressions he is come out of the hands of GOD,—with the very bias upon his nature, which prepares him for the character, which he was designed to fulfil.——But let us pass by the years which denote childhood, as no lawful evidence, you'll say, in this dispute; let us follow him to the period, when he is just got loose from tutors and governors, when his actions may be argued upon with less exception. If you observe, you will find, that one of the first and leading propensities of his nature, is that, which discovers itself in the desire of society, and the spontaneous love towards those of his kind. And tho' the natural wants and exigencies of his condition, are no doubt, one reason of this amiable impulse,—GOD having founded that in him, as a provisional security to make him social;—yet tho' it is a reason in nature,—'tis a reason, to him yet undiscover'd. Youth is not apt to philosophise so deeply—but follows,—as it feels itself prompted by the inward workings of benevolence—without view to itself, or previous calculation either of the loss or profit which may accrue. Agreeably to this, observe how warmly, how heartily he enters into friendships,—how disinterested, and unsuspicious in the choice of them,—how generous and open in his professions!—how sincere and honest in making them good!—When his friend is in distress,—what lengths he will go,—what hazards he will bring upon himself,—what embarassment upon his affairs to extricate and serve him! If man is altogether a selfish creature (as these moralisers would make him) 'tis certain he does not arrive at the full maturity of it, in this time of his life.—— No. If he deserves any accusation, 'tis in the other extream, 'That in his youth he is generally more FOOL than KNAVE,'°—and so far from being suspected of living to himself, that he lives rather to every body else; the unconsciousness of art and design in his own intentions, rendering him so utterly void of a suspicion of it in others, as to leave him too oft a bubble to every one who will take the advantage.—But you will say, he soon abates of these transports of disinterested love; and as he grows older,—grows wiser, and learns to live more to himself.

Let us examine.——

That a longer knowledge of the world, and some experience of insincerity,—will teach him a lesson of more caution in the choice of friendships, and less forwardness in the undistinguished offers of his services, is what I grant. But if he cools of these, does he not grow warmer still in connections of a different kind? Follow him, I pray you, into the next stage of life, where he has enter'd into engagements and appears as the father of a family, and, you will see, the passion still remains,—the stream somewhat more confined,—but, runs the stronger for it,—the same benevolence of heart alter'd only in its course, and the difference of objects towards which it tends. Take a short view of him in this light, as acting under the many tender claims which that relation lays upon him,—spending many weary days, and sleepless nights—utterly forgetful of himself,— intent only upon his family, and with an anxious heart contriving and labouring to preserve it from distress, against° that hour when he shall be taken from its protection. Does such a one live to himself?——He who rises early, late takes rest, and eats the bread of carefulness, to save others the sorrow of doing so after him. Does such a one live only to himself?——Ye who are parents answer this question for him. How oft have ye sacrificed your health,—your ease,—your pleasures,—nay, the very comforts of your lives, for the sake of your children?—How many indulgencies have ye given up?—What self-denials and difficulties have ye chearfully undergone for them?—In their sickness, or reports of their misconduct, how have ye *gone on your way sorrowing?* What alarms within you, when fancy forebodes but imaginary misfortunes hanging over them?—but when real ones have overtaken them, *and mischief befallen them in the way in which they have gone,*° how sharper than a sword have ye felt the workings of parental kindness? In whatever period of human life we look for proofs of selfishness,—let us not seek them in this relation of a parent, whose whole life, when truly known, is often little else but a succession of cares, heart-aches, and disquieting apprehensions,—enough to shew, that he is but an instrument in the hands of GOD to provide for the well-being of others, to serve their interest as well as his own.

If you try the truth of this reasoning upon every other part or situation of the same life, you will find it holds good in one degree or other; take a view of it out of these closer connections both of a friend and parent.—Consider him for a moment, under that natural alliance, in which even a heathen poet has placed him; namely that of *a man:*—and as such, to his honor, as one incapable of standing unconcern'd, in whatever concerns his fellow creatures.°— Compassion has so great a share in our nature, and the miseries of this world are so constant an exercise of it, as to leave it in no one's power (who deserves the name of man) in this respect, *to live to himself.*

He cannot stop his ears against the cries of the unfortunate.—The sad story of the fatherless and him that has no helper *must* be heard.—*The sorrowful sighing of the prisoners will come before him;*° and a thousand other untold cases of distress to which the life of man is subject, find a way to his heart.——Let interest guard the passage as it will, *if he has this world's goods, and seeth his brother have need, he will not be able to shut up his bowels of compassion from him.*°

Let any man of common humanity, look back upon his own life as subjected to these strong claims, and recollect the influence they have had upon him. How oft the mere impulses of generosity and compassion have led him out of his way?—In how many acts of charity and kindness, his fellow-feeling for others has made him forget himself?——In neighbourly offices, how oft he has acted against all considerations of profit, convenience, nay sometimes even of justice itself?—Let him add to this account, how much, in the progress of his life, has been given up even to the lesser obligations of civility and good manners?—What restraints they have laid him under? How large a portion of his time,—how much of his inclination and the plan of life he should most have wished, has from time to time been made a sacrifice, to his good nature and disinclination to give pain or disgust to others?

Whoever takes a view of the life of man, in this glass wherein I have shewn it, will find it so beset and hemm'd in with obligations of one kind or other, as to leave little room to suspect, that *man can live to himself:* and so closely has our creator link'd us together, (as well as all other parts of his works) for the preservation of that harmony in the frame and system of things which his wisdom has at first established,—That we find this bond of mutual dependence, however relax'd, is too strong to be broke, and I believe, that the most selfish men find it is so, and that they cannot, in fact, live so much to themselves, as the narrowness of their own hearts incline them. If these reflections are just upon the moral relations in which we stand to each other, let us close the examination with a short reflection upon the great relation in which we stand to GOD.

The first and most natural thought on this subject, which at one time or other will thrust itself upon every man's mind, is this,—— That there is a GOD who made me,—to whose gift I owe all the powers and faculties of my soul, to whose providence I owe all the blessings of my life, and by whose permission it is that I exercise and enjoy them; that I am placed in this world as a creature but of a day, hastening to the place from whence I shall not return.—That I am accountable for my conduct and behaviour to this great and wisest of beings, before whose judgment seat I must finally appear and receive the things done in my body,—whether they are good, or whether they are bad.

Can any one doubt but the most inconsiderate of men sometimes sit down coolly, and make some such plain reflections as these upon their state and condition,—or, that after they have made them, can one imagine, they lose all effect.——As little appearance as there is of religion in the world, there is a great deal of its influence felt, in its affairs,—nor can one so root out the principles of it, but like nature they will return again and give checks and interruptions to guilty pursuits. There are seasons, when the thought of a just GOD over-looking, and the terror of an after reckoning has made the most determined tremble, and stop short in the execution of a wicked purpose; and if we conceive that the worst of men lay some restraints upon themselves from the weight of this principle, what shall we think of the good and virtuous part of the world, who live under the perpetual influence of it,—who sacrifice their appetites and passions from conscience of their duty to GOD; and consider him as the object to whom they have dedicated their service, and make that the first principle, and ultimate end of all their actions.—How many real and unaffected instances there are in this world, of men, thus gov-ern'd, will not so much concern us to enquire, as to take care that we are of the number, which may GOD grant for the sake of Jesus Christ, *Amen*.

JOB's Account of the SHORTNESS and TROUBLES of LIFE, considered.°

JOB xiv. 1, 2.

Man that is born of a woman, is of few days, and full of trouble:—He cometh forth like a flower, and is cut down; he fleeth also as a shadow, and continueth not.

THERE is something in this reflection of holy Job's, upon the short-ness of life, and instability of human affairs, so beautiful and truly sublime;° that one might challenge the writings of the most cele-brated orators of antiquity, to produce a specimen of eloquence, so noble and thoroughly affecting. Whether this effect be owing in some measure, to the pathetic nature of the subject reflected on;—or to the eastern manner of expression, in a stile more exalted and suitable to so great a subject, or (which is the more likely account,) because they are properly the words of that being, who first inspired man with language, and taught his mouth to utter, who opened the lips of the dumb, and made the tongue of the infant eloquent;° --- to which of these we are to refer the beauty and sublimity of this, as well as that of numberless other passages in holy writ, may not seem now material; but surely without these helps, never man was better qualified to make just and noble reflections upon the shortness of life, and instability of human affairs, than Job was, who had himself waded through such a sea of troubles,° and in his passage had encountered many vicissitudes of storms and sunshine, and by turns had felt both the extremes, of all the happiness, and all the wretched-ness that mortal man is heir to.

The beginning of his days was crowned with every thing that ambition could wish for;—he was the greatest of all the men of the East,—had large and unbounded possessions, and no doubt enjoyed all the comforts and advantages of life, which they could adminis-ter.——Perhaps you will say, a wise man might not be inclined to give a full loose to this kind of happiness, without some better secur-ity for the support of it, than the mere possession of such goods of fortune, which often slip from under us, and sometimes unaccount-ably make themselves wings, and fly away.—But he had that security too,——for the hand of providence which had thus far protected, was still leading him forwards, and seemed engaged in the preservation and continuance of these blessings;—God had set a hedge about him, and about all that he had on every side, he had blessed all the works of his hands, and his substance increased every day. Indeed even with this security, riches to him that hath *neither child or brother*, as the wise man observes, instead of a comfort prove sometimes a sore travel and vexation.——The mind of man is not always satisfied with the reasonable assurance of its own enjoyments, but will look forwards, and if it discovers some imaginary void, the want of some beloved object to fill his place after him, will often disquiet itself in vain, and say—'For whom do I labour, and bereave myself of rest?'°

This bar to his happiness God had likewise taken away, in blessing him with a numerous offspring of sons and daughters, the apparent inheriters of all his present happiness.—Pleasing reflection! to think the blessings God has indulged one's self in, shall be handed and continued down to a man's own seed; how little does this differ from a second enjoyment of them, to an affectionate parent, who naturally looks forwards with as strong an interest upon his children, as if he was to live over again in his own posterity.

What could be wanting to finish such a picture of a happy man?——Surely nothing, except a virtuous disposition to give a relish to these blessings, and direct him to make a proper use of them.—He had that too, for—he was a perfect and upright man, one that feared God and eschewed evil.

In the midst of all this prosperity, which was as great as could well fall to the share of one man;—whilst all the world looked gay, and smiled upon him, and every thing round him seemed to promise, if possible, an increase of happiness, in one instant all is changed into sorrow and utter despair.——

It pleases God for wise purposes to blast the fortunes of his house, and cut off the hopes of his posterity, and in one mournful day, to bring this great prince from his palace down to the dunghill. His flocks and herds, in which consisted the abundance of his wealth, were part consumed by a fire from heaven, the remainder taken away by the sword of the enemy: his sons and daughters, whom 'tis natural to imagine so good a man had so brought up in a sense of their duty, as to give him all reasonable hopes of much joy and pleasure in their future lives;—natural prospect for a parent to look forwards at, to recompense him for the many cares and anxieties which their infancy had cost him; these dear pledges of his future happiness were all, all snatched from him at one blow, just at the time that one might imagine they were beginning to be the comfort and delight of his old age, which most wanted such staves° to lean on;——and as circumstances add to an evil, so they did to this;——for it fell out not only by a very calamitous accident, which was grievous enough in itself, but likewise upon the back of his other misfortunes, when he was ill prepared to bear such a shock; and what would still add to it, it happened at an hour when he had least reason to expect it, when he would naturally think his children secure and out of the way of danger. 'For whilst they were feasting and making merry in their eldest brother's house, a great wind out of the wilderness smote the four corners of the house, and it fell upon them.'°

Such a concurrence of misfortunes are not the common lot of many: and yet there are instances of some who have undergone as severe trials, and bravely struggled under them; perhaps by natural force of spirits, the advantages of health, and the cordial assistance of a friend. And with these helps, what may not a man sustain?——But this was not Job's case; for scarce had these evils fallen upon him, when he was not only borne down with a grievous distemper which afflicted him from the crown of his head to the sole of his foot, but likewise his three friends, in whose kind consolations he might have found a medicine,——even the wife of his bosom, whose duty it was with a gentle hand to have softened all his sorrows, instead of doing this, they cruelly insulted and became the reproachers of his integrity. O God! what is man when thou thus bruisest him, and makest his burthen heavier as his strength grows less?—Who, that had found himself thus an example of the many changes and chances of this mortal life;——when he considered himself now stripped and left destitute of so many valuable blessings which the moment before thy providence had poured upon his head;—when he reflected upon this gay delightsome structure, in appearance so strongly built, so pleasingly surrounded with every thing that could flatter his hopes and wishes, and beheld it all levelled with the ground in one moment, and the whole prospect vanish with it like the description of an enchantment;—who I say that had seen and felt the shock of so sudden a revolution, would not have been furnished with just and beautiful reflections upon the occasion, and said with Job in the words of the text, 'That man that is born of a woman, is of few days, and full of misery,—that he cometh forth like a flower, and is cut down; he fleeth also as a shadow and continueth not?'°

The words of the text are an epitome° of the *natural* and *moral* vanity of man, and contain two distinct declarations concerning his state and condition in each respect.

First, that he is a creature of few days; and secondly, that those days are full of trouble.

I shall make some reflections upon each of these in their order, and conclude with a practical lesson from the whole.

And first, That he is of few days. The comparison which Job makes use of, That man cometh forth like a flower, is extremely beautiful, and more to the purpose than the most elaborate proof, which in truth the subject will not easily admit of;——the shortness of life being a point so generally complained of in all ages since the flood, and so universally felt and acknowledged by the whole species, as to require no evidence beyond a similitude; the intent of which is not so much to prove the fact, as to illustrate and place it in such a light as to strike us, and bring the impression home to ourselves in a more affecting manner.

Man comes forth, says Job, like a flower, and is cut down;——he is sent into the world the fairest and noblest part of God's works— fashioned after the image of his creator with respect to reason and the great faculties of the mind; he comes forth glorious as the flower of the field;° as it surpasses the vegetable world in beauty, so does he the animal world in the glory and excellencies of his nature.

The one——if no untimely accident oppress it, soon arrives at the full period of its perfection,—is suffered to triumph for a few moments, and is plucked up by the roots in the very pride and gayest stage of its being:——or if it happens to escape the hands of violence, in a few days it necessarily sickens of itself and dies away.

Man likewise, though his progress is slower, and his duration something longer, yet the periods of his growth and declension° are nearly the same both in the nature and manner of them.

If he escapes the dangers which threaten his tenderer years, he is soon got into the full maturity and strength of life; and if he is so fortunate as not to be hurried out of it then by accidents, by his own folly or intemperance——if he escapes these, he naturally decays of himself;——a period comes fast upon him, beyond which he was not made to last.——Like a flower or fruit which may be plucked up by force before the time of their maturity, yet cannot be made to outgrow the period when they are to fade and drop of themselves; when that comes, the hand of nature then plucks them both off, and no art of the botanist can uphold the one, or skill of the physician preserve the other, beyond the periods to which their original frames and constitutions were made to extend. As God has appointed and determined the several growths and decays of the vegetable race, so he seems as evidently to have prescribed the same laws to man, as well as all living creatures, in the first rudiments of which, there are contained the specifick powers of their growth, duration and extinction; and when the evolutions of those animal powers are exhausted and run down, the creature expires and dies of itself, as ripe fruit falls from the tree, or a flower preserved beyond its bloom droops and perishes upon the stalk.°

Thus much for this comparison of Job's, which though it is very poetical, yet conveys a just idea of the thing referred to.——'That he fleeth also as a shadow, and continueth not'—is no less a faithful and fine representation of the shortness and vanity of human life, of which one cannot give a better explanation, than by referring to the original, from whence the picture was taken.——With how quick a succession, do days, months and years pass over our heads?°—how truely like a shadow that departeth do they flee away insensibly, and scarce leave an impression with us?——when we endeavour to call them back by reflection, and consider in what manner they have gone, how unable are the best of us to give a tolerable account?—and were it not for some of the more remarkable stages which have distinguished a few periods of this rapid progress—we should look back upon it all as Nebuchadnezzar did upon his dream when he awoke in the morning;——he was sensible many things had passed, and troubled him too; but had passed on so quickly, they had left no footsteps behind, by which he could be enabled to trace them back.°——Melancholy account of the life of man! which generally runs on in such a manner, as scarce to allow time to make reflections which way it has gone.

How many of our first years slide by, in the innocent sports of childhood, in which we are not able to make reflections upon them?—how many more thoughtless years escape us in our youth, when we are unwilling to do it, and are so eager in the pursuit of pleasure as to have no time to spare, to stop and consider them?

When graver and riper years come on, and we begin to think it time to reform and set up for men of sense and conduct, then the business and perplexing interests of this world, and the endless plotting and contriving how to make the most of it, do so wholly employ us, that we are too busy to waste reflections upon so unprofitable a subject.——As families and children increase, so do our affections, and with them are multiplied our cares and toils for their preservation and establishment;—all which take up our thoughts so closely, and possess them so long, that we are often overtaken by grey hairs before we see them, or have found leisure to consider how far we were got,—what we have been doing,—and for what purpose God sent us into the world. As man may justly be said to be of few days considered with respect to this hasty succession of things, which soon carries him into the decline of his life, so may he likewise be said to flee like a shadow and continue not, when his duration is compared with other parts of God's works, and even the works of his own hands, which outlast him many generations;—whilst his—as Homer observes,° like leaves, one generation drops, and another springs up to fall again and be forgotten.

But when we further consider his days in the light in which we ought chiefly to view them, as they appear in thy sight, O God! with whom a thousand years are but as yesterday; when we reflect that this hand-breadth of life is all that is measured out to us from that eternity for which he is created, how does his short span vanish to nothing in the comparison? 'Tis true, the greatest portion of time will do the same when compared with what is to come; and therefore so short and transitory a one, as threescore years and ten, beyond which all is declared to be labour and sorrow, may the easier be allowed: and yet how uncertain are we of that portion, short as it is? Do not ten thousand accidents break off the slender thread of human life, long before it can be drawn out to that extent?——The new-born babe falls down an easy prey, and moulders back again into dust, like a tender blossom put forth in an untimely hour.——The hopeful youth in the very pride and beauty of life is cut off, some cruel distemper or unthought of accident lays him prostrate upon the earth, to pursue Job's comparison, like a blooming flower smit and shrivelled up with a malignant blast.——In this stage of life chances multiply upon us,——the seeds of disorders are sown by intemperance or neglect,——infectious distempers are more easily contracted, when contracted they rage with greater violence, and the success in many cases is more doubtful, insomuch that they who have exercised themselves in computations of this kind tell us, 'That one half of the whole species which are born into the world, go out of it again, and are all dead in so short a space as the first seventeen years.'°

These reflections may be sufficient to illustrate the first part of Job's declaration, '*That man is of few days.*' Let us examine the truth of the other, and see, whether he is not likewise full of trouble.

And here we must not take our account from the flattering outside of things, which are generally set off with a glittering appearance enough, especially in what is called, *higher life.*—Nor can we safely trust the evidence of some of the more merry and thoughtless amongst us, who are so set upon the enjoyment of life as seldom to reflect upon the troubles of it;—or who, perhaps, because they are not yet come to this portion of their inheritance, imagine it is not their common lot.——Nor lastly, are we to form an idea of it, from the delusive stories of a few of the more prosperous passengers, who have fortunately sailed through and escaped the rougher toils and distresses. But we are to take our accounts from a close survey of human life, and the real face of things, stript of every thing that can palliate or gild it over. We must hear the general complaint of all ages, and read the histories of mankind. If we look into them, and examine them to the bottom, what do they contain but the history of sad and uncomfortable passages, which a good-natured man cannot read but with oppression of spirits.——Consider the dreadful succession of wars in one part or other of the earth, perpetuated from one century to another with so little intermission, that mankind have scarce had time to breathe from them, since ambition first came into the world; consider the horrid effects of them in all those barbarous devastations we read of, where whole nations have been put to the sword, or have been driven out to nakedness and famine to make room for new comers. For a specimen of this, let us reflect upon the story related by Plutarch, when by order of the Roman senate, seventy populous cities were unawares sacked and destroyed at one prefixed hour, by P. Æmilius, by whom one hundred and fifty thousand unhappy people were driven in one day into captivity, to be sold to the highest bidder to end their days in cruel anguish.°——

Consider how great a part of our species in all ages down to this, have been trod under the feet of cruel and capricious tyrants, who would neither hear their cries, nor pity their distresses.—— Consider slavery——what it is,——how bitter a draught, and how many millions have been made to drink of it;° — which if it can poison all earthly happiness when exercised barely upon our bodies, what must it be, when it comprehends both the slavery of body and mind?——To conceive this, look into the history of the Romish church and her tyrants, (or rather executioners) who seem to have taken pleasure in the pangs and convulsions of their fellow-creatures.——Examine the prisons of the inquisition, hear the melancholy notes sounded in every cell.——Consider the anguish of mock-trials, and the exquisite tortures consequent thereupon, mercilessly inflicted upon the unfortunate, where the racked and weary soul has so often wished to take its leave,——but cruelly not suffered to depart.——Consider how many of these helpless wretches have been haled from thence in all periods of this tyrannic usurpation, to undergo the massacres and flames to which a false and a bloody religion has condemned them.°

If this sad history and detail of the more public causes of the miseries of man are not sufficient, let us behold him in another light with respect to the more private causes of them, and see whether he is not full of trouble likewise there, and almost born to it as naturally as the sparks fly upwards.° If we consider man as a creature full of wants and necessities (whether real or imaginary) which he is not able to supply of himself, what a train of disappointments, vexations and dependencies are to be seen, issuing from thence to perplex and make his being uneasy?—How many justlings and hard struggles do we undergo, in making our way in the world?—How barbarously held back?—How often and basely overthrown, in aiming only at getting bread?——How many of us never attain it—at least not comfortably, -- but from various unknown causes——eat it all their lives long in bitterness?

If we shift the scene, and look upwards, towards those whose situation in life seems to place them above the sorrows of this kind, yet where are they exempt from others? Do not all ranks and conditions of men meet with sad accidents and numberless calamities in other respects which often make them go heavily all their lives long?

How many fall into chronical infirmities, which render both their days and nights restless and insupportable?—How many of the highest rank are tore up with ambition, or soured with disappointments, and how many more from a thousand secret causes of disquiet pine away in silence, and owe their deaths to sorrow and dejection of heart?——If we cast our eyes upon the lowest class and condition of life,——the scene is more melancholy still.—— Millions of our fellow-creatures, born to no inheritance but poverty and trouble,° forced by the necessity of their lots to drudgery and painful employments, and hard set with that too, to get enough to keep themselves and families alive.——So that upon the whole, when we have examined the true state and condition of human life, and have made some allowances for a few fugacious,° deceitful pleasures, there is scarce any thing to be found which contradicts Job's description of it.——Which ever way we look abroad, we see some legible characters of what God first denounced against us, 'That in sorrow we should eat our bread, till we returned to the ground, from whence we were taken.'†°

But some one will say, Why are we thus to be put out of love with human life? To what purpose is it to expose the dark sides of it to us, or enlarge upon the infirmities which are natural, and consequently out of our power to redress?

I answer, that the subject is nevertheless of great importance, since it is necessary every creature should understand his present state and condition, to put him in mind of behaving suitably to it.——Does not an impartial survey of man—the holding up this glass to shew him his defects and natural infirmities, naturally tend to cure his pride and cloath him with humility, which is a dress that best becomes a short-lived and a wretched creature?—Does not the consideration of the shortness of our life, convince us of the wisdom of dedicating so small a portion to the great purposes of eternity?—

Lastly, When we reflect that this span of life, short as it is, is chequered with so many troubles, that there is nothing in this world springs up, or can be enjoyed without a mixture of sorrow,° how insensibly does it incline us to turn our eyes and affections from so gloomy a prospect, and fix them upon that happier country, where afflictions cannot follow us, and where God will wipe away all tears from off our faces for ever and ever? Amen.

† N.B. Most of these reflections upon the miseries of life, are taken from Wollaston.°

The LEVITE and his CONCUBINE.°

JUDGES xix. 1, 2, 3.°

And it came to pass in those days, when there was no king in Israel, that there was a certain Levite sojourning on the side of mount Ephraim, who took unto him a concubine.——

——A CONCUBINE!—but the text accounts for it, *for in those days there was no king in Israel*, and the Levite, you will say, like every other man in it, did what was right in his own eyes,——and so, you may add, did his concubine too—*for she played the whore against him, and went away.*——

——Then shame and grief go with her, and wherever she seeks a shelter, may the hand of justice shut the door against her.——

Not so; for she went unto her father's house in Bethlehem-judah, and was with him four whole months.——Blessed interval for meditation upon the fickleness and vanity of this world and it's pleasures! I see the holy man upon his knees,——with hands compressed to his bosom, and with uplifted eyes, thanking heaven, that the object which had so long shared his affections, was fled.——

The text gives a different picture of his situation; *for he arose and went after her to speak friendly to her, and to bring her back again, having his servant with him, and a couple of asses; and she brought him unto her father's house; and when the father of the damsel saw him, he rejoiced to meet him.*——

——A most sentimental group! you'll say: and so it is, my good commentator, the world talks of every thing: give but the outlines of a story,——let *spleen* or *prudery* snatch the pencil, and they will finish it with so many hard strokes, and with so dirty a colouring, that *candour* and *courtesy* will sit in torture as they look at it.—Gentle and virtuous spirits! ye who know not what it is to be rigid interpreters, but of your own failings,——to you, I address myself, the unhired advocates for the conduct of the misguided,——whence is it, that the world is not more jealous of your office? How often must ye repeat it, 'That such a one's doing so or so,'—is not sufficient evidence by itself to overthrow the accused? That our actions stand surrounded with a thousand circumstances which do not present themselves at first sight;—that the first springs and motives which impell'd the unfortunate, lie deeper still;——and, that of the millions which every hour are arraign'd, thousands of them may have err'd merely from the *head*, and been actually outwitted into evil; and even when from the heart,°——that the difficulties and temptations under which they acted,——the force of the passions,——the suitableness of the object, and the many struggles of virtue before she fell,——may be so many appeals from justice to the judgment seat of pity.

Here then let us stop a moment, and give the story of the Levite and his Concubine a second hearing: like all others much of it depends upon the telling; and as the Scripture has left us no kind of comment upon it, 'tis a story on which the heart cannot be at a loss for what to say, or the imagination for what to suppose—the danger is, humanity may say too much.°

And it came to pass in those days when there was no king in Israel, that a certain Levite sojourning on the side of mount Ephraim, took unto himself a Concubine.——

O Abraham, thou father of the faithful! if this was wrong,—— Why didst thou set so ensnaring an example before the eyes of thy descendants? and, Why did the GOD of Abraham, the GOD of Isaac and Jacob, bless so often the seed of such intercourses, and promise to multiply and make princes come out of them?

GOD can dispense with his own laws; and accordingly we find the holiest of the patriarchs, and others in Scripture whose hearts cleaved most unto GOD, accommodating themselves as well as they could to the dispensation: that Abraham had Hagar;—that Jacob, besides his two wives, Rachael and Leah, took also unto him Zilpah and Bilhah, from whom many of the tribes descended:—that David had seven wives and ten concubines;——Rehoboam, sixty,—and that, in whatever cases it became reproachable, it seemed not so much the thing itself, as the abuse of it, which made it so; this was remarkable in that of Solomon, whose excess became an insult upon the privileges of mankind; for by the same plan of luxury, which made it necessary to have forty thousand stalls of horses,—he had unfortunately miscalculated his other wants, and so had seven hundred wives, and three hundred concubines.——

Wise——deluded man! was it not that thou madest some amends for thy bad practice, by thy good preaching, what had become of thee!——three hundred——but let us turn aside, I beseech you, from so sad a stumbling block.

The Levite had but one. The Hebrew word imports a woman a concubine, or a wife a concubine, to distinguish her from the more infamous species, who came under the roofs of the licentious without principle. Our annotators tell us, that in Jewish *œconomicks*,° these differ'd little from the wife, except in some outward ceremonies and stipulations, but agreed with her in all the true essences of marriage, and gave themselves up to the husband, (for so he is call'd) with faith plighted, with sentiments and with affection.

Such a one the Levite wanted to share his solitude, and fill up that uncomfortable blank in the heart in such a situation; for notwithstanding all we meet with in books, in many of which, no doubt, there are a good many handsome things said upon the sweets of retirement, &c. . . . Yet still, '*it is not good for man to be alone:*'° nor can all which the cold-hearted pedant stuns our ears with upon the subject, ever give one answer of satisfaction to the mind; in the midst of the loudest vauntings of philosophy, Nature will have her yearnings for society and friendship;——a good heart wants some object to be kind to——and the best parts of our blood, and the purest of our spirits suffer most under the destitution.°

Let the torpid Monk seek heaven comfortless and alone——GOD speed him! For my own part, I fear, I should never so find the way: let me be wise and religious——but let me be MAN: wherever thy Providence places me, or whatever be the road I take to get to thee——give me some companion in my journey, be it only to remark to, How our shadows lengthen as the sun goes down;——to whom I may say, How fresh is the face of nature! How sweet the flowers of the field! How delicious are these fruits!°

Alas! with bitter herbs, like his passover, did the Levite eat them: for as they thus walked the path of life together,——she wantonly turn'd aside unto another, and fled from him.

It is the mild and quiet half of the world, who are generally outraged and born down by the other half of it: but in this they have the advantage; whatever be the sense of their wrongs, that pride stands not so watchful a sentinel over their forgiveness, as it does in the breasts of the fierce and froward: we should all of us, I believe, be more forgiving than we are, would the world but give us leave; but it is apt to interpose it's ill offices in remissions, especially of this kind:

the truth is, it has it's laws, to which the heart is not always a party; and acts so like an unfeeling engine in all cases without distinction, that it requires all the firmness of the most settled humanity to bear up against it.

Many a bitter conflict would the Levite have to sustain with himself—his Concubine——and the sentiments of his tribe, upon the wrong done him:——much matter for pleading—and many an embarrassing account on all sides: in a period of four whole months, every passion would take it's empire by turns; and in the ebbs and flows of the less unfriendly ones, PITY would find some moments to be heard——RELIGION herself would not be silent,——CHARITY would have much to say,——and thus attun'd, every object he beheld on the borders of mount Ephraim,——every grot° and grove he pass'd by, would sollicit the recollection of former kindness, and awaken an advocate in her behalf, more powerful than them all.

'I grant——I grant it all,'—he would cry,——''tis foul! 'tis faithless!——but, Why is the door of mercy to be shut forever against it? and, Why is it to be the only sad crime that the injured may not remit, or reason or imagination pass over without a scar?——Is it the blackest? In what catalogue of human offences is it so marked? or, Is it, that of all others, 'tis a blow most grievous to be endured?—— the heart cries out, It is so: but let me ask my own, What passions are they which give edge and force to this weapon which has struck me? and, Whether it is not my own pride, as much as my virtues, which at this moment excite the greatest part of that intolerable anguish in the wound which I am laying to her charge? But merciful heaven! was it otherwise, Why is an unhappy creature of thine to be persecuted by me with so much cruel revenge and rancorous despite° as my first transport called for? Have faults no extenuations?—— Makes it nothing, that, when the trespass was committed, she forsook the partner of her guilt, and fled directly to her father's house? And is there no difference betwixt one propensely going out of the road and continuing there, thro' depravity of will——and a hapless wanderer straying by delusion, and warily treading back her steps?——Sweet is the look of sorrow for an offence, in a heart determined never to commit it more!——Upon that altar only, could I offer up my wrongs. Cruel is the punishment which an ingenuous mind will take upon itself, from the remorse of so hard a trespass against me,——and if that will not balance the

account,——just GOD! let me forgive the rest. Mercy well becomes
the heart of all thy creatures,——but most of thy servant, a Levite,
who offers up so many daily sacrifices to thee,° for the transgressions
of thy people.——

—'But to little purpose, he would add, have I served at thy altar,
where my business was to sue for mercy, had I not learn'd to practise
it.'

Peace and happiness rest upon the head and heart of every man
who can thus think!

So he arose, and went after her to speak friendly to her—in the original—'to speak to her heart;'——to apply to their former endear-
ments,—and to ask, How she could be so unkind to him, and so very
unkind to herself?——

——Even the upbraidings of the quiet and relenting are sweet:
not like the strivings of the fierce and inexorable, who bite and
devour all who have thwarted them in their way;—but they are calm
and courteous like the spirit which watches over their character:
How could such a temper woo the damsel and not bring her back? or,
How could the father of the damsel, in such a scene, have a heart
open to any impressions but those mentioned in the text;——*That
when he saw him, he rejoiced to meet him*;——urged his stay from day
to day, with that most irresistible of all invitations,—*'Comfort thy
heart, and tarry all night, and let thine heart be merry.'*°

If *Mercy* and *Truth* thus met together° in settling this account,
Love would surely be of the party: great—great is it's power in
cementing what has been broken, and wiping out wrongs even from
the memory itself: and so it was——for the Levite arose up, and
with him his Concubine and his servant, and they departed.

It serves no purpose to pursue the story further; the catastrophe is
horrid;° and would lead us beyond the particular purpose for which I
have enlarged upon thus much of it,—and that is, to discredit rash
judgment, and illustrate from the manner of conducting this drama,
the courtesy which the *dramatis personæ* of every other piece, may
have a right to. Almost one half of our time is spent in telling and
hearing evil of one another—some unfortunate knight is always
upon this stage——and every hour brings forth something strange
and terrible to fill up our discourse and our astonishment, 'How
people can be so foolish!'——and 'tis well if the compliment ends
there: so that there is not a social virtue for which there is so constant

a demand,——or, consequently, so well worth cultivating, as that
which opposes this unfriendly current——many and rapid are the
springs which feed it, and various and sudden, GOD knows, are the
gusts which render it unsafe to us in this short passage of our life: let
us make the discourse as serviceable as we can, by tracing some of
the most remarkable of them, up to their source.

And first, there is one miserable inlet to this evil; and which by the
way, if speculation is supposed to precede practice, may have been
derived, for aught I know, from some of our busiest enquirers after
nature,—and that is, when with more zeal than knowledge, we
account for phenomena, before we are sure of their existence.—*It is
not the manner of the Romans to condemn any man to death*, (much less
to be martyr'd) said Festus;——*and doth our law judge any man
before it hear him, and know what he doth?* cried Nicodemus; *and he
that answereth*, or determineth, *a matter before he has heard it,——it
is folly and a shame unto him.*°—We are generally in such a haste to
make our own decrees, that we pass over the justice of these,——and
then the scene is so changed by it, that 'tis our folly only which is
real, and that of the accused, which is imaginary: through too much
precipitancy it will happen so;—and then the jest is spoiled,—or we
have criticised our own shadow.

A second way is, when the process goes on more orderly, and we
begin with getting information,——but do it from those suspected
evidences, against which our SAVIOUR warns us, when he bids us
'*not to judge according to appearance:*'°——in truth, 'tis behind these,
that most of the things which blind human judgment, lie concealed,——and on the contrary, there are many things which appear
to be,——which are not:——*Christ came eating and drinking,—
behold a wine-bibber!*°——he sat with sinners—he was their
friend:——in many cases of which kind, *Truth*, like a modest
matron, scorns art——and disdains to press herself forwards into
the circle to be seen:——ground sufficient for *Suspicion* to draw up
the libel,——for *Malice* to give the torture,—or rash *Judgment* to
start up and pass a final sentence.

A third way is, when the facts which denote misconduct, are less
disputable, but are commented upon with an asperity of censure,
which a humane or a gracious temper would spare: an abhorrence
against what is criminal, is so fair a plea for this, and looks so like
virtue in the face, that in a sermon against rash judgment, it would

be unseasonable to call it in question,——and yet, I declare, in the fullest torrent of exclamations which the guilty can deserve, that the simple ápostrophè, 'Who made me to differ: why was not I an example?'° would touch my heart more, and give me a better earnest of the commentators,——than the most corrosive period° you could add. The punishment of the unhappy, I fear, is enough without it——and were it not,——'tis pitious, the tongue of a Christian, whose religion is all candour and courtesy, should be made the executioner. We find in the discourse between Abraham and the rich man, tho' the one was in heaven, and the other in hell, yet still the patriarch treated him with mild language:—*Son!*—*Son, remember that thou in thy life time*, &c. &c.°—and in the dispute about the body of Moses, between the Arch-angel and the devil, (himself,) St. Jude tells us, he durst not bring a railing° accusation against him;—'twas unworthy his high character,——and indeed, might have been impolitick too; for if he had, (as one of our divines notes upon the passage)° the devil had been too hard for him at railing,——'twas his own weapon,——and the basest spirits after his example are the most expert at it.

This leads me to the observation of a fourth cruel inlet to this evil, and that is, the desire of being thought men of wit and parts, and the vain expectation of coming honestly by the title, by shrewd and sarcastick reflections upon whatever is done in the world. This is setting up trade upon the broken stock of other people's failings,—perhaps their misfortunes:——so much good may't do them with what honour they can get,——the furthest extent of which, I think, is, to be praised, as we do some sauces, with tears in our eyes: It is a commerce most illiberal; and as it requires no vast capital, too many embark in it, and so long as there are bad passions to be gratified,—and bad heads to judge, with such it may pass for wit, or at least like some vile relation, whom all the family is ashamed of, claim kindred with it, even in better companies. Whatever be the degree of its affinity, it has helped to give wit a bad name, as if the main essence of it was satire: certainly there is a difference between *Bitterness* and *Saltness*,—that is,——between the malignity and the festivity of wit,°——the one is a mere quickness of apprehension, void of humanity,—and is a talent of the devil; the other comes down from the Father of Spirits, so pure and abstracted from persons, that willingly it hurts no man; or if it touches upon an indecorum, 'tis with that dexterity of true genius, which enables him rather to give a new colour to the absurdity, and let it pass.——He may smile at the shape of the obelisk raised to another's fame,——but the malignant wit will level it at once with the ground, and build his own upon the ruins of it.——

What then, ye rash censurers of the world! Have ye no mansions for your credit, but those from whence ye have extruded the right owners? Are there no regions for you to shine in, that ye descend for it, into the low caverns of abuse and crimination? Have ye no seats——but those of the scornful to sit down in? if *Honour* has mistook his road, or the *Virtues* in their excesses have approached too near the confines of VICE, Are they therefore to be cast down the precipice?° Must BEAUTY for ever be trampled upon in the dirt for one——one false step? And shall no one virtue or good quality, out of the thousand the fair penitent may have left,——shall not one of them be suffered to stand by her?——Just GOD of Heaven and Earth!——

——But thou art merciful, loving and righteous, and lookest down with pity upon these wrongs thy servants do unto each other: pardon us, we beseech thee, for them, and all our transgressions; let it not be remember'd, that we were brethren of the same flesh, the same feelings and infirmities.——O my GOD! write it not down in thy book, that thou madest us merciful, after thy own image;—— that thou hast given us a religion so courteous,——so good temper'd,——that every precept of it carries a balm along with it to heal the soreness of our natures, and sweeten our spirits, that we might live with such kind intercourse in this world, as will fit us to exist together in a better.

On Enthusiasm.°

ST. JOHN xv. 5.

——For without me, ye can do nothing.

OUR Saviour, in the former part of the verse, having told his disciples,—That he was the vine, and that they were only branches;—intimating, in what a degree their good fruits, as well as the success of all their endeavours, were to depend upon his communications with them;—he closes the illustration with the inference from it, in the words of the text,—For without me, ye can do nothing.—In the 11th chapter to the Romans, where the manner is explained in which a christian stands by faith,—there is a like illustration made use of, and probably with an eye to this,—where St. Paul instructs us,—that a good man stands as the branch of a wild olive does, when it is grafted into a good olive tree;—and that is,—it flourishes not through its own virtue, but in virtue of the root,—and such a root as is naturally not its own.

It is very remarkable in that passage,—that the apostle calls a bad man a wild olive *tree*;—not barely a branch, (as in the other case) but a tree, which having a root of its own, supports itself, and stands in its own strength, and brings forth its own fruit.—And so does every bad man in respect of the wild and sour fruit of a vicious and corrupt heart.—According to the resemblance,—if the apostle intended it,—he is a tree,—has a root of his own,—and fruitfulness, such as it is, with a power to bring it forth without help. But in respect of religion, and the moral improvements of virtue and goodness,—the apostle calls us, and reason tells us, we are no more than a branch; and all our fruitfulness, and all our support,—depend so much upon the influence and communications of God,—that without him we can do nothing,—as our Saviour declares in the text.—There is scarce any point in our religion wherein men have run into such violent extremes as in the senses given to this, and such like declarations in Scripture,—of our sufficiency being of God;°—some understanding them so, as to leave no meaning at all in them;—others,—too much:—the one interpreting the gifts and influences of the spirit, so as to destroy the truth of all such promises and declarations in the gospel;—the other carrying their notions of them so high, as to destroy the reason of the gospel itself,—and render the christian religion, which consists of sober and consistent doctrines,—the most intoxicated,—the most wild and unintelligible institution that ever was in the world.°

This being premised, I know not how I can more seasonably engage your attention this day, than by a short examination of each of these errors;—in doing which, as I shall take some pains to reduce both the extremes of them to reason,—it will necessarily lead me, at the same time, to mark the safe and true doctrine of our church, concerning the promised influences and operations of the spirit of God upon our hearts;—which, however depreciated through the first mistake,—or boasted of beyond measure through the second,—must nevertheless be so limited and understood,—as, on one hand, to make the gospel of Christ consistent with itself,—and, on the other, to make it consistent with reason and common sense.

If we consider the many express declarations, wherein our Saviour tells his followers, before his crucifixion,—That God would send his spirit the comforter amongst them, to supply his place in their hearts;—and, as in the text,—that without him, they could do nothing:—if we conceive them as spoken to his disciples with an immediate view to the emergencies they were under, from their *natural* incapacities of finishing the great work he had left them, and building upon that large foundation he had laid,—without some extraordinary help and guidance to carry them through,—no one can dispute that evidence and confirmation which was after given of its truth;—as our Lord's disciples were illiterate men, consequently unskilled in the arts and acquired ways of persuasion.—Unless this want had been supplied,—the first obstacle to their labours must have discouraged and put an end to them for ever.—As they had no language but their own, without the gift of tongues° they could not have preached the gospel except in Judea;—and as they had no authority of their own,—without the supernatural one of signs and wonders,—they could not vouch for the truth of it beyond the limits where it was first transacted.—In this work, doubtless, all their sufficiency and power of acting was immediately from God;—his holy spirit, as he had promised them, so it gave them a mouth and wisdom which all their adversaries were not able to gainsay or resist.—So that without him,—without these extraordinary gifts, in the most literal sense of the words, they *could* do nothing.—But besides this plain application of the text to those particular persons and times, when God's spirit was poured down in that signal manner held sacred to this day,—there is something in them to be extended further, which christians of all ages,—and, I hope, of all denominations, have still a claim and trust in,—and that is, the ordinary assistance and influences of the spirit of God in our hearts, for moral and virtuous improvements;—these, both in their natures as well as intentions, being altogether different from the others above-mentioned conferred upon the disciples of our Lord.—The one were miraculous gifts,—in which the endowed person contributed nothing, which advanced human nature above itself, and raised all its projectile springs above their fountains; enabling them to speak and act such things, and in such manner, as was impossible for men not inspired and preternaturally upheld.—In the other case, the helps spoken of were the influences of God's spirit, which upheld us from falling below the dignity of our nature:—that divine assistance which graciously kept us from falling, and enabled us to perform the holy professions of our religion.—Though these are equally called spiritual gifts,—they are not, as in the first case, the entire works of the spirit,—but the calm co-operations of it with our own endeavours; and are ordinarily what every sincere and well-disposed christian has reason to pray for, and expect from the same fountain of strength,—who has promised to give his holy spirit to them that ask it.

From this point, which is the true doctrine of our church,—the two parties begin to divide both from it and each other;—each of them equally misapplying these passages of Scripture, and wresting them to extremes equally pernicious.—

To begin with the first; of whom, should you enquire the explanation and meaning of this or of other texts,—wherein the assistance of God's grace and holy spirit is implied as necessary to sanctify our nature, and enable us to serve and please God?—They will answer,—That no doubt all our parts and abilities are the gifts of God,—who is the original author of our nature,—and, of consequence, of all that belongs thereto.—*That as by him we live, and move, and have our being,*°—we must in course depend upon him for all our actions whatsoever,—since we must depend upon him even for our life, and for every moment of its continuance.—That from this view of our state and natural dependence, it is certain they will say,—We can do nothing without his help.—But then they will add,—that it concerns us no farther as *christians*, than as we are *men*;—the sanctity of our lives, the religious habits and improvements of our hearts, in no other sense depending upon God, than the most indifferent of our actions, or the natural exercise of any of the other powers he has given us.—Agreeably with this,—that the spiritual gifts spoken of in Scripture, are to be understood by way of accommodation, to signify the natural or acquired gifts of a man's mind; such as memory, fancy, wit and eloquence; which, in a strict and philosophical sense, may be called spiritual;—because they transcend the mechanical powers of matter,—and proceed more or less from the rational soul, which is a spiritual substance.

Whether these ought, in propriety, to be called spiritual gifts, I shall not contend, as it seems a mere dispute about words;—but it is enough that the interpretation cuts the knot, instead of untying it;° and, besides, explains away all kind of meaning in the above promises.—And the error of them seems to arise, in the first place, from not distinguishing that these spiritual gifts,—if they must be called so,—such as memory, fancy and wit, and other endowments of the mind, which are known by the name of natural parts, belong merely to us as men; and whether the different degrees, by which we excel each other in them, arise from a natural difference of our souls,—or a happier disposition of the organical parts of us.—They are such, however, as God originally bestows upon us, and with which, in a great measure, we are sent into the world. But the moral gifts of the Holy Ghost,—which are more commonly called the fruits of the spirit,—cannot be confined within this description.—We come not into the world equipt with virtues, as we do with talents;—if we did, we should come into the world with that which robbed virtue of its best title both to present commendation and future reward.—The gift of continency° depends not, as these affirm, upon a mere coldness of the constitution—or patience and humility from an insensibility of it;—but they are virtues insensibly wrought in us by the endeavours of our own wills and concurrent influences of a gracious agent;—and the religious improvements arising from thence, are so far from being the effects of nature, and a fit disposition of the several parts and organical powers given us,—that the contrary is true;—namely,—that the stream of our affections and appetites but too naturally carry us the other way.—For this, let any man lay his hand upon his heart, and reflect what has past within him, in the several conflicts of meekness,—temperance,—chastity, and other self-denials,—and he will need no better argument for his conviction.—

This hint leads to the true answer to the above misinterpretation of the text,—That we depend upon God in no other sense for our virtues,—than we necessarily do for every thing else; and that the fruits of the spirit are merely the determinations and efforts of our own reason,—and as much our own accomplishments, as any other improvements are the effect of our own diligence and industry.

This account, by the way, is opposite to the apostle's;—who tells us,—It is God that worketh in us both to do and will, of his good pleasure.°—It is true,—though we are born ignorant,—we can make ourselves skillful;—we can acquire arts and sciences by our own application and study.—But the case is not the same in respect of goodness.—We can acquire arts and sciences, because we lay under no natural indisposition or backwardness to that acquirement.—For nature, though it be corrupt, yet still it is curious and busy after knowledge.—But it does not appear, that to goodness and sanctity of manners we have the same natural propensity.—Lusts within, and temptations without, set up so strong a confederacy against it, as we are never able to surmount by our own strength.—However firmly we may think we stand,—the best of us are but upheld, and graciously kept upright; and whenever this divine assistance is withdrawn,—or suspended,—all history, especially the sacred, is full of melancholy instances of what man is, when God leaves him to himself,—that he is even a thing of nought.

Whether it was from a conscious experience of this truth in themselves,—or some traditions handed from the Scripture account of it;—or that it was, in some measure, deducible from the principles of reason,—in the writings of some of the wisest of the heathen philosophers, we find the strongest traces of the persuasion of God's assisting men to virtue and probity of manners.—One of the greatest masters of reasoning amongst the ancients acknowledges, that nothing great and exalted can be atchieved, sine divino afflatu;°—and Seneca,° to the same purpose,—nulla mens bona sine deo;—that no soul can be good without divine assistance.—Now whatever comments may be put upon such passages in their writings,—it is certain those in Scripture can receive no other, to be consistent with themselves, than what has been given.—And though, in vindication of human liberty, it is as certain on the other hand,—that education, precepts, examples, pious inclinations, and practical diligence, are great and meritorious advances towards a religious state;—yet the state itself is got and finished by God's grace; and the concurrence of his spirit upon tempers thus happily pre-disposed,—and honestly making use of such fit means:—and unless thus much is understood from them,—the several expressions in Scripture, where the offices of the Holy Ghost conducive to this end, are enumerated;—such as cleansing, guiding, renewing, comforting, strengthening and establishing us,—are a set of unintelligible words, which may amuse, but can convey little light to the understanding.

This is all I have time left to say at present upon the first error of those, who, by too loose an interpretation of the gifts and fruits of the spirit, explain away the whole sense and meaning of them, and thereby render not only the promises, but the comforts of them too, of none effect.—Concerning which error, I have only to add this by way of extenuation of it,—that I believe the great and unedifying rout° made about sanctification and regeneration in the middle of the last century,°—and the enthusiastic extravagancies into which the communications of the spirit have been carried by so many deluded or deluding people in this, are two of the great causes which have driven many a sober man into the opposite extreme, against which I have argued.—Now if the dread of savouring too much of religion in their interpretations has done this ill service,—let us enquire, on the other hand, whether the affectation of too *much* religion in the other extreme, has not misled others full as far from truth, and further from the reason and sobriety of the gospel, than the first.

I have already proved by Scripture arguments, that the influence of the holy spirit of God is necessary to render the imperfect sacrifice of our obedience pleasing to our Maker.—He hath promised to *perfect his strength in our weakness.*°—With this assurance we ought to be satisfied;—especially since our Saviour hath thought proper to mortify all scrupulous enquiries into operations of this kind, by comparing them to the wind, *which bloweth where it listeth; and thou hearest the sound thereof, but canst not tell whence it cometh, or whither it goeth:—so is every one that is born of the spirit.*°—Let humble gratitude acknowledge the effect, unprompted by an idle curiosity to explain the cause.

We are told, without this assistance, we can do nothing;—we are told, from the same authority, we can do all through Christ that strengthens us.—We are commanded to *work out our own salvation with fear and trembling.* The reason immediately follows; *for it is God that worketh in you, both to will and to do, of his own good pleasure.*°— From these, and many other repeated passages, it is evident, that the assistances of grace were not intended to destroy, but to co-operate with the endeavours of man,—and are derived from God in the same manner as all natural powers.—Indeed, without this interpretation, how could the Almighty address himself to man as a rational being?—how could his actions be his own?—how could he be considered as a blameable or rewardable creature?

From this account of the consistent opinions of a sober-minded christian, let us take a view of the mistaken enthusiast.—See him ostentatiously cloathed with the outward garb of sanctity, to attract the eyes of the vulgar.—See a chearful demeanour, the natural result of an easy and self-applauding heart, studiously avoided as criminal.—See his countenance overspread with a melancholy gloom and despondence;—as if religion, which is evidently calculated to make us happy in this life as well as the next, was the parent of sullenness and discontent.—Hear him pouring forth his pharisaical° ejaculations on his journey, or in the streets.—Hear him boasting of extraordinary communications with the God of all knowledge, and at the same time offending against the common rules of his own native language, and the plainer dictates of common sense.—Hear him arrogantly thanking his God, that he is not as other men are; and, with more than papal uncharitableness, very liberally allotting the portion of the damned, to every christian whom he, partial judge, deems less perfect than himself—to every christian who is walking on in the paths of duty with sober vigilance, aspiring to perfection by progressive attainments, and seriously endeavouring, through a rational faith in his Redeemer, to make his calling and election sure.

There have been no sects in the christian world, however absurd, which have not endeavoured to support their opinions by arguments drawn from Scripture, misinterpreted or misapplied.

We had a melancholy instance of this in our own country, in the last century,—when the church of Christ, as well as the government, during that period of national confusion,° was torn asunder into various sects and factions;—when some men pretended to have Scripture precepts, parables, or prophecies to plead, in favour of the most impious absurdities that falsehood could advance. The same spirit which prevailed amongst the fanaticks, seems to have gone forth among these modern enthusiasts.—Faith, the distinguishing characteristick of a christian, is defined by them not as a rational assent of the understanding, to truths which are established by indisputable authority, but as a violent persuasion of mind, that they are instantaneously become the children of God—that the whole score of their sins is for ever blotted out, without the payment of one tear of repentance.—Pleasing doctrine this to the fears and passions of mankind!—promising fair to gain proselytes of the vicious and impenitent.

Pardons and indulgences° are the great support of papal power;—but these modern empiricks° in religion have improved upon the scheme, pretending to have discovered an infallible nostrum for all incurables; such as will preserve them for ever.—And notwithstanding we have instances of notorious offenders among the warmest advocates for sinless perfection,—the charm continues powerful.—Did these visionary notions of an heated imagination tend only to amuse the fancy, they might be treated with contempt;—but when they depreciate all moral attainments;—when the suggestions of a frantic brain are blasphemously ascribed to the holy spirit of God;—when faith and divine love are placed in opposition to practical virtues, they then become the objects of aversion. In one sense, indeed, many of these deluded people demand our tenderest compassion,—whose disorder is in the head rather than the heart: and who call for the aid of a physician who can cure the distempered state of the body, rather than one who may sooth the anxieties of the mind.

Indeed, in many cases, they seem so much above the skill of either,—that unless God in his mercy rebuke this spirit of enthusiasm, which is gone out amongst us, no one can pretend to say how far it may go, or what mischiefs it may do in these kingdoms.—Already it has taught us as much blasphemous language;—and, if it goes on, by the samples given us in their journals,° will fill us with as many legendary accounts of visions and revelations, as we have formerly had from the church of Rome. And for any security we have against it,—when time shall serve, it may as effectually convert the professors of it, even into popery itself,—consistent with their own principles;—for they have nothing more to do than to say, that the spirit which inspired them, has signified, that the pope is inspired as well as they,—and consequently is infallible.—After which I cannot see how they can possibly refrain going to mass, consistent with their own principles.—

Thus much for these two opposite errors;—the examination of which has taken up so much time,—that I have little left to add, but to beg of God, by the assistance of his holy spirit, to preserve us equally from both extremes, and enable us to form such right and worthy apprehensions of our holy religion,—that it may never suffer, through the coolness of our conceptions of it, on one hand,—or the immoderate heat of them, on the other;—but that we may at all times see it, as it is, and as it was designed by its blessed Founder, as the most rational, sober and consistent institution that could have been given to the sons of men.

Now to God, &c.

EXPLANATORY NOTES

For the present edition, Ian Jack's annotations have been augmented and in some instances rewritten. Jack's notes are initialled. Biographical information has been keyed to the two-volume standard life of Sterne by Arthur H. Cash. Translations of classical texts are taken from the editions of the Loeb Classical Library, Harvard University Press. References to *Tristram Shandy* are to original volume and chapter, followed by page number of the Florida edition.

T.P.

A SENTIMENTAL JOURNEY

3 *this matter*: although the enigma is deliberate, a number of commentators have sought to explain the 'matter' in question. As Ian Jack notes, *Yorick's Sentimental Journey Continued, By Eugenius* (1769) offers the following gloss: 'The subject in debate, was, the inconvenience of drinking healths whilst at meal, and toasts afterwards'. Matters are ordered better in France where: 'HEALTHS ARE ABOLISHED, AND TOASTS NEVER

WERE ADOPTED' (see Jack's letter in *TLS*, 4 Feb. 1977, p. 131). For the suggestion that Sterne is alluding to the philosophical materialism espoused by the likes of Baron d'Holbach and Diderot, see Martin C. Battestin, 'Sterne among the *Philosophes*: Body and Soul in *A Sentimental Journey*' *Eighteenth-Century Fiction*, 7 (1994), 27–8.

3 *my gentleman*: my manservant. [I.J.]

Dover stage: stage-coach bound for Dover.

packet: packet-boat.

Eliza: Elizabeth Sclater Draper (1744–78). For Sterne's relationship with Mrs Draper, see Introduction, pp. xxix–xxx. Sterne had a miniature of Eliza mounted not in a locket, but in the lid of his snuffbox. He refers to this passage in the entries in the *Journal* for 13 and 17 June (see pp. 130–1 and 132).

All the effects . . . redress: the footnote echoes *Travels through France and Italy* (1766) by Tobias Smollett (1721–71): 'If a foreigner dies in France, the king seizes all his effects, even though his heir should be upon the spot; and this tyranny is called the *droit d'aubaine*' (*Travels*, ii. 9). Sterne had had first-hand experience of the 'Villany & extortion' of the *droit d'aubaine* in Toulouse in 1763 (see *LY*, 161–2). For the 'farming' of taxes, see note to p. 92 below.

4 *for the accommodation*: as a result of settling the matter (in my own mind). [I.J.]

livres: a livre was a unit of French currency roughly equal to the modern franc. In eighteenth-century terms, it was worth about ten English pennies.

physical precieuse: once a term of approbation for a cultured woman, 'precieuse' became a pejorative epithet for a woman affecting fashionable learning and taste. Updating the type satirized in *Les Précieuses ridicules* (1659) by Molière (1622–73), Yorick sets his 'proof' of the mysterious and immaterial sources of human action against the imagined arguments of an advocate of the kind of atheistic materialism embodied in *L'Homme machine* (1748) by Julien Offray de la Mettrie (1709–51).

puissant: powerful.

sed non, quo ad hanc: the sense of this Latin phrase is perhaps best conveyed by Sterne's rough translation, 'or be it as it may'.

5 *sous*: a coin worth a twentieth of a livre and roughly equivalent in the eighteenth century to half an English penny.

Guido: Guido Reni (1575–1642), Bolognese painter, whose mainly religious works inspired much critical enthusiasm in the eighteenth century. According to Smollett, there 'is a tenderness and delicacy in his manner; and his figures are all exquisitely beautiful' (*Travels*, xxxi. 255).

fat contented ignorance: such a negative image of a bloated monk— embodying the kind of corruption, greed, and superstition that the rhetoric of Britishness typically associated with the French—takes centre stage in Hogarth's engraving, *Calais Gate, or the Roast Beef of Old England* (1749). The conventional symbolism of the monk figure in Protestant propaganda suggests that Sterne, in spite of regular swipes at Catholicism in *Tristram Shandy* and the sermons, may here be attempting to contest and revise the stereotype.

Bramin: a Brahmin is a member of the Hindu priestly caste, renowned for wisdom and austerity. In a double allusion to his own role as a priest and to Elizabeth Draper's associations with India, Sterne and Eliza used 'Bramin and Bramine' as pet names (see *Journal*, 107).

attitude of Intreaty: Sterne was keenly interested in painting, and in the attitudes conventionally associated with the various passions. [I.J.]

6 *order of mercy ... St. Francis*: while the Franciscans beg for their own subsistence, the Order of Our Lady of Mercy was instituted in 1218 to raise funds for the ransoming of Christians captured by the Moors.

for the love of God: a translation of the conventional appeal for charity, 'pour l'amour de Dieu'.

hectic: flush.

7 *chaise*: carriage.

Monsieur Dessein: proprietor of the Lyon d'Argent in Calais, where Sterne stayed in 1762. For further details about Dessein and the celebrity following from Sterne's use of his name in the *Journey*, see *LY*, 229 and Stout, 336–8.

8 *peripatetic philosopher*: because of Aristotle's habit of walking about as he taught, the phrase is used to describe his followers. Yorick is a 'peripatetic philosopher' insofar as he makes philosophical observations as he travels.

sentimental commerce: cf. 'The House of Feasting ...', p. 186 above: 'so benevolent a commerce'.

efficient ... final causes: in scholastic terminology, an efficient cause makes a thing to be what it is, while a final cause is the purpose for which something is done.

9 *peregrine*: 'upon a pilgrimage; travelling abroad' (*OED*).

with the benefit of the clergy: accompanied by clerical tutors, as was common for young 'milords' on the Grand Tour. Sterne is glancing humorously at the usual meaning of the phrase 'benefit of clergy'—exemption from the jurisdiction of the ordinary courts of law. [I.J.]

was it not necessary ... confusion of character: Tristram affects a similar anxiety in his portrayal of Uncle Toby (*TS*, II. ii. 98).

10 *besoin de Voyager*: need to travel, wanderlust.

my travels ... my Vehicle: writing to his daughter about his plans for a new work in February 1767, Sterne similarly stressed the originality of the *Journey*: 'I have laid a plan for something new, quite out of the beaten track' (*Letters*, 301).

10 *discovering his nakedness*: an allusion to the results of Noah's drunkenness in Genesis 9: 20–2.

11 *as Sancho Pança said to Don Quixote*: Miguel de Cervantes (1547–1616), *Don Quixote* (1605, 1615), II. v. Sancho was actually speaking to his wife.

Where then . . . are you going: echoing the question in the title of Joseph Hall's *Quo Vadis? A Just Censure of Travel, As it is Commonly Undertaken by the Gentlemen of our Nation* (1617). Although the comments in this paragraph on travel and the state of knowledge seem relevant to the mid-eighteenth century, many of them are verbatim borrowings from Hall (1574–1656). Hall appears to have been one of Sterne's favourite writers and is an important influence on the sermons.

Vis a Vis: a carriage for two people sitting face-to-face.

effectually: in fact.

out of conceit with: out of a favourable opinion of.

12 *vampt-up*: patched up, repaired.

Mount Sennis: Mt. Cenis on the French-Italian border. Because of the steepness of Mt. Cenis, carriages were dismantled and carried over the pass by mules.

Mon Dieu!: My God!

C'est bien vrai: It's very true, quite so.

d'un homme d'esprit: of a man of wit, of a wit.

casuistry: 'the art . . . of the casuist . . . often applied to a quibbling or evasive way of dealing with difficult cases of duty' (*OED*).

Remise: coach-house. On p. 62, however, 'remise' means a hired carriage. [I.J.]

magazine: storehouse.

13 *conventionist*: one who enters into a contract.

en face: in the face, full face.

louisd'ors: a louis d'or was a French gold coin worth about 20 livres and roughly equivalent to an eighteenth-century English pound.

thy hand . . . against thee: cf. Genesis 16: 12.

diabled: cursed, from French *diable* (devil).

14 *When the heart . . . world of pains*: cf. p. 37 and 'The Levite and his Concubine', p. 207 above. The privileging of heart over head is a commonplace which occurs regularly in Sterne's writing.

ductility: tractableness, docility.

as if . . . into the Tiber for it: an allusion to the recovery by archaeologists of the missing heads of statues from the Tiber. Cf. the musings of Fancy in *TS*, VIII. v. 661.

15 *rouge or powder*: it was common for English travellers to object to the use of cosmetics by Frenchwomen. Shortly before she was due to return to

England from France in 1767, Sterne urged his daughter to 'throw all your rouge pots into the Sorgue before you set out' (*Letters*, 391).

interesting: as Arthur Cash notes, for Sterne, 'interesting' meant 'affecting, appealing to the tender sentiments. . . . The *OED* cites *A Sentimental Journey* as its earliest example of this word in its second meaning—appealing to or able to arouse emotions' (*LY*, 27 and n. 61).

declension: decline, sunken condition.

bon ton: good manners, conventions.

Esdras . . . troubled: cf. 2 Esdras 10: 31 (Apocrypha).

felt benevolence for her: cf. Tristram's 'full force of an honest heart-ache' on seeing 'poor Maria' in *TS*, IX. xxiv. 783.

service: possibly punning on a number of meanings: a willingness to serve or help in a general sense, 'the devotion or suit of a lover' (*OED*), and to serve sexually.

16 *neither oil . . . to the wound*: cf. Luke 10: 33–4.

The pulsations . . . within me: the Widow Wadman seeks to make contact with Uncle Toby by a similar route (see *TS*, VIII. xvi. 676–7).

18 *revulsion*: 'the action of drawing, or the fact of being drawn, back or away' (*OED*).

19 *lousy prebendary*: Sterne himself was made Prebend of Givendale in 1741 and of North Newbald in the following year. To his disappointment, a church career failed to blossom after this early promise. The Yorick of *Tristram Shandy* is similarly torn between the demands of discretion and the promptings of his heteroclite nature.

tartufish: hypocritical, after the central character of Molière's *Le Tartuffe* (1664). For Tristram's and Sterne's contempt for 'Tartuffes', see *TS*, V. i. 409 and VIII. ii. 657 and *Letters*, 411.

20 *Vous n'etez pas . . . Lisle?*: the captain's questions might be translated as follows: 'You are not from London? . . . Apparently you are Flemish? . . . Perhaps, from Lisle?'

last war: during the War of the Austrian Succession (1740–8), the French besieged and finally captured Brussels from the Austrians, Dutch, and English.

pour cela: for that.

21 *Et Madame a son Mari?*: 'And Madame is with her husband?'

chaffer: haggle.

22 *C'EST bien comique*: It's very funny.

fort: strong point, forte.

pours and contres: points for and against, pros and cons.

grave people . . . name's sake: possibly an echo of the Preface to the Third Partition of the *Anatomy of Melancholy* (1621–51) by Robert Burton

(1577–1640). Introducing a ticklish subject for a divine, 'Love-Melancholy', Burton tries to forestall the criticisms of those who 'out of an affected gravity, will dislike all for the names [*sic*] sake'. Burton is an important source for Sterne in *Tristram Shandy*.

23 *having eyes to see*: cf. Mark 8: 18 and Luke 8: 10.

time and chance: cf. Ecclesiastes 9: 11. For Sterne's sermon on this text, see *Sermons*, 8. 74–80.

24 *assay*: test, experiment.

by him who . . . gross to sleep: cf. 'The Levite and his Concubine', p. 208 above.

Dan to Beersheba: cf. Judges 20: 1 in which the children of Israel are 'gathered together as one man, from Dan even to Beersheba'. Dan and Beersheba represent the extreme north and south of Canaan, and Sterne uses them figuratively to suggest the length and breadth of the country.

SMELFUNGUS: Smollett. The almost unremittingly negative response to French culture in the *Travels* led the reviewer in the *Gazette littéraire de l'Europe* to accuse Smollett of 'exposing our nudity in the eyes of the nations with an unexampled inhumanity' (see *LY*, 312–13). While the contrast between the sentimental and laughing Yorick and the splenetic Smollett suits Sterne's artistic purposes, his own letters from France sometimes savour more of spleen than of sentiment (see, for example, *Letters*, 182–3, 186, 209).

sweet myrtle . . . melancholy cypress: traditionally, the myrtle is associated with Venus and the cypress with death.

I met Smelfungus . . . in nature: although Sterne did meet Smollett in Montpellier in 1763, the meeting in the Pantheon has no basis in fact. Smollett was 'much disappointed at sight of the Pantheon, which . . . looks like a huge cockpit' (*Travels*, xxxi. 258). Smollett's criticisms of the Medici Venus are prefaced by an admission of possible 'want of taste', but he opened himself to Sterne's ridicule by noting that the statue's 'back parts especially are executed so happily, as to excite the admiration of the most indifferent spectator' (*Travels*, xxviii. 227).

'wherein . . . Anthropophagi': cf. *Othello* i. iii. 134 ff.

he had been flea'd . . . come at: as Tom Keymer suggests (*A Sentimental Journey and Other Writings* (London: J. M. Dent, 1994), 153), Sterne is probably punning on Smollett's description of 'St Bartholomew flaed alive, and . . . other pictures equally frightful' (*Travels*, xxxi. 257) and on his complaints about being 'half devoured by vermin' in 'abominably nasty' (*Travels*, xxxiv. 281, 280) Italian inns. For Sterne's own complaints about being 'eat up at night by bugs, and other unswept out vermin' on his journey to Toulouse, see *Letters*, 182–3.

Mundungus: traditionally identified as Dr Samuel Sharp (1700?–78), author of *Letters from Italy* (1766). Since, however, Sharp and Mundungus share neither fortune nor itinerary, it is safer to see the latter as a generalized figure. The *Lexicon Balatronicum* (1811) defines Mundungus thus: 'Bad or rank tobacco: from *mondongo*, a Spanish word signifying tripes, or the uncleaned entrails of a beast, full of filth'.

25 *Peace be to them! . . . eternity*: this passage finds some interesting parallels and echoes in Sterne's sermon, 'Our Conversation in Heaven' (*Sermons*, 29. 280).

postilion: one who rides the near horse of a carriage or post-chaise. The postilion takes the place of a driver in a two-horse carriage.

q'un my . . . Janatone: the landlord's French and Yorick's reply might be translated thus: 'that an English nobleman presented an ecu [a French silver crown piece] to the chamber-maid—So much the worse for Miss Janatone'. Janatone appears in *Tristram Shandy* as the most notable feature of Montreuil (*TS*, VII. ix. 588–90).

I should . . . Monsieur: 'I should not have said *so much the worse*—but, *so much the better. So much the better, always, Sir . . .*'

26 *Pardonnez moi*: Pardon me.

Mr. H—— . . . the poet: the surnames of the poet and playwright John Home (1722–1808) and the philosopher and historian David Hume (1711–76) were pronounced in the same way. Sterne met Hume in Paris in 1764, and although the faith of the vicar conflicted with the philosopher's scepticism, Sterne praised Hume for his 'placid and gentle nature' and the 'amiable turn of his character' (*Letters*, 218).

the mood I am in . . . the person I am to govern: Sterne is here playing with the terminology of grammar. [I.J.]

27 *fife*: 'a small shrill-toned instrument of the flute kind, used chiefly to accompany the drum in military music' (*OED*).

retired a ses terres: literally, retired 'to his estates'. As Stout notes, this is a euphemism for desertion.

comme il plaisoit a Dieu: as God pleased.

compagnon du voiage: travelling companion.

equivoque: pun or double meaning, referring to the dubious course of Yorick's argument from the literal to the figurative.

O qu'oui!: Yes, indeed!

spatterdashes: long gaiters or leggings worn in riding, to keep the trousers or stockings from being spattered. [I.J.]

play a bass myself: Sterne owned and played a bass viol.

28 *hunger . . . journeyings*: cf. 2 Corinthians 11: 23–7.

complexional: constitutional.

coxcomb: 'anciently, a fool. . . . At present, coxcomb signifies a fop, or vain self-conceited fellow' (*Lexicon Balatronicum*).

C'est un garçon . . . fortune: He is a very lucky lad, i.e. he is lucky in love.

eloge: encomium.

29 '*He is always in love*' ... *sin in it*: Yorick's endorsement of the bene-
ficial effects of love is echoed in a letter Sterne wrote in 1765: 'I am glad
that you are in love—'twill cure you (at least) of the spleen, which has a
bad effect on both man and woman—I myself must ever have some
dulcinea in my head—it harmonises the soul—and in those cases I first
endeavour to make the lady believe so, or rather I begin first to make
myself believe that I am in love—but I carry on my affairs quite in the
French way, sentimentally—"*l'amour*" (say they) "*n'est rien sans sentiment*"—Now notwithstanding they make such a pother about the *word*,
they have no precise idea annex'd to it—And so much for that same
subject called love' (*Letters*, 256).

The idea that a moderated love for the opposite sex—rather than the
perceived excesses of uncontrolled desire—had a role to play in reform-
ing more traditional and antisocial models of masculinity has been seen as
a significant element in the mid-eighteenth-century 'culture of sensibility' (see G. J. Barker-Benfield, *The Culture of Sensibility* (Chicago:
University of Chicago Press, 1992), 248–50 and *passim*). Writing of the
'social passions' in *The Theory of Moral Sentiments* (1759), Adam Smith
(1723–90) recommends the 'sentiment of love' because it 'sooths and
composes the breast, seems to favour the vital motions, and to promote
the healthful state of the human constitution' (I. ii. 4. 2).

A FRAGMENT: the fragmentary story is adapted by Sterne from an
anecdote in Burton's *Anatomy*, Pt. 3, Sect. 2. Mem. 2, Subs. 4. Burton
relays the tale as an example of the power of 'tales of lovers' and other
'artificial allurements' in arousing the passion of love.

THE town of Abdera ... all Thrace: head of the school of Abdera in
Thrace, Democritus (*c.*460–*c.*357 BC) was known as the 'laughing philosopher' because of his mirthful response to the follies of human beings.
He is the model for Burton's persona, 'Democritus Junior'. Sterne
alludes to both Democritus senior and junior in the epigraphs to the
third instalment of *Tristram Shandy*.

pasquinades: a pasquinade is 'a lampoon affixed to some public place; a
squib, libel, or piece of satire generally' (*OED*).

the Andromeda of Euripedes: only fragments of the play have survived.
[I.J.]

orchestra: the 'orchestra' in a Greek theatre was the semi-circular space
in front of the stage, where the chorus danced and sang. In the roman
theatre seats in the orchestra were reserved for senators and other people
of distinction. [I.J.]

spoke pure iambics: in imitation of the iambic metre of the play's verse.

pharmacopolist: pharmacist.

helebore: a drug concocted from hellebore once thought to cure
madness.

30 *the whole parterre*: the whole audience in the pit of a theatre. [I.J.]

Place aux dames: Ladies first.

politesse: politeness.

over-against: facing.

31   *Prenez . . . prenez*: Take some, do.

Vive le Roi!: Long live the King!

pour l'amour de Dieu: see note to p. 6 above.

Mon cher . . . Monsieur: 'My dear and most kind, Sir'.

pauvre honteux: shamefaced pauper.

Dieu vous . . . benisse encore: 'God bless you—and the good God bless you again'.

32   *bidet*: small horse.

c'est un cheval . . . du monde: 'this is the most stubborn horse in the world'.

Peste!: A plague on it!

mal a propos: out of place/inappropriate.

throwing once doublets: throwing a pair of ones in a game of dice where the object is to score as highly as possible.

33   *the cast*: the throw of the dice.

for the third: for two appropriate expletives, see *TS*, VII. xxv. 613–14.

Grant me . . . in distress!: cf. *TS*, VI. xxv. 545 and 'Job's Account', p. 197 above. All three passages derive from Wisdom 10: 21.

wallet: 'a bag for holding provisions, clothing, etc., especially on a journey' (*OED*).

apostrophe: exclamatory address.

Sancho's lamentation: *Don Quixote*, I. xxiii. Cf. *TS*, VII. xxxvi. 639.

pannel: a kind of saddle.

34   *St. Iago in Spain*: the shrine of the patron saint of Spain, St James the Great, in Santiago de Compostela.

it had . . . as a friend: a paraphrase of 2 Samuel 12: 3: 'But the poor man had nothing, save one little ewe lamb, which . . . did eat of his own meat, and drank of his own cup, and lay in his bosom, and was unto him as a daughter.' Cf. pp. 96 and 97.

35   *pavè*: pavement.

The thirstiest . . . cold water: an echo of Proverbs 25: 25. Cf. *Letters*, 117.

clue: the thread (the original sense of the word). [I.J.]

wight: man.

36   *billet*: note.

rout: route.

wiping . . . cheeks: cf. Isaiah 25: 8 and *Journal*, 149.

36 *reprobate*: disapproving, condemnatory.

37 *crisis of our separation*: cf. *Journal*, 136 and 141.

   In transports . . . too much: cf. p. 14 and note above and 'The Levite and his Concubine', p. 207 above.

   signalize: 'to display in a striking manner' (*OED*).

   Auberge: inn.

   hôtel: here, a town house or mansion. The word is used in the *Journey* to refer to both private town houses and inns.

   prevenancy: obliging manner.

38 *maitre d'hotel*: here, the Count's steward or butler. Sterne also uses the term (often translated simply as 'master of the hotel') to describe hoteliers such as Monsieur Dessein.

   au desespoire: in despair.

   en egards . . . femme: consideration for a woman.

   O qu'oui: see note to p. 27 above.

   fob: 'a small pocket formerly made in the waistband of the breeches and used for carrying a watch, money, etc.' (*OED*).

   Quelle etourderie!: How careless of me!

   par hazard: by chance.

39 *Le Diable l'emporte!*: The Devil take it!

   billet-doux: love-letter.

   La voila!: Here it is!

40 *L'amour . . . sentiment*: for Sterne's comments on this phrase, see note to p. 29 above.

   JE suis penetré . . . tout a vous: the drummer's letter may be translated: 'I am at once most deeply grief-stricken and driven to despair on account of the Corporal's unexpected return, which makes our meeting tonight a complete impossibility.

   But long live joy! and mine shall all be in thoughts of you.
   Love is *nothing* without sentiment.
   And sentiment is still *less* without love.
   As we are told, we should never give in to despair.
   I am also told that the Corporal mounts guard on Wednesday: then it will be my turn.

   Everyone has his turn.

   In the meantime—long live love! and long live trifling!
   I am, MADAME,
   with all the most respectful and tender sentiments, yours devotedly.'

41 *'Me voici! mes enfans'*: 'Here I am! my children'.

   running at the ring . . . fame and love: running at the ring is a chivalric exercise in which a rider attempts to pass the point of his lance through a suspended ring. The 'ring of pleasure' is also a slang term for the vagina, and in *Tristram Shandy* Sterne follows Rabelais in making the implication more explicit: 'They are running at the ring of pleasure, said I, giving him a prick' (VII. xliii. 649). In this passage, bawdy connotations are further suggested by 'armour' (an eighteenth-century euphemism for a condom) and the impotent broken lances of the old. For a comparably equivocal play with lances and vizardless helmets, see *Letters*, 294.

Alas, poor Yorick!: Hamlet, V. i. 178. Yorick's 'epitaph and elegy' in *TS*, I. xii. 35. See also *Journal*, 123.

tourniquet: turnstile.

flambeau: a lighted torch.

grisset: 'a French girl or young woman of the working class, e.g. a shop assistant or a seamstress' (*OED*).

buckle: curl of hair.

immerge: immerse.

42 *more in the word . . . less in the thing*: writing to Garrick from Paris in April 1762, Sterne noted that 'here every thing is hyperbolized—and if a woman is but simply pleased—'tis *Je suis charmée*—and if she is charmed 'tis nothing less, than that she is *ravi*-sh'd—and when ravi-sh'd . . . there is nothing left for her but to fly to the other world for a metaphor' (*Letters*, 161).

Opera comique: the Hôtel de Bourgogne where the newly combined companies of the Opéra Comique and the Comédiens Italiens performed comic operas from February 1762 onwards.

43 *ruffles*: strips of gathered lace and other material worn as ornamental frills on garments.

mais prenez guarde: but take care.

tittle: smallest part.

courtesy: curtsy.

Attendez!: Wait!

44 *temperature*: temperament.

Eugenius: the name means 'well born' or 'noble'. Eugenius is the literary type of the trustworthy and generous confidant and friend. Traditionally, Yorick's Eugenius, who is also addressed in *Tristram Shandy*, has been identified as Sterne's longtime friend, John Hall-Stevenson (1718–85).

45 *thrum*: made of waste threads of yarn, or of very coarse material. [I.J.]

is salique: observes the Salic law, 'the alleged fundamental law of the French monarchy, by which females were excluded from succession to the crown' (*OED*).

The genius of a people . . . to the women: the notion that French women were allowed too much power was a commonplace in British conceptions of the French. Writing in 1776, James Fordyce claimed that in 'France the women are supreme: they govern all from the court down to the cottage'.

45 *by a continual . . . brilliant*: as Mark Loveridge notes, Sterne seems to be recalling a passage from the Earl of Shaftesbury's essay on 'The Freedom of Wit and Humour' in the *Characteristics* (1711): 'All Politeness is owing to Liberty. We polish one another, and rub off our Corners and rough Sides by a sort of *amicable Collision*. To restrain this, is inevitably to bring a Rust upon Men's Understandings' (see Mark Loveridge, *Laurence Sterne and the Argument about Design* (London: Macmillan, 1982), 187). A brilliant is 'a diamond of the finest cut and brilliancy' (*OED*).

le Mari: the husband.

it is not good . . . sit alone: cf. Genesis 2: 18: 'And the LORD God said, It is not good that the man should be alone; I will make him an help meet for him.' Cf. 'The Levite and his Concubine', p. 208 above.

46 *languages of Babel*: for the confusion of tongues at Babel, see Genesis 11.

reins: 'in or after Biblical use: the seat of the feelings or affections' (*OED*).

I found I lost . . . feel she did: for the comparable effects of the Widow Wadman's eye on Uncle Toby, see *TS*, VIII. xxiv–xxv. 705–8.

M'en croyez capable?: Do you think me capable of it?

47 *Tobias Shandy . . . gush out with tears*: Sterne's own father was a lieutenant in the army and both his public and private writings suggest a lifelong affection for an idealized type of the noble and generous soldier. The Uncle Toby of *Tristram Shandy*, described by Hazlitt as 'one of the finest compliments ever paid to human nature', combines tender-hearted philanthropy—embodied most famously in the incident in which he releases a troublesome fly (*TS*, II. xii. 130–1) and 'The Story of Le Fever' (*TS*, VI. vi–x. 499–513)—and an obsession with warfare. For Toby's defence of the role of the soldier and the necessity for war, see his 'Apologetical Oration' (*TS*, VI. xxxii. 554–7).

shagreen: 'a species of untanned leather with a rough granular surface . . . and frequently dyed green' (*OED*).

worse than a German: as Stout notes, Yorick is travelling before the Seven Years War had formally ended, and the French and the Prussians were on opposite sides during the conflict.

48 *Martini's concert*: probably an allusion to Giovanni Battista Martini (1706–84), the Italian composer and musical theorist.

the Marquesina di F***: identified by Arthur Young in 1789 as the Marchesa Fagnani, with whom, according to Young, Sterne had a 'rencontre at Milan'. The identification is probably spurious (see Stout, 343–44 and *LY*, 235).

chichesbee: a cicisbeo is 'the recognized gallant or *cavalier servente* of a married woman' (*OED*).

St. Cecilia: the patron saint of music.

49 *I HAD never . . . that was*: an allusion to Smollett's speculations on the causes of deformity in his *Travels* (xxx. 245–6). The satire becomes more direct later in the chapter when Sterne refers to Smollett as a medical, splenetic, and inquisitive traveller.

parterre: see note to p. 30 above.

Mr. Shandy the elder: Walter Shandy, father to Tristram and brother to Uncle Toby. Walter's love of bizarre theories about the development and education of children provides frequent occasions for Sterne's satire throughout *Tristram Shandy*.

50 *Mr. Shandy being very short*: see *TS*, vi. xviii. 526–7.

orchestra: see note to p. 29 above.

A poor defenceless being . . . higher than himself: Sterne adapts this incident from the *Roman Comique* (1651) by Paul Scarron (1610–60). For Sterne's sense of kinship with Scarron, see *Letters*, 416 and the letter to the Marquis of Rockingham of December 1759 (*LY*, 360).

51 *apostrophe*: see note to p. 33 above.

queue: pigtail.

In England . . . at our ease: the notion that Protestant Britain possessed a peculiar degree of freedom not found in Catholic France informs eighteenth-century conceptions of Britishness.

bon mot: a good or witty saying, clever repartee.

'Haussez les mains, Monsieur l'Abbe': 'Raise your hands, Mr. Priest'.

loges: boxes, seats.

perdu: hidden.

52 *Quelle grossierte!*: What coarseness!

Le POUR . . . chaque nation: 'points for and against are found in every nation'. Writing to Lord Fauconberg from Montpellier in 1763, Sterne is less a citizen of the world than the French officer: 'I'm more than half tired of France, as fine a Country as it is—but there is the *Pour* & the *Contre* for every place,—all wch being ballanced, I think Old England preferable to any Kingdome in the world' (*Letters*, 201).

sçavoir vivre: 'ability in the conduct of life, knowledge of the world and of the usages of good society' (*OED*).

Madame de Rambouliet: recalling the Marquise de Ramboulliet (1588–1665), hostess of a renowned salon frequented by the précieuses satirized in Molière's *Les Précieuses ridicules* (see note to p. 4 above).

52 *Rein que pisser*: Nothing but to piss.

53 *pluck your rose*: 'to pluck a rose; an expression said to be used by women for going to the necessary house, which in the country usually stands in the garden' (*Lexicon Balatronicum*).

   CASTALIA: a nymph who threw herself into a spring on Mt. Parnassus in order to escape Apollo's amorous advances. The Castalian spring was sacred to the muses and its waters were supposed to inspire its drinkers with the gift of poetry.

54 *Polonius's advice to his son*: *Hamlet*, I. iii. 55–81.

   Comment!: What!

   Count de B****: Claude de Thiard (1721–1810), comte de Bissy, the Anglophile general who seems to have helped Sterne's application for a passport in Paris in 1762 (see *LY*, 128–9).

   C'est un Esprit fort: He's a brilliant mind.

   Les Egarments ... l'Esprit: by Claude-Prosper Jolyot de Crébillon ('Crébillon fils'), a tale of amorous adventure spiced with social satire and literary criticism (1736). Crébillon proposed to Sterne that each of them should write a pamphlet expostulating on the indecorums in the work of the other, and that the two pamphlets should be published together as a joke (*Letters*, 162). No such pamphlets are known. [I.J.] Crébillon's novel was translated into English as *The Wanderings of the Heart and Mind* (1751). Sterne alludes to the novel twice in his correspondence (*Letters*, 88 and 245).

   Le Dieu m'en guard!: God protect me/keep me from that!

55 *her sattin purse ... one in*: 'purse' has sexual connotations as in the broadside ballad, 'The Turnep Ground': '(When) gently down I L'ayed her, | She Op't a Purse as black as Coal, | To hold my Coin'.

   En verite ... argent apart: 'truly, Sir, I will put this money aside'.

56 *are we not all relations?*: cf. *Letters*, 287 and 408.

57 *at war with France*: Sterne travelled to Paris in January 1762 before the Seven Years War had been officially ended with the Treaty of Paris in February 1763. For Sterne's negotiation of the difficulties of travelling to a country technically at war with England, see *LY*, 116–23.

   packet: see note to p. 3 above.

   suite: retinue.

   trait: characteristic.

   apparament: apparently.

   certes: certainly, of course.

   au moins: at least.

   Cela n'empeche pas: that doesn't prevent it, it's all the same.

58 *Pardi! ... tres extraordinaires*: 'Golly! ... these English gentlemen are very extraordinary people'.

59 *sombre pencil*: dark colours (a reference to the terminology of art criticism). [I.J.]

fossè: ditch or moat.

I can't get out: possibly an echo of the words of Bunyan's Man of Despair in *Pilgrim's Progress* (1678): 'I cannot get out; O *now* I cannot' (see Stephen Derry, '*Mansfield Park*, Sterne's Starling, and Bunyan's Man of Despair', *N&Q* 44 (1997), 322–3).

60 *trellis*: the bars of the cage.

Disguise . . . account: cf. 'Job's Account', p. 204 above. In a letter of July 1766, Ignatius Sancho, an African freedman who had been born on a slave ship, wrote to Sterne expressing his admiration for the passage in the sermon that is reworked here. Sancho urged Sterne to 'give one half-hour's attention to slavery' in the hope that it might 'ease the yoke . . . of many'. In his reply, Sterne promised not to forget Sancho's letter and it is possible that the generalized condemnation of slavery here is, in part, a response to Sancho's plea.

shower down thy mitres: a reference to Sterne's frustrated efforts to gain preferment in the church and a paraphrase of Sancho's words to Don Quixote in *Don Quixote*, I. vii.

61 *millions . . . but slavery*: cf. 'Job's Account', p. 205, above.

I was going to begin . . . single captive: although the rapid transition from the millions born into slavery to a single captive has been read as an example of Yorick's egotism, it finds some support in Smith's understanding of the workings of sympathy. For Smith, as 'we have no immediate experience of what other men feel, we can form no idea of the manner in which they are affected, but by conceiving what we ourselves should feel in the like situation. . . . By the imagination we place ourselves in [the sufferer's] . . . situation, we conceive ourselves enduring all the same torments. . . . His agonies, when they are thus brought home to ourselves, when we have thus adopted and made them our own, begin at last to affect us, and we then tremble and shudder at the thought of what he feels' (*Theory of Moral Sentiments*, I. i. 1. 2). For Sterne's probable familiarity with this passage, see Melvyn New, Richard A. Davies, and W. G. Day, Florida edn., vol. iii, *Tristram Shandy: The Notes* (Gainesville, Fla.: University Press of Florida, 1984), 184–5. For the argument that Sterne views Smithean sympathy as a self-indulgence, see Kenneth MacLean, 'Imagination and Sympathy: Sterne and Adam Smith', *Journal of the History of Ideas*, 10 (1949), 399–410.

hope deferr'd: cf. Proverbs 13: 12, 'Hope deferred maketh the heart sick'.

the iron enter into his soul: cf. Psalm 105: 18 (Book of Common Prayer).

62 *Le Duke de Choiseul*: either César-Gabriel de Choiseul (1712–85), Minister for Foreign Affairs 1761–6, or his cousin Étienne-François de Choiseul-Stainville (1719–85), First Minister of France. The latter

was ultimately responsible for approving the issue of passports (see *LY*, 128).

63   *to get in*: to get on socially, to climb the social ladder. [I.J.]

I have borne . . . to my arms: the arms and crest pictured had been used by Sterne's great-grandfather Richard Sterne (d. 1683), archbishop of York, on his episcopal seal. Although the family may not have had a legal right to them, Sterne himself used a seal imprinted with the arms. The Sternes appear to have adopted the starling crest on the basis of a punning association between *starn* (Yorkshire dialect for starling) and the family name (see Stout, 205–6).

64   *in the field . . . in the cabinet*: the field of battle and the cabinet where political and other business is transacted. Cf. *TS*, III. xxv. 250. [I.J.]

succours: assistance, relief.

65   *meet it*: i.e. life. [I.J.]

maitre d'hotel: see note to p. 38 above.

C'est une autre affaire: That's another matter.

LE PATISSER: the pastry-maker or seller. In the popular eighteenth-century anthology of Sterne's writing, *The Beauties of Sterne*, the chapter heading was Anglicized as 'The Pieman'.

hotels: see note to p. 37 above.

66   *Chevalier de St. Louis*: member of the Order of St Louis, instituted by Louis XIV in 1693 to reward distinguished military service.

patès: pies or pastries.

damask: a fabric woven with designs.

propreté: cleanliness.

67   *the last peace*: probably the Treaty of Aix-la-Chapelle, which ended the War of the Austrian Succession in 1748.

patisserie: pastry-making.

declension: see note to p. 15 above.

68   *the mounting*: equipment, or here perhaps in general the expenses of keeping up the station of a man of honour. [I.J.]

In any other province . . . provision for this: in Brittany, nobles were permitted to undertake commercial activity without permanently losing their rank. The custom allowed a temporary suspension of nobility.

69   *The set of Shakespears . . . over*: cf. Sterne's letter to Garrick of January 1762: ' 'Twas an odd incident when I was introduced to the Count de Bissie . . . I found him reading Tristram—' (*Letters*, 151).

et ayez . . . cet honneur la: 'and have the goodness, my dear friend . . . to do me this honour'.

pale and sickly: Sterne had suffered from pulmonary tuberculosis all his adult life, and his own travels to France and Italy were undertaken in the hope of improving his health.

spy the nakedness of the land: cf. Genesis 42: 9: 'Ye are spies; to see the nakedness of the land ye are come'.

70 *C'est bien dit*: Well said.

Hèh bien! . . . Monsieur l'Anglois: Well then! my English friend.

ni encore: nor even.

par hazard: see note to p. 38 above.

71 *as a temple*: a biblical metaphor. See, for example, John 2: 21: 'But he spake of the temple of his body.'

transfiguration of Raphael: the celebrated altarpiece of the *Transfiguration of Christ*, on which Raphael (1483–1520) was working at his death.

'tis a quiet journey . . . better than we do: in a letter to Mrs James of November 1767, Sterne described the 'design' of the *Journey* thus: 'to teach us to love the world and our fellow creatures better than we do—so it runs most upon those gentler passions and affections, which aid so much to it' (*Letters*, 401).

THERE is not . . . who I am: cf. *TS*, VII. xxxiii. 633.

Me Voici!: Here I am!

72 *'He could not bear . . . Denmark's jester'*: no such response from a churchman has been recorded, but Sterne may be alluding to his falling out with the bishop of Gloucester, William Warburton (1698–1779), over the indelicate comedy of *Tristram Shandy*. More generally, Sterne is glancing at a wider critical response to the pseudonymous publication of the sermons. The first instalment of the *Sermons of Mr. Yorick* (1760) appeared with two title-pages, the second one giving Sterne's real name. In spite of a preface excusing the pseudonym as a concession to 'serve the bookseller's purpose', the reviewer in the *Monthly Review* (May 1760) was outraged: 'For who is this *Yorick*? We have heard of one of that name who was a *Jester*—we have read of a Yorick likewise, in an obscene Romance [*Tristram Shandy*].—But are the solemn dictates of religion fit to be conveyed from the mouths of Buffoons and ludicrous Romancers?' Significantly, the reviewer goes on to praise the content of the sermons.

Horwendillus's: in the *Historia Danica* of Saxo Grammaticus, Horwendillus, king of Denmark, is the father of Amlethus, Shakespeare's Hamlet. Cf. *TS*, I. xi. 25–6. [I.J.]

Alexander the Great . . . Copper-smith: Alexander the Great is discussed by Hamlet (*Hamlet*, v. i. 191–205), but Sterne is probably only concerned with a comparison between the great and the little. Alexander the coppersmith is mentioned in 2 Timothy 4: 14.

translated: a bishop is translated from one see to another. [I.J.]

Et, Monsieur . . . Yorick: the exchange might be translated: 'And, Sir, are you Yorick? . . . I am he . . . You?—Me—I who have the honour to speak with you, Count—My God! . . . You are Yorick'.

72 *number'd out my days*: cf. Psalms 90: 12.

73 *I force myself, like Eneas . . . miseries and dishonours*: Aeneas gains entry
into the Elysian Fields (paradise) in *Aeneid*, vi. 635–6 and meets Dido in
Hades in vi. 450–76.

Surely this is not . . . in vain: cf. Psalm 39: 7: 'For man walketh in a vain
shadow, and disquieteth himself in vain' (Book of Common Prayer).

commotions: 'mental perturbations, agitation' (*OED*).

beating up: 'to beat up for recruits' (or game) was a common phrase in
the eighteenth century. [I.J.]

Un homme . . . dangereuz: 'A man who laughs will never be dangerous'.

Et vous plaisantez?: And you jest?

at my own expence: the Yorick of Tristram Shandy loves 'a jest in his
heart—and as he saw himself in the true point of ridicule . . . he could
not be angry with others for seeing him in a light, in which he so strongly
saw himself' (*TS*, I. x. 19–20).

no jester at court . . . Charles IId: probably a reference to Charles II's
master of the revels, Thomas Killigrew (1612–83).

patriots: originally designating the group of Whig politicians who
opposed Walpole in the 1730s and early 1740s in terms of an ideology of
disinterested service of one's country. After the fall of Walpole in 1742,
the realization that the patriots were also concerned with their own
advancement helped bring the term into disrepute. It is this debasement
of a once privileged concept that informs Dr Johnson's famous comment
to Boswell: 'Patriotism is the last refuge of a scoundrel'.

Voila un persiflage!: Now there's raillery!

74 *But there is nothing unmixt . . . little better than a convulsion*: cf. 'Job's
Account', p. 205 above. As Melvyn New discovered, Sterne's source
appears to be *Of Wisdom* (1601) by Pierre Charron (1541–1603). According to Charron: 'Good things, delights and pleasures cannot be enjoyed
without some mixture of evil and discommodity. . . . The highest pleasure that is, hath a sigh and a complaint to accompany it; and being come
to perfection is but debility, a dejection of the mind, languishment'.
Charron is paraphrasing another of Sterne's favourite writers, Mon-
taigne, who similarly uses sexual climax to illustrate the mixed nature of
pleasure (see Melvyn New, 'Some Sterne Borrowings from Four Renaissance Authors', *PQ* 71 (1992), 302).

Bevoriskius: probably the Dutch theologian and physician, Johan van
Beverwyck (1594–1647), who discusses the lecherous sparrows in his
Schat der Gesontheyd (*Treasury of Health*). It seems likely, however, that
Sterne took the following anecdote from an intermediate source which is
yet to be identified.

Mais passe, pour cela: As for that, let it go.

Vraiment ... Les Francois sont polis: 'Truly ... the French are polite/ refined.'

75 *compass*: the range of a musical instrument from the highest to the lowest note obtainable.

politesse de cœur: instinctive good manners/civility. Writing to his daughter in August 1767, Sterne expresses similar scepticism about the value of French refinement: 'I will shew you more real politesses than any you have met with in France, as mine will come warm from the heart' (*Letters*, 391).

but should it ever be the case of the English ... from all the world besides: the notion that English climate and English 'Liberty' fosters quirky and whimsical character survives today in ideas of English eccentricity, but in the eighteenth century it was an important element in the construction of an emerging national identity. Such an identity was typically defined in opposition to the perceived defects in the French 'character'.

king William's shillings: issued during the reign of William III (1689– 1702).

they are become ... from another: writing from Toulouse in October 1762, Sterne complained that he was tired of France: 'the ground work of my *ennui* is ... the eternal platitude of the French characters—little variety, no originality in it at all ... they are very civil—but civility itself, in that uniform, wearies and bodders one to death' (*Letters*, 186).

they are too serious: although Tristram objects to the 'serious character' (*TS*, VII. xxxiv. 634) of the French, Sterne describes them elsewhere as a 'laughter-loving people' (*Letters*, 163).

76 *Mais vous plaisantez*: But you are in jest.

band-box: 'a slight box ... for collars, hats, caps, and millinery' (*OED*).

merchande de modes: milliner.

77 *super-induced*: introduced in addition to.

78 *I'll just shew you ... on one side of it*: for the sexual connotations of the purse see note to p. 55 above.

stock: 'an article of clerical attire, consisting of a piece of black silk or other material (worn on the chest and secured by a band round the neck)' (*OED*).

hussive: 'a pocket-case for needles, pins, thread, scissors etc.' (*OED*).

If nature ... as a man: cf. 'The Levite and his Concubine', pp. 208 and 213 above.

thou hast ... ourselves: cf. Psalm 100: 2: 'Be ye sure that the Lord he is God: it is he that hath made us, and not we ourselves' (Book of Common Prayer).

79 *it was ... musick*: ending a piece of music in a minor rather than a major key (implying dissonance rather than consonance).

79 *adust*: gloomy, parched.

propretè: see note to p. 66 above.

80 *Voyez vous, Monsieur*: See here, Sir.

81 *ruffles*: see note to p. 43 above.

et tout cela: and all that, et cetera.

en conscience: in good faith, honestly.

magazine: 'a portable receptacle for articles of value' (*OED*).

cullibility: gullibility.

82 *C'est deroger à noblesse . . . Et encore Monsieur*: 'That's demeaning to
your rank, Sir'. 'Deroger à noblesse' means literally to depart from nobility. 'Et encore Monsieur', 'And furthermore Sir'.

took away: cleared away the supper-things. [I.J.]

the philosopher's stone: the mythical substance supposed to transform
base metals into gold.

both the Indies: i.e. West and East.

I found my spirit . . . interpretation: for Nebuchadnezzar's dreams, see
Daniel 2: 1–11.

83 *pour s'adoniser*: to array himself.

Rue de friperie: *friperie* are second-hand clothes.

a new bag and a solitaire: a bag is 'a silken pouch to hold the back-hair
of a wig' and a solitaire 'a loose neck-tie of black silk or broad ribbon'
(*OED*).

bien brodées: 'well embroidered'.

pour faire . . . sa maitresse: 'to pay court to his mistress'.

84 *house of bondage*: a biblical phrase. See, for example, Exodus 13: 3.

Behold! . . . thy servant: 2 Samuel 9: 6. [I.J.]

petite demoiselle: young woman.

Happy people! . . . earth: cf. Yorick's claim that the French are too
serious, p. 75 above.

print of butter: pat of butter (moulded to a shape). [I.J.]

85 *traiteur*: 'a keeper of an eating house . . . who supplies or sends out
meals to order' (*OED*).

Rabelais's time: François Rabelais (*c.*1494–*c.*1553), author of *Gargantua and Pantagruel* (1533, 1532?) and one of Sterne's favourite writers.
The Yorick of *Tristram Shandy* carries a copy of *Gargantua and Pantagruel* in his pocket (*TS*, v. xxviii. 463).

I at it again: i.e. I went at it again. [I.J.]

Gruter or Jacob Spon: Jan Gruytère (1560–1627) and Jacob Spon
(1647–85). Both were antiquarian scholars.

notary: 'a person publicly authorized to draw up or attest contracts
etc.' (*OED*).

86 *a little fume of a woman*: i.e. a woman who readily got into a 'fume' or fury. [I.J.]

By this . . . Frenchman: French pride in the Pont Neuf had become a butt of English humour.

sacre Dieu'd: 'God Almighty-ed', cursed.

garde d'eau: 'beware water', the warning called out from upper windows when emptying slops.

gascon: Gascons were reputed to be braggarts and boasters.

harquebuss: an early type of portable gun.

lanthorn: lantern.

87 *castor*: a fur hat.

pontific: pertaining to a bridge (a facetious use of the word). [I.J.]

bandoleer: a broad belt worn over the shoulder and across the breast, used by soldiers to support the musket and carry charges.

Monsieur le Notaire: Mr Notary.

88 *that BOOK*: the book of life of Revelation 20: 12. Cf. *TS*, VI. viii. 511.

see if you canst get: because of a compositor's error, these words were mistakenly italicized in the first and subsequent editions of the *Journey*. I am grateful to Melvyn New for drawing my attention to this.

Juste ciel!: Good heavens!

89 *gage d'amour*: love token.

all the sentiments . . . compounded together: cf. Sterne's comments to Garrick about Elizabeth Griffith's translation of Diderot's *Fils Naturel*: 'It has too much sentiment in it, (at least for me) the speeches too long, and savour too much of *preaching*' (*Letters*, 162). Interestingly, Sterne uses 'sentiment' here to mean moral maxims rather than feeling or thought informed by emotion.

'Capadosia . . . Pamphilia': cf. Acts 2: 9–10.

90 *vestal sisters*: after the six vestal virgins who tended the sacred fire brought from Troy by Aeneas.

91 *concentre*: 'increase the vigour or intensity of' (*OED*).

92 *Cour d'amour*: court of love.

Mons. P**** the farmer-general: suggesting Alexandre-Jean-Joseph Le Riche de La Popelinière (1692–1762), who entertained Sterne in Paris in 1762 (see *Letters*, 132). The farmers-general collected indirect taxes and made a substantial profit in the process. According to Smollett, the farmers 'oppress the people in raising the taxes, not above two thirds of which are brought into the king's coffers: the rest enriches themselves' (*Travels*, v. 37).

esprit: a wit, with possible implications of freethinking.

deist . . . devôte: a deist is strictly someone who rejects Christian notions of revelation and the supernatural (revealed religion) and believes that the divine can be accessed through reason alone. From the late seventeenth century onwards, however, deist was often used as a synonym for a sceptic or atheist. In the context of the Parisian salons of the 1760s, it seems likely that Sterne is thinking particularly of the atheistic materialism of the philosophes (see notes to pp. 3 and 4 above). A 'devôte' is a woman characterized by religious devotion of an extreme or superstitious kind.

93 *adamant*: 'a poetic or rhetorical name for impregnable hardness' (*OED*).

Mons. D*** . . . against it: Monsieur D*** is Denis Diderot (1713–84), principal editor of and contributor to the *Encyclopédie* (1751–80), whose meeting with Sterne bore fruit in a radically Shandean novel, *Jaques le fataliste* (1796). Abbe M*** has been identified as another contributor to the *Encyclopédie*, André Morellet (1727–1819). Informed as it is by sceptical rationalism and aiming at universal knowledge, the *Encyclopédie* has come to stand for the project of the French Enlightenment.

first cause: God.

Count de Faineant: Cash suggests 'Lord Lounger' or 'Count Sloth' as suitable translations (*LY*, 135).

solitaire: see note to p. 83 above.

plus badinant: looser.

Pardi! . . . enfant: 'By golly! this Mr. Yorick is as much of a wit as us . . . He reasons well . . . he is a sound fellow'.

94 *children of Art . . . those of Nature*: cf. Sterne's letter from Paris to Lady D. of July 1762: 'My wife and daughter are arrived—the latter does nothing but look out of the window, and complain of the torment of being frizled.—I wish she may ever remain a child of nature—I hate children of art' (*Letters*, 179).

poor Maria . . . near Moulines: see *TS*, IX. xxiv. 780–4. The story of Maria in *Tristram Shandy* is often seen as an advertisement of sorts for the *Journey* (see *LY*, 256).

Knight of the Woeful Countenance: Don Quixote, so dubbed by Sancho. See *Don Quixote*, I. xix.

95 *'Thou shalt not . . . Sylvio*: for the possibility that Sterne is alluding to Andrew Marvell's 'Nymph Complaining for the Death of Her Faun', and an interesting discussion of its significance, see Tom Keymer, 'Marvell, Thomas Hollis, and Sterne's Maria: Parody in *A Sentimental Journey*', *The Shandean*, 5 (1993), 9–31.

96 *God tempers . . . shorn lamb*: Sterne's rendering of the French proverb, 'A brebis tondue Dieu mesure le vent'.

where I have a cottage . . . shelter thee: cf. *Journal*, 108.

eat of my . . . own cup: cf. pp. 34 and 97 above. For Sterne's source, see note to p. 34 above.

97 *salutations . . . market-place*: unlike the Pharisees of Mark 12: 38.

not only eat . . . daughter: see note to p. 34 above. In an unsent letter to Elizabeth Draper's husband, Daniel, Sterne wrote: 'I fell in Love with y^r Wife—but tis a Love, You would honour me for—for tis so like that I bear my own daughter . . . that I scarse distinguish a difference betwixt it' (*Letters*, 349).

imbibe the oil . . . for ever: an allusion to the compassion of the good Samaritan (Luke 10: 33–4).

98 *Dear sensibility . . . sorrows*: cf. Sterne's letter of September 1767: 'my Sentimental Journey will . . . convince you that my feelings are from the heart, and that that heart is not of the worst of molds—praised be God for my sensibility! Though it has often made me wretched, yet I would not exchange it for all the pleasures the grossest sensualist ever felt' (*Letters*, 395–6).

thy divinity . . . at destruction: paraphrased from *Cato* (1713), v. i. 2–9 by Joseph Addison (1672–1719).

SENSORIUM: 'the seat of sensation in the brain of man and other animals; the percipient centre to which sense-impressions are transmitted by the nerves' (*OED*). Discussing the comfort to be derived from comprehending God's omniscience and omnipresence, Addison draws on Newton's *Opticks* (1704) for an understanding of the divinity's presence in infinite space: 'the noblest and most exalted way of considering this infinite Space is that of Sir *Isaac Newton*, who calls it the *Sensorium* of the Godhead. Brutes and Men have their *Sensoriola*, or little *Sensoriums*, by which they apprehend the Presence, and perceive the Actions of a few Objects that lie contiguous to them. . . . But as God Almighty cannot but perceive and know every thing in which he resides, Infinite Space gives room to Infinite Knowledge, and is, as it were, an Organ to Omniscience' (*Spectator*, No. 565). For an illuminating discussion of the significance of Sterne's use of the image of the sensorium and the notion of vibrations, see John A. Dussinger, 'The Sensorium in the World of *A Sentimental Journey*', *Ariel*, 13 (1982), 3–16.

if a hair . . . the ground: cf. Matthew 10: 29–31.

Eugenius . . . languish: cf. *TS*, I. xii. 33.

thill-horse: 'the shaft-horse or wheeler in a team' (*OED*).

99 *potagerie*: a kitchen or vegetable garden.

feast of love: an allusion to the love-feast, or *agape*, held by the early Christians in conjunction with the Lord's supper.

luncheon: 'a thick piece' (*OED*).

100 *sabots*: wooden shoes.

vielle: 'a musical instrument with four strings played by means of a small wheel; a hurdy-gurdy' (*OED*).

I beheld Religion . . . dance: cf. Sterne's sermon, 'The Prodigal Son' (*Sermons*, 20. 190–1).

100 *Voiturin*: carriage-driver.

101 *when a voiture . . . servant-maid*: Sterne apparently adapted the following story from an anecdote relayed to him by John Craufurd (d. 1814) (see *LY*, 231).

nicety: delicacy.

103 *corking pins*: pins of the largest size.

robe de chambre: dressing gown.

protesting . . . his own imagination: in a letter of November 1767, Sterne makes a similar point about the *Journey*: 'If it is not thought a chaste book, mercy on them that read it, for they must have warm imaginations indeed!' (*Letters*, 403).

104 *no more than an ejaculation*: allowing for two possible meanings: 'the hasty utterance of prayers, emotional exclamations etc.' and 'the sudden ejection or emission (of seeds, fluids, etc.)' (*OED*).

Fille de Chambre's . . . END: some early editions left less room for the reader's warm imagination by inserting a dash between 'Chambre's' and 'END'. The suggestive ambiguity is, of course, deliberate.

THE JOURNAL TO ELIZA

107 *Bramin and Bramine*: see note to p. 5 above.

a Copy . . . the Lady's Account: as Cash notes, the invention of a manuscript source reverses a literary convention: 'instead of passing off a fictional diary as a real one, Sterne seemed to be passing off a real diary as a fiction' (*LY*, 285). Elizabeth Draper's 'Counterpart' has never been found.

Continuation . . . Journal: Sterne had begun the journal before he and Eliza separated. Two earlier portions of the journal had been sent to Eliza.

April 13: as Curtis points out, Sunday fell on 12 April. The other entries for the week are also one day in advance. [I.J.]

dined with Hall . . . Pandamonium: Hall is John Hall-Stevenson (see note to p. 44 above). 'Pandemonium' is Milton's name for the principal city in Hell, but Sterne is alluding more particularly to its literal meaning, 'all the demons'. The 'Demoniacs' was Sterne's playful name for the informal club of friends who frequently met at Hall-Stevenson's Skelton Castle (*see EMY*, 185–95).

108 *worn out . . . again*: this, like a number of other passages in the *Journal*, echoes a letter Sterne supposedly wrote to his wife-to-be, Elizabeth Lumley, in 1739/40. It is as likely that Sterne's daughter concocted the letter from passages in the *Journal* as it is that Sterne copied from the letter while writing to Eliza (see *EMY*, 81–2 and *Letters*, 10–15).

Mrs James: Anne James, close friend of Eliza and wife of Commodore

William James, a 'retired commander-in-chief of the marine forces of the East India Company' (*LY*, 268). Sterne met and made friends with the Jameses in the first weeks of 1767. Writing to his daughter in February 1767, Sterne described Mrs James as 'kind—and friendly—of a senti-mental turn of mind—and so sweet a disposition, that she is too good for the world she lives in' (*Letters*, 302).

James's Powder: a medicine invented by Dr Robert James (1703–76) administered to induce sweating.

Help-mate: see note to p. 45 above.

Elysium: in Greek mythology, the abode assigned to the blessed after death. The word is used figuratively, as here, to describe a state of ideal happiness.

Cordelia's Spirit: a ghostly nun Sterne imagined inhabiting the ruins of Byland Abbey near Coxwold. Cordelia also appears in a letter Sterne sent to both a Countess ****** and to Eliza (see *Letters*, 360–2 and *LY*, 218–21).

invite her to his Cottage: cf. *Journey*, 96.

when Molly . . . distressing: cf. p. 119. Molly was the servant of the land-lady of Sterne's lodgings in Old Bond Street.

109 *meek and gentle . . . disinherited of it*: cf. Matthew 5: 5: 'Blessed are the meek: for they shall inherit the earth.'

Orm's account of India: *History of the Military Transactions of the British in Indostan* (1763–78) by Robert Orme (1728–1801). Because of its com-plimentary allusions to William James, Sterne promised to send his daughter a copy of Orme's book (*Letters*, 301).

loving thee: here and elsewhere in the *Journal* Sterne made a cross (x), no doubt for a kiss. [I.J.]

110 *Corporal Trim's . . . in his head*: see *TS*, VIII. xx. 699.

111 *Newnhams*: a family of London merchants and politicians who evidently tried to warn Eliza against a relationship with Sterne. In response, Sterne effected a break between Eliza and the Newnhams by what, in a letter to friend, he called a 'falsity': 'I wrote her word that the most amiable of women [Anne James] reiterated my request, that she should not write to them' (*Letters*, 369). See *LY*, 278–9.

112 *as comically disastrous . . . fools to it*: alluding to three of the most comical disasters in Tristram Shandy's early life: the crushing of his nose by the man-midwife's forceps (*TS*, III. xxvii. 253), his misnaming by Yorick's curate (*TS*, IV. xiv. 344), and his accidental circumcision by a sash win-dow (*TS*, V. xvii. 449–50).

The Injury I did myself . . . acted like a Saint: although it seems unlikely that Sterne had had 'no commerce' with the opposite sex for fifteen years, acute pain in the testicles is not a symptom of syphilis, and is more likely to have been an effect of tuberculosis. Sterne's willingness to undergo a dangerous mercury cure, however, may, as Cash suggests, indicate that he accepted the doctors' diagnosis (see *LY*, 289–91). Sterne relays the same 'whimsical' story, almost verbatim, in a letter to the Earl of Shelburne (*Letters*, 343).

112 *father of mischief*: the devil.

113 *sensibilities . . . Sensualist*: cf. Sterne's letter of September 1767, quoted in note to p. 98 above.

    Gotham: a village proverbial for the folly of its inhabitants. 'The wise men of Gotham' = fools. [I.J.]

114 *round house*: 'a cabin or set of cabins on the after-part of the quarter deck' (*OED*).

    philtre: a love-potion, or simply a magic-potion.

115 *recruited*: restored to vigour.

    Van Sweeten's: named after the physician, Gerard Van Swieten (1700–72).

    sublimated . . . etherial Substance: punning on the sublimated mercury of Van Sweeten's cure and 'sublimate', meaning to transmute into a higher, purer state.

    Cast: a punning allusion to the division of Indian society according to hereditary castes, and the word's etymological relationship to 'casto', meaning pure or chaste.

    Communion: both the Eucharist and 'spiritual intercourse' (*OED*).

    Hyde park . . . Salt hill: Sterne was living about half a mile from Hyde Park and 25 miles from Salt Hill.

116 *matins and Vespers*: morning and evening prayers.

    our mutual friend: presumably, Anne James.

117 *thatchd Cottage*: Sterne's Coxwold home was actually roofed with stone tiles.

    Sheba: if Sterne had a particular woman in mind, she has not been positively identified. The broader allusion is to the biblical story of the Queen of Sheba's testing of Solomon's reputed wisdom (1 Kings 10: 1–13 and 2 Chronicles 9: 1–12).

118 *Skin for Skin . . . his Life*: cf. Job 2: 4.

    Wings of the Morning: cf. Psalms 139: 9: 'If I take the wings of the morning, and dwell in the uttermost parts of the sea'.

    Ranelagh: a fashionable pleasure garden opened in Chelsea in 1742.

119 *Molly . . . think of her*: cf. p. 108.

    Lord Shelburn: William Petty (1737–1805), earl of Shelburne.

    Earl of Chatham: the ship on which Eliza sailed to India.

    the Line: the equator.

120 *Bussorah*: the port city of Basra in Iraq (part of the Ottoman Empire in

the eighteenth century), where the East India Company had a long established trading base.

l'Extraite de Saturne . . . french Nostrum: a treatment for venereal disease
and other 'chirurgical disorders' invented by Thomas Goulard, Surgeon-
Major to the Royal and Military Hospital at Montpellier. The medicine
was made by boiling lead in wine vinegar or wine (I am indebted to
Melvyn New for this information).

Soho Concert: a series of concerts organized by Theresa Cornelys for a
select group of subscribers at Carlisle House in Soho Square. The con-
certs were conducted alternately by Karl Friedrich Abel and Johann
Christian Bach. Having attended one of the concerts in January 1767,
Sterne described it as 'the best . . . I ever had the honour to be at'
(*Letters*, 296).

121 *Aleppo*: city in Syria, formerly in the Ottoman Empire and an important
centre of trade between Europe and Asia.

Lamb to the Slaughter: cf. Isaiah 53: 7.

'Man delights . . . nor Woman': cf. *Hamlet*, II. ii. 309–10.

Lord and Lady Bellasys: Thomas Belasyse (1699–1774), first Earl Fauconberg of Newburgh and his wife. Lord Fauconberg had presented Sterne
to the perpetual curacy of Coxwold in March 1760.

Seneca, or Socrates: Seneca (*c*.4 BC–AD 65), the Roman tragic poet and
Stoic philosopher and Socrates (469–399 BC), the Greek philosopher
who took his own life when condemned to death.

Lady Spencer: Margaret Georgiana Spencer, wife of Sterne's friend and
patron John Spencer (1734–83). The story of Le Fever in the sixth
volume of *Tristram Shandy* is dedicated to Lady Spencer.

Ranelagh: see note to p. 118 above.

At Court: Curtis notes that Sterne attended 'a very grand Court at St.
James's, at which all the Royal Family except the Princess Dowager, of
Wales, were present' (*Public Advertiser*, Monday, 18 May 1767).

122 *apprehend*: to anticipate with fear, worry.

monitory: 'giving or conveying a warning' (*OED*).

123 *detaind . . . Books*: this passage is used again in a letter to the earl of
Shelburne (*Letters*, 342).

the Downs: collective name for the South and North Downs, a series of
undulating chalk hills, south of the Thames. Deal in Kent, the port from
which Eliza probably sailed for India (see *LY*, 280), is situated in the
North Downs.

Archbishops of Yorks: the home of Archbishop Robert Hay Drummond
(1711–76) in Brodsworth, 5 miles north-west of Doncaster.

'remember thee! . . . trivial men: a paraphrase of Hamlet's words to his
father's ghost in *Hamlet*, I. v. 95–9. For 'Alas! Poor Yorick!', see note to
p. 41 above.

123 *Cholicks*: biliousness.

    the Faculty: doctors.

    Ecclesiastick Rhum: a euphemism for venereal disease.

124 *Uncle Toby . . . quietness sake*: *TS*, VIII. vi. 662.

    Lydia . . . Mama: Sterne's daughter and wife.

    parole: word, formal promise.

    strait: limited.

125 *Magazeens*: see note to p. 81 above.

    Capitals: suggesting both heads and accumulated wealth.

    catechize: 'to examine with or as with a catechism' (*OED*).

126 *Hussy!*: an abbreviation of housewife. A playful term of endearment.

    Straitness: narrowness, meanness.

127 *Disquietudes . . . few feel*: cf. *TS*, IV. 319–20, where Julia suffers 'the many disquietudes of a tender heart, which all talk of—but few feel'.

    he has orderd . . . Steps: cf. Psalms 37: 23: 'The steps of a good man are ordered by the Lord'.

    Tabernacles: places of worship.

    Sash: sash-window.

128 *India Man*: a ship from India.

130 *Cosway*: Richard Cosway (1742–1821), the most fashionable miniature painter of his day, who had painted Eliza for the Jameses (see *LY*, 274).

    gawsy: thin.

    my Convent: see note to p. 108, above.

    Enthusiasm: imaginative inspiration and fervour.

    against: in preparation for.

    Ecritoire: possibly a writing desk, but more likely the silver ink stand Lord Spencer had sent Sterne in October 1765 (see *LY*, 226–7).

    immortalized . . . Journey: see *Journey*, 3.

131 *Stock*: see note to p. 78 above.

    Ovid's Tomb: the tomb of the Roman writer, Publius Ovidius Naso (43 BC–AD 18). Sterne refers to Ovid's mock-didactic verse, *Ars Amatoria*.

    Sculptures . . . Rome: Sterne reworks this passage in a letter of February 1768 (*Letters*, 412).

    Lord ffauconberg's: see note to p. 121 above.

    so Crawford's like: probably John Craufurd (d. 1814), the source of the anecdote that formed the basis of the last episode in the *Journey* (see note to p. 101 above). According to Curtis, Craufurd was 'as much in love with pose as with play' (*Letters*, 263 n. 7).

132 *This last Sheet*: i.e. the prophecy that Sterne and Eliza would become free to marry. [I.J.]

133 *after her Lying in*: after giving birth.

post: express.

Rib: wife. A playful allusion to the creation of Eve from one of Adam's ribs (Genesis 2: 22–3).

depart in peace: cf. Luke 2: 29: 'Lord, now lettest thy servant depart in peace'.

other side of this Leaf: see note to p. 132 above.

Crasy Castle: the Demoniacs' name for Hall-Stevenson's Skelton Castle (see note to p. 107 above).

134 *with a friend . . . to Salt hill, and Enfield Wash*: possibly a reference to journeys with one of Eliza's children. Salt Hill, where the children may have been at school, is west of London and Enfield Wash to the north.

Arno's Vale . . . Eliza's Visit: Sterne had visited Florence, which is situated on the banks of the Arno, on his trip to Italy in 1765. In the penultimate letter sent to Eliza before she sailed for India, Sterne similarly imagines an idyllic return to Italy: 'We shall fish upon the banks of Arno, and lose ourselves in the sweet labyrinths of its vallies' (*Letters*, 318). There may also be an allusion here to 'Arno's Vale, A Song' by the Duke of Dorset. The poem begins with a celebration of pastoral paradise—'All look'd as joy could never fail, | Among the sweets of Arno's vale'—but concludes lamenting that the 'taste of pleasure now is o'er'.

here: at Skelton [I.J.].

Bombay-Lascelles: Peter Lascelles, who made three voyages to India for the East India Company, before retiring in 1766.

135 *with my Snuff . . . face opposite to mine*: see note to p. 3 above.

clew: see note to p. 35 above.

136 *Dreamer . . . Scripture Language*: cf. Deuteronomy 13: 1.

ride myself . . . Sand: this passage is used again in a letter of 30 June (*Letters*, 368–9).

that Crisis: cf. *Journey*, 37 and 141 above.

137 *your Nymph*: presumably, Eliza's maid.

Bandboxes: see note to p. 76 above.

Aleppo: see note to p. 121 above.

Dillon: John Talbot Dillon (1734–1806).

138 *pecuniary chances . . . my Prebend*: presumably, monies arising from Sterne's status as prebendary of York.

I wish . . . Arno's Vale: see note to p. 134 above.

139 *Coxwould . . . as an Offering*: a slight revision of a passage from a letter of 7 June (*Letters*, 353).

140 *flea*: flay, to strip of money.

140 *Spare my life . . . all I have*: cf. George Farquhar's *The Beaux' Stratagem* (1707), v. ii: 'Spare all I have, and take my life'.

break faith with the world: a reference to Sterne's obligations to the 334 people who had subscribed in advance for the *Journey*.

141 *Albion*: an ancient and poetical name for Britain, probably deriving from the Latin *albus*, 'white'.

dismal Crisis: cf. *Journey*, 37 and p. 136.

143 *as melancholly and sad as a Cat*: proverbial. Cf. Gay, *New Similes* (1720): 'I melancholy as a cat, am kept awake to weep'.

pianissimo: musical term for 'very softly'. Cf. Yorick's system of grading his sermons by musical terms (*TS*, VI. xi. 514–15).

Behold . . . for Wife: cf. Genesis 3: 12.

dun: to importune for debt.

Lascelles has told me: according to Cash, Peter Lascelles 'frightened [Sterne] by telling him about the terrible dangers that ships encountered in Indian waters' (*LY*, 297).

145 *'We hear . . . expected'*: a modified version of a notice that appeared in the *Public Advertiser* for Monday, 20 July 1767: 'Skelton-Castle is, at present, the place of rendezvous of the most celebrated wits: The humourous author of Tristram Shandy, and Mr. G——, author of several ingenious pieces, have been there some time: some other persons of distinguished rank and abilities in the literary world, are daily expected' (quoted by Curtis, *Letters*, 382 n. 4). Although it is not impossible that Garrick visited Skelton, it seems more likely that Sterne inserted his name to impress Eliza.

Time and Chance: see note to p. 23 above.

Die: dice.

146 *Mr Turner's . . . herself*: Charles Turner (?1726–83) and his wife Elizabeth (1731–68).

et caetera: used here 'as substitute for a suppressed substantive, generally a coarse or indelicate one' (*OED*). Cf. *TS*, II. vi. 116 and *Shamela* (1741) by Henry Fielding (1707–54): 'naked in Bed, with his Hand on her Breasts, &c . . .'

place tis in: see note to p. 3 above.

Shandy Hall: Sterne's Coxwold home, named after the family residence of Tristram Shandy.

Vally . . . Jehosophat: cf. Joel 3: 2.

our Archbishop: see note to p. 123 above.

147 *his name in a List*: as a subscriber to the *Journey*. See note to p. 140 above.

Chamber . . . Candlestick: 2 Kings 4: 10.

Harrogate . . . waters here: like other Spa towns, Harrogate (15 miles to

the west of Coxwold) was visited both for the supposed medicinal benefits of its springs and for the entertainments it offered.

York. Races: York Race Week was held annually in August and from 16 to
23 August in 1767. It appears that Sterne added 'Races' at a later date to
make his subsequent tinkering with chronology seem consistent. See
note to p. 148 below.

Packets from Iago: letters posted from Santiago or St Jago, in the Cape
Verde islands.

148 *I'll love . . . hast past*: cf. *Othello*, I. iii. 167: 'She lov'd me for the dangers I
had pass'd'.

I now want . . . Festivity over: given the gap between the date of this entry
and the actual Race Week, Cash suggests that it was made after a three-
week break from the *Journal*. Although he was writing in August, Sterne
continued to antedate his entries so as to maintain the pretence that he
had written every day (see *LY*, 301–2).

sad Story . . . Dutch Ship: probably a second set of letters, sent by Eliza
via a Dutch ship and received by Sterne during Race Week (*LY*, 302).

'it can no be': in a letter to Eliza of March 1767, Sterne quotes a similar
phrase: '*It can no be masser*' (*Letters*, 315).

furnace of Affliction: cf. Isaiah 48: 10: 'I have chosen thee in the furnace of
affliction'.

149 *The Bishop of Cork and Ross*: Dr Jemmett Browne (?1703–82). He entertained Sterne in Scarborough in September.

I have had an offer . . . my brow: as Curtis notes, Sterne reworks this
passage in a letter to his daughter of December 1767. In the letter, it is
Lydia rather than Eliza who will make the mitre sit easily upon Sterne's
brow (*Letters*, 406).

not only wipe away . . . for ever: cf. *Journey*, p. 36 and note, above.

August 4: Sterne expected his wife and daughter to arrive at the end of
September, although they in fact arrived on 1 October. While it is possible that Sterne lied in order to excuse breaking off the *Journal* pre-
maturely, it is more likely, as Cash argues persuasively, that he actually
made this entry in late September (*LY*, 303).

150 *November 1st*: Sterne writes just after Elizabeth and Lydia had moved to
York at the end of October.

2 Months: see note to p. 149 above.

on the edge of sixty: Elizabeth Sterne was 53.

A POLITICAL ROMANCE

151 *Ridiculum . . . Res*: Horace (65–8 BC), *Satires*, I. x. 14–15: 'Jesting oft cuts
hard knots more forcefully and effectively than gravity'.

153 *Fending and Proving*: argument, wrangling. [I.J.]

153 *old-cast . . . Breeches*: the Commissaryship of Pickering and Pocklington, which was in the gift of Dr John Fountayne (1714–1802), dean of York (represented here by '*John*, our Parish-Clerk'). Sterne was sworn into the post on 12 July 1751.

Trim: Dr Francis Topham (1713–70), who had his eyes on the Pickering and Pocklington post before Sterne's appointment denied him it. Although Trim is also the name of Uncle Toby's faithful servant in *Tristram Shandy*, the negative implications of 'trimming'—'cheating, changing side, or beating' (*Lexicon Balatronicum*)—clearly inform Sterne's choice of name here. Topham comes in for more ridicule in the generalized lawyer figure, Didius, in *Tristram Shandy*.

Watch-Coat: the commissaryship of the Exchequer and Prerogative Court. Although the position was in the gift of the archbishop ('the Parson of the Parish'), Dr John Gilbert (1693–1761), Topham sought to alter his current patent so that his son could inherit the preferment. Having learnt of Topham's plan (possibly from Dean Fountayne), the archbishop put a stop to it. Topham, who blamed Fountayne for the frustrated ambitions of nearly a decade, complained bitterly of breach of promise.

155 *Militia-List*: the Militia Act of 1757 empowered the government to conscript all males of military age for three years' service. The act provoked riots among the disenfranchised poor.

Groat: a proverbially insignificant denomination of coin.

Lord of the Manor: Henry VIII.

Complines, Passing-Bells: the compline-bell was rung for the last service of the day and the passing-bell, or death-knell, when someone was on their deathbed.

Tythes: produce and money due to the church.

156 *Against*: see note to p. 130 above.

Church-Wardens . . . old Man: the church wardens represent the prebendaries of the minster and the sides-men the archbishop's officers. The 'knowing' old man is Dr William Herring (1691–1762).

pettifogging, ambidextrous: a pettifogger is 'a little dirty attorney, ready to undertake any litigious or bad cause' (*Lexicon Balatronicum*). Ambidextrous means double-dealing.

just got down to his Living: Gilbert became archbishop of York in 1757.

157 *in Verbo Sacerdotis*: 'on the word of a priest'.

whetted: sharpened.

to charr: to do housework.

158 *Close-stool*: a chamber pot enclosed in a stool or box. The allegory of the close stool represents Topham's failed attempt to rush Gilbert's brother into a post as prebendary when the archbishop was seriously ill.

call: invoke.

Uproar . . . about it: Topham made his grievances public by publishing *A Letter Address'd to the Reverend the Dean of York; in which is given a full Detail of some very extraordinary Behaviour of his, in relation to his Denial of a Promise made by him to Dr. Topham* (1758).

Battle of the Breeches: recalling *The Battle of the Books* (1704) by Jonathan Swift (1667–1745), one of a number of Scriblerian satires to which the *Romance* is indebted.

159 *the late Parson of the Parish*: Dr Matthew Hutton, archbishop of York 1748–57.

John's Desk . . . should be: a power struggle, fuelled by Topham, between the dean and the archbishop.

make his Market: to do some bargaining. [I.J.]

a good creditable cast Coat: Topham secured the commissaryship of the Exchequer and Prerogative Court in 1751.

160 *Mark Slender*: Dr Mark Braithwaite. Out of sympathy for Braithwaite's poverty and ill health, the then commissary, Dr Ward, allowed the old lawyer to act as his surrogate in the Pickering and Pocklington post in April 1749. Braithwaite died in August of the following year.

161 *Green . . . Cushion*: the commissaryship of the dean and chapter of York.

William Doe: William Stables, appointed commissary of the dean and chapter court in 1751.

Lorry Slim: Laurence Sterne, so named for his tall and spare figure. For his possession of the 'old Breeches', see note to p. 153 above.

162 *The Pinder's Place*: a pinder was 'an officer of the manor, having the duty of impounding stray beasts' (*OED*).

CONIES: rabbits. As Cash notes, coney-catching 'was a cant term for both swindling and fornicating' (*EMY*, 272).

163 *Sow-Gelder's Horn*: cf. Samuel Butler (1612–80), *Hudibras*, I. ii. 537–8: 'No *Sow-gelder* did blow his Horn | To geld a Cat, But cry'd *Reform*'. [I.J.]

But . . . over again: Fountayne had responded to Topham's first pamphlet with the *Answer to a Letter Address'd to the Dean of York* (1758). Topham responded in turn with *A Reply to the Answer to a Letter Lately Addressed to the Dean of York* (1759).

twelve Men . . . in Kendal Green: alluding to Falstaff's lying bravado in *I Henry IV*, II. iv. 189–213.

164 *Hold*: refuge.

Close-Stool: see note to p. 158 above.

be Book-sworn: swear on the Bible.

165 *trimm'd*: beaten or thrashed.

167 *Gross*: main body.

Wipe: a blow, or reproach.

168 *Partition-Treaty*: of either 1698 or 1700. Both treaties attempted to settle the question of the Spanish Succession.

Ichnography: ground-plan.

Slops: legs.

169 *what Ichnography meant*: cf. *TS*, II. v. 110.

Investiture: 'a conveyance of the fee-simple, right, or interest in lands . . . giving first the possession, and afterwards the interest in the estate conveyed' (*OED*).

170 *looking too high*: writing to an admirer of *Tristram Shandy* who had commented on the tendency of readers to look for hidden meanings in the book, Sterne responded: 'they all look too high—tis ever the fate of low minds' (*Letters*, 122).

171 *Panegyric*: eulogy.

a Third: a musical term. A third is an interval of three notes in a scale.

concenter: concentrate.

Raillery: ridicule, banter.

Reproof Valiant: *As You Like It*, v. iv. 93.

172 *Gird*: jibe, dig.

found to lay hid . . . Pantagruel: cf. *TS*, III. xxxvi. 268. For *Gargantua and Pantagruel*, see note to p. 85 above.

Whitesmith: metal worker, locksmith.

174 *To . . . of York*: probably Caesar Ward (1711–59), who printed *A Political Romance*.

Child of many Fathers: an allegation made in Topham's *Reply*. Sterne may well have been one of the fathers of the dean's *Answer*.

Bays's plea . . . Child at all: cf. George Villiers, 2nd duke of Buckingham (1628–87) *et al.*, *The Rehearsal* (1672), III. iv. 68–9.

Curl: Edmund Curll (1683–1747), publisher and literary pirate who notoriously published an unauthorized edition of Pope's letters in 1735.

quaint Conceit: perhaps a reference to the little vignette of two fighting cocks subsequently set at the end of the text of *A Political Romance*. [I.J.]

176 *Instrument*: 'a formal writing of any kind' (*OED*).

Dr. Herring, Mr. Berdmore: Dr William Herring and William Berdmore, supporters, along with Sterne, of the dean. Their names had appeared in Fountayne's *Answer*.

Veniam petimus, demusque vicissim: a slight misquotation from Horace's *Ars Poetica*, line 11: 'Painters and poets have always had an equal right in hazarding anything'.

177 *Mr. Ricard's*: Arthur Ricard, a York attorney.

178 *Peine fort et dure*: pressing to death (a punishment inflicted on felons who refused to plead). [I.J.]

prima est hæc Ultio: Juvenal (*c.* AD 60–*c.*136), *Satires*, xiii. 2: 'The first punishment is this: that no guilty man is acquitted at the bar of his own conscience'.

SERMONS

183 *The House . . . Described*: sermon 2 in *The Sermons of Mr. Yorick*, I–II (1760). Writing to his daughter in 1767, Sterne described the sermon as 'one of the best' (*Letters*, 301). As Sterne's note on p. 187 suggests, the content of the sermon is partly determined by its delivery during the period of Lenten fast preceding Easter.

Carthusian monks: an order founded in 1084 by St Bruno of Cologne.

Sierra Morena: mountainous desert region in south-west Spain, through which Don Quixote travels in *Don Quixote*, I. xxiii.

fugacious: evanescent, fugitive.

caravansera's: 'a kind of inn in the East where caravans put up' (*OED*).

184 *saint errantry*: saint errant is an ironic term for a 'saint who travelled in quest of spiritual adventures' (*OED*).

185 *originals*: sources, examples.

186 *so benevolent a commerce*: cf. *Journey*, 8: 'sentimental commerce'.

mechanically: automatically.

singing men . . . singing women: cf. 2 Samuel 19: 35.

like the unclean spirit . . . from him: Matthew 17: 14–18; Mark 9: 17–29; Luke 9: 38–42.

188 *glass*: mirror.

the wise man: Solomon.

189 *debt of nature*: death. In this metaphor, life is a loan and death the repayment.

house of mirth: Ecclesiastes 7: 4.

naked as it is: cf. *TS*, I. xxiii. 82–3.

nor can gravity . . . the other: cf. *TS*, I. xi. 28–9.

190 *Vindication of Human Nature*: sermon 7 in *The Sermons of Mr. Yorick*, I–II (1760). The sermon was almost certainly first delivered as a charity sermon. Such sermons sought not only to recommend 'social virtue and public spirit', but also to persuade the congregation to make charitable donations.

For none . . . himself: as the next verse makes clear, the text is tradition-ally interpreted as an injunction to live for God: 'For whether we live, we live unto the Lord; and whether we die unto the Lord: whether we live therefore, or die, we are the Lord's'. There is at least one precedent for Sterne's interpretation of the text in 'A Sermon Preached before King George I' by Richard Bentley (1662–1742). Sterne uses material derived from Bentley later in the sermon (see *Sermons: Notes*, 120 and 123–4).

190 *such an enquirer*: Sterne probably has Thomas Hobbes (1588–1679) or Bernard de Mandeville (1670–1733) in mind. Both philosophers argue for the essentially selfish basis of human actions. For the Anglican response to Hobbes, see Introduction, pp. xv–xvi above.

bubble: gull, dupe.

191 *GOD made . . . own image*: Genesis 1: 27.

sensitive: endowed with sensation or sensuous perception.

the fall of man, in our first parents: recounted in Genesis 3.

super-inductions: see note to p. 77 above.

French writers: as New suggests, Sterne may be thinking of François de la Rochefoucauld (1613–80). The idea that French writers in particular characterized human nature in relentlessly negative terms was a commonplace (see *Sermons: Notes*, 122–3).

to judge . . . bad sample: cf. Tom Jones's comment to the Man of the Hill: 'you . . . fall into an error, which . . . I have observed to be a very common one, by taking the character of mankind from the worst and basest among them; whereas . . . nothing should be esteemed as characteristical of a species but what is to be found among the best and most perfect individuals' (Fielding, *Tom Jones* (1749), VIII. xv).

strait-hearted: mean-hearted.

192 *God made man upright*: Ecclesiastes 7: 29.

193 *more FOOL . . . KNAVE*: proverbial.

194 *against*: see note to p. 130 above.

and mischief . . . have gone: Genesis 42: 38.

195 *heathen poet . . . fellow creatures*: Terence (*c.* 190–159 BC), *Heauton Timorumenos*, I. i. 77: 'Homo sum; humani nil a me alienum puto' ('I am a man, I count nothing human foreign to me').

The sorrowful . . . before him: cf. Psalm 79: 11 (Book of Common Prayer).

if he has . . . compassion from him: 1 John 3: 17.

197 *JOB's Account . . . considered*: sermon 10 in *The Sermons of Mr. Yorick*, I–II (1760). That a second sermon, 'Job's Expostulation with his Wife', also focuses on the Book of Job, is an indication of its importance for the eighteenth century in general and for Sterne in particular.

sublime: a concept that became increasingly important in mid- to late eighteenth-century discussions of aesthetic response. New points out that Robert Lowth's *Lectures on the Sacred Poetry of the Hebrews* (1753) finds the Book of Job 'universally animated with the true spirit of sublimity' (*Sermons: Notes*, 141).

the words . . . infant eloquent: Wisdom 10: 21. Cf. p. 33 and note, above.

sea of troubles: *Hamlet*, III. i. 59.

198 *Indeed even . . . myself of rest*: a paraphrase of Ecclesiastes 4: 8.

199 *staves*: staffs.

For whilst . . . upon them: cf. Job 1: 18–19.

200 *That man . . . continueth not*: Job 14: 1–2. The phrase 'full of misery' is the Book of Common Prayer's rendering of the first verse of ch. 14 (Order for the Burial of the Dead).

epitome: 'a condensed record or representation in miniature' (*OED*).

flower of the field: Isaiah 40: 6. Cf. *TS*, v. ix. 435.

declension: see note to p. 15 above.

201 *if he escapes . . . upon the stalk*: in this paragraph, Sterne reworks material from Bentley's 'A Sermon Preached before King George I' (see note to p. 190 above).

With how quick . . . over our heads: cf. *TS*, IX. viii. 754.

Nebuchadnezzar . . . trace them back: Daniel 2: 5–8.

202 *as Homer observes*: cf. *Iliad*, vi. 146: 'Like that of leaves is a generation of men'.

203 *That one . . . seventeen years*: Sterne's source has not been identified.

story related by Plutarch . . . cruel anguish: Sterne takes this anecdote not from Plutarch's *Lives*, but from *The Religion of Nature Delineated*, 2nd edn. (1724) by William Wollaston (1660–1724). The reflections on the effects of war are derived from Wollaston.

204 *Consider how great a part . . . drink of it*: cf. *Journey*, 60 and note, above. This is the passage quoted by Sancho in his letter to Sterne.

To conceive this . . . condemned them: the Inquisition was often invoked in Anglican sermons to highlight the 'tyrannical' Catholic threat and to underscore a sense of the value of Protestant freedoms. Contemporary newspapers and periodicals regularly carried lurid and pathetic tales of continuing Inquisition activity in Portugal and Spain. Sterne paints a similarly graphic picture of the Inquisition in the 'Abuses of Conscience' sermon, which Trim reads in *Tristram Shandy* (*TS*, II. xvii. 161–3).

full of trouble . . . sparks fly upwards: Job 5: 7.

205 *Millions . . . trouble*: cf. *Journey*, 61.

fugacious: see note to p. 183 above.

'That in sorrow . . . were taken': Genesis 3: 19.

Wollaston: see note to p. 203 above. Sterne is, in effect, acknowledging the sermon's broader indebtedness to Wollaston.

there is nothing . . . mixture of sorrow: cf. *Journey*, 74.

206 *The LEVITE and his CONCUBINE*: sermon 3 in *The Sermons of Mr Yorick*, III–IV (1766).

JUDGES xix. 1, 2, 3: Sterne's text is Judges 19: 1, but he quotes a portion of the second verse and all of the third on this opening page.

207 *from the head . . . heart*: cf. *Journey*, 14 and note, above.

'*tis a story . . . too much*: cf. *Journey*, 37 and note, above.

208 *œconomicks*: household management.

it is not good . . . alone: cf. *Journey*, 45 and note, above.

Nature will . . . destitution: cf. *Journey*, 24.

Let the torpid Monk . . . fruits: cf. *Journey*, 78.

209 *grot*: grotto.

despite: scorn, disdain.

210 *but most . . . to thee*: the Levites acted as assistants to the priests in temple worship.

Comfort . . . be merry: Judges 19: 5–6.

Mercy . . . met together: Psalm 85: 10.

the catastrophe is horrid: grotesquely, the concubine is raped by a group of men, cut 'into twelve pieces' and the pieces 'sent into all the coasts of Israel' (see Judges 19: 24–9).

211 *It is not . . . shame unto him*: as New notes, 'Sterne weaves together three biblical passages, Acts 25: 16, John 7: 51, and Proverbs 18: 13' (*Sermons: Notes*, 211).

not to . . . appearance: John 7: 24.

Christ came . . . wine-bibber: Matthew 11: 19.

212 *ápostrophè*, '*Who made . . . example*: 1 Corinthians 4: 7. For apostrophe, see note to p. 33 above.

period: sentence.

Son! . . . &c.: Luke 16: 25.

railing: harsh and abusive reviling, often distinguished in the eighteenth century from more good-natured raillery.

as one . . . passage: an acknowledgement of this paragraph's indebtedness to 'The Parable of the Rich Man and Lazarus' by John Tillotson (1630–94), archbishop of Canterbury.

difference between . . . of wit: Sterne borrows this distinction and other elements of his discussion of 'sarcastick reflections' from Walter Charleton's *A Brief Discourse Concerning the Different Wits of Men*, 2nd edn. (1675) (see *Sermons: Notes*, 212–13).

213 *if Honour . . . precipice*: cf. *Journey*, 78.

214 *On Enthusiasm*: sermon 11 in the *Sermons of the late Rev. Mr. Sterne*, V–VII (1769). While Sterne seems to have made few changes to his published sermons, the sermons printed after his death offer, perhaps, the clearest insight into the kinds of sermon he preached to his parishioners. Probably first delivered at a Whitsuntide or Pentecost service, the sermon reveals the grounds on which orthodox Anglicans attacked Methodism, and offers a powerful reminder of the continuing Anglican

resistance to largely secular notions of human self-sufficiency and innate goodness.

'Enthusiasm' derives from the Greek word for being inspired or possessed by the god, but in the late seventeenth and eighteenth centuries, it became a pejorative term for the claims of direct contact with the Holy Spirit associated with puritanism. More broadly, in the latitudinarian tradition of which Sterne's sermons are a part, enthusiasm meant 'any manifestations of puritanism that divorced faith from reason or stressed faith at the expense of works' (Rivers, *Reason, Grace, and Sentiment* (1991), 34).

our sufficiency . . . God: 2 Corinthians 3: 5.

215 *There is scarce . . . the world*: this paragraph is indebted, like many of the sermon's other arguments against enthusiasm, to George Hickes's *The Spirit of Enthusiasm Exorcised* (1680). Interestingly, as New observes, 'Sterne takes the language of a Restoration attack on dissenters and turns it against the Methodists'. See Melvyn New, 'Some Sterne Borrowings from Four Renaissance Authors', *PQ* 71 (1992), 306–10.

gift of tongues: see Acts 2: 1–11.

216 *That as . . . being*: Acts 17: 28.

217 *cuts the knot . . . untying it*: cf. *TS*, IV. vii. 332, where Walter is disappointed by Toby's willingness to cut the knot.

continency: self-restraint.

218 *It is God . . . good pleasure*: cf. Philippians 2: 13, quoted again on p. 220.

One of the . . . sine divino afflatu: the Latin means 'without divine inspiration'. As New notes, the master of reasoning in question is Marcus Tullius Cicero (106–43 BC).

Seneca: for Seneca see note to p. 121 above. Sterne is borrowing here, as elsewhere in the sermon, from 'Of Nature and Grace' by Edward Young (1642?–1705).

219 *rout*: fuss, clamour.

sanctification . . . last century: contested doctrines especially associated with Calvinist fundamentalists of the mid-seventeenth century. Sanctification, 'the action of the Holy Ghost in sanctifying or making holy the believer, by the implanting within him of the Christian graces and the destruction of sinful affections' (*OED*). Regeneration, 'the process or fact of being born again spiritually' (*OED*).

perfect . . . weakness: 2 Corinthians 12: 9.

which bloweth . . . spirit: John 3: 8.

220 *work out . . . good pleasure*: Philippians 2: 12–13.

pharisaical: self-righteous.

221 *period of national confusion*: the Civil Wars (1642–9) and the Interregnum (1649–60).

221 *Pardons and indulgences*: in Catholicism, an indulgence granted by the church allows for a remission of the punishment due for sin after sacramental absolution. The selling of indulgences in Germany incurred Luther's displeasure and helped precipitate the Reformation.

empiricks: an ancient sect of physicians, but the word came to be applied to untrained and fraudulent quack doctors.

in their journals: probably a reference to the published *Journals* of George Whitefield (1714–1770), a key figure in the founding of Methodism.

Women's Writing 1778–1838

WILLIAM BECKFORD	Vathek
JAMES BOSWELL	Life of Johnson
FRANCES BURNEY	Camilla Cecilia Evelina The Wanderer
LORD CHESTERFIELD	Lord Chesterfield's Letters
JOHN CLELAND	Memoirs of a Woman of Pleasure
DANIEL DEFOE	A Journal of the Plague Year Moll Flanders Robinson Crusoe Roxana
HENRY FIELDING	Joseph Andrews and Shamela A Journey from This World to the Next and The Journal of a Voyage to Lisbon Tom Jones
WILLIAM GODWIN	Caleb Williams
OLIVER GOLDSMITH	The Vicar of Wakefield
MARY HAYS	Memoirs of Emma Courtney
ELIZABETH HAYWOOD	The History of Miss Betsy Thoughtless
ELIZABETH INCHBALD	A Simple Story
SAMUEL JOHNSON	The History of Rasselas The Major Works
CHARLOTTE LENNOX	The Female Quixote
MATTHEW LEWIS	Journal of a West India Proprietor The Monk
HENRY MACKENZIE	The Man of Feeling
ALEXANDER POPE	Selected Poetry

JANE AUSTEN	Emma
	Mansfield Park
	Persuasion
	Pride and Prejudice
	Sense and Sensibility
MRS BEETON	Book of Household Management
LADY ELIZABETH BRADDON	Lady Audley's Secret
ANNE BRONTË	The Tenant of Wildfell Hall
CHARLOTTE BRONTË	Jane Eyre
	Shirley
	Villette
EMILY BRONTË	Wuthering Heights
SAMUEL TAYLOR COLERIDGE	The Major Works
WILKIE COLLINS	The Moonstone
	No Name
	The Woman in White
CHARLES DARWIN	The Origin of Species
CHARLES DICKENS	The Adventures of Oliver Twist
	Bleak House
	David Copperfield
	Great Expectations
	Nicholas Nickleby
	The Old Curiosity Shop
	Our Mutual Friend
	The Pickwick Papers
	A Tale of Two Cities
GEORGE DU MAURIER	Trilby
MARIA EDGEWORTH	Castle Rackrent

	Eirik the Red and Other Icelandic Sagas
	The German-Jewish Dialogue
	The Kalevala
	The Poetic Edda
LUDOVICO ARIOSTO	Orlando Furioso
GIOVANNI BOCCACCIO	The Decameron
GEORG BÜCHNER	Danton's Death, Leonce and Lena, and Woyzeck
LUIS VAZ DE CAMÕES	The Lusiads
MIGUEL DE CERVANTES	Don Quixote Exemplary Stories
CARLO COLLODI	The Adventures of Pinocchio
DANTE ALIGHIERI	The Divine Comedy Vita Nuova
LOPE DE VEGA	Three Major Plays
J. W. VON GOETHE	Elective Affinities Erotic Poems Faust: Part One and Part Two The Flight to Italy
E. T. A. HOFFMANN	The Golden Pot and Other Tales
HENRIK IBSEN	An Enemy of the People, The Wild Duck, Rosmersholm Four Major Plays Peer Gynt
LEONARDO DA VINCI	Selections from the Notebooks
FEDERICO GARCIA LORCA	Four Major Plays
MICHELANGELO BUONARROTI	Life, Letters, and Poetry

The Oxford World's Classics Website

www.worldsclassics.co.uk

- Information about new titles
- Explore the full range of Oxford World's Classics
- Links to other literary sites and the main OUP webpage
- Imaginative competitions, with bookish prizes
- Peruse the Oxford World's Classics Magazine
- Articles by editors
- Extracts from Introductions
- A forum for discussion and feedback on the series
- Special information for teachers and lecturers

www.worldsclassics.co.uk

American Literature

British and Irish Literature

Children's Literature

Classics and Ancient Literature

Colonial Literature

Eastern Literature

European Literature

History

Medieval Literature

Oxford English Drama

Poetry

Philosophy

Politics

Religion

The Oxford Shakespeare

A complete list of Oxford Paperbacks, including Oxford World's Classics, Oxford Shakespeare, Oxford Drama, and Oxford Paperback Reference, is available in the UK from the Academic Division Publicity Department, Oxford University Press, Great Clarendon Street, Oxford OX2 6DP.

In the USA, complete lists are available from the Paperbacks Marketing Manager, Oxford University Press, 198 Madison Avenue, New York, NY 10016.

Oxford Paperbacks are available from all good bookshops. In case of difficulty, customers in the UK can order direct from Oxford University Press Bookshop, Freepost, 116 High Street, Oxford OX1 4BR, enclosing full payment. Please add 10 per cent of published price for postage and packing.